The Rewind

Also by Allison Winn Scotch

The Rewind

Allison Winn Scotch

WITHDRAWN

Berkley Romance | New York

BERKLEY ROMANCE
Published by Berkley
An imprint of Penguin Random House LLC
penguinrandomhouse.com

Library of Congress Cataloging-in-Publication Data

Names: Scotch, Allison Winn, author.
Title: The rewind / Allison Winn Scotch.
Description: First Edition. | New York: Berkley Romance, 2022.
Identifiers: LCCN 2022001935 (print) | LCCN 2022001936 (ebook) |
ISBN 9780593546536 (trade paperback) | ISBN 9780593546543 (ebook)
Classification: LCC PS3619.C64 R49 2022 (print) | LCC PS3619.C64 (ebook) |
DDC 813/.6—dc23
LC record available at https://lccn.loc.gov/2022001935
LC ebook record available at https://lccn.loc.gov/2022001936

First Edition: November 2022

Printed in the United States of America
1st Printing

Book design by Elke Sigal

*For Campbell, who was a newborn when I wrote
my debut and who is now eighteen and grown.
What a joy it has been to watch you fly.*

We're running with the shadows of the night,
So baby, take my hand, it'll be all right.
Surrender all your dreams to me tonight,
They'll come true in the end.

—PAT BENATAR, "SHADOWS OF THE NIGHT"

The Rewind

PROLOGUE

Frankie Harriman took a long last look in the mirror on the back of the bathroom door of her decently appointed hotel room. The lighting was, as expected, quite grim, but even without the shadowing and the unflattering overtone of yellow, she startled herself. She fidgeted with the hem of her oversize wool sweater, tried tucking it into the waist of her Levi's, then decided that made her look like she was trying too hard, so untucked it, but she still wasn't happy. She turned to the side and gave herself a final once-over. It would have to do. The rehearsal dinner invite had called for *College Chic!* and this was all she had: her old J.Crew fisherman sweater that she'd dug out of a box in the back of her closet in her Los Feliz apartment and her vintage Levi's, which she now bought at a used-clothing store on Fairfax, but she may just as well have been wearing the ones from 1989, the year they graduated. The last time she'd set foot on campus at Middleton University.

She had been as surprised as anyone that she willingly accepted her freshman-year roommate's request to be a bridesmaid (how do you really turn that sort of thing down?). Months later, she checked off "Yes! Party Like It's 1999," rather than "Y2Nay," on the invitation, and after sealing the envelope and dropping it in the mailbox on the corner outside her office, it wouldn't be a lie to say that she regretted it and immediately thought of a million and one excuses as to how she could bail last minute. She always had excuses at the ready, and to be honest, half of them weren't even lies: her artists inevitably got themselves into trouble or she was headed out on tour or there was some sort of unforeseeable crisis to manage.

But here she was despite all of that. At April and Connor's wedding. At Middleton after a decade. With a magenta taffeta bridesmaid's dress with an oversize bow on one shoulder hanging in the closet next to the hotel robe. There were so many places she would rather be—anywhere, really—but she knew she owed it to April to show up and stand beside her when she vowed herself to Connor for life.

She'd tried to convince herself otherwise. She'd poured herself a whiskey a few months back, the day before she had to go to a wedding shop in Beverly Hills to pick up her bridesmaid's dress, and dialed Laila Simpson, the college friend she was still tightest with, and ran through why her presence wasn't really necessary. She'd stayed in closer touch with Laila than April in the years since they graduated; whenever Laila was in LA, they toasted each other and got drunk at whichever hotel bar Laila's pharmaceutical company was putting her up at. That afternoon, Laila went quiet on the other end of the line for a beat, then said, "You know, Frankie, you have this big, incredible life, and I'm never here to tell you how to live it, but April gave you a shoulder to lean on when you needed it, and it's probably time that you reciprocated." Frankie knew she was referring to the night they graduated from college, when the two of them—Laila and April—had hailed her a cab and hugged her goodbye and called her the next morning to make sure she was ok, but she hadn't thought about all of that in so long. It was easier not to think about any of that. Because that's how Frankie marched forward. By never looking back.

Frankie wanted to protest, to say, *But there are bigger reasons, more terrifying reasons for me not to come.* But that wasn't true. There was just one.

Ezra Jones.

Tonight at the hotel, Frankie tousled her blond hair one last time in front of the mirror and swiped on bright red lipstick. She checked her teeth and ran her fingers under her armpits because she couldn't remember if she'd put on deodorant. She knew she was more frazzled than usual (as a former child piano prodigy, Frankie Harriman had been trained like a show dog to overcome any nerves), so she stared at her reflection until her pulse slowed, and she told herself that Ezra Jones was just a small sliver of her past, a hiccup, a forgotten glimpse. She didn't have to speak to him, she didn't even know if he'd be here at April and Connor's wedding, and she certainly didn't ask. Frankie often advised her musical artists on how to avoid drawing unnecessary attention to their weaknesses, and she thus knew that asking was doing just that.

Her phone beeped on the nightstand, and she turned away from the mirror and flipped it open.

"You ready?" Laila asked. "I'm almost there. I'll be in the lobby in five."

Laila was crashing with a girl Frankie didn't remember who was two years behind them in college but who had returned to get her master's in something related to literature. (Laila had told Frankie, but she hadn't been paying close attention.) Laila had stayed in touch with this woman all these years because she was better at those things than Frankie.

Frankie pushed her shoulders back and reached for her coat, then her purse. She stuffed her CD player into her jacket's oversize pocket and flipped her yellow Sony headphones atop her hair. She had Night Vixen's early cut of their new album but never gave them feedback until she'd listened to it at least twenty times. She kept hearing new things, new nuances with each spin, but then that's what made her the best at what she did.

Frankie held her head high as she swung the door open and strode down the hall toward the elevator. She heard the door latch behind her and told herself that she was Frankie Harriman, music manager to the stars, and she was capable of anything. She'd eradicated Ezra Jones from her life once before. How hard could it be to do for one weekend more?

———

Ezra Jones popped open the black velvet box one last time. The ring, naturally, was still there. He didn't know why he worried it wouldn't be. But nevertheless, it was reassuring to see it secured away in its place, sparkling and magnificent, a single two-carat solitaire. He thought of his mother and how much he wished she were here so he could call her and share the news. She was always happy for him, whatever his choices.

A knock on the door startled him, and he closed the box with a start and tucked it into the inside pocket of his coat, which was slung around the mahogany wood chair in front of a matching desk. Ezra had sprung for a suite, which felt a little foolish now—he didn't want his old college friends to think he was being flashy about his bank account—but it was too late to do anything about it. Besides, he wanted tomorrow night, New Year's Eve, to be special. Mimi was coming, and it felt like exactly the right time, the right moment to make a new start, even if this was the place where plenty of things had come to an end.

"Hello?" he called from behind the door, then unlatched the safety lock.

"Dude!" He opened the door to find Gregory Mason standing there with open arms, double fisting two large bottles of booze. Gregory, whose brown hair was shaggy and who still looked about twenty-two despite a half-hearted attempt at a mustache, bear-hugged him like they hadn't seen each other in years, which wasn't quite true. Gregory had moved to Portland three summers ago, but they'd stayed close. They'd planned a trip to Prague last summer that Ezra bailed on last minute—instead, he went to Nantucket with Mimi for her work retreat—and Ezra was relieved that Gregory didn't seem to hold a grudge.

Gregory entered like Ezra's suite was his own, plunked the alcohol onto the mahogany desk, and flopped on the bed, rolling onto his back to unwrap his scarf and unzip his bright red puffer jacket. "Drink, my friend, you must drink. It's the only way to see this through." He rolled back over, then pushed up to his elbows and eyed Ezra.

"I'm fine," Ezra said. "I'm totally fine. I'm better than fine."

Gregory gave him a long up-and-down stare, as if his gaze were a lie detector, then he hopped to his feet and grabbed one of the bottles and took a swig. "You know that she's here, right?" Gregory didn't need to elaborate: *she* was Frankie. Ezra didn't bother to ask how he knew such things because Gregory always knew such things.

"Mimi's coming," Ezra offered. "So I'm honestly fine. She's flying from Kansas City to Chicago tonight, Hartford in the morning—I have a car bringing her." He grabbed his bright blue iBook from the desk. "I was just about to check on her flight."

"Mimi." Gregory sniffed.

"I'm sorry again," Ezra said.

Gregory shrugged like he knew there was no use in holding it against him. "I'm just saying that Prague is significantly more awesome than Nantucket."

"I know." Ezra nodded. Because he did. "It was just . . . it turned into a thing." He didn't mean to sigh but did anyway. How could he explain that Mimi was upset that everyone else was bringing a plus-one to the retreat while her plus-one was in Prague with his college buddy, and so, rather than disappoint her, he canceled his own plans.

Gregory moved on and refocused. "Your shirt is buttoned wrong," he said, and Ezra glanced down at his plaid flannel (*College Chic!*). Gregory's always-animated face slowed for a beat, and Ezra knew he was worried. He was one of just a handful of Ezra's friends, well, really his only friend, plus Frankie, who knew how deeply his anxiety used to run straight through him.

"This doesn't mean I'm not fine," Ezra said, unbuttoning, then rebuttoning, but Gregory held the bottle between them until Ezra finally sighed and reached for it and drank. It burned all the way down, deep into his gut, and he shuddered.

"Special Portland blend." Gregory smiled. "I know a guy." He paused. "We used to know each other intimately but fortunately now are still on speaking terms. Because, you know, the booze."

Ezra took this to mean that Gregory was still happily single, as he had nearly always been since he'd come out their senior year. Ezra never understood his rotating lineup of men, how it didn't unnerve him not to have a steady partner, how Gregory seemed to delight in the chase. For Ezra, the chase was the most arduous, exhausting part. Give him the evenings in pajamas and Blockbuster rentals, give him morning breath and bed head, give him the assured companionship over dinner, the shared *New York Times* crossword, the intimacy of being on a first-name basis with her parents.

"Have another," Gregory said. "I suspect you'll need it."

Ezra tipped the bottle back and drank again, and this time, it burned a little less, felt a little better. "I don't even have to see her," he said. "I mean, I guess I have to see her, but I don't have to *see* her. It's been ten years. Who said I have to care?"

Gregory cupped his shoulder and said, "My man," and shook his head, like he was in on a secret that Ezra didn't yet understand, and then he grabbed his scarf and his red puffer and also the two bottles of booze and said, "Let's hit it. We have an hour at the hotel bar before we head to Burton."

Ezra didn't want to make a big scene about the ring in front of Gregory, who, he knew, would make it into an even bigger thing because Gregory was all about delighting in the dramatic. Until Ezra got on bended knee and slipped his grandmother's ring on Mimi's finger, he just wanted this for himself. He'd planned to put the ring in the hotel room safe, but that would draw attention to it, so instead, he reached for his coat where it was stuffed in the inside pocket and said, "Ok, just promise me one thing."

And Gregory turned, with the door ajar, and said, "Anything."

"Just don't let me . . . I mean . . . Look, I don't want to turn this into a *drama*. You know, with Frankie."

"I got you," Gregory said. "I'll be the buffer."

Ezra didn't really know what exactly that meant. He envisioned Gregory rushing over to form a human wall between Frankie and him if ever they were in the same vicinity. But Gregory said it with such confidence, with such enthusiasm that he decided to trust him; he seemed to be an expert in making peace with exes, and when peace couldn't be found, at exorcising their ghosts. Ezra had never exorcised a ghost in his life.

Ezra thought of Frankie again, of her ghost. He'd been off his anxiety medication for a few years now but always kept a solitary pill on hand. His break-in-case-of-emergency supply. His pulse was already racing at the news of her proximity, and he wondered if this weren't a bit of an emergency.

"One sec," he said to Gregory, then dipped into the bathroom and rooted around in his Dopp kit for his pill container: his multivitamins, his calcium, and a single Xanax. He stared into the mirror and resolved he was fine; he really could white-knuckle it out. But then Gregory said from around the corner, "You good, man?" And just to be sure that he really *was good*, he placed the pill on the back of his tongue and swallowed.

"All set," Ezra said, emerging from the bathroom. Gregory held the hotel door open and flourished his arm as if he were an usher.

The Portland vodka was already making Ezra's legs feel rubbery, and he held a hand up against the wall as they lolled down the hallway toward the elevator. Gregory jabbed the button, and the two of them glanced upward as the floor ticked downward.

"Don't worry," Gregory said again. "I got you."

Ezra nodded perfunctorily because this seemed like the only reasonable reaction. Why did he care if he ran into his ex-girlfriend from a decade ago? Why was his heart thumping through his flannel shirt? Why was his mind racing a million miles an hour like it used to?

He waited for the Xanax to kick in. What sweet relief that would be.

The elevator number settled on THREE, and the gold doors whooshed open.

It took Ezra's brain a good four seconds to get what he was looking at: a blonde staring at the floor, her Doc Martens tapping out a beat, her black down jacket zipped to the neck. He stepped forward as if magnetically drawn toward her, as if he couldn't stop himself even when he'd spent the previous hour reminding himself of all the ways he'd need to do just that. Then he felt Gregory's hand reach over and grab his forearm, pulling him back, like the elevator was full or like they were bracing for impact.

By the time Frankie Harriman looked up from her Motorola and snapped it closed, the door was already easing shut. But there was just enough time—a few seconds that morphed into a decade—for Frankie to gasp and for Ezra to both recoil and retreat, and for each of them to vow to themselves that this would be the only time they'd be within spitting distance the rest of the weekend through.

SIXTEEN HOURS LATER

ONE

Frankie

Frankie awoke to a headache that felt akin to a leech sucking the blood straight from her spinal cord. The throbbing started low in her skull, right at the nape of her neck, and reverberated out with each heartbeat, each pulse, into every vein, every cerebral fold, every nerve. She squeezed her eyes closed, willing for sleep for one more moment, but the pain was unbearable, too much to allow for rest to settle back in. This, certainly, was one of a hundred hangovers she had endured, and yet this one felt different. Harrowing.

She allowed her eyes to flutter open and found herself staring at a white wall. To be sure, this was not the first wall she had woken in close proximity to, but certainly, she knew immediately that it wasn't her own. She'd painted one of her bedroom walls a vibrant purple last year, and though all her friends in LA thought it was a little *much*, Frankie had yet to grow weary of it, unlike so many other things in her life. (Really, she only had, like, three friends in LA, and mostly, those friendships were work friendships, but still. They really all did think she'd get sick of the purple wall.)

Frankie rolled to her back, emitted a groan, and noticed a heat emanating from beside her. The naked back of a man rose and fell next to her. This was also not a highly unusual experience for Frankie, who often took advice from Prince and partied like it was the end of the world, or at least the end of the century. Who could blame her: hot men and tequila went with her business.

This morning, however, Frankie narrowed her crusty eyes and took stock. The room was dim, the shades still pulled, and low light filtered in. The bed was small, *very* small. True, she occasionally woke up in a shabby studio with an aspiring drummer or the like (Frankie did prefer drummers, as they knew what to do with their hands; guitarists were pretty all right, too), but as adults, nearly everyone had at least a decent-sized bed. Sometimes, yes, there were futons involved. She rarely even bothered to give those aspirings her number. Futon-guys were fun, but they were not on Frankie's long-term radar. Laila would argue that Frankie didn't have long-term radar, while April would urge Frankie to find her long-term radar. "It's very fulfilling once you do," she'd once said, while Frankie made groaning noises over the phone that she hoped April could interpret three thousand miles away.

Frankie pushed up to her elbows and glanced around. The furnishings were . . . She tried to place them. The furnishings were familiar but only in a vague, back-of-her-mind way. They were utilitarian, basic, standard-issue beige wood. Frankie squinted, her brain running in the way that it sometimes did before she either had a brilliant epiphany or needed to take an Ativan.

This did not seem right. This did not *feel* right, and if Frankie Harriman was good at anything, it was tapping into a *feeling* and riding that wave. That's how she discovered Night Vixen in a dank club off Sunset and brought them from bickering post–high school naïfs to the A-lister girl band who currently had the number two record and five singles on the charts. No small thing for a girl band in the late '90s, when—despite the success of, well, Frankie would just say it: ugh, the Spice Girls—girl bands still had to fight for both respect and airplay. It was how she'd navigated the boys' club of her industry and landed on *Hollywood Reporter*'s 30 Under 30 at twenty-eight: by tapping into *feelings* about up-and-comers and massaging egos and wiping tears and sending ridiculously large bottles of champagne to front doors when a single got its first spin on 102.7 KISS FM.

This morning, with alarming and rapid acuity, Frankie realized that her feelings bleated, *Something is not right.*

Gingerly, she eased closer to the man beside her, craning her neck until she hovered just above his face.

She recognized him both too slowly and too quickly, in the way that you might when you slam on your brakes before you hit a biker who runs a light. How quickly you react determines everything that comes next. An adrenaline rush but nothing except tire marks in the street or a man dead in the crosswalk. Half a second makes all the difference.

Frankie Harriman, who was accustomed to finding herself in plenty of oncoming traffic, did not react well. She stared at the stubble and the chestnut hair and the long eyelashes and the straight nose, and she screamed.

TWO

Ezra

Ezra woke to someone screaming, so loud, too loud. Oh God. Why was it so loud?

"Stop," he mumbled, his eyes still closed. "Stop."

The screaming abated, and he curled into the fetal position, tugging the sheets closer. A tug back. He yanked in reply and cocooned himself further in the bed.

Then, an unwanted poking at his hip. *Poke. Poke. Poke.*

He groaned and exhaled, his eyes still shut.

"*You,*" he heard, and felt hot breath in his ear. "You!"

Now his eyes were open, and he took a sliver of a beat to process where he had unceremoniously woken.

A dorm room? His brain discarded the notion. Then revisited it.

He tilted his head up an inch from the pillow. No, this was definitely a dorm room.

His heart accelerated in a way he could feel acutely in his

chest. Did he actually go home with a college student last night? He did the math: while one hundred percent disgusting, it would not be illegal. Ezra had gone to law school and knew that while there were plenty of things that were unsavory, they could not land you in prison.

He felt the finger pressing his hip again. *Please don't be eighteen. Please be clothed. Please be Mimi. Please please please be Mimi.*

"You! What are *you* doing here?" From behind him. And then he instantly knew the voice; he'd heard it a million times back when he was young enough to live in a dorm room. In fact, when he did. When she did. Their junior and senior years. They'd lived together even if it hadn't been official.

Oh shit. It hadn't occurred to him to plead for a reprieve from Frankie Harriman because never in ten billion years— no, more than that—would it have occurred to him that she could be the woman next to him.

He didn't want to turn around to face her, and yet, it appeared to be too late to slink out unnoticed, to leave a note and a promise to call. Not that Ezra had ever done such a thing even once in his life. He was a Big Brother. He spearheaded a free legal aid group in law school. He was a monogamous commitment-fiend who'd never had a one-night stand because he valued the relationship, not just the sex.

He steeled himself before he turned to face her. How he'd ended up in a twin bed in a dorm room with Frankie Harriman was truly beyond him at the moment. But turn he must.

So he did.

And she screamed again.

And he, startled at both the decibel and the proximity of her face for the first time in ten years, screamed back. Louder. *Louder.* Because he'd vowed the last time he'd seen her that she would never get the better of him again.

THREE

Frankie

What are you doing here?" Frankie shrieked, pushing her palms flat against Ezra's bare chest, then pulling them back as if she incurred an electric shock. "Why are you in bed with me?"

Her head throbbed with each syllable, so she quieted and waited for what she hoped was a suitable explanation. How could there be a suitable explanation? She had pledged never to speak to him again, never to *think* of him again, and now, here they were, skin to skin, tucked under his sheets as if they still knew each other in the ways that they used to.

She watched Ezra blanch and swallow. He scrunched his face, a habit from back in the time when they were crazy in love and he was tackling an Eastern European history paper or a group project he'd wind up doing the bulk of the work on. A decade ago, she found this perplexed look endearing. Now, its breezy intimacy made her ill. But that could have been the hangover too. How could he be so familiar to her, so exactly the same?

Of course, Ezra *had* grown up (she heard things, ok?)—law school, Manhattan, last she'd been told. But she hadn't really kept up with him over the years. Had never once been tempted to seek out his phone number, had never whiled away late evening hours (even when tipsy) in an AOL search spiral. When she and Ezra split the day of their graduation, Frankie put it behind her entirely. She had barely given a second thought to Ezra Jones, except to occasionally consider how much she hated him, how deeply he had offended her, how gravely he had misunderstood her. That was the one that really stung. That after two years, he'd gotten her all wrong.

Of course, Laila and April occasionally couldn't help themselves—April would mention that Connor had crashed with him for a boys' weekend in New York; Laila would say that she heard he was single again, as if Frankie had known that he wasn't single in the first place. There was one trip to New York about five years after graduation when the record company put Frankie up at the Gramercy Park Hotel, so Laila had come up from North Carolina and April had trained down from her graduate studies in Boston, and they were at the lobby bar, and Laila gasped and said, "Holy shit, is that Ezra?" And Frankie froze like a cornered animal, her adrenaline seizing her intestines, and then Laila said, "Oh, no, my bad, not him," but Frankie was already shaking. Later, they were tipsy and flopped on the king bed, and Frankie said, "Guys, please, I don't want to hear his name again, like, ever, ok?" And she saw a look pass between them, but they nodded all the same. That's how Frankie did it, that's how she organized her life, and that's how she left Ezra Jones behind. By any means necessary.

Now, Ezra's face unwound, and he hiccupped, his breath smelling like day-old alcohol. Then his features comported themselves again. He didn't look much different than he had back in college, Frankie thought. His cheeks had shed the last of their baby fat, and his stubble was fuller now, as if he really could grow an actual beard, which had seemed just out of reach at twenty-one. But he was still boyish, his dark eyes still protected by full lashes, the line of freckles that ran from his left eye to his ear still prominent and shaped like the curve of a moon.

Frankie remembered running her fingers over that curve, awed by the perfect crescent on what she used to think was a perfect face. Though she hated to acknowledge it, even under the veil of sleep and in need of a shower, Ezra Jones was beautiful.

"Why are you in bed with *me?*" Ezra responded, bringing her back. "And what . . . I mean . . . Are we in a dorm room?"

"A dorm room?" Frankie snapped. "I'm staying at the Inn. Why would we be in a—"

She stopped, as something clicked into place. The beige furniture, the vague familiarity, the generic blandness of it all. They had, indeed, inexplicably landed in bed together *in a dorm room.* If this were a rom-com, someone in the audience would squeal. This was not a rom-com, however. Neither of them squealed. Both of them were horrified.

Frankie arched and tilted her head back. The wall behind them was covered in posters. The Backstreet Boys. The Cranberries. Nirvana. Night Vixen. (*Hooray*, Frankie thought, despite everything else.)

"Yeah," she said. "I guess this is a dorm room. What the fuck."

She thought about pointing out that her clients were on the wall above them but decided she didn't care about impressing Ezra. She regretted that she even had the instinct to impress Ezra Jones.

"Did we . . . ?" Ezra gestured back and forth between them. "I mean, do you remember what happened? Like, with us? Was there—"

"Oh my God, no!" Frankie said, though she honestly had no idea if they did or didn't. She sure as shit hoped they didn't though. Frankie had a motto that if something was over, it was *over*, which wasn't to equate that motto with the fact that she had zero inkling of what happened last night. Still, it felt more solid, more concrete to simply rule it out. "No," she said again. "For sure not. We did not."

She ran her hands down to her waist. She still had on her underwear, so that was . . . promising. She raised the sheets and sighed: though Ezra's flannel shirt was flung to the floor, he was also still in his jeans, although his belt, disturbingly, was undone.

She focused on the positive: "Your belt's still on," she said. "And I'm in my tank top. I'll take that as a good sign."

He stared at her for a beat, as if he were going to argue, but instead, let it wash over him.

Well, well, Frankie thought, a little annoyed that he didn't take her bait, a little relieved too. Back then, he'd rarely pushed back, and they'd never argued. Until they finally did in the archway of Burton Library on a clear day in May when their divide became a crevasse, when she'd said goodbye to Ezra forever and didn't lay eyes on him again until now.

"Are we in Homer?" Ezra asked. "Doesn't this look like Homer?"

Homer. Their freshman dorm.

Frankie screwed up her face into something that she hoped connoted: *That's the dumbest thing I've ever heard.* Inarguably, Ezra was almost always the smartest person in the room— he'd gotten a full merit scholarship to Middleton and was easily the brains of their group, so she never minded one-upping him when she had the chance.

She wanted to prove to him that she'd grown up too. And yet, she heard herself saying:

"How would we be in Homer?"

Ezra rubbed his eyes. "I don't remember anything from last night."

Frankie considered this. To be honest, she didn't either. She remembered getting ready in her hotel room; she remembered getting a call from Laila; she remembered—a jolt ran through her—locking eyes with Ezra as the elevator door closed. But then, well, she tried to find the rest of the night somewhere hidden in her cerebral folds. Nothing. There was nothing else there.

But she was not about to admit that to him, the brains, the ex.

"I loathe you," she said instead. "I can't imagine that I wanted to sleep with you."

"So." He paused. "You don't remember either?"

Ezra always did have a way of cutting through her horseshit.

She recalled that clearly now too. It helped that they'd been friends before they'd fallen desperately in love at the start of their junior year.

"Of course I remember." She tutted. "I remember that I absolutely do not want to sleep with you. I remember that the last time I saw you, I swore that if I ever saw you naked again, I'd run into a pit of fire before anything happened between the two of us."

"You didn't swear that," he said. "I have a very clear memory of that scene. Anyone who was walking by probably did too. I'm surprised it didn't make the evening news."

"I didn't swear it aloud, maybe. But to myself, yes, I did."

Ezra sighed and swung his feet over the bed to scrounge his shirt off the floor. Frankie wanted to look away, but she didn't. He was fitter than a decade ago, certainly. Back then, he had the torso of a twenty-one-year-old former cross-country runner with a good metabolism, who occasionally played a game of pickup basketball but who also had a McDonald's habit, which was just off campus for drivers passing through to the bigger Berkshire towns. She remembered the game they invented: whenever Frankie would look at him and say *run*, Ezra had to. He *had* to. They could be at Burton pulling an all-nighter; he could be wearing a towel fresh from the shower; he could be standing in line at the cereal bar in the dining hall. If she said *run*, he had to race her, and Frankie, sometimes because she would cheat and sometimes because he would let her, would always win. Now, she eyed him, saw his six-pack, the way his back was lean and sinewy, and thought she wouldn't stand a chance.

Ezra reached down, swiped a balled-up ivory sweater from

the foot of the bed and held it up, and Frankie nodded, so he tossed it to her wordlessly. She tugged her wool cable knit over her head like it was a suit of armor; in fact, she'd worn it so often their senior year that Ezra sometimes joked it was a third wheel. Her parents had split up by then, and her mom tried to overcompensate for both the divorce and the wreckage of her junior year summer by sending enormous packages from the J.Crew catalog.

Frankie felt Ezra watching her now. He remembered the sweater, just as she had, and blood rose to her cheeks.

"Stop staring at me," she said.

She ran her palms over her now-blond hair, flattening the overnight flyaways. She wondered if she looked different to him or if he were thinking she was the same, just older. She had never gone blond in college, and she liked to think that she'd grown more comfortable in her skin since then. But her eyeliner was surely smudged, and she wore much more of it anyway, and she was certain she had dark circles under her eyes—she always had them these days because she was never in the same time zone long enough for her circadian rhythm to settle.

"I'm not staring." Ezra sighed. "I'm just surprised that you still have that sweater. I figured you dumped everything that had to do with back then."

"Not everything," Frankie said. "Just the dead weight."

Ezra rolled his eyes at her overt pettiness, and Frankie wanted to regret it, to be less petty, but she found that she could not. And since she had come to accept herself for exactly who she was, nothing more, nothing less, she jutted her chin and said not another word.

Ezra spun around and in two steps, he was at the window, which had steamed up along the bottom corner from the radiator heat below. These dorm room heaters were shit, Frankie remembered. Always too scalding or not working at all. A relic from the 1950s. Middleton prided itself on its traditions, on its two-hundred-year history, and on campus, everything old was new again: radiators, stodgy library books, ancient professors, and evidently, previous lovers too.

At the window, Ezra raised the drawn shade.

"It's snowing."

Frankie pressed her palms into the mattress and straightened up to catch a glimpse out the window, as if he were lying to her. Ezra saw this too.

"We can agree on the basic facts of the weather, ok? It's snowing." Then he cocked his head and really assessed the situation. He loped ten paces to the door, opened it, twisted his head right and left out the front, then walked the ten paces back to the window.

"Holy shit," he said. "That's what I thought. This is my freshman-year dorm room."

"I didn't know you then," Frankie replied, as if this were a way to prove him wrong. She felt so desperate to prove him wrong about something. Snow, the sweater, that they'd slept together. It didn't matter. Anything!

"Well, it is. I used to count my paces back and forth whenever I needed to calm down." He paused, then quieted. "It was my mom's idea."

Frankie softened for a moment. She'd heard his mom had died a few years ago. Ovarian cancer, which she'd fought off and on since Ezra was a teen. Ezra was unusually close to her: his dad had left when he was a toddler, and his brother, Henry, older by six years, was busy being a grown-up by then. So it was just the two of them. Frankie used to be jealous of their bond. Even with a deadbeat dad and a mom who was chronically exhausted trying to pay their mortgage while going through treatments, he never doubted his mother's commitment to him. Her unconditional love for him. When she died, Laila had called and left a message on Frankie's machine, but she had been in Tokyo with Ashlee Cooper, a young up-and-comer who they thought they could launch in Asia before the States. (Alas, Ashlee developed a raging coke habit before her first single blew up, and she never really made much happen beyond that. Last Frankie had heard, Ashlee was auditioning for the first season of a show that marooned twenty contestants on an island.) By the time Frankie returned from Japan and heard Laila's message, she told herself that too much time had passed to reach out, and besides, who was she to call him and say how sorry she was? They weren't friends. They weren't anything. His mom had always been kind to her, though: pretended not to notice that she snuck into Ezra's bedroom the times she stayed with them over Thanksgiving or Christmas, went out of her way to send Frankie care packages whenever she sent ones to Ezra, and they always had homemade cookies. *I should have called*, Frankie thought now, a tickle forming at the back of her nose, a pinch of tears building too. She started to say something—condolences, perhaps—but Ezra cut her off before she could compose herself.

"Holy shit," Ezra said again. "This is definitely Homer, and this is definitely my old room. And I have absolutely no idea how we got here. Or why." He looked toward her for an answer, but Frankie happened to glance down at that exact moment and was in a bit of shock herself. In, well, actually a compete spiral, albeit for a totally different reason.

"Holy shit," Frankie said in reply. She'd just noticed a weight on her left hand, on her ring finger, in fact. A solitaire diamond in a platinum setting.

"*HOLY SHIT, EZRA!*" she said louder. "Why am I wearing an engagement ring?"

FOUR

Ezra

Ezra could feel his panic rising, and it had just about reached his boiling point. He didn't know if Frankie remembered this: flushed skin, shallow breathing, tremors in his fingers, all the signs of an oncoming anxiety attack. He was clutching her hand, staring at the ring on her finger—his grandmother's ring, the one meant for Mimi. And she was clutching his: staring at a band around his own left ring finger, which, until this very moment, he had never seen, much less owned or worn, before in his life.

Frankie yanked the ring on her finger, but it wouldn't budge: either her knuckle had swollen overnight or she'd shoved it on with such force last night that it was just stuck there. He pulled the gold band off his own hand, but she yelped, "If I have to wear this, so do you, so don't you dare!" which really didn't make all that much sense rationally, but they had bigger fish to fry, so he slid his back on.

"What the hell, Ezra?" Frankie started again and threw her arms into the air, then was on her feet, the sheets (whose sheets?) in his old dorm room tossed on the floor. One of the sleeves of her sweater caught a prong from the ring, and she spent a good five seconds waving her left arm spasmodically trying to release herself. When she did, she circled around in search of her jeans, finding them under the wood-laminate desk, and jumped into them like an old-timey cartoon character.

Ezra watched all of this and was struck by how little she had changed; how much she reminded him as she so often had done in college of a tornado: always in motion, occasionally a thing of beauty, too often destructive. Her hair was blond now—he'd never pictured her as a blonde, always a broody brunette, but he gazed at her and thought that it suited her. Maybe because it gave the veneer of sunshine but then you noticed the darker roots and wondered if there weren't something more menacing below. That's who Frankie was. A blonde with dark roots, all the way down. She was leaner than a decade ago, reflected not just in her taut shoulders and arms (which he couldn't help but notice in her tank top before she covered herself), but in her austere cheekbones too. He knew she was a big deal in the music world and jetted from city to glittery city, but Ezra thought that she looked like she could use a home-cooked meal. Not for the nutrition but for the nourishment. Even with the blond hair and the lithe body, she seemed nearly unchanged. Ten years had come and gone, and here they were, exactly as they had been.

Frankie caught her breath and then rubbed her temples. Then she was at it again.

"What the actual fuck, Ezra?! Please tell me that we did

not get . . ." She paused here, and Ezra thought she might actually gag. "Please tell me that we did not *get married* last night?!"

"I thought you remembered last night clearly," he said. "If memory serves, not even five minutes ago, you reassured me that you remembered everything." He felt himself slide into unemotional work mode, which calmed him, slowed his racing heart.

"Stop being such a goddamned lawyer," she scoffed. "I'm not on the witness stand here."

Ezra did not bother correcting her, but it stung a bit, that she thought of him as a lawyer, that she hadn't kept up on his life enough to know that he'd never given it much of a go. It's not like he *wanted* her to be plugged in to his life, but standing there in front of her, he realized it's not like he hadn't wanted that either. He'd heard things over the years, didn't mind perking up his ears whenever her name came up in conversation. Usually, it only served to remind him that they were better off apart, that they'd always been combustible. Still. It would have been nice to know her ears were perking up too.

They'd been best friends since the early winter of their sophomore year—even then, he was a serial monogamist who had split with his high school girlfriend the summer before Middleton (well, she'd split from him) and then committed to a flighty girl named Bethany. Frankie had plopped down next to him one night at the bar at Lemonhead, every student's favorite drinking joint, and said: "I'm not a therapist, but you look like you need some life advice," and he surprised himself and told her everything: about Bethany's odd disappearances for days at a time, about his mother's newly returned cancer.

And Frankie said, "Well, if this is like where we spill our darkest secrets, I guess I can tell you, stranger, that my mom is 99 percent having an affair with my old piano teacher?" Ezra remembered that she said it like a question but then recalibrated and said, "No, she definitely is. She 100 percent is fucking him." And he really didn't know what to say, because what he wanted most in his world was to veer away from any messiness, and here was this girl who simply purged her messiness onto the bar. When he didn't reply, she clicked her tongue and said, "Yeah, but anyway, I don't understand why you're with a girl who seems to have very few redeeming qualities? Just, like, to be with someone? That doesn't seem healthy." She was blunt, even back then.

Gregory had been hovering nearby, and he poked his chin between them and said, "Oh, hey, I'm Gregory, not Greg, just Gregory, and for the record, you—you're Frankie, right?—you are totally right, and Ez, really, you'll be ok if you dump her because it's not the end of the world if you're single, ok?"

Frankie had lit up at being validated, her eyebrows raised, the edges of her grin pointing northward too, and Ezra decided right then that she could be good for him, even with her messiness, even with her blunt force. She added, just to drive the point home: "Yeah, what are you even doing with her, with your life? Don't you know that you're in control of your own destiny?"

And then someone cued up "You Give Love a Bad Name" on the jukebox, and everyone behind them cheered, so Frankie dragged a reluctant Ezra to the dance floor, where they all screamed the chorus so loudly the walls shook.

"So . . . you don't remember last night?" Ezra said now, twelve years after they'd first met, more gently than before because he didn't know what other tack to take here. Frankie scowled, but then she was never particularly good at acknowledging mistakes. Much less apologizing for them. "We couldn't have . . . gotten married," Ezra continued. "I only had that ring on me because . . . it's for Mimi. And now you . . . I mean . . . No . . . it's impossible. Besides, where would we have done that . . . here?" He waved a hand as if to acknowledge this idyllic gem of a college town in Western Massachusetts, which had three bed-and-breakfasts and a used bookstore and a bakery that specialized in cinnamon buns but certainly no all-night wedding chapels. "It's not exactly Vegas."

But then Ezra remembered that Connor had asked one of his Middleton hockey teammates, Alec Barstow, to get ordained online, which sounded completely preposterous, but Connor swore it was legit.

"Mimi?" Frankie asked flatly.

"My girlfriend? Obviously."

"You planned to ask her to marry you at April and Connor's wedding?" Frankie made a face like he should know better.

"No," he said. "I did not plan on asking her to marry me at a wedding. I was planning on—afterward—" He stopped. He didn't need to justify himself to his college girlfriend.

"Oh," she said, but said it like: *ooooooooh*, a guise of understanding riddled with sarcasm. "The gesture grandé. Your specialty."

"Hey." He held up a finger. "Do not."

"Do not what?"

It was true that Ezra had long been a fan of a grand gesture. A decade ago, he'd probably overcompensated for his feelings for Frankie by using any opportunity to go big. The time he'd brought Paris to her behind their dorm; the ill-fated, heady decision in front of Burton Library that led to their destruction; the hotel room he booked the night he was certain they were going to sleep together for the first time. It was one of those quaint B and Bs because his only other choice was the Red Roof Inn on the outskirts of town, and even if Ezra didn't understand Frankie in the ways that he wanted to by then, he knew well enough that she'd grown up in a four- or five-star hotel kind of way. So he put the room on his close-to-maxed-out card, and scrambled around lighting too many candles and tossing literal rose petals on the duvet, and he cued up music from Sade because Frankie had once said that her songs were "pure sex." Frankie arrived after her last lecture, just as dusk was settling in, and he swung open the door, ready to woo her, and she took it all in and tilted her head, laughed, then said, "Is this all just to get me to sleep with you? Ez, I would have done that in the dorm." Then she took off all of her clothes and pulled him on top of the rose-petaled duvet.

"Well, thank goodness, Mimi isn't you," he said now, his voice dull. "So please do not insert your opinion where it isn't welcome."

Indeed, Mimi, like Ezra, loved a grand gesture—she'd been clear on that from the night they met when they were deemed "100% compatible" by a questionnaire they both filled out at a work event she was hosting. A proposal at midnight of the new millennium would be exactly what she wanted. He didn't have to stand here and explain all this to the woman who wouldn't get that in the first place.

"Anyway," Ezra continued, "later. Not at the wedding."

"Shit!" Frankie yelped, already over it. "The wedding! What time is it? I can't be late!"

The wedding. The reason they were back on campus in the first place. April and Connor worked here now—April taught nineteenth-century literature, and Connor was the assistant coach for the Division 2 hockey team. When Ezra got the invite, he thought of Frankie briefly—*Will she be there?*—but Frankie had such a big life in Los Angeles, so far removed from most of their social circle, that he didn't linger on the worry of seeing her again.

"What time is it?" Frankie said again. "How is there not a clock in this room?"

"I have a phone," Ezra replied.

"So do I. Everyone does!" Frankie tutted. "It's 1999. That doesn't make you special."

Ezra blew out his breath, and then they both cast about. Frankie patted down the bed; Ezra dropped to his knees looking on the floor. Frankie opened the closet, which was still full of a student's belonging. Ezra found his down coat by the front door and checked the pockets.

"Where are our phones?" he said finally, when there were no corners to scour, no flat surfaces they might be overlooking.

"So we may be married and we're missing our phones and we are in your old dorm room," Frankie cried. "And I'm supposed to believe that you have no memory of this?"

"What? You think I, like, did this intentionally? Like . . . with drugs?"

Frankie made a face like she didn't really think that because Ezra Jones had never even smoked a joint, but she had to start with a theory somewhere.

"Who's to say this isn't on you?" he jabbed back. "You and your . . ." He threw up his hands. "Rock-and-roll lifestyle." He was immediately mortified and wished he could recant.

"You are, like, literally the last person in the world I would want to hook up with!" Frankie snapped, then quieted. "Besides, I mean, I would also never do that—drug you. For obvious moral reasons. I don't need to drug someone to get them naked." Then she squeezed her eyes closed and looked wobbly on her feet.

"Are you ok?" Ezra asked.

"I am obviously not."

"I meant . . . I mean, not about all of this. But physically. Are you ok?"

"I have a blistering headache. Not a hangover headache, just that it feels like—" She reached up to touch the top of her head and assess.

But before she could say another word, the lock on the door clicked and the door swung open. A young woman, no taller than five feet and bundled in wool from tip to toes, appeared in front of them. Her eyes widened, and she froze.

Ezra had the bad luck of being the one standing within striking distance, so when she unfroze and screamed and reached for something that was buckled to her backpack, he was the one who was unfortunately blinded by her Mace.

FIVE

Frankie

Frankie did feel badly to see Ezra in such a state, even if she preferred not to see him at all. She rubbed her temples and tried to pray her headache away, but it felt selfish to worry about the pounding in her own head when he could barely crack open his eyes. She thought of that poor student, returning home from her walk of shame (Frankie didn't know if she was still allowed to say that?) to find two strangers in her dorm room. She could hardly blame her for dousing Ezra, then fleeing the scene. Frankie had scrambled around and grabbed what she could: her Doc Martens, their jackets, her purse, before tugging Ezra, who was alternating between whimpers and hysteria, out into the dorm hallway, then down the steps to the frigid outside air. It occurred to her now that she was missing her Walkman. And Night Vixen's early cuts.

Holy hell, this was turning into a ten-alarm fire.

She refocused. One problem at a time.

"We need to take you to a hospital," she said.

Ezra was sitting on a concrete step outside Homer, its brick facade glimmering in the snow, and muttering, "My eyes, my eyes, my eyes," his breath puffing out into clouds in front of him. Ezra had always been a bit of a hypochondriac, which in hindsight might have just been a cry for someone to take care of him. That had never been her strong suit, back then, maybe not now either. But today, Frankie, in a moment of genuine pity, wrapped Ezra's coat over his shoulders and sat beside him to rub his back.

It was odd, she thought, touching him again. With no memory of the night before, this was essentially the first time she'd made contact with Ezra Jones in a decade. A third of her life, really. A significant enough swath of time that he felt like both a stranger and also a familiar puzzle piece that clicked so easily into place. They'd fallen in love organically, simply, like learning a song stanza by stanza.

The night she sidled up to him at the bar at Lemonhead, he'd told her that she was the easiest person to talk to he'd ever met, that she made him want to tell her his secrets. Frankie remembered being flattered: she had been called many things, but amiable and approachable had never been among them. And he was easy to talk to too: like someone she needed to know, like someone who made her like herself more than she realized she could. And so she decided that they were going to be great friends, and they had been. They spent the remainder of their sophomore year swapping stories at the library or splitting buttered bagels while they crammed for their art history exams (they discovered they were in the same lecture), and once Bethany dumped him that spring, they metaphorically leaned closer and closer into each other like magnets until there was no space between them. And they stayed that way until they didn't, the day of graduation.

Now, Frankie's hand worked in concentric circles over his shoulder blades, and she reminded herself that this was a temporary balm, a short-lasting kindness. She did not want to be entwined with Ezra again. She had new people with whom to swap her stories, to share her secrets. She couldn't think of any at the moment, but she was sure that she did all the same.

Then she remembered the ring. Rings. Plural. She pressed her eyes closed and tried, *tried* to recollect what had happened. She met Laila in the lobby, and they'd taxied over to Lemonhead—the hotel, set back from campus and newly built for high-end donors and guest lecturers, was too far a walk even in Doc Martens. They ordered drinks, and Frankie was proud of herself for starting with a club soda. They toasted to seeing each other again. She had a vague image of the bar: not much had changed in the ensuing decade, but then students hadn't flocked there for the dingy decor. Rather, they were liberal with their ID policy, and pitchers of beer were five bucks. The floor was still sticky from spilled drinks; the pleather on the backs of the booth seats still crackled beneath their weight; the light was still dim enough to conceal all sorts of misdeeds. It was oddly crowded for winter break, but then plenty of students opted to stick around over the holidays— either by choice or by circumstance. Frankie had been one of them until she started going home with Ezra instead. Middleton forged new families—she wasn't so many years out that she didn't remember that.

The first time Ezra had invited her home, it had been

Christmas break, they'd been together for four months, they were seamless in the way that early love is. After they first slept together in the B and B that Ezra had splurged on—a memory that Frankie revisited now for the first time in years, flooding her cheeks with heat—they wanted always to be naked, and when they weren't naked, they wanted always to be together. At lectures, in the library, at the dining hall. It didn't matter. The span of a two-week break felt interminably long to the both of them, and Frankie's parents were splintering by then: she couldn't bear to decamp to West Palm Beach, where they spent most Christmases, and be the glue that held her parents together.

Frankie was surprised to remember this now—how easy it had been to say yes to spending break with him, how easy the two weeks had been in a home that wasn't hers. She was a near-professional at performing for strangers, even several years after quitting performing entirely, but she found that his mom asked for no artifice, and Ezra demanded even less of it.

"Just you," he would say. "Just you."

That holiday break, he'd suggested ice skating. There was a pond over in Bryn Mawr that was shallow enough to freeze by mid-December, and all the local kids made an event out of it: the first skate out. Frankie could borrow his mom's skates, Ezra had said. Someone always set up speakers and a boom box and blasted whatever was charting on the radio. And someone else always inevitably sold hot chocolate for a quarter, fifty cents if you wanted marshmallows.

But Frankie had never learned to skate. She didn't explain the why of it because she wasn't yet ready to trust anyone with her history—it had been because she'd had one singular focus in childhood, and anything beyond that, *any childhood things*, were simply not on the docket. She'd barely even told him that she played piano by that point, by that magical Christmas. When he suggested that they head to the pond for the evening, she shook her head and burst into tears. It had to be the first time he'd seen her cry. It was one of the last times too, in fact.

He told her that he didn't care if she were the world's worst ice skater; he didn't care if she dug her fingers into his elbow or spent the bulk of the evening on her butt. He thought it would be amazingly endearing if either of those proved true. But Frankie simply would not budge. She didn't want to learn something new; she didn't want to be the only one at the pond who looked like a fool. Later, Ezra realized that what she really meant was: I only like to do something when I am the best at it.

They agreed to go to the movies instead. They saw *Moonstruck*, and Frankie had laughed until she got a cramp in her side. But he made her promise that she would take lessons at Abel Rink, Middleton's hockey arena, when they got back. She didn't know why he cared, why that was so important to him.

"It's not like ice skating is, like, a critical life skill," she said while they were waiting in the concession line for a large popcorn and Red Vines.

"No." He shook his head and smiled. "But what if I want to take you skating some time? Just because I want to? Wouldn't it be nice if you said yes?"

Now, a decade later, the cold from the step outside Homer was seeping through her Levi's, just like it had all those years ago on the ice, and Frankie pushed the memory away. She wasn't here for nostalgia; she wasn't interested in a trip down memory lane. Getting swept up in emotion today wasn't going to help anything. She nodded to herself, an exclamation mark on her proclamation. Beside her, Ezra shoved his arms through the sleeves of his North Face puffer, and Frankie hopped to her feet, happy for a respite from the chilly concrete, a respite from her thoughts.

"Can you walk? We really need to get you somewhere." She paused. "Isn't student health . . ." She glanced to her left and right, tried to get her bearings. In contrast to the pulse at Lemonhead the night before, the campus was quiet, the snow falling in wet, fat flakes and starting to stick. The gray Gothic buildings seemed to shiver, so Frankie did too. She thought again of the ring on her finger and wondered, if she managed to wrestle it off and dropped it in the snow and let it sink to the ground below, if that would mean that whatever happened simply hadn't. Could you erase a moment or an act just by burying it? Frankie knew well enough the answer, but that didn't mean she didn't consider it all the same.

Ezra was still whimpering on the chilly steps beside her. His eyes were swelling at an alarmingly rapid rate, his lids and surrounding skin a bright angry pink. Frankie didn't want to play nursemaid, but she also didn't know what other choice she had, and she'd done it often enough for work: a harried trip to the ER for a pumped stomach in Milan, a backstage IV of fluids if it meant getting the artist onstage in London.

"Goddamned Mace!" Ezra squawked, and Frankie wasn't sure if he was genuinely crying or just unable to stop his tears from the spray. Ezra had always been an easy crier. In college, she first found this lovable, but by the end, she thought it was all a little melodramatic. "I mean," he continued, "who maces a perfectly nice guy standing there trying to explain himself?"

Frankie didn't think this was the time to get into the dynamics of a young woman returning home to find a strange man in her room or point out that she also kept Mace not only in her purse but in her glove compartment too.

"Come on," she said. "You need help."

She offered him a hand. They both froze for a beat, his grandmother's engagement ring twinkling in the morning light between them, then she reconsidered and thrust out her other one.

"Shit," he muttered. "*Shit shit shit.*"

"Let's just go back to the hotel," Frankie offered. "Shower, get some sleep, pretend this never happened."

"No," Ezra said in the urgent way that was just so Ezra. "I'm proposing tonight. This needs to be over ASAP."

"You can still propose tonight."

"How can I propose tonight if we're already married? I can't . . ." He flung a hand into the air as if to say, *I'm not a polygamist, my God, come on!* "Also, Mimi should be at the hotel by now, her flight landed this morning, I can't just—" He stopped and sighed.

"Fine," Frankie said, her chest tight, her patience tried. "Just fine. There must be a reasonable explanation. We'll figure it out, *then* we'll go back to the hotel and move on. Act like it never happened. Annul this if we need to. *Obviously*, legally or not, we're not married."

Ezra started to reply, but his face folded into confusion. His hands, tucked deep into his coat pockets, moved with urgency.

"The lining of my pocket is torn . . ." he offered, as a way of explanation. He paused again, wrestling something free. "Something's caught in here."

Frankie raised her eyebrows because the Ezra she knew—summa cum laude, matching socks, organized Filofax, never late for a deadline—would never have a hole in his pocket. But Ezra shimmied something out of the right side of his jacket. Then he held up a set of keys and peered at them the best he could with his donut-sized eyes and faulty focus.

"I don't suppose these are yours?" he asked.

"Mine?" Frankie said. "Why would my keys be stuffed inside the lining of your coat?"

"Why are you wearing my grandmother's engagement ring?" he rebutted.

"Why did we wake up in a twin bed in Homer?" Frankie barked back.

Ezra sighed, his shoulders deflating like someone had punctured him. He ran his hands over his stubble, and something was so familiar, too familiar about it. Not from years back but from last night. Frankie tried to hold steady, to hold still, but she was nearly bowled over with a memory: *of mistletoe, of Ezra running his hands over his face, of Frankie leaning in closer, and of kissing him.* Frankie thought she felt her breath leave her body.

Ezra, fortunately, paid her no mind.

"Well, these aren't mine." He dropped his head into his hands. "I've never seen these before in my life."

"Fabulous," Frankie said, and she hoped her voice didn't wobble.

"Fucking A," Ezra replied, too loudly. His voice reverberated off the exterior dorm walls and then bounced right back at them. Though she tried not to betray it, Frankie was screaming on the inside too.

SIX

Ezra

Ezra was trying to think only of Mimi but found it increasingly difficult to stay focused. His face was throbbing, Frankie was wearing his grandmother's ring, and the snow was coming down in sheets. They trudged away from campus in search of shelter, finally landing at a coffee shop that used to be a Chinese restaurant where they'd gone for Friday night dinners with April, Connor, Gregory, and Laila. But Chinese food reminded him of Mimi, who liked to crack open fortune cookies and intuit the deeper meaning, and brought his brain and anxiety circling right back to where he started.

Mimi! Sweet Mimi, who he'd planned to ask to marry him at the stroke of midnight when the world ushered in a new century. He'd written a small speech, he'd ensured that his tux had enough give for him to get down on one knee, he'd even inscribed the ring with the date: 12/31/99. Mimi came from a sprawling midwestern family who spent Christmas every year at her childhood home outside Kansas City, and she had agreed to cut the visit short to join him at Middleton. To be honest, Ezra had pleaded: it was about a month ago, and Ezra was late to mail back the RSVP because he wasn't sure if she would join him.

"Please, I want you to meet my college friends." They were splitting Chinese food on the sofa in their one-bedroom, and it occurred to Ezra how separate his lives had been until now: there was his college life and the friends he kept in touch with (mostly just Gregory and Connor), and there was his Mimi life. Mimi worked for a dating start-up, Datify.com—she was insistent that meeting your spouse on the internet was about to become the next big trend in romance, though Ezra was dubious. Who would ever admit to such a thing? Didn't it sound embarrassing, impersonal, desperate? But she was constantly dragging him to various events; in fact, they'd met at one. Datify frequently gauged compatibility algorithms, so they held meet and greets with free wine and cheese for singles who agreed to fill out questionnaires in exchange for a shot at love. Ezra happened to be at the bar with a poker buddy when Mimi descended and corralled him into joining.

"Here," she'd said, flipping back her shiny red hair, handing him a clipboard. "Trust me, you'll be awed, amazed, bowled over at what is about to happen." Ezra was already fairly swoony at her beauty, and she probably knew it, so she turned on a magnanimous smile, and he ticked off various likes and dislikes: Was he a morning person? Was education important? Was he religious? Did he want children? What was his favorite city? Did he like hiking, did he like movies, did he like quiet time, reading, concerts, cooking, spicy foods, far-flung vacations, museums, Valentine's Day, and baseball games? He handed the clipboard back to Mimi, and she ran her finger over each of his answers, her eyes widening as she went.

"Wait!" she squealed. "WAIT! I cannot allow you to meet anyone here."

"That doesn't seem fair," Ezra said, half-heartedly. He didn't really care all that much because the whole thing seemed like a gimmick. But he was trying to play along mostly because she was adorable.

Mimi ran into the back of the bar and emerged a few minutes later, her pale cheeks flushed. She pushed a different clipboard with a completed form into his hands.

"Look," she said, nearly breathless. "Look!"

He looked. Then he raised his eyes to hers. She was grinning and thrust out a hand, and said, "I'm Mimi. I think you're my perfect match." And Ezra took her hand and raised it to his lips and kissed it. Because they'd both checked off "chivalrous," and they'd also both checked off "romantic" and "honest" and "loyal," and he knew that she would appreciate the gesture and not find it cheesy or patronizing. She giggled, then held her hand to her heart, like she'd been shot with Cupid's arrow. They were a couple within a day. And from there, his life was about Mimi, about their future, not his past.

But April and Connor's invitation had reminded him of those bonds he'd forged at college, of how they'd both shown up for his mother's funeral, even though he hadn't asked. Of course, Frankie hadn't shown. They hadn't spoken in years. He wouldn't have expected her to.

"Come on, Meems, you'll love them," he had said that night over Chinese food. "April and Connor, and Gregory, oh my God, you'd love him, and . . . just . . . we were all inseparable."

"I met Gregory," Mimi said without looking up. "In the Hamptons."

Ezra had forgotten—two summers ago, when they were newly together, when Gregory was back from Portland for the week and joined them.

"Right, and he's great, right? But I want you to meet the rest of them."

Mimi had raised an eyebrow and her chopsticks hovered in the air and she said: "Is this because of *her*?"

"Her?" Ezra honest to God didn't even know who she meant at first.

"*Her*," Mimi said, and then Ezra understood. *Her.* He and Mimi had never had to have the talk about exclusivity or if they were going to be serious. Ezra always wanted things to be serious, with any new girlfriend. And besides, they'd both ticked those same boxes: monogamy and fidelity were of utmost importance. When they started dating, he was already apartment hunting—he'd gotten too old for roommates, and he made enough money to splurge on a prewar rental with decent plumbing and a doorman—so she started apartment hunting with him. She moved in with him after he signed the lease, and honestly, Ezra was happy. They were a perfect match of two people who both wanted the exact same amount of loyalty (all of it), who both required the exact same amount of honesty (also all of it). It had been this way since the start, and with expectations so clear, it had always been easy, exactly what Ezra thought a relationship should be. They'd talked about their exes in passing—the sort of conversations you had, and then set aside, when you were both so relieved to finally find the right fit—and just like everything else in their relationship, they landed on the same page: that those relationships were so far in the rearview mirror they couldn't be seen, that those were shadows who felt like distant memories. Ezra was surprised that Mimi was even mentioning Frankie. He certainly never did.

That night, he put down his own set of chopsticks and cracked open a fortune cookie that fortuitously read: *You have a great adventure in your future!* And he held it up for Mimi to read, and she laughed and pushed her copper hair behind her ears and said: "You planned that, didn't you?" And he grinned in reply, and said, "Please come? I really want you there. And it has nothing to do with *her.*" And she acquiesced and then she promised she would call to find a flight from Kansas City to Boston or Hartford, Connecticut. They never discussed *her* after that, and when he thought about this later, he was never quite sure if this was a blessing or a warning. Maybe both.

Today, Ezra watched Frankie shake her blond hair free of damp snowflakes and wondered if Mimi hadn't been right all along, that part of him wanted her there as protection, as a shield against Frankie Harriman. But Ezra truly hadn't known if Frankie would even attend: her showing up to celebrate a life event for old friends, much less as a willing bridesmaid, felt totally out of character, and while there were a slew of surprises to behold this morning, it only just dawned on him that one of the biggest was that Frankie opted back into their circle.

Frankie swung open the door to the coffee shop, and the heat assaulted them.

"Oh, thank the sweet Lord," Frankie said, more to herself than to him. "Heat and sustenance. I'd forgotten how cold it is here. LA is seventy degrees any day of the year."

"I need to call the hotel," Ezra said.

"I can't do anything without caffeine," Frankie said. "Can we agree, drinks first, call second?"

Ezra acquiesced. He could really use some coffee, and besides, what was he going to say? *Hello, I may be married, but if I'm not, please accept my grandmother's engagement ring?*

Frankie scooted out a chair for him, he plopped down, and she went to the counter.

He didn't bother telling her what to order: it was exactly what he'd always gotten, and he assumed she knew as much. Ezra never cared much about change, which he thought was overrated. He liked what he liked; he was who he was. Frankie, though, had always been like an impressionist painting: different from every angle, different in each light. But Ezra was just Ezra. He liked his coffee with a splash of cream and one sugar, and it had been that way since he was eighteen and started drinking coffee once he was done growing. He'd read research that caffeine could stunt your growth, and he was nothing if not a faithful abider of the rules.

Frankie returned to the table, pushed the to-go cup his way.

"Splash of cream, one sugar." She also got two buttered bagels.

"Hasn't changed." He nodded.

She raised her eyebrows as if to say: *I figured*, and he hated that he wanted to apologize for this. Like morphing his coffee order into something more interesting might mean that he had evolved into someone more interesting too. But this was always part of their flawed foundation: that she gravitated toward the storm, while he preferred locking the doors and shuttering the windows until the storm passed. Ezra studied her and again thought of Mimi: how he could have loved two women so wildly different. Mimi, like him, was ordered, measured, reliable, *grown-up*. They'd been, after all, a perfect match in their meet-and-greet questionnaire. Ezra eyed Frankie across the table and corrected himself: Frankie didn't gravitate toward the storm, she *was* the storm. Who, he regretted having to remind himself, he may have married last night. Whether it was the coffee or the notion, Ezra's intestines contracted.

Frankie pulled out a chair, drank her own coffee for a quiet beat and broke off half her bagel and swallowed it in a few quick bites, and then folded her hands in front of her, resting them on the table.

"So," she said.

"So," he replied. His stomach lurched, but he knew he needed to eat too, so he nibbled on the bagel, then found himself hungrier than he realized and kept going.

"It seems improbable that you don't remember what happened . . ." Her voice drifted as she tried to drill down on what she really wanted to say, though Frankie often said one thing and meant something else entirely. "I mean, you were always the smart one."

Ezra wondered if maybe she didn't think she knew him like he still believed that he knew her. That wouldn't shock him—he'd always been more sentimental. It wasn't that he thought of her often. Sometimes, sure, but often? Not really. Sitting here, across from her in the cozy coffee shop, with Christmas carols lilting from the overhead speakers and with Middleton all around them, it was easy to imagine that he'd never forgotten her, hadn't really stopped thinking of her at all.

Which was insane, he told himself. Insane! Frankie Harriman had driven him crazy, had split him in two, had withered him into a shell of himself, and once he departed Middleton, having packed up his (their) dorm room the day after graduation and driven to New York City with his mom, who was in remission again by then, he told himself that leaving her behind, leaving her *anywhere*, was the only possible solution. There was a quick phone call a week later, he remembered. A finality, the nail in the proverbial coffin. *Closure*, his mom said at the time, even though she'd liked Frankie, but then his mom had liked everyone. A decade ago, Ezra found it reassuring to tell himself that he was in control of his choices and his destiny, and so, on the winding drive down the Taconic Parkway, and in the days and weeks later, as he unpacked his boxes in his brother's one-bedroom apartment (they built a temporary wall in the living room to create a small room for Ezra) a few blocks from NYU School of Law, he repeated this mantra: *Frankie Harriman is out of your life. This is a very good thing.*

Now, he sipped the coffee she had brought him and wished that he were in less pain, that his vision weren't fuzzy, that his older brother, Henry, weren't all the way in London or that Mimi or Gregory were here to tell him he was ok. He wasn't ok, but just hearing them say it might make it more true all the same. What Ezra wanted was a support system. What Ezra had (mostly) was a brother in Great Britain, a wonderful but flaky friend in Gregory, and a girlfriend whom he wanted to marry but who would assuredly and messily ditch him when she discovered whatever it was that he couldn't remember about last night.

"Why would I lie to you?" he asked. "Why would I tell you I don't remember last night if I did?" Besides, he wanted to add: the one thing he'd never been with her was untruthful.

"I don't know. Maybe because you're a lawyer. Isn't getting married and breaking and entering the type of stuff you guys manipulate, like, daily?" Frankie winced and massaged the back of her head. "My head is killing me." Her hand lingered. "I think . . . I think I have a bump here?"

Her eyes met his, and he waited for her to ask. Because after that dig, he wasn't going to offer, and he wasn't going to assume that she wanted his help.

"I mean, can you look?" she said finally.

"I'm not sure I'm in the best position to assess—"

She yanked his hand from his side of the table and jutted her head forward.

"Here," she said, placing his palm on the back of her head. "Do you feel anything?"

It was odd, Ezra thought, to be touching her again. This woman whose body he once knew so intimately, whose body he had loved so intimately. Running his fingers through her hair was as personal an act as he knew.

His hand found the egg-like bump on the back right of her skull.

"Ow! Shit!" Frankie yelped. "I didn't ask for a cranium massage!"

He pulled his fingers back and noticed a light film of what looked like blood.

"Is this . . . I can't see well . . . but are you bleeding?"

Frankie went pale in front of him. He'd forgotten how bad she was with blood. They used to play "all's fair football" on the quad with Gregory and Connor and Laila and Alec Barstow, and once April and Connor started dating, with April too. This mostly meant that when Frankie was on the opposite team, she'd climb on his back and try to pin him down while howling with laughter because she was hypercompetitive and tiny, and he was not, but sometimes he played along and fell to the ground just so he could kiss her while she giggled. During one outing when they admittedly all had a beer too many, Connor beaned Gregory square in the nose, which sent blood spurting, and they would later learn, after X-rays at student health, that he had broken it. And this was when Ezra learned that his hardened New York City girlfriend was extremely bad with blood: she literally fainted right there on the quad. Now, he wondered if she had changed as little as he had: still scared of her own insides, in more ways than one.

He tested the waters.

"Remember Gregory and that football?" he asked.

"Are you trying to make me pass out?"

So she did remember. *Interesting,* Ezra thought. *How far she'd run away from this place without possibly running far at all.*

"Is his nose still crooked?" she asked. "Remember how it looked off-center for the rest of senior year?"

Ezra almost laughed, because it really had: if you looked at Gregory straight on, you'd wonder if you were having a bit of a stroke because his nose just never sat right on his face again.

But Ezra found that he was in too much pain for any joy: his eyes were really killing him now, and he started to notice that his throat didn't feel so hot either.

"I think I may have inhaled that pepper spray," he said. He swigged from his coffee cup, and it stung going down but maybe helped a little bit.

They sat in silence for a long minute. The songs switched and "All I Want For Christmas Is You" started up, instantly recognizable.

"Mariah," Frankie said, like Ezra didn't know who sang it.

"Obviously," he replied.

"She bailed out one of my artists—let us sample a song when we were up shit's creek. So, like, I have her number in my phone."

"I'm not sure Mariah Carey would be the one to call in an emergency." Ezra knew that wasn't what she meant, that she was only showing off, throwing around her self-importance, but he wanted to needle her anyway.

"Well, this is a different type of emergency, ok? So don't be a dickhead." Frankie winced and squeezed her eyes shut. "Goddammit, my head hurts."

"I think maybe you're the one who needs to go to student health?" Ezra said.

Frankie made a noise that sounded like indignant disdain, as if seeking help was a weakness. Ezra blew out his breath and scanned his brain once more for any speck of information that could help him sort it out—something about Alec Barstow being an ordained minister worried him, like as preposterous as this all was, as banged up as they both were, there was a not-zero chance that the damage could be, might be, far worse.

Shit. He tugged out the keys from his pocket, ran his fingers over the beveled edges, then spun the gold band around his left ring finger.

"Look," he said finally. "The only way we figure this out is if we do this together." He paused, really considered it. *Would they do it together? Could they do it together?* "So," he finally continued and held out his right hand. "Truce?"

SEVEN

Frankie

Frankie fiddled with the set of keys—four total on a Middleton key chain—and watched Ezra while he asked the nice girl at the coffee shop if he could borrow the phone. They'd agreed to a truce, but Frankie wondered, really, how long either of them would stick with it. Fidelity had never been their problem, but maybe loyalty had.

The barista passed him the cordless. She seemed young enough to be in high school and had a nose ring and a messy topknot bun and was looking at him oddly, but then he did look like a figurative dumpster fire, like maybe he'd just emerged from a fistfight or possibly a run-in with a swarm of hornets. Ezra asked for a phone book and flipped the pages until he found the hotel, and Frankie overheard him requesting a connection for room number 303. Then his mangled face fell when, clearly, it rang and rang and rang.

"No answer," he said, plopping back in the chair, then swiping the keys and tucking them back into his coat pocket.

"Try her cell?"

"She doesn't answer unknown numbers. She gets personally involved with work sometimes—gives people her cell. It usually backfires, so she's learned. Or she's trying to learn, anyway."

"Isn't being personally involved at work a good thing?" Frankie was always personally involved; she didn't know any other way with her artists.

Ezra shook his head. "No. Not with this. Have you heard of Datify?"

Frankie made a face. *No.* Also: *What?*

"Online dating," Ezra said, then Frankie started laughing. "Stop! It's a thing. Or it will be. Anyway, she also does off-line setups from her events. She gets paid when they match." Ezra shrugged, and Frankie bit her lip. "Look," he said, "she thinks it's promising, and since I believe in her, I think it's promising too."

"Sure," Frankie said and considered needling him, but honestly, the whole thing was so embarrassing it wasn't even worth it. She suspected Ezra already agreed. "Okay then, maybe she's out for a jog."

They both turned toward the window where the snow had blanketed the street.

"Don't be an asshole, Frankie," Ezra said. "I mean, if you can help it."

"I can't."

"That's the problem." He stood, as if to go. "Forget it. I thought we could make this work, and literally two minutes ago we agreed to a truce, but fine. I'll do this on my own."

"Godspeed," Frankie offered.

Ezra steeled his jaw, brushed his hair off his forehead, which Frankie was disturbed to find as sexy as it had always been. "There are a lot of surprising things about this morning, but your . . . your . . ." Ezra continued, waving his hands around searching for the right word. "Your pain-in-the-assness is absolutely not one. God, can you just not be an asshole?"

"Oh shut up," Frankie retorted. She didn't really care if she offended him. Truthfully, she probably wanted to. But even she could see that he wasn't wrong: in order to sort out their evening, they had to rely on each other. So she tried again. "Fine. It was a joke. I mean, obviously. No one is jogging in this weather."

"Make your jokes funny then. Also, Mimi doesn't run. She does the StairMaster—low impact. We go together five times a week."

"You hate the gym," Frankie said.

"You don't know me anymore," Ezra replied, though Frankie thought his voice was wavering, like she knew him better than he thought.

"Okay, fine, you love the gym now. Good for you, good for her. Yay, Mimi." Frankie waited. He remained standing. "That wasn't the problem back then, me being an asshole." Still, Ezra scowled. Frankie sighed. "Sit down. Don't be an idiot."

Ezra pulled back a chair and sat, though he jutted his chin as if he weren't relenting.

"Maybe we should start with the keys," she said, ignoring his theatrics. "To the dorm? To an apartment? To a car?"

"The dorms use key cards now," he said. "Everything's gone tech."

Frankie sighed. In college, she was constantly losing her

keys to the main gate of their building. She didn't know why. Theoretically, she was disciplined and organized after years of childhood commitment to learning her craft. In practice, she was half falling apart. There was a pay phone on the corner just down the block from the upperclassman dorms, so not infrequently, she would call Ezra collect, then hang up once he intentionally refused the charges, and he would lumber down the steps from his third-floor room to the gate. He never seemed to mind and always greeted her with a raised eyebrow but a happy smile, like he was the only one who could grant her entry. And in a lot of ways, he was right.

Ezra was staring now, a leveled, steely glare. "Why did you come back, anyway?"

A simple question.

"Because April asked me to be a bridesmaid," Frankie said.

"No." Ezra shook his head. "That's not a reason."

Frankie opened her mouth as if to protest, then closed it. She didn't want to tell Ezra that of course her instinct had been to say no. That when April reached her in Vancouver to tell her that Connor had proposed and to ask if she would be in the wedding, Frankie thought of all of the excuses she could offer. April was always so kind, and honestly, she wouldn't have argued, wouldn't have even doubted if Frankie were being truthful. But then Frankie remembered their freshman year together: even if they now lived such different lives that they often ran out of things to talk about whenever they did talk, April had that unique quality of making friendships easy, of being an ideally perfect freshman year roommate who wasn't put off by Frankie's moodiness, who made sure she always invited her to join her at the dining hall so Frankie had someone to sit with, who showed Frankie—who'd had a housekeeper her whole life—how to do the laundry so her whites didn't turn pink, so her sweaters didn't get tossed in the dryer and emerge infant-sized.

There were people who saved you in big and small ways.

Frankie was old enough now to know this, and April had saved her in so many small ways over that first year, when Frankie was still uncomfortable in her skin, still awkward with her identity, that she couldn't bring herself to be cruel and say no to the bridesmaid request. Also, there was the kindness the day of graduation too—the no-questions-asked call to the taxi, the hug before the drive to the airport.

It wouldn't be fair to say that she didn't regret saying yes to the bridesmaid request: she did. But then she dialed Laila, who was asleep in her apartment in Charlotte and who said: "You think I want to wear a magenta taffeta gown? Sometimes we do things that we just don't want to do for the people we love." They hung up, and Frankie sat in the silence of her hotel room, like so many hotel rooms she'd sat in for the past few years, and wondered why she so often found herself alone. And maybe if she showed up for the people she really did love, she'd find herself less alone when it mattered. She wasn't about to say any of this to Ezra though.

Frankie reached up and palmed the lump on her head, as if that could circumvent the blood flow. She thought of the time in Bangkok when she had gotten a concussion after she'd beaned her head against load-in equipment. There, she'd lain flat on a couch in the greenroom until her balance recalibrated, and after a few hours, her disorientation and spotty memory issues cleared up. She assumed the same would happen today.

Besides, she didn't want Ezra's sympathies. He'd already suggested student health, and the last thing she wanted was to be stuck in an exam room with Ezra looking worried and making calming but annoying comments to whatever resident was on call from the Pittsfield hospital.

Then, from behind the pastry display, Frankie heard: "Excuse me, oh my God."

She turned, and Ezra's gaze followed. The barista swung open the little door from behind the counter and stepped forward.

"I just realized," she said. "I didn't, I mean, I didn't recognize you from . . . well . . . your face. Are you ok?"

"Semi," Ezra said, as his eyes watered and tears streaked down his cheeks. "Not great, I guess."

"I didn't make the connection at first," she said. "But it's you from last night."

Frankie perked up, her headache momentarily forgotten. Ezra, best that he could, perked up too.

"You saw me last night?"

The barista—Frankie noticed now that she wore a name tag that read *Joni*—frowned.

"Well, yeah? Five card draw?"

"Is that some sort of drinking game?" Frankie interjected, because a drinking game would at least explain the situation. She hoped not though. What she hadn't told Ezra because, well, there hadn't been a great time to raise it, and besides, her booze habit was none of his business, is that she'd sworn off alcohol for two months now. She'd made the decision right before Halloween. She hadn't checked herself in anywhere; she wasn't attending AA. She didn't, like, have a formal problem.

But she found that at thirty-two, her hangovers were sticking like ugly bruises, and it was true that she could no longer party with Night Vixen, who was now a multimillion-dollar brand, the way she did early in her career. Someone needed to be the goddamned adult, someone needed, dare she say it, to be the Girl Scout! Frankie didn't want it to be her, but alas, who else was it going to be?

"No, not a drinking game," Joni replied to Frankie. "Poker."

"*Poker?*" Ezra yelped. "I was playing poker?"

Frankie rested her elbows on the table, silently relieved that she hadn't been driven to drink by Ezra Jones, and folded her hands beneath her face and parked her chin there. Now *this* was getting interesting. She remembered that Ezra, at least the last she had heard, had been banned from the Bellagio *and* the MGM when he was caught counting cards a year or two after college. She couldn't remember the specifics (and hadn't totally believed them, if she was being honest), only that Laila had been dating a mutual friend who spilled the details, and Laila, even though she was fully aware of Frankie's moratorium on Ezra Jones news, called her up breathless to gossip all about it. The whole thing was lurid, shocking—Frankie kept saying, "No way, no way, that *can't* be right," but indeed, it evidently was. A decade ago, Ezra had never had any sort of edge to him: he was a baseball hat–wearing, khaki pants, Boy Scout kind of guy. In fact, Frankie remembered now, he had been an actual Boy Scout until his freshman year in high school when Henry, older and significantly cooler, pulled him aside at Christmas and said: *Dude, you gotta quit, ok? No one will ever make out with you if you don't.* You couldn't judge a book by its cover, but with Ezra, you kind of could. He was *nice*, he was *smart*, he was *all-American handsome* in the way that suburban Philly boys could be in 1987, and he was the sort of committed that most girls wanted. He was Bruce Springsteen, not Axl Rose.

"I think you have the wrong guy," Ezra said. "I don't play poker."

"You play poker," Frankie interjected. "At least last I heard."

"Not anymore I don't." He waved a hand as if to end the discussion, and Frankie was honest to God a little turned-on by his dismissiveness.

"No, it was definitely you." Joni hesitated. "Ezra, right?"

If Ezra's face hadn't been so mangled, Frankie was certain she would have seen the blood rise to his cheeks. As it was, he was already a piggish shade of pink.

"Was I there?" Frankie asked.

"You don't remember if you were there?" Joni said, not unkindly, rather just because it was a reasonable question. "But . . . I'm not sure? We were over at Waverly's—"

"Waverly's . . . the pool hall? That's still around?" Frankie said.

At this Joni looked even more perplexed.

"We went to school here," Ezra offered. "But we haven't gotten around to exploring just yet."

"Oh! Cute. Married college sweethearts."

"Oh no—" Ezra started to explain.

"So we were at Waverly's, not Lemonhead?" Frankie talked over him. "Because I was definitely at Lemonhead." She thought again of Laila and wished she'd paid better attention to the last name of the girl she was crashing with. At least then she could call directory assistance and track her down to sleuth out the messy spiral of their evening.

Her phone, she needed her phone, where was her phone? She had it on her last night in the elevator when she'd locked eyes with Ezra. Had she and Laila even made it to the rehearsal dinner? Had Ezra? Some part of her brain tingled—she imagined her neurons waking up after being sucker punched—and she tried to lean in and pay attention. Why was she thinking she'd been on—no, this didn't seem possible. Had she participated in . . . a scavenger hunt? Frankie thought she must be hallucinating now. Never in her wildest dreams would she do such a thing. Even for April. So why was it prickling at her subconscious, why did it feel so real?

But then the barista was talking again, and Frankie swallowed the thought.

"No, Waverly's isn't really a 'pool hall' now—just a bar, but with a . . . back room. Lemonhead is just good for the dance floor. Maybe it wasn't that way when you went here?" Joni looked at Frankie with an almost pitying look, and Frankie wanted to scream that she was only thirty-two and hadn't even entered the prime of her life, but she found that she just didn't have the energy.

"Ok," Frankie said. "So *he* was at Waverly's. My whereabouts are still unknown."

"I don't want to get anyone in trouble," Joni said, as if Frankie were about to rap Ezra on the knuckles, like a chiding wife, a possessive partner. "I was just coming over to say that you were the best player I've ever gone up against. And, like, I'm easily the best in our senior class."

"Wait, did he take your money?" Frankie asked.

"Oh . . . well," Joni said stoically, then stared at the floor.

Frankie leveled Ezra with a look she knew he'd understand. He reached into his pocket, first removing the keys, then pulling out his wallet. He fingered through the billfold, and sure enough, Frankie noted that there must have been at least seven hundred dollars, probably more, in there. Ezra's swollen eyes managed to pop just enough that Frankie knew Joni was telling the truth.

"How much?" Frankie asked.

"No, no, really, that's not why—" Joni started.

"Do you know what this man does for a living?" Frankie said.

"Stop," Ezra cut her off.

"He's a high-powered Manhattan attorney at one of the top law firms in the city. Have you seen *Ally McBeal*? Like that. But . . . less singing." Frankie realized she wasn't making her point, but she forged ahead. "And you're here, slinging coffee, which is great for your work ethic but not for your tuition payments. Let him pay you back."

"Seventy-five. He took about seventy-five." Joni shrugged. "But it's ok. I got out a little too far over my skis. I can be a cocky bastard."

"Coincidentally, so can he." Frankie reached over, took Ezra's wallet and handed Joni five twenties. "That's your tip for today. Thank you."

Ezra sighed and then picked up the keys.

"I don't suppose these belong to you?"

Joni shook her head.

"And I don't suppose you know the people I was with last night? It's all . . . kind of fuzzy," Ezra said. "Neither of us remember much."

Joni scrunched up her face with no judgment. In the corner of the shop, the stereo speakers quieted, then a new song started. Frankie immediately recognized the opening clang: "We Are the World." She wondered if the song stirred up the same memory for Ezra—that first winter break she'd gone home with him to the Philadelphia suburbs. Ezra's mom was in remission but due for scans after the holiday, and he was understandably jittery. Ezra was often jittery, but this was a lot even for him. Frankie wanted to soothe him, but she wasn't used to caretaking, didn't really know how to, since she didn't exactly have exemplary role models, and she was barely used to taking care of herself. She hadn't yet told him about her child prodigy years, about the mess of her youth, which is how she'd come to think of it; about the fact that she could hear the notes in any piece of music and just somehow see them. But this song came on the radio as they were driving in his beat-up Jeep, and she'd started singing, because if Ezra could be vulnerable, maybe she could be too.

And she had looked at him and said: "You trade off with me."

Ezra scoffed like she was crazy. "I can't sing. Do you not know that about me? I really can't sing."

"Anyone can sing," she said. Then, as if to demonstrate, she proceeded to belt Paul Simon's line pitch-perfectly.

"No, really, I'm tone-deaf," he said, and she made a face as if to signal she didn't think Ezra was less than wonderful at anything, and so he'd tried Tina Turner's lyric—*We're all a part of God's great big family*—and he was right. He was truly awful. Frankie didn't mean to laugh, but honestly, he wasn't even in the right octave much less the right key, and Ezra cried, "I told you!" and because he was making her smile, he sang the next line too: *And the truth, you know, love is all we need.* But soon she was laughing so hard she thought she was going to pee in her pants, and when she told him as much through her hiccups, he started laughing too.

Finally, she got a hold of herself and said, "Well, I think if you're really that terrible at something, the only thing to do is lean into it." So she unlatched her seat belt and opened up the Jeep's sunroof, her torso craning out, her cheeks chapped from the cold air, and shouted, *"We are the world!"* Then she heard Ezra from the driver's side: *"We are the children!"* Then together: *"We are the ones who make a brighter day, so let's start giving."* Ezra let Frankie take the high notes as they finished up the chorus. And then Frankie shouted, "This time with feeling, Ezra!" And they did that over and over again, louder each time, until the song ended. And she eased back into the seat and then he pulled over, and they made out on the side of the quiet street peppered with homes flashing green and red Christmas lights until the windows fogged up.

If the song meant anything to Ezra now, he betrayed nothing.

"Really, was I with anyone you can remember?" he said to Joni. "It would be really helpful."

"I think . . . well . . . there were a few of us regulars at the table. I'm not even sure how you ended up there."

Frankie heard Cyndi Lauper wail her solo now, and she tried again not to think of that night in Ezra's Jeep. By then, he had already told her he loved her; he'd done that early on, shortly after he decorated that B and B where they first slept together, because that's what Ezra did. But when he'd pulled back from kissing her, the heat blasting from his Jeep's vents, her shirt off, her skin exposed, she surprised herself by laying the rest of herself bare too.

"I love you, Ezra Jones," she'd said, because it was true and also because she thought it might help soothe him, calm the pulse of anxiety that raced through him because of his sick mom but also because he'd probably been born that way.

"I already know that," he said, his voice husky and low. Then he kissed her again and took off the rest of her clothes.

Now, Joni's brow unfurrowed, as if something just came to her. "Wait, you did go on a rant for a few minutes."

"Was it about her?" Ezra pointed to Frankie.

"No, at least, I don't think so?" Joni shook her head slowly. "I kind of lose myself when I'm playing a hand," she said finally. "I could tell you what cards I was holding, I could even probably tell you what cards *you* were holding. But the rest of it . . ." She shrugged.

"Well, he can count cards," Frankie piped up. "So don't feel too badly." At this, Ezra audibly blew out his breath, then took another hundred from his wallet, slid it across the table.

To Frankie he snapped: "Just so you know, the card counting is for blackjack, not poker. You don't even know what you're talking about." Then to Joni, softer, he said: "But still, that's probably only reasonable."

"Oh!" Joni brightened. "Actually, you did say something like that: 'I don't think I'm being unreasonable!'" Joni faltered, trying to bring it back. "I think . . . wait, maybe someone couldn't get here? Her flight was canceled?" She considered this, her eyes narrow, her lips pressed into a line. "Yes! Yes, that was it. She couldn't get here because of the weather, and you were, well, look, you were pretty frazzled. More like . . . irate. You were irate. And probably . . . drunk? That's why I couldn't believe you kept winning."

"The card counting," Frankie said again dryly. Ezra slapped a hand down on the table and glared at her. "I guess that would explain why she's not at the hotel," Frankie continued, as if this were helpful.

"Shit!" Ezra ignored her. He sank his face into his hands. "Shit! I had a plan!" He dropped his hands to his lap, closed his eyes, and inhaled. "I can fix this," he said. "I'll just fix this."

Frankie, who really did know better than to keep stirring the pot, couldn't help herself. "How? How do you fix this?" Did Ezra have access to a jet? To the weather? How did one fix this? Frankie was honestly intrigued.

"Not *now*, Frankie," Ezra buzzed, and there it was again: Frankie found herself attracted to Ezra's newfound backbone. Frankie hadn't known that he, metaphorically, had it in him. He slouched over, resting his forehead on the table, and her impulse evaporated.

"Oh!" Joni brightened again. "And there was a scavenger hunt."

"A scavenger hunt?" Frankie echoed back, her decibel too high, too loud, as Ezra groaned again, dropping his face into his hands.

"I think, I mean, again, please don't take this as gospel, but I think you guys were a team?"

"That can't be right," Frankie said, even though she'd thought of such a thing just a few minutes prior. How? Why? Under what circumstances would Frankie Harriman ever agree to participate in a game that was most likely to be found at a ten-year-old's birthday party? Especially . . . with Ezra Jones?

Before Frankie could give the notion any breathing room,

however, Ezra, being so quintessentially Ezra, leaned over and flopped to the floor.

"Man down," Frankie said to no one.

Old patterns, familiar habits, a warning. All of it surprised her, even though none of it should.

EIGHT

Ezra

Ezra found himself staring at the stucco on the ceiling, inexplicably flattened against the rustic wood floor of the coffee shop. He had no memory of why he was down there; he had no memory of how he got down there.

Frankie's face moved into his frame, then hovered.

"Ezra, come on, you have to get control of yourself." She paused. "It's after ten o'clock already. Pictures are in six hours at the chapel, and Laila threatened my life if I'm not on time."

Frankie always ran late. He'd forgotten about that. He could tell that she was trying to be patient, but she'd never much been one for patience. He shifted his eyes from hers back to the ceiling. A refusal.

Then Joni, the barista, spoke up.

"Should I call someone? Like, 911?" He watched her gaze move from him to Frankie then back to him. "Campus is pretty dead, but someone could come? I know they have some patrols in case of Y2K."

"Y2K is really not a thing." Frankie scoffed. "Also, he does this occasionally."

Ezra wanted to state that he hadn't, frankly, had a panic attack in ten years—coincidentally, since Frankie Harriman exited his life—not even when his mom died, because at least he'd steeled himself for that.

"You're a sweet wife," Joni said, and Ezra's panic went straight through the roof again.

"No, we're not really . . ." Frankie started.

"No," Ezra managed, cutting her off. "No. I had a plan."

"His brain works too quickly," Frankie explained to Joni, as if he weren't there. "And then, sometimes, it just stops. Like being on a treadmill, you know? It just stops suddenly, and you're flattened on the ground behind it." She looked down at Ezra and pointed. "That's his brain. And that's probably what happened last night—he just got too caught up in the moment, went blank."

Ezra stared at the ceiling and thought of the time when, shortly after Frankie had come home with him the first time for Christmas of their junior year, his mother called him in his third-floor dorm room to tell him that they'd found lesions on her liver. How Frankie had lumbered to his room from a skating lesson at Abel, how her cheeks were pink and she was bubbling about a spin she'd managed to master—just one rotation, but still, she'd said—when she noticed he was catatonic on the floor. How she sat with him and sang "Summer of '69" to distract him, which she said they were playing at the rink, and how her voice sounded like a miracle. How she kept going until he was ready to ease into sitting. Then she kissed his cheeks and pulled him to his feet and suggested they break into the pool at the athletic center because she thought he needed to be reckless for a night, to be anyone other than Responsible Ezra Jones With a Very Sick Mom. He was surprised, back then, that he agreed, and he was further surprised by how much it had helped, even if for just a few hours.

"It's nice that you guys understand each other so well," Joni said, as if Frankie were recounting some goddamned fairy tale in which she was the hero.

I am the hero! Ezra wanted to shout. *I was going to propose to my beautiful girlfriend in an unforgettable display of romantic chivalry tonight. I am a knight in shining armor!*

Frankie squatted down, then plopped on the floor.

"Ezra, you're going to close your eyes, and you're going to breathe in and count to five and breathe out and count to five. And we're going to do that seven times, and then I'm going to heave you up." Just like she used to.

Ezra pressed his still-swollen eyes shut as best he could. But now, he didn't want Frankie's help. He didn't want to be pancaked on the floor of this cozy café while the snow dumped down on his college campus and while Mimi was stranded in Kansas City with her four brothers and nieces and nephews and mom and dad who would spend the holiday watching football and drinking beers with three-layer dip. (Ezra could not imagine Mimi eating three-layer dip or drinking long-necked Bud Lights because, despite checking off "adventurous eater" on her original questionnaire, she was quite meticulous about her calories and also her taste in alcohol, which started at chardonnay and ended at sauvignon blanc.) He didn't want to consider that he had won almost a grand last night in cards, a sum that despite Ezra's now comfortable lifestyle still shocked him. And how Mimi would feel about all of it because she didn't understand that part of him, just like she might not understand his previous panic attacks and breathing exercises and inability to turn off his brain when he needed to most.

Maybe she would; Ezra didn't know. He'd stitched himself together just enough by the time they met that he hadn't had to find out, and besides, Mimi liked their seamless life, one uninterrupted by drama. So too did Ezra. Which was why he gave up the poker and the blackjack and the online gambling when she tutted about it. He really did stop cold, but it wasn't his fault that his brain was wired for formulas and gaming the system and winning betting pots as easily as some people won Go Fish. He didn't even know why he was at Waverly's in the first place! He certainly didn't know that they had a back room with a card table, or else he'd probably have failed out of Middleton when he'd attended, rather than graduating summa cum laude without even trying. Then he wondered if maybe it were for the best that Mimi hadn't made it this morning. Which furthered his despair. He'd never been the guy who was relieved not to have his girlfriend show up. He was the guy who always wanted his girlfriend to show up! He didn't understand this new dichotomy, but he felt, deep in his bones, that he could blame it on Frankie Harriman's resurrection in his life.

Ezra groaned as Frankie counted slowly and aloud. "One . . . two . . . three . . . four . . . five. And now exhale: five . . . four . . . three . . . two . . . one."

The three of them breathed in and out in sync, as if they weren't a band of misfits who were trying to find their way out of a crisis that none of them understood. Then Ezra felt Frankie's palms on his back, and he was sitting upright, the blood draining quickly from his brain, the floor tilting ever so slightly until his mind settled.

"I think your swelling's going down a little," Joni offered. "I mean, your eyes."

Frankie stood and extended her hands toward him for the second time this morning, much as she had so many years back. "Come on, I'll help you up."

Ezra winced and declined. Instead, he sort of rolled forward and over and onto all fours, then grasped a nearby chair.

"So," Frankie said. "Do you remember a scavenger hunt, like Joni said?"

Ezra did not.

"Of course not." Frankie sighed. "Look, I have a hideous taffeta dress waiting for me at the hotel, so I sort of need to speed things along. We need to start at Lemonhead."

"I was never at Lemonhead."

"You have no clue where you were."

"What's the last thing you remember?" Joni asked. "That's how they do it in the movies."

Ezra dug in. He remembered checking into the hotel. He remembered trying Mimi's cell, but reception was spotty in both Western Mass and her Missouri suburb, so he logged on to his laptop and paid for the hotel dial-up to send her an email. She planned to fly to Chicago that evening, then was on the first flight out to Hartford, and a car would take her from there. He intended to send her the itinerary one more time because Ezra was the type of boyfriend who did that sort of thing.

He remembered right as he was about to send the email, Gregory knocked on his door and showed up with some home-brewed vodka that, when Ezra thought about it now, was probably the beginning of his problems. How he wobbled down the hallway to the elevator. How, after he saw Frankie with her yellow headphones and her Doc Martens, all his trouble began.

Now, on the floor of the café, he realized that he had no memory of what came next. Maybe he *was* at Lemonhead with Frankie and Laila. Maybe they were fucking married. Maybe he'd stolen someone's car with those keys. They could have done anything. They could have robbed a bank; they could have torched the library. He didn't know.

He reached for the leg of a chair and hoisted himself up. He needed to get his wits together, get his brain involved. Ezra had always been a whiz kid, a bit of a logical genius, which was why everyone had pushed him toward law and why he'd gotten a full ride at Middleton. He could, at least on paper, outsmart anyone. There's no reason why he couldn't methodically piece together their night. If he had to do it with Frankie, so be it. It would probably be easier to do without her, mostly because she knew exactly which buttons to push to send him skyrocketing to the penthouse of frustration, but still, he could do it if it meant proposing to Mimi at midnight and putting Frankie behind him once and for all.

"I think we need to work backward," he said, once he had settled himself in the chair.

"And I think we should start at the beginning," Frankie countered, sitting opposite him back at the table.

Ezra sighed. Long. Slow. Exhausted.

"I'm just saying!" she snapped. "I remember being at Lemon-head. The only solid info we have is that you were then at

Waverly's, and we inexplicably slept together at Homer. So why wouldn't we start at the one place we're sure of?"

"We didn't sleep together!" Ezra barked.

"Semantics," Frankie said.

"Well, what about the rehearsal dinner at Burton?" Ezra lobbed back.

He saw Frankie steel her jaw, and her nostrils flared just a touch, and beyond that, he thought he saw something like recognition. April and Connor had set the dinner in a private room at Burton Library—but there was too much about Burton to unpack right now.

"We will not discuss Burton until we need to. God, do we have to make everything about *that afternoon*? It was a decade ago!" Frankie said.

"Fine," Ezra said. "Just fine."

A concession. And then he realized: yes, he really could always outsmart anyone. Unless, of course, it was Frankie Harriman.

NINE

Frankie

Ezra insisted on checking his answering machine before they headed to Lemonhead, which Joni noted probably wouldn't even be open yet. Frankie admired her street smarts and wondered what she'd do after graduating. She was half-inclined to offer her a job like someone had done for her: an olive branch, a lifeline, out in LA.

"Maybe Mimi left me a message this morning," Ezra said, partially to himself, as he punched in his number, then his code. "She'd know that I could fix it."

Frankie rolled her eyes and thought about how paternal he sounded, and she knew that sounding paternal shouldn't annoy her but it did all the same. Her own dad was somewhere in the Caribbean with his new girlfriend and certainly unconcerned with Frankie's holiday itinerary, though he had sent her five hundred dollars for Christmas. Her mom had called and pleaded to meet up in Los Angeles after she and her new husband wrapped up in Cabo, but Frankie had told her she was leaving for Middleton early and concocted dates so her mother wouldn't push it. Her family was exhausting, and besides, her mom would only needle her about why she was managing half-talented, nubile, partially dressed twenty-three-year-olds rather than pursuing her own musical talents.

And anyway, she was thirty-two now, too old to embark on a new career when being young and having round breasts and flat abs was as important as any sort of talent. And yet, about a year ago, she found herself at home for a whole weekend—no travel, no concerts, no evening plans—and grew wistful about her neglected musicality, like it was a sunflower plant she'd left out to die. Without even thinking about it, she'd driven down Western Avenue to an out-of-the-way haunt where one of her artists picked up collectable guitars, and she bought an upright piano. It wasn't the grand piano she'd grown up with, but then, a grand was out of the question in her apartment. She paid an extra three hundred dollars for delivery, and then she just sat and stared at it from across the room for the rest of the weekend. She didn't know what she was thinking. She called to return it but was told it was final sale.

Today, she watched Ezra behind the espresso bar counter, the phone pressed to his ear, his eyes floating toward the ceiling, and she saw him mutter under his breath. Then he handed the phone back to Joni and returned to the table, swinging his coat over his shoulders and around his torso in one fluid motion. Somehow, Frankie had adjusted to his mangled face. It was odd, she thought, how something so shocking not even an hour ago felt digestible now. His cheeks still looked like roadkill, but now this was just an accepted fact of their morning.

Her own head was still throbbing, but she didn't want to make a big deal of it. She knew Ezra would become paternal with her too, and the last thing Frankie wanted was a father figure. Her parents had been trust fund kids who got pregnant too young and decided to valiantly keep it—keep her—but neither of them had been ready to be the type of parents who raised a well-rounded kid. So however Frankie turned out, she figured it wasn't her fault. They'd been twenty years old and had too much money and not enough interest or life experience. And like Ezra's face, it seemed completely fucked-up for a period in her childhood, but years later, it was what it was. For a while there, the three of them had united behind her musical genius: they had something to focus on collectively rather than recognize that they were simultaneously wholly dysfunctional. When she abandoned her music, they abandoned one another. She used to blame herself, but that got tiring quickly, so she settled into a new mantra: Who ever said family had to be forever?

She was a city kid seeking an escape when she'd arrived at Middleton at eighteen. Her parents and her school counselors at LaGuardia (everyone knew it as the *Fame* school by then) and her music teacher, Fred, were pushing her toward a conservatory, toward Juilliard. Middleton, a smaller liberal arts school in the middle of the Berkshires, had only a budding music department. So she said yes as soon as the oversize envelope arrived in the mail.

She'd shown up for college admittedly unformed. She'd spent the bulk of high school in music labs, collaborating with teachers or semiprofessionals or performing in competitions where sometimes, afterward, the kids would sneak away from their parents and try to act like normals, but they, all of them, were one-degree abnormal, which her mom always told her was necessary for great talent, for prodigies. But mostly that meant that her high school social experience, at least until her senior year, was spent in deserted classrooms post-concert sipping off-brand soda and eating powdered donuts left over from the reception. By seventeen, however, she was done with all of that. But still, it was no surprise that she landed at Middleton a bit of a mess.

"Well," Ezra said today, heaving his shoulders like he bore the weight of the world on them. "It's true: her flight got canceled. I guess she called my machine last night too. So"—he flapped his arms in the air—"that's that."

"You know you can propose literally any day of the year," Frankie offered.

Ezra leveled her with a look the best he could. One of his eyes spasmed under its own weight. "Do you ever just not have an opinion?"

Frankie considered this. No, she rarely did *not* have an opinion. Her opinions were what literally defined her, what made her career. As far as she was concerned, this was part of her charm. She thought this was something he used to love about her: that whenever he was waffling, he would tell her the two options and ask her to choose. Advanced art history or abnormal psych? Chinese chicken salad or beef with broccoli? Absolut or Amstel? Frankie would make an unequivocal choice for him and always chose, she thought, correctly. If she didn't or hadn't, he never said otherwise. Who chose for him now? she wondered. She suspected it might be Mimi. But even as they chipped away at each other, she hoped, for his sake, this wasn't the case.

"We need to get moving," she said, standing quickly. The room spun, and she flattened her hand against the table. Ezra was by her side immediately, grasping her elbow, keeping her steady.

"You ok?"

Frankie nodded. Of course, this was a preposterous question because she wasn't ok. But she found herself in the unusual position of merely wanting to be compliant. Things were messy enough already.

"You both could probably use a doctor," Joni offered from the cash register. "Is there a reason you're here and not there?"

Frankie looked at her for a beat and didn't reply. How to answer a question that felt loaded, too complicated to explain to this nice stranger. Neither of them wanted to admit weakness, neither of them wanted to be the first to say mercy, neither of them wanted to simply say: *help.*

Beside her, she heard Ezra sigh.

"Do you have anyone you could call from last night?" he asked. "Maybe to help us sort this out?"

Frankie shook her head. She knew that her voicemail would be only work emergencies or her mother. She didn't know how to reach Laila without her cell—she hadn't committed her number to memory. Who else was there? No one. Her artists were used to her rescuing *them*, not vice versa. Frankie had set up what she deemed a perfect hierarchy in her life: she was at the top, everyone else clung to rungs below her, and until this very moment, she'd never considered the ways that this might not serve her.

"What about Gregory?" Frankie said. For reasons she didn't yet remember, she felt sure that he'd been part of the debacle last night. Perhaps he was with them at the scavenger hunt? She jostled with the idea. Something about it felt familiar. "I think he was with us?"

Ezra scowled. "Like I didn't think of that. I tried his room too. He's not picking up."

They thanked Joni, who told them she'd be at the café until three p.m. if they needed anything but no later because she had a second gig tonight, and Ezra held the door for Frankie, and then they were padding through the snow, headed west through the main artery of the grounds. Middleton was a sprawling, sleepy campus: rolling hills, Gothic architecture, lawns of bright green grass when they weren't blanketed with leaves in the fall and snow in the winter. Statues of founding fathers sprung up in front of fountains, footpaths with raised wooden bridges crossing small bubbling brooks. It was all so postcard beautiful, as if you could become more serene just by looking at it.

Frankie flipped the hood of her jacket over her head and tugged the cord to seal in the warmth. Ezra squinted as the flakes landed on his eyelashes and then melted. His ears were a salmony pink from the cold, and he pressed his chin into the zipper of his coat to conserve body heat. They marched silently toward the bar, his Sambas and her Doc Martens crunching the ground beneath them.

Frankie wondered what he was thinking. In the ten years since she'd left Middleton, she'd convinced herself that her time here hadn't been transformative. That she'd been looking for an escape from her parents and the pressure of their musical aspirations and that Middleton had been a temporary fix. But as she tilted her head left, then right, she found herself pregnant with nostalgia. For the night when they, along with their friends, decided to camp out on the North Lawn because Gregory had said there was going to be a meteor shower (there was not); for the spring fair fundraiser where the campus turned into a literal circus, and fire-eaters and jugglers and men on stilts wobbled by, and Ezra taught her how to play Skee-Ball at the makeshift arcade. She was exceptional at it from the get-go and delighted at beating him each time, and he, ever the good sport, laughed until he ran out of tickets, and she, flush with them, went to the prize booth and bought him a stuffed zebra with a sad look on its face because it reminded her of him when he pretended to pout at losing.

They stomped by Steinway Auditorium, an imposing stone building that was one of the newer builds on campus. The Steinway family, of the piano fame, had donated several million dollars to attract top talent shortly before Frankie matriculated. It was one of the reasons her parents conceded and made peace with her decision to skip Juilliard and the like: though Frankie was done with *all of that* by then, they held out hope that she'd return to her roots, to "her gift" as her mother liked to say while Frankie often made vomit sounds.

As if reminding himself of the building's significance, Ezra did a double take and stopped.

"No," Frankie said, still so in tune with him. "We wouldn't have gone in there."

Ezra fished the keys from his pocket, ignoring her.

"Ezra!" she cried. "I wouldn't have gone in there!"

Her head throbbed when she raised her voice, and she tried to still herself to make the pain dissolve.

He turned to face her. "So you still don't play?"

"What business is it of yours if I do or do not?"

"Nothing about you is my business anymore, Frankie. And yet here we are."

"No," she said. "I'm still not playing. Ok? Can we go to Lemonhead, like we agreed?"

Ezra gave her a long stare, and even with his jelly donut–sized eyes, Frankie knew that he had her number. She wasn't about to tell him that a few months ago—nearly nine months after she bought the upright piano on Western Avenue and then let it collect dust for the better part of a year—she woke up pressed against her purple wall and felt the tug again: like an addict in search of another hit. And for the first time in years, she scooted out the piano bench and felt her fingers curve, then fly over the keys. She didn't know why: nostalgia, comfort, pain, maybe all three wrapped up together. Not unlike her decision to come back for the weekend: nostalgia, comfort, pain. Maybe they were all related.

"Don't look at me as if you have the right to my secrets anymore," she said finally. "I don't owe that to you." She fumbled for her jacket zipper and tugged it up an inch, as if this were any sort of protection from his permeating stare.

Ezra blew out his breath, the whirl of air pillowing around him.

"Listen," Frankie continued. "I've set foot in Steinway Auditorium exactly twice in my entire life. And just because one of them was with you doesn't mean that I relived those days last night."

"Both of them were with me, by the way," he countered. "So who's to say that last night—"

"Jesus Christ!" Frankie yelped into the empty campus, the

barren trees. "Are we relitigating our senior year or are we trying to find out if we are married?!"

"Fine, just fine. Perfect," he said, and started walking again, not waiting for her to catch him.

Frankie slunk along beside him until they reached the corner just across from a strip of dilapidated storefronts. The Soup Café, a Chinese restaurant, a campus clothing shop, a rinky-dink drugstore, and Lemonhead. The lights on the marquis were illuminated, but the L had burned out, so it read EMONHEAD, which struck Frankie as more depressing than it probably was.

Both of them stopped and stared across the street. It felt like a resurrection of sorts, of her old life, of their lives. Frankie felt an unwelcome swell of emotions—nostalgia, comfort, pain—rise through her: she didn't even know for what, specifically, but she thought that maybe it was just for lost time. How can you unexpectedly split from your boyfriend after a no-holds-barred fight in front of Burton Library and then wake up in a bed with him ten years later and grieve for those years, even if you wouldn't do any of it differently? Frankie hadn't allowed herself to mourn all that she lost after graduation. It was easier to move on, to force her way through. Now, she wondered if never mourning at all had been its own form of sorrow. It's not like pain just evaporated, she considered. It needed to go somewhere, and maybe shards of it were still lying dormant inside of her, waiting for a resurrection.

There was a Toyota Corolla in the tiny parking lot, and an open dumpster filled to the brim with black garbage bags, which gave Frankie hope that at least a janitor might be working at the bar this morning. But it was New Year's Eve, and she knew that would just be dumb luck. Of the many things that Frankie Harriman believed in, dumb luck wasn't one of them.

"Ready?" Ezra asked.

No, she wanted to say.

But in reply, she stepped ahead of him. She wasn't going to let Ezra Jones see her wilt. She never had. She wouldn't now.

TEN

Ezra

Ezra knew he had struck a nerve outside Steinway Auditorium, but he decided that Frankie had a point: Why did he care if she was playing piano again or not? Why did he care what her skeletons were? He knew why he did, actually: because when he watched her at the piano from the back row of the auditorium, he had seen a sort of release, an awakening, and it stirred something in him that he wasn't even aware he could feel. Unbridled joy. Total liberation. He could close his eyes and listen to her genius and tap into something that felt like freedom from everything else—his mom, his anxiety, her prognosis. Ezra hadn't expected that, from music, much less *her* music, which he hadn't even known about. Later, he'd discover this same hypnotic calm behind a hand of cards, but at Middleton, standing in the shadows of Steinway, listening to her brilliance, well, that was the closest he'd come to out-of-body serenity in a long time. But still, he reminded himself now, her decision to abandon her musicality wasn't his problem. He wasn't her therapist. He wasn't her boyfriend. They weren't even friends. They were friends once, even before they fell in love, but that's not the kind of thing you can return to after you've so deeply drawn blood.

He fiddled with the gold band on the ring finger of his left hand, which was jammed into the pocket of his North Face jacket, and he assured himself there must be a reasonable explanation for why they appeared to be married. Maybe it had been a fun game that April and Connor had set up last night. Maybe it had been some sort of joke. Could Alec Barstow really have married them? Ezra didn't even remember seeing Alec last night, though this was not particularly soothing because he remembered nothing at all.

By now, they'd crossed the street and wrestled with the door, which was padlocked shut. He'd tried the keys, but that would have been just too easy, and predictably, none of them worked. He pressed his forehead to the glass window and tried to peer in, but there was nothing to see, so then he stepped back and tipped his head back toward the sky and screamed, "FUUUUUUCK!" He knew it was a mistake to come here first. Why would this bar be open at eleven o'clock in the morning? Why didn't he push back harder against her stupid plan when he was the problem solver among the two of them?

"There's a back entrance," Frankie said.

He brushed snow off his hair and stared at her. "Frankie, can we—"

"Just come on," she said, and flagged him around the side

of the building. Ezra started to argue, but she'd already vanished around the corner.

Obviously, the back door was locked as well. Frankie tugged the handle and grunted for about ten seconds, but surely even she knew she was no match for the dead bolt. Ezra watched her glance around, wondering if she'd concede defeat.

But instead she said, "Well, I didn't want it to come to this, but alas."

Before he could stop her, she reached down for the brick by the door that appeared to serve as a doorjamb, and casually, as if she were a Little League pitcher, tossed it through a pane of glass just to her left. The shattering was high-pitched, startling, and Ezra nearly jumped out of his skin.

"Holy shit!" he yelled. "What are you doing? Have you lost your mind?"

She brushed shards of glass off the surrounding pane and then hoisted herself over the threshold and disappeared.

"Frankie!—" Ezra said, but found himself striding toward the broken window and peering in. "This is officially a crime!"

Silence. He glanced around to see if anyone had noticed, if he'd hear sirens cutting through the still campus air. But there was just the soft hush of falling snow, of branches shifting under the snow's weight.

The back door swung open, and Frankie looked triumphant.

"You're welcome!" she said.

"*You're welcome?*" Ezra held his ground, which he quickly realized was futile because they both knew he was going to follow her in.

Frankie rolled her eyes as he scrunched his hands into fists and literally shook them at the sky, then she raised her eyebrows, and he said, "Fine!" and she held the door as if she were being chivalrous.

Once inside, Ezra patted the wall until he found a light switch.

The lights flickered and then eked on, as if they needed coaxing. Ezra looked around. The bar hadn't changed much in a decade: same stench of spilled beer, same faux-wood bar top, same mismatched counter stools. The back wall had signed photographs of celebrities who had passed through the area, probably for a summer concert series or a stay at the exclusive spa twenty minutes down the road. None of the faces had been updated or changed in ten years, which made Ezra feel old. Older, anyway. Above them, someone had haphazardly taped up a HAPPY NEW YEAR banner, along with purple and gold streamers, Middleton colors, which floated toward the floor. Ezra had never spent the holidays on campus: he'd always been happy, even eager, to get home. Not because he was homesick. Rather, as if by being there, he ensured that his mom was okay. New Year's Eve meant they could throw out the shit from the calendar the year prior, and too often, that shit was chemo, radiation, and abject terror. A fresh start was the most he could ask for. Once Frankie began joining him, he sometimes wondered if he could just stop time, stay in his boyhood room forever, with his mom down the hall and his girlfriend under his comforter, and his Eagles and Phillies posters pinned on the walls, so that nothing could ever shatter the stability of those moments.

"No, no, turn the lights off," Frankie called from over her

shoulder. She was already behind the bar searching for something, which Ezra could only assume was extremely high-proof tequila. "No need to draw unnecessary attention. I know what I'm looking for."

"*Unnecessary attention?*" Ezra barked. "You just threw a brick through a window!"

"Yeah, but that was in the back alley," she replied. "No one notices that sort of thing for at least an hour."

Ezra did not want to know how she knew this. In fact, it seemed perfectly normal that Frankie Harriman would know how to pull off a low-level heist. Nevertheless, he turned off the lights.

He stepped further inside and ran his hands over the paneled wood of the bar. He and Frankie had met here, a memory he hadn't revisited in years. It came to him quickly: how it felt like luck that night, when she sat down next to him and he inexplicably spilled his guts about his girlfriend, Bethany, who started off as alluringly mysterious but soon left him emotionally itchy; that she was always coming and going, that he always felt like an afterthought. Still, Ezra was loyal and preferred monogamy even if it made him miserable. Part of this may have been, he could see now, that he so often walked on a knife's edge because of his mother's diagnosis; he simply didn't know how to live differently. The anxiety, the occasional self-loathing were baked in, not because he'd been born anxious but because he was constantly worried about another phone call, about a worsening prognosis, about losing her. Still, though, he couldn't blame his mother's chemo schedule on his inability to cut himself loose of Bethany; he'd just never been great at extricating himself from situations that didn't serve him. Years later, when he was offered six figures and an expense account and a fancy ergonomic chair at the white-shoe law firm where he'd worked for both summers in law school, he remembered that night with Frankie at the bar, how she'd plopped down next to him, a stranger, and he'd poured his miseries out to her, and she'd said in reply: "What are you even doing with her, with your life? Don't you know that you're in control of your own destiny?"

He and Frankie had done two rounds of shots that night, and then Gregory had joined them for two more, all of which surely made her advice and aura more legendary than they may have been in the sober light of morning. But once he recognized Frankie's face, he started seeing her everywhere, and she seemed to soothe him, calm him in ways he felt palpably, almost like she was a drug. Prozac. Frankie was like his Prozac. He ran into her at the cafeteria a day later during lunch, and she greeted him with no artifice, as if they were long-lost friends. He found her poring over the card catalog at Burton Library later in the week, and she said, "Oh rad, it's you. Go put your bag down with mine by the back stacks, then let's go get bagels." It was midafternoon, but Ezra adored eating breakfast foods at all hours of the day, and he soon discovered so did Frankie. It didn't take long for them to be inseparable. And then, it took even less time for them to fall in love.

This morning, Ezra squeezed his eyes closed and inhaled the dank scent of malty yeast and wondered if he needed to give Frankie more credit. *No.* His consciousness pushed back. He'd offered her everything he could: loyalty, love, commitment.

"I found it!" Frankie popped up from the bar area with a

box stuffed with electronic equipment. She glanced around the room, then headed to the back wall by the framed headshots where there was an abandoned TV sitting on a Formica table.

Frankie fiddled with various cords and muttered to herself while plugging one thing into another, and then she wedged herself around the back of the TV and pressed a button and piped: "Is it on yet?" And Ezra watched the screen come to life and said: "Yeah, but can you clue me in here?"

She righted herself and pressed a palm against the lump on her head.

"Ouch, shit." She wobbled for a few seconds but then turned to Ezra. "Don't you remember? They keep a record of who comes in and out, to cover their asses against underage drinking."

Ezra did remember now. Henry had given him his expired driver's license when he headed off to Middleton so Ezra could use it at bars, and he got nervous every time, which became a running joke among his friends, especially Frankie, who gave him a pretend pep talk every night when they headed out. "Ok, Ez, you can do this. Your name is Henry Jones, you are twenty-six but still a junior in college for reasons no one can explain." Then she'd fake roar and pound her chest, which he thought was meant to pump him up but mostly made all of them giggle, and that was enough; that was, in fact, just what he needed.

Today, Frankie turned on the VCR that she'd connected to the TV and dug out a remote control from the box.

"How do you know how to do all of this?" Ezra asked.

"Connect a VCR? This is like the bare minimum of my job requirements," Frankie said. "Do you know how many amps I've scrambled to fix, how many guitar plugs I've scrounged up?"

Ezra didn't mean connect a VCR, because no one was that ignorant, but he stopped himself from arguing. Instead, he walked over to the broken window and wondered if he could tape it back together. There were some larger shards on the ground, and some might have been salvageable if he put them back like puzzle pieces. He squatted down, and his knees cracked. No, there were too many—hundreds, really—of minuscule shards, the ones that are nearly impossible to see with the naked eye but could still draw blood when they pierced the skin. *Just like Frankie*, he thought. He stood and jutted his head out the window. Still, the alleyway was quiet.

"Hey," he heard her call from the barroom. "It's working!"

He lingered one more moment in the silence and the snow, and then turned back toward her. He found her fast-forwarding through the frames, as various students stood in front of the camera and held up IDs as if an ID were verification of the truth. How odd, it occurred to Ezra now, that they just took everyone at their words for this. Obviously, the bouncers knew plenty of kids were breaking the law, yet they all mutually agreed to be part of the ruse. *Lie to me well, and we'll all pretend that's enough to be mistaken for honesty.* Ezra rolled the gold band on his left ring finger and considered the multitude of sins this ruse could explain away. Where had he even found a gold band last night in the first place?

"Wait, wait, I just saw me!" Frankie bounced on her toes, and the screen rewound. Indeed, there she was on screen, with Laila beside her. She wore her fuzzy fisherman's sweater, her parka slung over her arm, and looked more pulled together than today, her hair brushed out and without the tight ache of pain ever present across her face right now.

Frankie leaned toward the TV and squinted.

"Ok, the time stamp says 5:47. I remember Laila saying it would give us an hour to catch up before the rehearsal dinner, which was at, what?" She turned toward Ezra. "Seven? Seven thirty?"

Ezra couldn't help himself; he laughed. She widened her eyes and frowned.

"Is there something that's hilarious about this? Being drugged, being married?"

"No one knows if we were drugged," he answered. Frankie looked doubtful. "No, nothing's hilarious about this at all. It's only that—" He drifted, remembering how initially, when they were first heady in love, her loose relationship with time was adorable. Frankie was always late. To everything. Not because she intended to be rude or even meant to keep others waiting. Just because, he sensed, she'd been tethered so tightly to the rigors of her old life, that once she hit college, she found that she could be. Freedom came in many iterations, and for Frankie, no longer being micromanaged by parents manifested in all sorts of ways. Remarkably, he hadn't even known she was a prodigy until a good nine months into their time together— and that was only by accident, when he stumbled upon her at Steinway Auditorium, and he watched breathless, like a Peeping Tom, from the back row. Even as they shared their secrets, Frankie had the freedom to keep parts of her concealed too.

"Seven thirty," he said now. "The rehearsal dinner started at seven thirty."

She didn't reply. Just refocused on the TV and skimmed through the faces as they appeared in front of her. Ezra didn't see what use he was, a second set of eyes when she knew what she was looking for, so he again thought of Mimi and went in search of a phone. He found a darkened office through a door to the left of the bar and poked his head in, as if he worried someone might pop out and startle him. He plunked down in the rolling chair in front of a worn and notched wooden desk, found the cordless under a pile of papers, and tucked the phone between his shoulder and neck and dialed. Five rings and then straight to voicemail, and he'd already left her a message when they were at the café.

Ezra rested the phone back in the cradle and ran his fingers over the computer mouse. In front of him, a desktop breathed to life. *Password protected, of course*, Ezra thought. He glanced over his shoulder—Frankie was still preoccupied. He didn't need her to know that his skill set postcollege included various iterations of learning how to crack passwords. It's not something he ever abused, but when he dipped his foot into the tech world, he made a point of learning everything that he could: both the rules and how to break them.

"Frankie," he called. "You still ok out there?"

"Hmmm, yeah, fine," she called back.

With that, Ezra rebooted the computer into safe mode and typed in a variety of prompts, and soon enough, he was in. He clicked on Netscape, then to American Airlines. If Mimi's flight had been canceled, surely they could just rebook the ticket. He set up his search terms: Kansas City to Hartford. Chicago to Hartford. Or Boston. He'd even take Boston and send her a car if it meant she could still arrive at Middleton by midnight and he could somehow ascertain that he and Frankie were *not* wed to each other. And even if they were, he'd wrestle the ring off her finger and assume he could get it annulled and still right things with Mimi. She never even had to know. Who said she had to know? He'd never thought to keep a secret from Mimi, not since the day that they met and discovered they were so alike that secrets were unnecessary. And yet. And yet.

He circled all of these notions as he waited for the search results to load.

He was surprised, when they did, that all the flights were operating on time. Hadn't Mimi's voicemail said that hers was canceled because of weather? Wouldn't that mean, he realized, that she could have just flown out today? Wouldn't that also mean, he felt himself scowl, that the airline would have put her on the first flight out?

He moved the mouse over to "Flight Status" and typed in yesterday's date, then pulled up all the flights from Kansas City to Chicago. The dial-up internet was interminably slow, and sure, it could have been that his nervous system was completely out of whack, what with the pepper spray and the morning wake-up and the unwelcome reunion with Frankie Harriman, but part of him already knew why his pulse was racing, why he could feel his mind starting to spin. Over the years, Ezra had learned to listen to his gut, which wasn't really something he'd fine-tuned at Middleton but later, once he had whittled himself into a bit of a professional poker player, he came to trust it inherently. His gut was rarely wrong.

And then it was in front of him.

Mimi's flight had landed on time yesterday. But for reasons that eluded him, the woman he was about to propose to simply wasn't on it.

ELEVEN

Frankie

Frankie needed to get out of Lemonhead, like, yesterday. First, actually, she needed a drink. The quick glimpse she'd seen on the video-tape had been alarming—how had she inexplicably ended up back at Lemonhead several hours after her first stopover with Laila, and why was she leaning into Ezra, her head on his shoulder, his arm slung around her waist? Then the start of a memory she had been searching for came to her: there had indeed been a scavenger hunt, and when struck with this lightning bolt, she further remembered that—inexplicably—there had been Polaroid cameras involved, actual proof. Fever-ishly, with Ezra still in the back office, she dug through her purse once again. There was a zippered pocket inside the middle fold where she often tucked her passport for safekeeping when flying internationally. With everything else going on, she'd overlooked that in Homer. Her fingers grasped exactly what she already knew would be there, and she pulled out a floppy square photograph. Their faces were out of focus, and Ezra was gazing past the camera. But Frankie was turned toward him, not exactly smiling but not exactly not. Behind them, blurry but clear enough to identify, was a swimming pool. Frankie squeezed her eyes shut, willing the rest of the evening to come to her. But there was nothing. She shoved the image back into her purse and jammed the zipper so tight, she nearly pulled the slider off.

So now she was desperate to get a grip on herself. She flipped off the TV, tossed the remote into the cardboard box, and slunk behind the bar to prepare herself a cocktail. True, she'd been sober for a few months, at least until last night, but if there were ever a time for throwing back a shot, surely, it was now. Was it possible that she and Ezra had reconnected last night and somehow that had spiraled into a spontaneous wedding? She shuddered and reached for the Absolut, just like she would have ten years ago.

Ezra emerged from the back office, and perhaps it was because, in the span of fifteen minutes or so, Frankie had forgotten how mangled his face was, or perhaps his face had gotten . . . worse . . . over that respite, but either way, he looked broken. His shoulders drooped and his head hung lower, and goddammit, Frankie found herself attracted to his mess. She'd never been a fixer. She was intuitive enough to know that you couldn't fix anyone if they couldn't heal themselves. Or maybe it wasn't intuition, maybe it was her childhood and its traumas that made her wise. But either way, here now with Ezra, something fluttered in her. She couldn't remember a time when he'd ever been so unkempt, and there was something honest about it, even if none of it were by choice.

"I'm drinking," she said, and hoped her hands didn't jitter. "I've decided. It's the only way through."

He lifted his head just enough to level her with a look.

"That seems like a decidedly terrible idea." He flopped a hand. "So naturally, Frankie Harriman would come up with it."

Frankie set down the Absolut with a little too much force, and it rattled the bottles on the rest of the bar.

"Also," he said, "it's eleven thirty in the morning, and I realize this wouldn't be the first time you've been drunk before noon, but don't you think we should try to show up to April and Connor's wedding still standing? Aren't you a bridesmaid?"

Frankie opened her mouth to reply, then closed it. She remembered all the things she didn't like about Ezra Jones just then: his condescension, his rigidness, his total lack of *fun*. How could she have married him? How, it must be asked, could she have loved him? She squeezed the contented-looking images from the VCR and the Polaroid out of the corners of her mind.

"Fine, fine!" she said, waving her own hand in the air. The engagement ring caught the light from the ceiling, and they both let their eyes linger, then fall to the floor. "What were you doing back there? Let me guess: trying to reach your future wife?"

Frankie regretted it as soon as it was out of her mouth. She knew she should at least be trying to be a little bit less of a bitch, but then she was often at her sharpest, some might even say at her best, when she felt cornered. She couldn't help it. She wasn't going to apologize for it.

"No." He shook his head. "Still going to voicemail."

"Well, where to next? I suggested Lemonhead, and I con-

firmed that I was here. So, that's something. More than you."
She should probably suggest the athletic complex, tell him
about the pool. Disclose the rest about the scavenger hunt. But
she didn't.

"And you confirmed I wasn't with you?" Ezra pulled out a
stool and sat, as if he were too weary to remain on his feet for
another second. "Before the rehearsal dinner? You'd think I
could remember that at least. I didn't think I was *that* wasted
when I left the hotel."

Frankie hesitated. Ezra's initial premise was correct: he
hadn't been at Lemonhead before the rehearsal dinner. It was
only hours later that he'd dropped by, that she spotted them
together on the VCR tape, and until she understood why,
Frankie wasn't yet ready to tell Ezra that yes, at around 10
p.m. last night, they were arm in arm in the lobby of Lemonhead; that twelve hours ago, they appeared happy.

"No," she said. "Just Laila and me."

"So let's find Laila," he said.

"Like I haven't thought of that."

He rubbed his temples. "Well, I guess we could go back to
the Inn?"

Frankie considered this. It wasn't a bad suggestion. They
could knock on doors until they found someone who was with
them. She glanced down. She was still wearing the same clothes
as she left in though, and she assumed as much about Ezra.

"I'm pretty sure I didn't go back there," she said. "Also, it's
a long way to walk in a blizzard."

Ezra nodded because she wasn't wrong: without the snow,
they could probably get back in forty-five minutes. Today, un-
doable. Frankie supposed they could call a taxi, but then what?

They'd be stuck off-campus when seemingly everything they needed to solve for was here.

He looked down at his own attire and exhaled. "Let me try Gregory again."

"Maybe he was our best man," Frankie said, and she meant it to be funny, to lighten the gloom of the moment because it was all just so *ridiculous.*

"Don't even joke." Ezra slapped his hand on the bar. "Do not even joke."

He rose as if he had the weight of their shared history on his shoulders and returned to the back room. "I'll try to reach him. You come up with plan B."

"We are already on plan C," she said.

"Wonderful," he replied before she heard the office door close.

Frankie didn't know what to do now. Ezra was right: she probably shouldn't be drinking this early, and besides, her concussion felt like it was progressing from bad to worse. Could concussions do that? She didn't know. Maybe it was a brain bleed; maybe she was actually dying. She shuddered. Now she was spiraling like Ezra would. She tilted over and tried to see the lump on the shiny gold railing that decorated the side of the bar. Her back spasmed, and she righted herself. She headed to the bathroom for a better view.

As she pushed open the red-painted door that read GRRRLS, she felt bile rise up in her throat. Not because she was ill, rather because she remembered. She tripped her way toward the sink and gripped the porcelain edges and told herself not to vomit.

The memory from twelve years ago was fuzzy, then came

more clearly into focus. She and Ezra had been friends for months by then, spinning closer to each other once he ended things with Bethany. She herself had left a series of paramours by the wayside her first two years at college: she'd graduated from LaGuardia a virgin, though there had been some pretty decent grinding on the dance floor of Studio 54 her senior year once she'd quit music and was attempting to make herself over into someone new. By the time she got to Middleton, Frankie was reborn and had resolved to make up for a lack of sexual experience by having a lot of it. She didn't have many male friends—men weren't of particular interest to her unless solely for her pleasure—and yet she and Ezra, after their serendipitous meeting, built a quixotic, consuming friendship.

They'd spent that summer between their sophomore and junior years apart. She was back in Manhattan at her parents' apartment for the break; her dad was at their Hamptons' house, and her mom had been so happy to be relieved of him that she agreed to stay put in the city. Ezra had returned to Lower Merion for an internship at a friend's dad's law firm. Frankie remembered this now: how he'd always known what he wanted, how it was just a straight shot for him, from A to B, and maybe that's part of what tugged her toward him. How what she was innately brilliant at and what she thought she wanted for herself were two wildly opposing things. Instead, that summer, she found herself working at Tower Records in the Village on 4th and Broadway, which drove her mom through the beamed ceiling of their Park Avenue apartment. But she didn't want a stuffy internship at some corporate gig, and she had no other idea what to do with her life, and she knew the manager at Tower because she'd been in there so often in high school.

"I think it's absurd that you're working for minimum wage selling other people's music," her mom had said one morning in her bright blue leotard and neon-pink headband after her ritual of a doubleheader of two Jane Fonda workouts. Her mother had just turned forty, and the unspoken agreement between them was that they would not discuss her basically confirmed affair with Fred, Frankie's old music teacher. Her mom was in the best shape of her life.

Frankie had recounted this to Ezra on the phone one summer night. How her mom was standing there in her ritzy apartment in her royal-blue spandex and her scrunchy socks and her too-white Reeboks and pretending that she wasn't cheating on Frankie's dad with her childhood piano teacher, with no career to speak of herself, and somehow judging her for being directionless.

"Like, shouldn't she look in the mirror? A little self-reflection before she starts talking to me about my choices?" Frankie was out on the balcony of her bedroom smoking a cigarette.

Ezra started laughing, which hadn't been Frankie's intent, but she dragged on her Marlboro and joined him. Soon, she was curled up in a ball on a lounger barely able to catch her breath. Her mom. Spandex. Jane Fonda. Fred. She hadn't realized how absurd it was.

"It sounds like a plotline from *Dynasty*," Ezra said, and Frankie could feel his grin through the line. "Aerobics instructor seduces her child's tennis instructor."

"If it were my tennis instructor, at least I'd understand," Frankie had howled. "You've never seen Fred!"

They laughed until Ezra's mom needed him—she was in remission now but only just, and relied on Ezra when her energy was low, and he said, "Hey, I gotta go, but you know, I just realized that I didn't even know you played piano."

"Oh," Frankie said. "Yeah. Just one of those things that all kids outgrow, you know? It's not really part of my deal anymore."

"Same time tomorrow?" Ezra asked before hanging up, and Frankie, staring into darkened apartment windows in the building across the street—the whole of Park Avenue fled town for the summer—responded simply, "Yes."

Frankie didn't know what to expect, come fall. Over the summer, she had relied on Laila for relationship advice. Laila was back home in Atlanta working at Orange Julius during the day (*You don't even want to see my uniform*, she'd whined) and babysitting at night, so once she put her charges to sleep, she would call Frankie collect, and they would dig into every detail, every sentence, every nuance. Laila was more experienced in the ways of love; she'd had a high school boyfriend and also dated someone for most of her freshman year before she dumped him after he got so drunk that he streaked naked as part of a fraternity pledge prank. So whenever Frankie worried she was wildly misreading Ezra's intentions, Laila would soothe her like she knew everything, and Frankie, uncharacteristically, believed her.

Back on campus that fall, Frankie, Laila, and April unpacked their bags and boxes and met in the mail room of the dorm for their first night out. She hadn't seen Ezra, and she didn't know his phone number on campus, and she felt too vulnerable to just show up and knock. So the three of them had headed to Lemonhead. The night was warm and star speckled, and as they made their way through campus, the optimism of a new year and new possibilities hung in the air. Everyone felt it. Even Frankie.

"This is going to be *our year!*" Laila had screamed into the open sky.

"Fuck yeah!" a lacrosse bro screamed back from across Middie Walk.

April had turned and curtseyed just as Frankie was flipping him off. They laughed about it all the way to the bar.

Frankie was three beers deep when her bladder pressed against the waist of her Levi's. Laila was on the dance floor, and April was flirting with a boy a year behind them who she'd made out with a few times last spring. The AC had broken, so everyone was sticky and shiny, but none of it mattered: there was a joy at being back together, a joy at the possibility the new school year held. Frankie squeezed through the crowd to the bathroom. A new song came on, one that would empty the dance floor or push bodies closer together, depending on how drunk or how frisky any of them were. Frankie heard Bono wail *I can't live, with or without you.*

She looked in the mirror and felt the music penetrate all the way down, like it was changing her on a cellular level. It wasn't *her* music that mattered, it was *any* music that mattered, she thought, and she didn't regret for a moment that she had abandoned chasing the genius of someone like Bono when it was so much easier to listen rather than create. After spending the entirety of her childhood with only a singular goal, be *better*, be *the best*—a goal that too often wasn't even her own—she never regretted walking away. Her world could still be filled with noise, with melody, even if it wasn't of her own making. Her parents hadn't understood this; Fred hadn't understood this. But Frankie did, and that's all that mattered. She suspected Ezra might too, but what if he didn't? What if he pushed her just like her parents, shamed her the way that they had when she'd quit, nagged her the way that they still did now? It was nearly impossible to be in the same room with her parents without the tension of her choice cutting between them. Frankie didn't want to ruin the one pure thing in her life, the one pure person, so this was her secret to keep.

Bono wailed again, his voice clear even through the bathroom door. Frankie was so moved, she almost started to cry, just standing there, washing her hands, listening to his perfect tenor. Then the door swung open.

"Frankie," Ezra had said, like a gasp, like he'd searched the world over for her. Frankie drank him in. He was skinnier and tanner than when she last saw him in May. The cut of his jaw looked sharper, the blaze in his eyes felt acute.

"In the flesh," Frankie had said, uncharacteristically shy. "Have you been looking for me?"

"Yes," he said, catching his breath.

"Where?" she asked, moving forward.

"Everywhere," he said. "I've been looking for you everywhere." And then he'd pressed her back against the porcelain sink, pausing just long enough to meet her gaze. And with no hesitation, no ounce of self-doubt, he'd kissed her. Exactly like the Ezra Jones she'd come to love.

"Frankie," he'd managed, his voice husky, almost broken, then again, "Frankie."

He ran his lips over her neck, down her collarbone, and Frankie dipped her head back, electricity running through her like a current she knew she was going to be unable to stop, like an addiction from which she wouldn't recover.

Ezra's hands were all over her, making up for the summer spent connected by nothing but a phone line. His fingers wound their way under her shirt, over her bra, and then she wasn't wearing a bra at all.

"Jesus," he'd said. "You are so fucking beautiful."

Then his mouth had covered her right breast, and Frankie moved her hips closer to his, urgency coursing through her. Sex had always been casual, distant, but now she *needed* Ezra in a way she never had. The button fly of her jeans unpopped— *pop pop pop pop pop*—and then his fingers were inside her underwear, and Frankie gasped at how he set her ablaze. He lifted her onto the sink, and his fingers sank deeper inside her. "Ezra," she managed. "*Ezra . . .*" She reached for him but he shifted ever so slightly away.

"Not yet, not here," he'd said. "First, let me do everything I've been thinking about all summer. To you."

And so she'd let him. With her arms around his shoulders, he'd explored every last inch of her there. And even now, after they'd ruined it all, Frankie remembered that it was the most solid thing that she'd ever held on to her whole life through.

TWELVE

Ezra

Ezra found Frankie on the floor of the ladies' room. Her eyes were closed, and she was leaning against the wall, and for a moment, he worried she was unconscious.

"Frankie," he whispered and nudged her shoulder. "Frankie!"

Her eyes fluttered open, and he squatted down to her level.

"What happened? Are you ok?"

Frankie inhaled and looked upward toward the flickering halogen lights. Then her mouth pointed downward in her trademark frown, and a look of disgust washed over her face.

"Ew. Am I on the bathroom floor?" she said. "I got a little dizzy, I guess."

Ezra pushed himself upright and extended his hand, which she accepted with surprisingly little reluctance. When they were both on their feet, Frankie wobbled a bit and her hands landed against his chest.

"Whoa, ok, come on, I got you. Let's get you some water," he said.

Ezra felt her hesitate, and he wasn't sure if it was because she was going to spurn his help or because they were close enough to feel intimate. He supposed that both things were akin to the same feeling: even Frankie would tell you that she too often panicked at the first sign of emotional surrender. He gazed down at her while she steadied herself. No, that wasn't fair. Not the first sign. But at the first *real* sign of emotional surrender, at the most honest sign.

Of course he remembered what had happened here in this dank, dingy bathroom, how he'd been going crazy all summer, delicately trying to get to know everything there was to know in the Frankie Harriman oeuvre without terrifying her and scaring her off. It was obvious to him even back then that he had to proceed carefully, that he had to tiptoe right up to the line that she had drawn for whatever romantic criteria she concocted for herself. Though it didn't occur to him until much later that he was risking his own heart as much as he risked hers.

That summer, they spent every night on the phone—she always called him to incur the long-distance charges, and what started out as late-night check-ins in their childhood bedrooms when their mothers were asleep soon became conversations over dinner or time spent watching sitcom reruns with the phone held to their ears, neither one of them saying much, just laughing at the same jokes, groaning at the clunkers. Frankie had never seen *Cheers* or *Night Court* because she didn't watch much TV as a kid, she'd told him, so Ezra made sure that Thursday nights were appointment TV.

When he got back on campus—he took the train up by himself because his mother had an oncology appointment in

Center City—he'd dropped his bags, and before even unpacking, he went to find her. As if he literally couldn't wait another beat, another minute, without touching her, without inhaling her. For Ezra, Frankie Harriman was like a full-body infection: once he felt it, there was no way to ignore the way it pulsed through his veins. She wasn't in her room and she wasn't in the library, so he'd walked to the bookstore in case she was loading up on supplies, but she wasn't there either. He checked Laila's room and then April's, and he poked his head in to see Gregory, who was sharing a double with a transfer kid from Michigan State named Connor. Gregory, who'd spent the summer at an internship in Houston, bear-hugged him and said, "I'd try Lemonhead, but give me a sec, and I'll head there with you. It's five o'clock somewhere." Gregory was always full of those little idioms, like he carried a quote book around with him.

It wasn't even dinnertime, so it hadn't occurred to him that they'd already be drinking. The bar was crowded when they got there. Laila sucked on a cigarette and waved to him from the dance floor, then threw her arms around him when he made his way through.

"Frankie?" he asked.

And her face cracked open with a Cheshire cat grin, like she was in on his mission, and she nudged her head to the back.

"Bathroom," she said, then gave him a little push. "I heard about this all summer. So go and make it stick."

And he felt something swell in him, a confirmation, an affirmation, and he pressed through the rest of the afternoon revelers and swung open the door to the ladies' room, and there she was, the voice on the other end of the line. He couldn't remember now if he kissed her or if she kissed him, but it didn't matter either way. Time stood still, and something electric raced through him from his toes to his heart and clear up to the top of his skull until he pulled back to catch his breath, and she'd said with no small amount of surprise, "You found me." And then he took off her clothes and explored her body right there in the Lemonhead bathroom, doing everything to her that he'd been imagining doing all summer. Not sex, because that, after so long, he wanted to make special, but there were so many other things to do besides sex.

Now, a decade later, with plenty of scars to show for it, Frankie moaned and said: "Look, I don't want to alarm you, but I guess I need to tell you that I'm ninety-nine percent sure that I have a concussion. This happened once before in . . ." She stopped and searched for the word. "Oh right, this happened in Bangkok." Then, as if remembering the whole shitstorm of a situation they were in, she added: "Did you reach Gregory? Does he know if you're my legally wed husband?" She pushed past him and out the bathroom door, weaving her way toward a barstool.

In fact, this time Ezra *had* reached Gregory, who was no help at all. He picked up the hotel phone after three rings and mumbled, "Yeah?" And when Ezra asked him if they'd been together last night, Gregory said, "One second dude," and seemed to rest the phone down on the nightstand. Ezra heard thumping footsteps and water running and some low-level groaning, and then Gregory returned and said, "Fucking booze-filled scavenger hunt, never again, *never again*," and Ezra said: "So there really was a scavenger hunt?" and Gregory said, "Come on, dude, it's too early for this bullshit," and then hung up on him.

"So I think there . . . possibly . . . could have been a scavenger hunt?" Ezra said to Frankie now. "And that sounds . . . insane? Because I honestly have no recollection of it. At all." He shook his head, trying to free a memory.

Surprisingly, this was not the only scavenger hunt that Ezra had participated in as of late. About six months ago, just at the start of summer, Mimi's company had been trial-running an in-person dating option. The site was still in beta testing, and they'd had another influx of Silicon Valley funding (though Mimi was still mostly paid in stock options and thus constantly tight on money), and their cash on hand meant they could throw additional parties and events and test-drive user satisfaction and algorithms. (Ezra never really got the sense that anyone in charge knew exactly what they were doing.) The event was in San Francisco, so Ezra had tagged along: he was in talks to join a new search engine start-up, the unfortunately named "Google," and Mimi always preferred to have a plus-one (ergo the aborted trip to Prague with Gregory six weeks later). The scavenger hunt was mostly a bar crawl through downtown on a Saturday afternoon; Ezra had a dinner with the Google executives that night, so he sipped his beers and deflected when Mimi kept pushing shots on the gathered figurative guinea pigs. Mimi herself was not much of a drinker. She enjoyed white wine and an occasional spritzer, but she, like him, preferred to remain in control. Also, Mimi didn't need booze: she got drunk off social situations—she literally grew more animated in a crowd, as if she were a rechargeable battery, and what jazzed her up, what turned her on, was people. It made her perfectly suited for the job—sober but still riotous; clearheaded but an absolute ball of a good time. Admittedly, Ezra found this side of her draining.

But it was such a small thing, her manic energy, her overzealous cacophony at a party, that in the scheme of their perfect match, he ignored it. She tried to egg him on, to sweep him up in her tornado, but all of it mainly left him exhausted. Despite his reluctance, she liked it when he joined her because she would often stand in front of the crowd, arm linked into his, and say something like: *You might be skeptical about Datify. I get it! I was too! But then I met my literal perfect match.* Ezra would see people in the back of the room stand on their tippy-toes to catch sight of him, and he'd do something like take a small bow or kiss her on the cheek, and then everyone else would glance around to see if their match was among them too. Being in front of a crowd made Ezra grind his teeth, set off small flares of anxiety. Sometimes he would chew the inside of his lip to quell the nerves, and sometimes he'd have to stuff his hands into his pockets so they didn't outwardly tremble, but he did it for Mimi because he loved her. And she never seemed to notice his anxiety, which was probably for the best, since he'd never explained it all.

The night of the scavenger hunt in San Francisco they were at their twelfth bar somewhere in the Mission District, traveling in a horde of fifty or so singles, when Ezra tried to leave for his Google dinner. As it was, he doubted he'd make dinner on time, and naturally, punctuality (and first impressions) mattered to Ezra. He'd tried to peel off, and Mimi said, "No! Ez! You can't go! Why would you leave me for some silly dinner?" She was at her most gregarious by now, her not-technically-drunk-but-still-exhausting extroverted self.

"Meems, it's not silly. I have to go. It's for work."

"Work?" Her face folded in confusion. "But you came out here with me." She looked around. "And we're the example.

We're Project Zero. These people need to know that the questionnaires are the real deal!"

Ezra sighed. He'd told her about the dinner but hadn't stressed its importance. He hadn't told her about the job offer because he didn't know if she, who had come to think of herself as a New Yorker, would want to move, and maybe more honestly, he didn't know if he'd break something fragile between them. But also, at these events, he was starting to feel like an animal in a zoo: always on display.

"No," he said. "I mean, yes. I'm here as your plus-one. But I do have some work."

"But this is my *thing*!" He knew that it mattered to her; he knew that she wanted to impress her bosses. She'd recently been told that she'd get a bonus for every person who signed up for the site from her events. "I wanted you here to do *my thing* with *me*."

Ezra nodded. He really, really did not want to fight. He really, really did not want to skip this dinner, if only because it was in thirty minutes and canceling now would be rude. But Mimi's arms were crossed and she was staring at him with a quiet fury.

"Mimi," he started, but she cut him off, which was just as well because he didn't know what, or how, he was going to decide.

"I'm sorry, Ezra," she said, though she didn't sound sorry at all. "By all means, go to dinner. You know, this doesn't exactly come easy to me. But, fine, whatever, ok. Go."

Ezra didn't even know what this meant, because the last thing he'd done was come to any of this easily either. He, like Mimi, had grown up without any of the perks of his new world order—having not much more than just what they needed, living mostly month to month with maybe a little savings if the sky fell down—and walked away from the law job to live off ramen and pizza slices for a year while he waited for one of his gaming ideas to break and pay him a salary. He'd buried his mom. He'd lost touch with most of his old friends. He'd managed to forge a bigger life than he'd planned, but it hadn't in any way come easily, and besides, he no longer knew if he wanted it now that it was his. He'd fallen into the work in tech, which was filled with bros who talked about expensive tire rims and twenty-thousand-dollar Rolexes, so far from his Philadelphia roots and values. He hadn't said any of that out loud, of course.

Mimi approached tears, so he conceded and rescheduled his dinner to brunch the next day, which was just as well because the Google guys were stuck at the office and running late, so no one really minded. Well, Ezra had minded being made to feel as if he were an unsupportive boyfriend. He needed Mimi as much as she needed him. He resolved that maybe they just needed to get married so she knew, really *knew*, that she was as necessary to him as air.

Ezra eyed Frankie for a long beat this morning, with Mimi inexplicably absent and a gold band even more inexplicably on his left ring finger. That night in San Francisco, they had finally trudged back to their hotel, and Mimi passed out, and Ezra watched her for a few minutes and eventually turned out the light on his side of the bed and slept fitfully. They woke up the next morning and apologized like grown-ups, and she took his credit card at his insistence because money didn't matter to him now, even though he knew how awful that sounded, and she went shopping while Ezra met the Google guys and they told him all about how they were going to revolutionize the internet.

He stared again at Frankie today. He didn't even know why he was thinking about all of that. "Hey," he said, sliding onto the stool next to her at the bar. "I know there's a lot of shit to sort through, but I really think we need to get you some medical attention. The rest of it can wait."

She dropped her head between her arms and onto the bar and moaned. Finally, she raised her head and drew in her breath and said, "Ok."

"Ok?"

"Ok!" she hissed, as if she couldn't believe he were making her repeat it. "Let's go to the hospital."

Ezra honestly couldn't believe it. A concession. He helped her off the stool, and she clutched his elbow, and he thought: *Wow, this is kind of sweet, maybe I have her wrong, maybe she's changed, maybe we really are in this together, and I've misread her this whole morning.* And just as they were headed toward the broken window and the back door, the door swung open, and two security officers shouted: "You inside, don't move! We have reports of a break-in!"

THIRTEEN

Frankie

Quite obviously, this was not Frankie's first run-in with the authorities. There was that time in Dallas when Shawnee Patterson, lead singer of Night Vixen, trashed her suite at the Four Seasons and had to be forcibly removed by two beefy officers; there was another time in Nashville when Paxton Sunshine, a wildly talented yet emotionally unbalanced midlist country singer, made Frankie his first call after being arrested for a DUI. There had been situations at airports with intoxicated clients; there had been nightclub brawls and cocaine arrests and her own father's dustups with the IRS every few years, for which he was always cleared although never quite exonerated. Frankie herself had managed to never yet be arrested personally, however. So this was new. Although technically, they were campus security, not cops, so she didn't really feel the need to take them particularly seriously.

"The window was broken before we got here," she said. "We thought maybe that meant it was open, like, the bar. It's

New Year's Eve, you know? We wanted to start early. We've only been here a few minutes." She glanced behind her. "Go check. Everything's there. Nothing's missing."

She was standing shoulder to shoulder with Ezra, just outside the doorframe, the two security guys blocking their exit down the alley. One of them clutched what she was sure was a Taser. (She'd seen some things, ok?) She dropped her hands, which were nearly numb from the frozen air. Her pulse was racing like a ticking time bomb, which sent the blood even faster to the lump in her head, which now throbbed like a metronome. But she was flying on adrenaline, and she knew herself well enough to know she could ride the wave until she couldn't. Still, she'd delay the crash for as long as possible.

"This really feels a little unnecessary," she added. "You know, we're just two alumni in search of a beer at our old bar." She felt Ezra twitch beside her.

The younger officer, baby-faced with a scuff of a beard, gave the older one a side glance, then his eyes moved back to Ezra. He tugged his wool hat over his ears.

"Sir, what happened to your face?"

"Allergic reaction," Frankie said before Ezra could. She'd never known him to be nearly as adept on his feet or, well, frankly, as loose with the truth as she was. "Accidental brush with shellfish for breakfast. We try to be so careful, but sometimes these things happen."

"Sir?" the officer said to Ezra, like Frankie was the one who had mauled him, like she, tiny lady that she was, had inflicted such damage on him. Frankie was honestly a little flattered that he thought she had it in her, though she knew he hadn't meant it as a compliment.

"Shellfish," Ezra said. "We're over at the Inn, and the chef got a little crazy with the omelet."

The officers looked warily from Frankie to Ezra then back again, and she took it as her opportunity to move on. She didn't see how mentioning that he had been pepper-sprayed at Homer would in any way help their cause, and she needed to keep things humming along before Ezra admitted to the truth. Because he would. Give it time. Then she remembered that he had somehow reinvented himself as an expert poker player, which always required a bluff, and wondered if maybe she were getting this wrong.

"It's New Year's Eve," Frankie said, because she also knew she could talk her way out of anything. "Wouldn't you guys rather be home with your families instead of investigating the case of a broken window?" She glanced up and down the street. "Honestly, the back door was open. We couldn't have known. And really, do we look like people who would smash a window?" She gestured back and forth between them but stopped suddenly when she realized that neither she nor Ezra exactly looked presentable. Her wild hair and smeared makeup, his mashed-up angry red face. She wondered just how long it took for the effects of pepper spray to wear off. She should know this—she sent all her clients on the road with at least one bottle to attach to their key chains, sometimes a second one to stow in their luggage in case anything got too out of hand in a hotel room.

"Ma'am, please empty your pockets," the older guard, who looked like he was fighting middle-age weight gain and badly needed a good night's sleep, said. "We need to know if anything is missing."

"I already told you—" she started, then looked to Ezra. He was the lawyer. She'd covered for the pepper spray; maybe it was time he handled the legalese.

"Don't you have anything to say?" She nudged her chin in his direction. "Shouldn't this now be your territory? Like, our Miranda rights or whatever?"

Frankie didn't technically even know when Miranda rights were called for, but she'd watched enough episodes of *Law & Order* in hotel rooms to know that it sounded official. She had to be in the shower by no later than 3:30 p.m. to make the photos at the chapel, and getting hauled into campus jail (was there such a thing as campus jail?) was not part of her timeline, not part of her plan. It was true, she considered, that she actually didn't have much of a plan after Lemonhead, as she had somehow convinced herself that the VCR would hold all the answers. It quite obviously did not. Indeed, just the contrary: it only added to the mounting list of questions. They could go to the athletic complex, they *should* go to the athletic complex, but that would mean coming clean to Ezra about the slivers of the night that she remembered—the mistletoe, the kiss under the mistletoe, snippets of the scavenger hunt—and at the moment, that was obviously out of the question. She didn't trust him to stay calm. She didn't trust him at all.

"Miranda rights are for when police actually arrest you," Ezra said.

"You went to NYU Law for that?" Frankie replied.

"I went to NYU Law for—" Ezra stopped himself and emitted a long, tense sigh, and Frankie saw his jaw flex, which he always used to do when he was trying not to argue with her. In fact, they were so aligned that for just about the whole of their relationship, they honestly never did. She wanted what he wanted; he wanted what she wanted. Frankie couldn't believe that a partnership could be so harmonious; Ezra couldn't believe that she was always waiting for something to blow up. Maybe that was half of their problem, Frankie thought now, as she stared at Ezra and campus security stared at them both. That if you never fight, you never learn how to fight fair, how to fight well. Instead, there's just a void, and inevitably, eventually, that becomes combustible. Just like it did for them.

"Your pockets," the younger guard said.

"Do you think we, like, smuggled out Crystal Gayle's headshot? Rolled it up and stuffed it down our pants or something?" Frankie asked. Crystal Gayle was the only one she could think of in the heat of the moment. She knew there were better, snappier names back there. Carly Simon maybe? James Taylor? "There is literally nothing of value inside. Absolut vodka? What is that? Like, fifteen bucks?"

"Can you ever just be quiet?" Ezra said, a little too sharply. He pulled out the linings of his pockets. Frankie already knew what he'd find because he'd done as much not an hour ago at the coffee shop. "Anything you say can and will be used against you."

"Oh, so *now* you're the lawyer," Frankie said.

"Now you, ma'am." The older officer nodded at her.

Frankie started to protest—she was debating mentioning something about a warrant, which she thought sounded official and she suspected was far above campus security's station—when she felt Ezra level her with his gaze.

"Just. Do. It," he hissed, as a gust of wind kicked up and

blew the snow sideways. They all steeled themselves until it passed.

"The more you protest, ma'am, the likelier we're going to have to call in reinforcement," the older one said. He adjusted his pants, which were both too tight and too loose. Frankie wondered if his wife nagged him to be less slovenly. Maybe his wife didn't care about things like that. Maybe he didn't have a wife. Maybe he sat home each night drinking Budweiser and flipping through basic cable. She wondered if he couldn't inspire a song for Paxton Sunshine. She wished she had a pencil and paper to take notes, to write down a riff or a lyric, an instinct that hadn't tugged at her for years. She felt herself inhale, a short little hiccup, at the notion: that she could write again, that she should play again.

"Forgive my wife," Ezra replied, turning his swollen, stony face into a sincere one. "She had her heart set on revisiting the place where we first met." His hand landed on her arm like a clamp. "Empty your pockets, darling. Then I'm sure they'll see that this was just a harmless trip down memory lane." He smiled at the officers. "Hopeless romantic, you know? You should see her on our anniversary. Balloons, wine, Barry Manilow on the stereo."

Frankie tutted. *Barry Manilow?* She had a lot to say about that. Still, it wasn't lost on her that Ezra remembered what she remembered: that Lemonhead had been where they'd met, where it all started.

"Darling?" he said, releasing his grip. "Come on. I'm sure they have other places to be. It's New Year's Eve, after all. Let's not make them wait all day."

Frankie sighed and fished out her pockets, which proved to be as mundane as she knew they'd be. She didn't know why she had made such a fuss in the first place. They could have wrapped this up ten minutes ago if she'd just acquiesced.

"Step aside, then. We'll take a look inside. Do not leave the premises. Understood?" The older guard looked from one to the other. "Even a trip down memory lane can constitute trespassing."

Frankie started to protest, but Ezra bugged his eyes at her, so she nodded.

"Yes, fine. We'll be here."

As soon as they disappeared inside, Ezra turned to Frankie. Or she turned to him. It didn't really matter. The pretense was gone.

"*Your wife?*" she whispered.

"*Would it have killed you to just follow instructions?*" he said at the same time.

They each scowled at the other. Ezra folded his arms. Frankie thrust her hands onto her hips.

"This was your idea," he said finally. "The brick, the . . . whole thing! *We need to start at Lemonhead*, you said."

"If you want to get something done, send a woman to do it." As soon as it was out of her mouth, she realized it was not really the defense she'd hoped to mount.

"If I want to get something done, I tend to do it legally, regardless of gender," he retorted.

"Please," she said. "I heard the stories about the card counting."

"It was *once*." He leaned in close to her face.

"Twice," she said.

"Fine! It was twice."

"You got *caught* twice." Frankie couldn't cite other examples of when he'd been anything less than a Boy Scout, so she hoped they changed the subject soon.

Ezra threw his hands into the air. "Look, can we just agree to stand here in silence before you make this any worse? Because I do not feel like landing in a squad car when I have plenty of other shit to deal with right now."

"They're not arresting us! They're campus security! I don't even think they have that authority!" Frankie prepared to launch into a story of this one time, in Nashville, with Paxton Sunshine, but Ezra cut her off.

"How do you have any idea what they're doing? Are you the lawyer now? Did you not see his Taser? My God, this is not the time to deal with your issues with authority."

"Well." She pouted. "I would not say that your legal skills did us any good."

"You are the most infuriating person who has ever walked the planet."

She was about to point out that *he* was in fact the most infuriating person to ever walk the planet, and she'd circled the globe more than a few times so she would know, but one of the guards called to the other inside, and both Ezra and Frankie fell quiet.

Frankie tapped her foot. Her toes were getting cold, but that wasn't the reason why. What were they doing here? Why were they wasting time? Who *cared* what campus security threatened them with? Frankie had tangled with real cops in Bangkok (not the same trip as the concussion); she'd talked her way out of *situations* in cities across Europe. This was petty crime shit, and she wasn't going to wait around to see if they ticketed her for a broken window.

She felt Ezra staring at her.

"No," he said. "Do not. *No.*"

She raised her finger to her lips. *Yes.* She nodded.

No, he mouthed back. Then louder: "Goddammit, Frankie!"

She cocked her head around the doorframe, but there was no sign of the security guards.

Before she could give herself another second to hesitate, she looked at Ezra and then she whispered, "Run."

FOURTEEN

Ezra

Ezra had never seen Frankie run that fast, even while palming the lump on her head, which didn't seem to slow her down. She flew around corners, she raced up the footpaths in the middle of the campus's rolling hills, she tucked into alleyways.

"Shit, shit, shit, shit, shit, shit, shit," he heaved as he raced to catch up to her. The wind and the snow pierced his already angry skin, and he felt his fury rising. All they had to do was stay! And be compliant. He was certain he could have cleared them. Why was everything with Frankie a level-five shit-storm?

He and Frankie used to do this all the time. Not flee from the campus security (obviously) but race all over campus. She'd just look at him whenever, wherever, and say: *Run!* And it was their unspoken agreement that they'd throw themselves into an all-out sprint. Usually, she'd end up grabbing his arm and tugging him back in an attempt to slow him down or clinging to the waistband of his jeans and trying to pants him. Frankie would do anything for a win, which meant that Ezra got to retaliate by picking her up and throwing her over his shoulder or by lumbering down the sidewalk with her hugging his leg. It was impossible not to end somewhere on the ground, limbs intertwined, tears streaking down their faces. The innocent hilarity of young love.

Today though, he saw only her back. She never slowed, she never turned around toward him, she never let him take the lead. How she moved so quickly in the snow would have been a thing of beauty if Ezra were in a generous mood. (He was not.) Middleton's campus was a roll of hills with grayscale buildings springing up in various spots as if they were old English manors. Ivy crept up some of the facades; others were bestowed with jewel-toned windows. A few were adorned with scaffolding, awaiting a makeover. The blanket of white made the whole landscape appear a bit like a fairy tale. How Frankie remembered which footpath led to the next, he couldn't say. But she had always flown on intuition: there were moments when this was his very favorite thing about her. There were also moments when he knew it could be the death of them both.

Frankie turned down a narrow opening not visible from the street, and he followed, panting, like a parent chasing a runaway toddler.

Ezra finally stopped, a cramp building in his side, and slapped a hand against the back of whatever building they were behind. He wheezed and tried to catch his breath and felt the residue from the pepper spray deep in his lungs. He didn't want to panic; he told himself not to panic. He used to be able to tell when these anxiety attacks were incoming: like a spider creeping up the back of his neck, like a surge of toxins infecting his bloodstream. But now, until today at least, it had been so long since his last one that he couldn't trust himself, couldn't trust those warning signs anymore. He breathed in and out, like he had done with Frankie on the floor of the coffee shop. He told himself, even though he knew it was untrue, it was akin to the rush of adrenaline he got while playing cards, and that he should just ride the wave.

"Frankie!" he sputtered. "Frankie."

He cocked his head up and saw her slow to a jog, then finally, blessedly, a stop. She spun around. He took another long inhale and exhale, and he felt the fever pitch of his disquietude ebb just enough to reassure him that he had himself under control.

"Well," she called down the alley in which they'd landed. "Looks like one of us has greeted their thirties a little better than the other one."

Ezra tried to right himself, but the pinch in his side barked back. He dug his fingers into his abdomen, an old trick from when he was forced to do cross-country in high school for PE credit. He'd never been the fastest, but by his senior spring, he was the one who could push himself through any sort of pain because he just went numb: there was too much else in his life to worry about than the onset of a cramp while competing against Radnor High School. Sometimes, when she was up for it, his mom stood at the finish line with red Gatorade, as if they were a perfectly normal family, as if the two of them weren't carrying the weight of her mortality on each of their shoulders. He ran faster because of that weight; he pushed himself further for her. But today, Frankie had beaten him.

Across the alleyway, she appeared—Ezra couldn't believe it—exhilarated. Was she honestly exhilarated? Her cheeks were flushed, she bounced again on her toes, and she had to bite her lip to keep from grinning.

"What *was* that?" he finally bleated.

"I feel that I should share that I one hundred percent have a concussion," she said, as if this were an answer to his question. "So I beat you even with a concussion. I'm not a doctor but I play one on TV." He could tell that she found this fucking hilarious.

"*Frankie.*" He eased himself to standing. "You just made things considerably worse."

"Please. No offense but I was seriously underwhelmed with your legal defense."

Ezra stared up at the gray sky and counted to ten before he absolutely blew his top.

"Like, remind me who *not* to call the next time I'm in a jam in New York," she added. Then: "Besides, it's New Year's Eve, Y2K, *Y2Nay!* Don't you think they'll have bigger things to deal with?"

"Well, yes," Ezra said. "That was my whole point. Diffuse the situation, then move on. So now, you've made us look guilty."

"We *are* guilty. Hello? And I thought lawyers didn't care about guilt or innocence."

"You're the one who chucked the brick through the window! For what? What did you even learn from going to Lemonhead?" Ezra did not want to consider what he had learned: the knowledge that his girlfriend, near-fiancée, had perhaps not shown up by choice. He really needed to find his phone and call her.

Frankie fell quiet, and he wondered if he'd struck a nerve. "What?" he said. "Tell me or I walk."

"Walk?" Frankie said, too loud. "To where? Am I keeping you here—"

"Actually, you still have my grandmother's ring—" Ezra's voice rose several decibels. "I don't exactly trust you with a family heirloom."

"Fine! Don't let me hold you up!" She tried to yank it off her finger again. The ring still didn't budge.

A window opened a few stories up and a head popped out.

"Can you guys please shut the fuck up? Some of us are trying to sleep!" The window slammed shut.

Ezra peered skyward and connected the dots. They were behind the upperclassman dorms; he knew it looked familiar. He'd only been back here once before, and the snowfall today made it look more romantic than it had been back then, with its three dumpsters and faded brick facade in need of a pressure wash. It was the fall of their senior year, and they were still happy. Mostly, anyway. Frankie had spent the summer with her mom in the Hamptons. By now, her parents had split for good—Frankie had known it was coming after a phone call in late spring—and her mom got the house in Sagaponack. Ezra shared a dorm room with Gregory at Fordham where they both took summer classes at night and worked at low-paying internships during the day. He took the Jitney out to see Frankie in early July for the long holiday weekend, his only visit that summer. Not because he didn't want to be with her all day, every day; rather because that one weekend visit had gone so poorly. It was clear upon his arrival that she was fighting with her mom. She didn't want to elaborate about the details, and every time Ezra asked, she snapped things like, "Ezra, you can't fix this, so please stop," or "This goes way back, ok? Like ages back. You don't seem to get it." He suspected it had to do with her music, but he'd promised never to ask her about it again, since their fight a few months earlier in Steinway when he'd first seen her playing, just after her parents had told her about their separation. And a promise to Ezra was a promise, even if he committed to it before he understood how breaking it may have saved them.

He wasn't emotionally mature enough that weekend in the Hamptons to suggest to her that her problems were his problems and that he would have just been fine hearing her out, listening to her vent. Because he *did* want to fix it; he *did* want to fix her. So they spent the weekend in a tense, noiseless bubble, with her mother pretending everything was perfectly fine whenever he was in the room, and with the two of them whispering out their rage when he wasn't. He was blessedly relieved when he finally kissed her goodbye and stepped on the Jitney to return to the city.

A decade ago, he'd ended up in this same alleyway behind the dorms shortly after they got back to campus from the summer. It was Frankie's twenty-first birthday, and the rule among their friends was they couldn't just drink themselves to oblivion for their twenty-first; they had to come up with a fitting celebration each time. For Gregory's birthday, they had gone to a Chuck E. Cheese in Pittsfield, followed by a depressing strip bar (he came out a few weeks later, and Ezra wondered if he finally just had enough boob to realize that it wasn't working for him); April had rented out a room for hers at one of the few haute cuisine restaurants in town (there were only two, and it was understood that these were exclusively reserved for professors or parents who came for a visit) for a very-adult sit-down dinner with a printed menu and wine pairings. All of them had felt a little foolish swirling their glasses and pretending they had any idea what they were doing—who knew a pinot from a Syrah back then?—but they were tipsy soon enough, and it proved hilarious to act like full-blown grown-ups for the evening. Connor, who had a black eye from hockey practice, wore an ascot; April had spoken in a British accent; Gregory had insisted everyone call him James Bond. Ezra had even worn his suit, which his mom had splurged on for his summer internship. Frankie had actually understood all the various ingredients on the menu—squab and ramps and some sort of rare sea urchin that she'd tried once in the city with her father—and had explained each course to them as they were served, like she was the adult in the room. So they were all pretending more than just a little bit.

But he wanted Frankie's twenty-first to be personal, to be unique in a different way. He wanted it to be just the two of them. She hadn't quite stabilized from her summer with her mother, but instead of talking about it, she was simply moodier than normal. He knew she was fighting to free an albatross from around her neck, so he tried to let it go. But he didn't know how to help her, and her refusal to want his help bruised him. Wasn't that his job? To try? Whenever he suggested that, much like over the summer, she snapped, and then later acted like nothing had ever happened. She never apologized, though that was something Ezra only realized once they'd cratered for good.

Anyway, it was Frankie's birthday. She'd called him from the Hamptons over the summer and repeatedly lamented that she regretted her choice to spend the summer with her mom.

"I should have gone to Paris," she said at least twice during every phone call.

Her dad, having lost the beach house in the separation, was in Paris with his new girlfriend, and although Frankie rarely spoke of her relationship with him, Ezra assumed it was less rocky than the one with her mom. Though he also didn't understand why her relationship with her mom was so tenuous. He'd asked. He'd asked often. Frankie often just tutted and said, "It's complicated."

"The music teacher?" Ezra pressed once.

Frankie went silent for so long that Ezra wondered if they'd been disconnected. Then finally, she said: "No, not Fred." Then, "Just so you know, I'm the one who made the choice to stop playing." Ezra didn't know and, further, didn't understand why that specific fact mattered.

But on Frankie's birthday, he knew how he could at least make her smile. He borrowed a ladder from the janitor's closet in their dorm, and Connor and Gregory held the legs while he strung fairy lights back and forth in the alley behind her second-floor room. He used some of his summer earnings to pay an art student for sketches of both the Eiffel Tower and the Arc de Triomphe, which he hung on the brick wall that was ten feet from her window. He ran to the grocery store and bought baguettes and Brie and red grapes. He splurged on a wine he didn't understand and couldn't afford.

Frankie had a late-afternoon lecture—he remembered now that it was Econ 101, which she hated but took because she was preparing for postcollege life and thought maybe she wanted to be music adjacent: a producer, an agent; she didn't know but it seemed like econ might come in handy. As long as she wasn't an artist, she'd say. *I'll be anything but the talent.* They'd talk about this late at night in bed together, and he always assumed he was part of those plans. He'd never questioned it; she'd never given him reason to. So for her birthday and while she was at Econ 101, he snuck into her room and donned a beret and turned out the lights so when dusk settled in, the alley glowed behind him. She swung open the door, and her weary face morphed into a delighted one, and he swept her into his arms and said, "Happy birthday, mademoiselle" (the most French he knew—he had studied Latin), and uncharacteristically, Frankie burst into tears. And Frankie never cried.

"Happy tears," she said. And Ezra believed her.

And from then on, at least until early spring, six or so months later, the two of them were better, they were fixed. Ezra had fixed them. Ezra, he'd liked to think, had fixed *her.* It only took Paris. And the alley that they'd find themselves in again eleven years later.

FIFTEEN

Frankie

Frankie knew that Ezra was thinking about that birthday, the one where he'd brought Paris to her, but she didn't want to get into all of that. It was easier to keep this clean: the past was what it was; the present was also what it was. Ezra had always been a hopeless romantic. She had enough road between the two of them now to understand that this was at least part of why they were incompatible.

He was staring at her now, and she didn't want to squirm, but it was admittedly difficult not to.

"So were you going to propose to her here? Like, in Paris?" she blurted out.

She hated that she said that. She hated more that it bothered her to think he would re-create that moment, that magnificent moment when time had stood still for her twenty-first birthday, for anyone other than her. She'd had a shit-awful summer. Her mom was all over her about returning to the concert stage because in late May, she'd received a prestigious invitation to play at a rising stars event in Aspen. Her mother wouldn't stop nagging, couldn't leave it be. She threatened to stop paying for Middleton; she questioned, cruelly, what other skills Frankie had. Which was Frankie's entire point. She still kept in touch with a few of her peers from back then, and nearly all of them excelled at one thing and one thing only. They were geniuses at the violin or the cello or even the harp, but Frankie's mother wasn't that far off: they were in many ways stunted young adults who didn't have a significant list of actionable other merits. They didn't seek adventure; they didn't envision any sort of big, wild life beyond their talent. Frankie had never wanted to be the kid who was brilliant at music but sucked at living. She didn't want to be the girl who was known simply because she was born with some kind of genius. Because that was actually just luck. Frankie wanted to earn her way through life: that's what the discipline of long practice days and relentless competitions had taught her. It felt important to her that her future be of her own making. Which was ultimately why she quit at seventeen. Why she woke up one morning and stared at the ceiling and knew she was going to disappoint every adult in her orbit. But she simply didn't want it anymore. She wasn't even sure if she ever had or if they were the ones who had wanted it for her.

So when the invitation came to perform in Aspen, all sorts of ugly things were rearing their heads between her and her mom during Ezra's Fourth of July visit. Explosions of arguments about her talent, about her *wasted* talent, about what Fred thought (her mom was screwing Fred, so Frankie gave less than zero shits about his opinion), about how she was squandering her life at a liberal arts college when she could be playing at Carnegie Hall. And finally, when her mom really cut to the truth of her accusation, about why she was so wrapped up in a *boy* who surely was nothing but a distraction from what she should be doing. Was Frankie staying at Middleton for him? Was Frankie throwing away her future for him? Frankie had thought that was pretty fucking rich, coming from her mom who'd gotten knocked up at twenty, and she said as much. Frankie already knew, even though she loved Ezra desperately, even though he was her one real thing in the world by then, that he'd never trump her desire to live a grand life, to grab it wholly and jump in.

This, of all the wreckage of that summer, proved in the end to be the truest thing she learned about herself, though she forgot about it all when she returned to Middleton in August and Ezra threw her a birthday party in Paris.

Today, Ezra, looking noticeably winded, made his way toward her.

"I was not going to propose to her here. I was—" He stopped, and she grinned because she knew she was under his skin. Triumph. Then he took a beat and moved past it. "Don't shit on that night because you feel like picking a fight with me. That night was perfect. And you can rewrite history all you want, but you can't rewrite that." He sighed. "Look, I should have told you this, but Alec Barstow got ordained to be April and Connor's officiant. It's not . . . I mean . . . is it totally beyond possibility that we got married?" His voice cracked, and Frankie willed him to hold it together.

Frankie leveled her eyes at him and thought about how cozy they'd looked on the VCR, her memory of the mistletoe, that picture by the pool. Something struck her: a flash, a crystal clear recollection, and she felt her heart accelerate. The start of the scavenger hunt: how they had been at Burton Library, how they had toasted the happy couple, and then April and Connor clinked their glasses and announced that they were going to scatter all over campus to track down clues and win prizes. She and Laila had glanced at each other and rolled their eyes, and then April shouted: "I see you, Frankie Harriman! You are not too good for this! You're the most competitive bitch I know, so I expect you to bring your A game!" And indeed, Alec Barstow had been there too. *Shit.*

"Look," she said to Ezra now, deflecting. "Even *if* we got married last night, can't we just annul it? Is that really a reason to panic?"

Ezra laughed, his pitch too high and decibel too loud. He removed his hands from his parka pockets, where they'd been warming, and ran his fingers through his hair, so it stood at attention, then tucked them back away.

"Of course this would be disposable to you, like just another bridge you blew up then walked away from."

"What is *that* supposed to mean?" Frankie said.

Ezra stared up at the gray sky rather than answer. Frankie knew what it meant; she didn't even know why she asked. It was a shot across the bow, a shot about their ending.

"Fine," she huffed. "What's your advice then? You're the lawyer here. Please, enlighten me."

"I'm not a lawyer," he said, his face a grimace.

"What do you mean, you're not a lawyer?" Frankie was as surprised as she sounded.

"I'm not a lawyer, ok?"

"So what *are* you?" Surely, the Ezra Jones she knew had to be *something.* "A DA? A US attorney?"

"Those are all just different names for a lawyer," he said.

"Well, I am not the expert!" She flopped her hands to her sides.

"Look, I . . . I never took the bar exam. My mom got sick again that summer, so I went home. And then I missed the test, and they obviously couldn't hire me—"

"But the Ezra I knew was obsessed with being a lawyer!"

"The Ezra you knew isn't me anymore," he said, leveling her with a look. And the sharpness in his voice indicated that was true: the Ezra she knew was compliant, avoidant, nonconfrontational. "Anyway, I probably could have retaken it but . . . I realized I didn't want to. Weren't you the one who always told me to think bigger, to take control of my own destiny?" He shrugged. "So I did."

Frankie was gobsmacked, flabbergasted. Fifty percent of Ezra's whole deal was that he always knew which direction he was pointed toward. He was unflappable against her chaos. He was the anchor to her sails.

"So what do you do? I mean, I assume you're gainfully employed?"

"I work in tech."

"Tech?" Frankie said, like she'd never heard of such a thing.

"A start-up."

"A start-up?!" Frankie flailed her hand, the diamond ring stuck below her knuckle. She'd heard of start-ups, obviously. But they were for risk-seeking, fast-action types. Not Ezra, who had always been linear, always conservative, and she didn't think he had it in him, if she were being honest. Frankie sighed. She wanted to ignore these revelations, because if she got into the meat of them, she'd be forced to consider that she had underestimated him, that who he was at twenty-two and who he was at thirty-two were different entities. And then everything from last night would get much more complicated.

"I built something——" He paused and dipped his head, as if he were embarrassed. "Well, I built an online platform for . . . card games."

"Card games? Like . . . Uno?" Frankie remembered now that they had sometimes played strip Uno late at night when neither one of them wanted to study but each of them was too wired to sleep.

"No, like poker." He stuttered. "Not like poker. Poker. I built a gaming model, and I sold it to Yahoo."

"Wow. That's actually . . . amazing," Frankie said, surprising herself that she meant it. "You always were the smartest guy in the room."

"It's complicated."

"What's complicated about being paid for something you're good at?"

Ezra sighed. "Mimi . . . Mimi isn't a fan of gambling."

"*Mimi isn't a fan of* . . . Why would you even begin a sentence like that, like she's your mom?" Frankie realized how terrible that sounded as soon as it was out of her mouth. Blood rushed to her cheeks and then to her head wound. She flattened her palm on the top of her head to try to slow the throbbing.

"You don't even know her," Ezra said tensely. "You don't know the first thing about her."

"And to think I've lived my whole life without that and have gotten by totally fine." Frankie looked around. "But she's not here, so why is that even relevant?"

"It's relevant because when you're in a relationship, you try to meet the other person's needs!" Ezra threw his arms up as if his point were so obvious that he couldn't believe he had to state it.

"Like I don't know that," Frankie said.

"Do you?" Ezra said more loudly, and now she could see this was about significantly more than his stupid girlfriend.

"Of course I do. You know, you don't know anything about me anymore either."

"Fine!" Ezra said. "That is actually totally fine! Have you noticed you haven't heard from me? That, like, I haven't messaged you on AOL?"

"I'm not even *on* AOL messenger!" Frankie said, as if that made her side of the argument more potent.

"Jesus Christ," Ezra yelled, louder than Frankie had ever heard for the whole of their two-year relationship. He really was different; he really had changed. "Why are we still doing this? I have a girlfriend I love, and a job offer in San Francisco—"

"I don't know, Ezra, why *are* we still doing this?" Frankie yelled back. "I spent the past ten years of my life in total bliss without you!" This wasn't true, but Frankie didn't think Ezra would be any the wiser.

Above them, they heard the window open again, and they both cocked their heads north and quieted. Three books came barreling down, spines open, pages flapping, followed by, "Get a fucking room, lovebirds!" then the window slamming shut.

Frankie pressed herself against the brick facade, but Ezra raised his hands over his head, then realized he was still in the line of fire, when another book—a hardcover, no less—smacked him right in the middle of his shoulder blades, sending him barreling forward and straight into her.

They both froze. Ezra's hands flattened against the brick wall on both sides of her face, Frankie's wide eyes matching his right in front of her. She felt his breath on her cheek, and for a moment, they breathed together, and honest to God, Frankie wondered if he were going to kiss her. Or she was going to kiss him. She didn't know where the instinct came from. It felt animalistic, reckless, totally inappropriate, and yet it rose up in her all the same.

After a beat or two, Ezra broke the spell and gingerly eased a step back.

"You know what, Frankie? This isn't working. I don't know what happened last night. I don't care that my grandmother's ring is tethered to your finger. I don't know if we're married, and I don't know where our phones are, and I don't know if we slept together—though I pray we did not." He took a slow breath, and she narrowed her eyes at him. "But what I do know is that this is a waste of my time. I've grown up enough to know that. I have to go find Mimi. I have to go clean up. I have a million better things to do than stand here relitigating my past with a girl who never wanted to be a part of my future."

He brushed himself off and took a long look at her, and Frankie felt her insides roil. He reached into his left side pocket and pulled out the keys, tossing them to her. On instinct, she held her hand out and caught them.

"Here," he said. "I'm done with this. You solve it because you always know everything anyway."

Frankie started to protest because she had *never* said that, that she knew everything; she just did happen to know a lot about a lot of things, and she wouldn't apologize for it! But Ezra talked over her.

"If you find out we're married, send me the divorce papers. Then we can finally be done. *Forever.*" He spun back around and kept going.

Frankie leaned against the wall because the ground no longer felt level. And then for the first time in her life, Frankie Harriman watched Ezra Jones walk away.

SIXTEEN

Ezra

Ezra was pretty sure that a grapefruit-sized bruise was blossoming in the middle of his back where the book had careened and knocked the wind out of him. As soon as he rounded the bend from the alley, he hunched over and tried to breathe. His brain was moving at a million miles an hour, and he couldn't find his focus: there were too many things to home in on. His pain. Mimi. The security guards. *Frankie*. Goddammit, Frankie!

He hadn't wanted to walk away; he knew that, theoretically, two minds in this situation were better than one, but he just couldn't take it. Couldn't take *her*. Frankie Harriman was honestly the most exasperating person in the history of the world, and though he was intuitive enough to know that this was part of their attraction—he was a straight arrow, and she was a moving target—he was also intuitive enough to know what he could and couldn't handle now. Also, he had the unnerving sense back there that she was, inexplicably, about to kiss him, and just as unsettling, he realized that he wouldn't have protested.

Mimi. Ezra forced himself to refocus. Mimi was exactly what he could handle. Mimi wasn't uncomplicated; that wouldn't be fair to say. But she certainly wasn't Frankie, and though he didn't think he was running from their history, he did have to admit, doubled over and grimacing outside the upperclassman dorm, that for now, simply being *not Frankie* would have been sufficient enough to say *I do.*

Of course, there were plenty of other reasons why he wanted to marry Mimi, just as their initial questionnaire had told them: they both wanted three kids; they both liked the same snack at the movies: a large buttered popcorn with Milk Duds dumped in; they both (remarkably) liked the same movies too: brainy period pieces preferably with British accents. They agreed on where they would live (the suburbs outside the city), on dogs or cats (dogs, always; besides, Ezra was allergic to cats), they both were early risers and were polite enough to tiptoe around if the other was sleeping. He took window seats, and she preferred aisles; he liked the soft middle of bread rolls, and she exclusively ate the crusts. It was true that of late, she was always on the go—to a Datify rock climbing event or a softball game in Central Park or a Rollerblade 5K—and that she had started hinting that Ezra needed more hobbies. But Ezra had hobbies—he liked reading, and he still ran in the park at sunrise whenever his company wasn't required alongside hers at the gym, and if he really wanted to get into it (he didn't), he'd given up his one passion—poker, cards, blackjack—because she'd asked him. So he begrudgingly tried rock climbing and attended an event at the Met with her (opera was really not his thing) and he put on a smile because that made Mimi smile, and really, it wasn't all that hard, even if he was exhausted by it all too. He literally showed up for her because she figuratively showed up for him, and honestly, in a world where plenty of people didn't, Ezra thought that was really something. He was thirty-two; he wanted to be married. He'd wanted to be married really his whole adult life. He found a woman he loved who wanted to build a life that echoed his own. That felt magnificent.

Admittedly, Mimi was puritanical about Ezra's gambling. For one thing, Mimi liked control. She found being *out of control*, she'd say with a grimace, unattractive. On this, she and Ezra actually agreed! They were both so measured that nothing about their lives felt complicated. But Mimi also explained that for a span in her childhood, her uncle lost his house, had to move into their garage. He couldn't stop, Mimi said: he went to the track; he routinely lost money on sports all the way down to Triple-A baseball; he'd try to lure her dad or her brothers into any sort of bet: who could run down the sidewalk the fastest, who could beat him at Donkey Kong, who could drink a can of Tab in under thirty seconds? He didn't have to be at a card table in Vegas to feed his habit, Mimi said. It was everywhere; it was all-consuming. It was, she noted, a cautionary tale.

Ezra wanted to explain that he was different. His wasn't an impulse; he wasn't an addict. He just happened to know how to do it, how to win, and besides, it wasn't her money to lose (though he rarely, rarely lost). But the corners of her mouth turned down whenever they discussed it—going to Vegas for some blackjack or a casual poker night with his law school friends (who he really didn't see much of now anyway)—and Ezra didn't want to argue. Avoiding the issue by agreeing with her felt like the best tack to take. It didn't even feel like that big of a sacrifice—who can't stop playing poker for the woman he loves? So though he had actually jump-started his career with his innate ability to count cards, win hands, read the room, he more or less stopped. No, he stopped. He sold his platform for more money than he ever imagined would come his way, and Google recruited him to build part of their back end if he were willing to relocate to San Francisco, and that was that. Poker was in his rearview mirror. Until last night, evidently.

The snow had begun to slow, and Ezra pushed himself upward and took a few steps east, then west, then east again. He didn't want to be around when Frankie came to her senses and chased after him. He shook his head. *Who was he kidding? Since when had Frankie been in the business of apologizing?* Never. *Never once.* She was undoubtedly stewing back there, waiting for him to return and offer his own apologies. *Well*, he huffed to himself, *no dice.*

Ezra scooped up a handful of snow and molded it into a tight ball, then pressed it against his right eye. Instant relief. He moved it over to his left. Then his right. Then his left again, until the snow began to melt from his body heat and was leaving only frigid streaks down his cheeks. Still, he felt certain that his swelling was subsiding. He peered over his shoulder toward the alley. Still, Frankie hadn't emerged. *What was she doing back there now?* He told himself not to care.

So he simply began to walk. Away from her. The more distance he put between them, the better. But where to go? *Waverly's.* He could try there. Joni from the coffee shop had at least placed him there. He felt his hands shaking and squeezed them into tight fists, as if that could stop him from trembling. He hadn't even gambled in college. After Ezra moved into Henry's apartment, his brother had been the one to invite him to his weekly card night, where they mostly played poker but sometimes switched it up to blackjack. At first, the table ribbed him on being such a newbie, and they were more than happy to take what little money he had before he inevitably folded early and then nursed his Amstels for the rest of the evening. But something happened in the weeks that followed. Ezra felt his brain percolating, like a twinge somewhere in his cerebrum that was awakening. He went to Barnes & Noble and picked up a book on card counting, and discovered that he could teach himself strategies in a night. Easy, no sweat. And from there, it was as if he could *see* the cards, move all the numbers around in his head, and had a sixth sense about who was playing what and which cards were left to be laid down. And then he became unbeatable. Not right away, of course. Poker and especially blackjack weren't like addition where simple mastery meant you knew everything. But eventually, a few months later, yes. Then Henry took him to Atlantic City, and then they started playing high-stakes games when he had breathers from law school, and one thing led to another. He didn't have a problem (other than getting caught in Vegas that one time). He merely loved it. *He loved it.* The rush, the assuredness, the way his brain hummed along like a machine that was built for it.

Three years later, the summer his mom's cancer returned, the summer he was set to take the bar, he sat in his boyhood bedroom and read some books on coding, which was still the Wild West, and built a new way to play with strangers from all over the world. And then he sold it, and now, he never had to work a day in his life again. But he wanted to. He loved to work, and maybe that was one thing that he and Frankie had in common. They both understood that the work was part of what defined them: he just never thought she'd be a talent manager when she *was* the actual talent. God, she was so fucking talented. He hated that he still remembered this so clearly about her, even if he'd only seen her play two times in the entirety of their relationship. She was that good; it was that memorable.

Steinway Auditorium. There was something that was nicking a part of him from last night. But maybe he was just caught up in the memory of Frankie sitting at a piano bench from all those years ago, the first time he saw her play. He tucked his chin into the neck of his parka and braced against a blast of wind. *No*, he was headed to Waverly's. Maybe his beloved Nokia had fallen under the poker table.

He would go to Waverly's, and find his phone, and call Mimi and arrange a new flight, and take some Tylenol, and attend the wedding (ignoring Frankie the whole time), and propose at midnight when the world crossed over to a new century. *Yes*. He told himself *yes* as he turned around and headed in the opposite direction toward the north side of campus. That didn't sound so hard. That felt extremely doable. What Ezra Jones always needed was a plan. What Frankie Harriman always needed was a foil. They never could have worked. They were always a thunderstorm of impending doom.

SEVENTEEN

Frankie

In the back alley behind the dorm where Ezra had brought her Paris, Frankie flexed her jaw and chewed on her lip and stewed for a good three minutes—about the fact that he left her, about the fact that she had the impulse to kiss him, about, well, all of it—before her ears got too cold and her fingertips went numb. Also, she needed the world to stop spinning. Eventually, when she was no longer dizzy, she started forming plan D. To the best of her calculation, she had about three hours before she had to make herself presentable and get to the chapel for photos, where she'd paste on a smile, just like she used to in her piano competitions, and pretend that everything was ok. Even all these years later, Frankie could endure any sort of version of pretend as long as she knew it was temporary.

It was better that she hadn't told him—about the mistletoe, about looking cozy at Lemonhead, about a scavenger hunt in which . . . She squeezed her eyes closed and tried to remember how they had possibly ended up as partners. None of this meant—she hoped—that they'd somehow gotten so wasted that they indeed wed themselves to each other. Not just because Frankie didn't believe in marriage, didn't believe in a stupid piece of paper that made you promise the rest of your life to someone. In fact, Frankie could think of almost no one she knew who was happily married. Maybe April and Connor would give it a real go. Maybe monogamy wouldn't bore them. Maybe exchanging emails with grocery lists was their type of kink. Maybe renting movies at Blockbuster and driving to Vermont for a week of maple syrup tasting for summer vacation was their idea of fun. She didn't know. It wasn't her life.

Fine. She blew out her breath. Fine! She would solve this herself, just as he'd suggested. Frankie was always a better solo operator than team player anyway, if she were being honest. School orchestra was the *worst* because she wanted only to do her own thing, and obviously, sports were out because, well, she was a fairly low-tone, highly protected bubble kid who spent her weekends at music competitions. She couldn't risk any injuries to her fingers or her hands or really her arms or elbows, so anything remotely fun was out. Also, she was an only child and, therefore, perhaps unsurprisingly, had never been a fan of collaboration. You would think this would be critical for a music manager, but in fact, what worked for her and her clients was simply that Frankie knew best, and they all understood this and so they listened. When they didn't listen, well, that's when the trouble started, and Frankie would be called in to clean it up. For someone who appeared re-markably undisciplined, Frankie was actually quite rigid. You don't practice piano for four hours a day throughout your childhood and transform into a different person as an adult. If she could have, she would have—she gave it her best go at Middleton, for God's sake. She'd triple-pierced her ear, worn acid-washed jeans with rubber bracelets and fringy tank tops, watched hours of MTV rather than rewrite her term papers, but none of that changed anything about her DNA, about the bones of who she was inherently. So now here she was, fully formed. Quite volatile, which could be misconstrued as wildly spontaneous, but those were not the same things. Not even close to being the same things.

So plan D it was.

Frankie emerged from the alley behind their old dorm where Ezra had once brought Paris to her. There was no sign of him when she looked to either side, though she could see the tracks from his Sambas—the little circles from the soles still clearly defined—heading back toward the north part of campus. She was certain he was going to try Waverly's, so she assessed she should go anywhere but.

A heavy gust of wind caught her off guard, whipping the snow against her cheeks, seizing her hood and sending it aloft, nearly propelling her backward and onto the ground. The world tilted for a good five seconds, and Frankie held her hands in front of her as if she were going to topple again. Her legs felt wobbly, her energy totally zapped.

She made her way to a bench along the walkway just a few buildings down from Steinway Auditorium, then tucked her hand inside the arm of her parka sleeve and dusted the snow from the seat. She'd been so annoyed with Ezra back there that she hadn't even had a moment to consider that he wasn't the buttoned-up lawyer he'd always promised to be.

"Why law?" Frankie would say every few weeks while he was studying for the LSAT, and then later, while he was doing his applications, mostly because she didn't have the slightest idea what she was going to do with the rest of her life, but also because she didn't understand what made it so appealing. Every lawyer she knew, mostly men through her father, was dull and waxy.

"The rules," Ezra would say, every time, as if Frankie thought he might have come up with a different reason. "There's always a firm set of rules. And you either follow them or there's a consequence. That makes sense to me."

Frankie still loved him enough not to point out that the law was open to all sorts of interpretation and not exactly equitable to all. Also, she loved him too much to note that his need for things to be black and white, to be so clear-cut and controlled, was about much more than the law and mostly about the uncertainty and destabilization of having a mother who was in and out of chemo. And there was nothing Ezra could do to change that. So Frankie would just sit on his bed with him while he typed into his gray PC with the interminable hum of his dot matrix printer in the background, and offer encouraging edits to his essays, and then, when she got really bored with it all, she'd take off her shirt and lay there topless, counting the seconds in her head until he noticed. The highest she ever got to was eighty-seven, and that was only because Ezra was extremely focused that night.

When Ezra was accepted to NYU in February of their senior year, he assumed she would move to New York with him. Frankie didn't know what she was doing with her post-college life, but she was certain she didn't want to repeat her past and move to the same city with the same streets and the same haunts and the same people she'd already experienced. She didn't want to stomp out his joy though, so she held her breath and hoped he got in elsewhere. She would have considered moving anywhere else with him. She really would have.

Thus, after all that steady certainty, after how much he loved the law and after he chose NYU because they gave him a full scholarship and a research job that paid well enough for him to start saving (she understood why he couldn't turn it down, and she didn't ask him to) and was also close to his mother who he still worried about, Frankie was genuinely shocked that he was some big-time tech guy now. She'd met plenty of these new "internet" dudes at swanky LA parties, and Ezra, at least *her* Ezra, didn't strike her as that type at all: flashy cars with subwoofers, girlfriends with enormous fake breasts, expense accounts to cover a multitude of sins. They talked about stock options and second homes and remote Caribbean islands that they jetted to for the weekend.

She shook her head and corrected herself. *Her* Ezra was not a thing. It was odd though, she had to admit. How the span of a decade had opened between them, and as much as they no longer knew each other, to Frankie—and she wondered if it were the same for Ezra—she couldn't shake the notion that she still knew him as intimately as ever.

Suddenly, she had a memory. *Her* Ezra. No wonder that sounded familiar: those very words resounded in the private room at Burton last night. There had been about forty of them there. The ceilings were high and the walls stacked with books, and portraits of the college's founders in gold frames hung over the fireplace mantels. Fancy canapés that were meant to mimic their college fare—oversize spoonfuls of ramen, delicate wedge sandwiches of PB&J—were carted around by waitstaff, students who lingered behind for the holiday to earn catering tips. There was an open bar, but still, Frankie managed to sip Diet Coke, and then, just so no one asked, a Sprite, which she told everyone was a vodka soda. She'd seen Ezra across the expanse of the room. She'd tried to look everywhere but at him, but of course, that was physically humanly impossible, because when your brain tells you not to stare, the only thing you do is stare. Laila was already tipsy. Frankie remembered this now too. She'd done two shots at Lemonhead, just as a warm-up, and also because she had her eye on Alec Barstow, who she'd heard had recently moved to Asheville, which she noted was close enough to Charlotte that maybe they could become something more than friends.

"He's officiating," Laila had said. "Like off the internet." She flopped her shoulders as if to say she didn't really understand how such things worked—Frankie didn't either—and then Laila wiggled her eyebrows like she thought it would be amazing to land the centerpiece of tomorrow night's ceremony.

At some point, April and Connor gathered them around, and April had raised her champagne glass triumphantly and said, "Don't think we were letting you get out of here without a trip down memory lane!" And someone—Frankie couldn't see who through the crowd, and also she was trying *very* hard not to look in that direction because Ezra was in the vicinity—called out, "This whole thing is a trip down memory lane, and not necessarily a good one!" And someone else called out, "Look, Scotty, just because you got put on academic probation

junior year doesn't mean the rest of us can't have some fun!"
And everyone laughed, and Frankie realized they were talking
about Scotty Quinnlan, who she literally hadn't given a single
thought to since leaving campus. Like, she had completely forgotten that he existed. That he lived somewhere on planet
Earth.

April and Connor were laughing at all of this, then Connor
reached for the microphone and said: "We're doing a scavenger hunt! All of your names are in the basket back there—
we'll break off into pairs—and there will be a grand prize
for the winner!" And someone, Frankie thought it was Alec
Barstow, yelled, "Let's make it threesomes! I'm always up for a
threesome!" And then they moved en masse to the back of the
room to draw names. Frankie did the math and thought how
unlucky she could be: she had a one in twenty or so chance to
be with Ezra, and though those weren't great odds—not something she would, say, bet her life on—she also had nineteen
other chances not to be with him.

The rules were that whoever picked your name was on
your team. You then picked another name to kick off the next
pairing. Gregory, who Frankie hadn't seen since graduation
and who, she thought, looked exactly the same as when she
last did see him, barring a sad wispy mustache, selected her
after being partnered with Alec Barstow. *Frankie Harriman*, he
said dryly, his eyebrows raised. But then he found her in the
crowd and steered her out to face the basket and slung his arm
around her like this whole thing was ridiculously wild and did
a little bow as if he were her butler. *M'lady*, he added for a
flourish.

Frankie stuck her hand into the basket—she could feel

herself shaking and honestly couldn't believe that she was going along with this preposterous situation, but Laila was shooting her the stink eye, as if to say: *April was a generous friend to you when you showed up freshman year as a moody loner, so you will shut up and enjoy yourself.* Remarkably, whether it was because she didn't have time to recalculate or because she was becoming an actual adult, Frankie understood this. This was not the moment to turn something that could be nothing—a one-in-twenty shot—into a full-on calamity. So she reached her hand into the basket and prayed silently, *Not Ezra not Ezra not Ezra.* And she pulled out a piece of paper, and she felt her cheeks flush with blood and she said:

"Oh. Ezra Jones."

And to her right, April squealed, "Your Ezra!" *Her Ezra.* And Frankie wanted to throttle her because April really did know the weight of their history, but April was also a hopeless romantic who adored things like Valentine's Day and red roses and believed in the tradition of not letting her husband see her in her wedding dress before the ceremony and also in second chances. If memory served, she and Connor had split for a few months in their midtwenties. No wonder April didn't give the pairing a second thought. And anyway, Frankie was too shell-shocked to do anything other than shuffle to the side for Ezra to make his way to the front.

Now, on the bench at midday, with the snow beginning to slow, Frankie connected the puzzle pieces to how she ended up with Ezra last night. They had been partners. She tilted over and thought she might be sick. The nausea passed, and she pushed her palms into her knees and righted herself.

Campus was starting to wake now. There was a smat-
tering of students making their way past, a few who looked
hungover, a few who looked like they were rushing because
they had somewhere to be. Frankie remembered that about
college: how even though there was so little that was actually
important, everything *felt* important. Maybe it was because it
was the first time she'd truly been in control of her choices, or
maybe things like her friendships and simply the experience of
being on her own, of being wholly independent, actually were
the most foundationally important part of her growth. Since
the age of five, Frankie had always been told who she was
going to be, and at Middleton, where no one knew what she
was capable of at a piano bench—at least until Ezra caught her
playing their junior year—she had the chance to be whatever
it was she chose.

Awash in memories of her younger life, Frankie tried to
envision what she would have done last night if she wanted to
pretend that she was twenty-one again and inhabit that ghost.
Well, she would have gone to Lemonhead; she already knew
that. Her fingers reached for the set of keys in her pocket. She
stood wearily and supposed she needed to at least check
Steinway Auditorium. It was such a cliché. Good God! Did she
get wasted and end up screwing Ezra in a music room? Honestly, she thought she was better than that, but the truth of it
was that she knew that this wouldn't have been unheard of.
The question was not really if they ended up sleeping together,
because for Frankie, the sex was beside the point. That was
just a physical thing that bodies were designed to do. No, it
was the vulnerability. The moments or hours leading up to it.

To the intimacy, to the tenderness, to the space between how much she thought she hated Ezra Jones and somehow kissing him beneath the mistletoe.

She trudged up the steps to Steinway and pulled out the keys. But surprisingly, there was no padlock on the door, and instead, she reached for the gold handle and simply swung it open. *No.* This was not it. Not what she was looking for. She let the door close and stood and stared at her reflection in the glass. God, if her mother could see her now, she'd have an absolute fit. Disheveled hair, wrinkled clothes, wan face, slouched shoulders. Standing outside of the auditorium where Frankie should have come into her greatness.

She turned and walked away before she allowed herself another thought about that. She didn't miss performing. This wasn't a do-over story about a child prodigy who second-guessed casting aside her talent. Her talent had been an anchor that dragged her down so deeply she had to make the choice to either drown in it or cut herself free. She didn't regret any of that.

A mountain bike passed in front of her, then came to an abrupt stop and skidded across the brick walkway. The biker hopped off, and the bike rattled to the ground. Then the rider turned and pointed herself toward Frankie.

"You!" she said.

It took Frankie a second to place her. She was still swaddled in wool but now had on earmuffs and a scarf tightly bundled around her neck. Her parka threatened to eat her whole.

"I'm sorry?" Frankie said, and then the glimmer of recognition formed a complete picture. *Shit.* The girl from Homer with the pepper spray. "Oh," she said. "Yeah, it's me."

"I called the police!" the girl said.

"Well, that wasn't necessary. We left as soon as you got there."

Also, Frankie thought, if she were to get arrested at some point in her life, she hoped it was at least for something exotic, like setting tigers free from a zoo or inventing a new strain of weed. Not breaking into her lame freshman-year dorm.

"You slept in my bed!" she said.

"If it helps, I don't remember any of it," Frankie said.

"Do you have any idea how disgusting it is to know that someone else"—she lowered her voice now, and Frankie tilted herself forward—"to know that someone else *had sex* in your bed? Like, do you understand how gross that is?"

"Oh." Calm coasted over her. If that's what this was about, she could clear the air and be on her way. "We didn't have sex. We really just fell asleep."

She tugged the keys from her pocket, thinking she could ask this girl if they belonged to her. Maybe they simply belonged to her! Wouldn't that be incredible, Frankie thought. If there were just a reasonable explanation, and Ezra had inadvertently picked up this girl's keys? She already felt relief washing over her.

"I think these are yours?" Frankie said, offering them to her.

"What? No." The girl scrunched up her face, then pulled out her own set of keys from her pocket. "But like, I'm sorry to tell you that you're wrong."

"About what?" Frankie felt her hope deflating and dropped the keys back into her own jacket pocket.

"About the sex," the girl said flatly. *"About your trespassing sex."*

"No." Frankie shook her head. "That's not the type of thing I'm wrong about."

"Look, I don't know you and I don't know what kind of person breaks into a dorm room to have sex, but I found a three-pack of condoms under my bed."

Frankie felt what she thought was a mild heart attack, a jolt of pain coursing through her. Her heart literally paused for a moment. She didn't think she could blame this on the concussion.

"No . . . I don't—" Frankie started then stopped.

A very, very hazy memory came to the front of her brain. Her asking Ezra if he had a something—protection. But that could have been from years ago. She had no idea if it was actually from *last night*. When they first hooked up in college, they used condoms because there were posters plastered everywhere on campus about herpes and genital warts and the terrifying notion of AIDS. Eventually, once they were together for a few months in college, they both got tested, and then she'd gone to student health and gotten a prescription for the pill. She'd never been in a steady enough relationship to go on the pill before that. She'd theoretically never been in a relationship at all.

"I . . . I don't think you're right," Frankie said, but each protest was getting weaker.

The girl gave her a pitying look. "You don't even remember having sex with him?"

"It's almost the twenty-first century," Frankie bleated. "I'm allowed to sleep with whomever I want!"

A barely postpubescent boy nearby turned and stared.

"It's true!" Frankie shouted at him and at anyone else. "My body, my choice!" She didn't know why she had to turn this into a bigger thing, a public spectacle, and she wished that she would just shut up. She was always doing this—stepping further into the shit instead of backing away. She considered briefly now that it was not the best way to manage a healthy personal life.

"You can do whatever you want with your body," the girl said. "But just not in my bed." She grimaced and gave Frankie a long look from head to toe. Then she reached into her pocket and said, "I'm calling the cops again. You can't just, like, get away with this. Someone has to be held accountable."

EIGHTEEN

Ezra

Ezra knew before he got there that Waverly's would be closed. But he wasn't someone who left things to chance and wanted to be sure. Then there it was. Shuttered and dark. He wasn't about to be as reckless as Frankie and vandalize a window to solve his problem. He pressed his forehead against the glass and tried to peer in, hoping to, he didn't know, jog a memory or stumble upon a clue. But the windows were tinted, and the glare from the gray skies meant that he was only staring back at his own reflection. His face looked a bit better now, cooled from the snowball and given some time. Ezra had quite obviously never been pepper-sprayed before—he was the *opposite* of the type of guy who would have been pepper-sprayed before—so he wasn't certain how long it would take to normalize. (How had it been only four hours since he'd woken up with Frankie? This day felt like a lifetime.) He did the mental math though and thought that surely, by the time he figured out how to get Mimi to Middleton, all would be well; his face would be the face of the man she loved.

Obviously, there was still the mess of last night to sort out before her arrival. Ezra was not in the habit of keeping secrets. If anything, he opened himself up quickly. Too quickly. Gregory used to rib him that he fell in love with anyone who loved him back. This had been true his whole life through, so he couldn't even blame his mother's diagnosis, which would be the easy thing to point to. Fear of abandonment and all of that. But this was simply how he was wired. He wanted a partner; he liked the notion of companionship. He pulled back from the window of Waverly's and stared at himself and was honestly astonished that he ever thought he'd get that from Frankie Harriman.

He turned and headed back toward campus. It was almost 1 p.m. by now. Surely, Gregory would be awake. Surely, someone must know if he'd gotten married last night. *But at least we didn't sleep together,* he told himself as he crossed back onto Middie Walk. At least I don't have to tell Mimi about that. Sleeping in a bed with Frankie was not the same thing as *sleeping with Frankie.* He'd gotten in over his head with that Portland booze (he really needed to speak with Gregory), which, he realized now, he certainly should *not* have combined with his emergency Xanax, and had been swept up in a wave of nostalgia and broken into Homer. But that was it. That was it! That was not a reason not to get engaged to the woman he loved. He knew, granularly, like he knew when he had a winning hand, that this was all horseshit: that Mimi was not the type of woman who excused falling asleep in the same bed with an ex-girlfriend as an *oops*. He couldn't expect her to be, wouldn't have wanted her to be. They'd said as much on their questionnaires: that when faced with infidelity, they'd each have a no-tolerance policy. But Ezra had to cling to something. He was a relentless optimist right up until the cancer spread to the bones.

Ezra slowed as he passed Burton Library, but even with his relentless optimism, he couldn't ignore that his stomach curled at the notion of going in: he was wise enough to know that something had probably happened there last night, because you almost always inevitably return to the scene of the crime, and this was where he had been robbed of Frankie. *No, he wasn't robbed of her. He was freed from her.* He didn't even know why he thought of it in those terms in the first place.

Screw it. He doubled back abruptly and scaled the library steps two by two, his back barking, but nothing was going to stop him now. Face your demons head-on, *that's* really how you free yourself. His mom had said something along those lines when it became clear she was dying, and Henry had moved to London for work, and so it really was just the two of them and the grief of knowing that time was finite. She was wisp-thin and had nothing more than downy hair by then, but she took his cheeks in her frail hands and told him: *Don't shy away from the darker corners, love. Life is hard. Face it anyway.* He was trying but suspected he wasn't quite there.

He swung the door open, and the first thing he noticed was the smell. How a decade had passed, and it still smelled exactly the same. Like floor wax and old books and a faint note of burned coffee because somewhere sometime enough students had spilled their to-go cups here and there that the scent stuck. Ezra stood in the open foyer with its marbled floors and its rotunda ceiling, and for the first time all morning, he allowed himself to breathe.

A security guard sat at a desk about ten feet away and glanced his sleepy eyes upward.

"ID?" he asked.

"Oh," Ezra said. "I'm not a student. I mean, I was but—"

"Visitors' passes have to go through the alumni office." He flipped over his wrist and checked his watch. "But it closes in fifteen minutes. So."

"Can't I . . ." Ezra put on his most pleasant face, the one he used to woo investors, the one he wore at all of those ridiculous events with Mimi where he was shuttled to the front of the crowd and made an example of. (In the best of ways, Mimi thought. *Who wouldn't want to be us?* she always said.) "I was here last night. I think. For a dinner? I may have dropped my phone." Ezra flashed a grin, which almost always worked. "I'll be in and out."

The guard squinted. "I worked last night. I don't remember anyone complaining about a lost phone."

"Right," Ezra said, relaxing. Finally! He found someone who could be helpful. "I only just realized this morning."

The guard had already lost interest. "Lost and found is closed."

"Yes, sure, but if I could just have five minutes."

"Visitors' pass required." He shrugged like he didn't make the rules but was more than happy to refuse to bend them.

"Ok, but I just—I'm proposing to my girlfriend, and I really need my cell to reach her. Come on, surely you can make an—"

The guard picked up his newspaper and put on his reading glasses, so Ezra stopped talking. If he were Frankie, he'd probably just blow right past him. He'd probably get a running start and hurdle the turnstile and leave the security guard wondering just what the hell happened, like he'd mistakenly seen the flash of a superhero. And by the time he tracked Ezra down in the stacks of the microfiche or the open reading room, he would have solved all of his problems. But he was not Frankie. His shoulders sagged, and he turned to leave.

To his right was a bank of pay phones.

"Can I at least make a phone call?" Ezra said. My God, he knew he sounded pathetic.

"You can do whatever you want," the guard said without even looking up from his crossword. "As long as it's on the other side of this line." He pointed toward an imaginary border between the lobby and the actual library.

Boundaries, Ezra thought. Something he'd respect even if he didn't want to. He nodded to himself, as if he'd found the key to the differences between him and his ex.

He dug into his pocket and found three dimes, then flipped through the white pages that were discarded on the floor of the booth. He dialed the hotel and again asked for Gregory's room. He had a vague memory that Gregory was training for the Portland biathlon or half-marathon or something. He hadn't read the fundraising email closely and hadn't figured it really mattered, since he'd typed in his credit card number and donated a hundred dollars. But whatever it was, even in this weather, Gregory, who was part of the reason Ezra had blacked out, could get his ass out of bed and over to campus. It was a three-mile jog. He could be here in twenty minutes.

Gregory grunted upon answering on the fourth ring.

"I'm at Burton," Ezra said. "I need your help."

Gregory groaned then said: "Fucking A, fine. Give me a few." Then he clicked off.

Ezra hung up and felt more settled, more assured that this was all going to be ok. There must have been some sort of giant misunderstanding, but there was nothing he couldn't solve if he really put his mind to it.

As he strolled out of the foyer toward the front steps to wait for Gregory, he happened to glance upward and was surprised to see a big bushel of mistletoe. How he even recognized it as mistletoe was only coincidence: he was not generally known to be savvy in the ways of horticulture. But he and Mimi had attended a holiday party sponsored by Datify just a few weeks back. It was bonus season, and Mimi's bosses had upped their cash promises from in-person matches to extra incentives for anyone she signed up, so she was even more romantically ravenous than usual. The theme was "Anything for a Kiss," which Ezra thought was a little predatory, but since Mimi had organized the whole thing, he stayed mum. He knew how much she needed the cash, and besides, he didn't want to be the guy who took one look at something and deconstructed all the ways it wasn't working. He'd save that for Google. The ballroom had TV screens running famous movie kisses on loop; the corners of the room had spin the bottle stations set up for anyone who was brave enough; the bar served a heavy pour of a peppermint schnapps drink called "Minty Kisses" (everyone would have fresh breath, Mimi said); and of course, there was mistletoe in every doorframe. Mimi put on such a display for the potential registrants that Ezra's lips were swollen from all the kissing. By the end, he had extremely minty breath and absolutely no desire to go home and sleep with her.

Today, Ezra glanced upward. "This seems like a lawsuit waiting to happen."

The guard floated his eyes toward the bushel. "I didn't hear any complaints from you people last night."

Ezra opened his mouth to ask more, but then panic set in: he knew himself well enough to know that he wasn't prepared enough, steely enough to hear whatever came next. Instead, he quickened his step and scurried out into the winter storm.

NINETEEN

Frankie

Frankie could not believe that after all the land mines she'd averted in the past few hours, this tiny girl swaddled in puffy layers and wearing bright green earmuffs was going to be the narc who ruined everything. The girl cradled her phone in a mittened hand and held it between them like it was a grenade.

"If you're gonna call the cops, call the cops," Frankie said. "Don't threaten me with a good time."

The girl hesitated, and Frankie was certain that she'd called her bluff. Police meant statements and back-and-forths and this and that, and honestly, it would kill this girl's whole afternoon, possibly her New Year's Eve plans.

But then the girl tugged off her other mitten with her teeth, flipped the phone open, and punched the buttons.

"Wait!" Frankie bleated. "Wait!"

Frankie had never been the type to beg. She couldn't think of a time she'd had to beg! Sometimes, yes, well, she wore different hats with different clients, and of course there were lecherous producers and managers, but that was just how it all went as one of the few female powerhouses in the industry. So she danced the dance for her clients because that was part of the gig: she protected them from the sleazebags who wanted to ply them with coke and then screw; she shielded them from dickheads who promised the moon but paid them a penny on the dollar. Women were constantly undervalued and underestimated in her business, so she had to work with all of the cards in her deck. This made her think of Ezra, and for a moment, she was distracted by just how much she could not wrap her head around how significantly he had changed.

The girl snapped her out of it.

"Why should I not? Give me one reason why I shouldn't call the cops."

And then Frankie remembered to use all the cards in her deck. She couldn't outrun a bike; she could barely run at all with the blood pooling in the lump on her head. But she remembered the posters over the bed.

"Night Vixen," she said.

The girl's brow furrowed. "*Night Vixen?* I shouldn't call the cops because of Night Vixen?"

"I'm their manager. I discovered them. I saw the poster in your room."

The girl wrinkled her nose like she couldn't decide if Frankie were lying or if it even mattered. "Please."

"It's true. I swear," Frankie said. "Do you want a signed CD? Tickets to their next tour?"

"Do I look like someone who can be bought off with a bribe?" But the hand holding the phone dropped into her parka pocket, and she took a beat, considering. "Oh, actually, I didn't just find condoms. I found this."

She reached into her crossbody bag and pulled out Frankie's CD Walkman. Frankie had forgotten about it in the mess of everything else. The Walkman itself wasn't important. The Night Vixen rough cut CD was. A leak could get her fired. Night Vixen would never dream of letting her go, but everyone answered to someone, and Frankie still had a boss at the management company, even if she pretended that she alone played God.

"Oh, wow!" Frankie said, trying to keep her cool. "Yes, thank you, I lost that last night."

She took a step closer to retrieve it, and the girl inched her arm away.

"What do I have to give you to take it off you?" Frankie asked.

"The dignity of not having screwed in my bed last night?"

Frankie sighed, low, long, exhausted. "I really don't think—" She stopped herself. She was already pressed for time and arguing with a freshman about her sex life was doing no one any good. Still, she was begrudgingly impressed that this girl was holding her own, that she hadn't already bent to Frankie's plan. Few things wowed Frankie Harriman more than independent thinking. In the end, that might have been the reason she and Ezra never would have worked. He wanted what she wanted; he was fine with what she was fine with. At least initially.

They had had their first fight just before the end of their junior year, after they'd been together for a full nine months. Who goes nine months in a relationship without ever expressing a dissatisfaction, without ever diverging on opinions? She could see how, in hindsight, the tipping point that led to that fight—that she hadn't told Ezra she was a prodigy, that she'd spent most of her childhood awing grown-ups in concert halls, and that he only learned of it by stumbling upon her playing at Steinway—may have felt like its own sort of betrayal. But Frankie had gotten so used to her college persona, the free spirit who was responsible to no one, that she hadn't wanted to let her old persona show; she hadn't wanted to do anything other than pretend she'd buried it at seventeen.

Frankie hadn't known she had an audience that day in April of her junior year. She'd just gotten off the phone with her mother, who had announced that she and Frankie's dad were splitting, and though Frankie had always assumed that this news, this official split, would come as a relief, she instead was consumed with grief. She couldn't explain it: she knew her parents didn't love each other; she knew that her talent and potential was what glued their trio together. But there it was all the same: anguish, and when the grief rolled over her, she surprised herself and raced through the rolling hills of campus to Steinway. Someone at the dorm must have told Ezra she'd left in a fit or that they saw her fly into Steinway, but he didn't hear it from her. This was Frankie's thing, her private thing, and as much as she loved him, she still wanted some things just for herself. She didn't think this made her selfish.

When she pulled her hands back from the keys, she was startled to hear applause from the back of the auditorium. She stood quickly, pushing the piano bench back with such force that it toppled over, and then there he was, her Ezra, leaping onto the stage, sweeping her up and into his arms like he'd just witnessed something magnificent, something just in its nascency, when what Frankie was there for was to honor the end of something else. He wouldn't stop talking. He wouldn't stop marveling. Frankie had fled her dorm and retreated to the one place she knew she could find security—behind the black and white keys of the grand piano center stage in an auditorium—and he invaded that space and shattered it. If she had explained this to him, maybe he would have understood. Instead, he kept saying things like, "Is this what you meant when you said you played piano? Because this is definitely not, like, 'Chopsticks,'" and "Holy shit, why would you not tell me that you are basically Beethoven or . . . ?" He searched around for another great composer, another master performer, but Ezra wasn't fluent in her old language, which was part of what she loved about him. She thought he was looking at her differently, inhaling her differently. And then he said, "I don't understand—if you are this brilliant, why would you ever stop? Don't you owe it to yourself to keep going?"

And that was it. That was all it took for Frankie to believe that her instinct not to trust him with who she had been before had been correct. That of course she shouldn't have told him about her secret, inexplicable gift, which she hadn't asked for, didn't want, which made her feel like a bird inside a gilded cage for the entirety of her childhood. Ezra didn't understand that to be the greatest at something, you could never relent—and even if he understood this, he wouldn't have found relentlessness a deterrent. Just look at his passion, at his direction toward law. But at least that was *his* decision, Frankie had thought back then. At least Ezra got to throw himself toward his own choice of relentlessness. Frankie had never had a say in hers, had never been behind the decision-making. So when she was finally old enough to choose for herself, the only thing she cared about was freedom, about independence, about having the right to make whatever fucking choices she wanted *for herself* in the first place. Her parents would never understand it. LaGuardia never understood it. Fred didn't, conservatories didn't, her nerd friends from the competition circuit didn't even try to. But Frankie did. Frankie *did.*

And of all people to choose everyone else's side: Ezra.

She went from zero to a thousand in an instant, and looking back, she could have, would have, done it very differently. But she exploded about how little he knew about her, how right she was not to trust him with her secrets, how the only person she could count on in this whole fucking world had let her down. She left him in the aisle of Steinway, pushing past him and running to her dorm room, indignant, furious, burned. Eventually, he knocked and looked like he'd been crying, and he said he was sorry and he'd never bring it up again. He hadn't realized that he was pressing into a bruise that was already purple. In his defense, he said, how could he have? She'd never let him take a look.

Finally, she said: "Ask me anything you want to, and then we'll never talk about this again."

So Ezra stared up at the ceiling for a long minute and said: "Do you ever miss it? Do you ever feel like you should have made different choices?"

And Frankie, unequivocally, emphatically said: "No."

So Ezra nodded, and then, because he was a man who honored his promises, he never said another word, not when she and her mom were fighting a few months later that summer in the Hamptons when he visited, not when she was starting her job search their senior year and he could have applied to law school at UCLA or USC or anywhere that they could have lived parallel lives. And years later, it dawned on Frankie that maybe if she hadn't asked so much of him, maybe if he'd pushed her, they'd have found a better way to battle. Maybe a better way to love. But they didn't; they hadn't. And so the next time they did indeed fight, fully a year later, it was the one that broke them.

Today, Frankie stared at the girl whose room she'd crashed in last night, and the girl stared back, unwavering, her flip phone in her hand again, poised to call the cops.

"Look," Frankie said, "I'm sure we can work this out." She was tired, so goddamned tired. "What's your name? I'm Frankie."

After a long, skeptical pause, the girl said, "I'm Zoe."

And Frankie said, "Great, Zoe, let's make a deal. I absolutely must get the CD back. Technically, it's stealing if you keep it."

"Technically, it's breaking and entering if I report it."

Frankie felt her nostrils flare. She didn't have time to waste here, and yet she couldn't keep going without the disc.

"What do you want? Money?" She pulled out her pockets. "I have no money."

Zoe tapped her foot and stared past Frankie thinking. Then: "If you need this so badly, then this is what I want: I want an apology."

Frankie flexed her jaw. She could do that. What was so hard about doing that?

Zoe laughed, though Frankie could tell it was pitying, not humorous. It was true that Frankie Harriman was spectacularly bad at apologies, but so what. For her clients, she'd do anything.

"Fine," Frankie said. "I'm sorry."

Zoe laughed again and popped the CD out of the Discman, then threw it toward her. "That wasn't really all that difficult, was it?"

It was, though Frankie didn't know why it had to be.

"I'm keeping the Walkman," Zoe added. "Consider it my overnight fee."

"Sure, sure—" Frankie started, but then Zoe gazed off, distracted by something in the distance. Her eyes narrowed, and she jutted her head forward.

"Isn't that your boyfriend?" she said, gesturing toward a building down the way. "I've changed my mind. I want to hear his side before I agree to anything about the cops."

So Frankie looked where Zoe did, and there was Ezra, sitting on the steps of stupid Burton Library. Before she could protest, Zoe had mounted her bike, which had enormous treaded tires and pushed through the snow, and was headed toward him like a bullet, Frankie's apology be damned.

TWENTY

Ezra

Sitting on the steps outside Burton, chewing on the security guard's new information about the mistletoe, Ezra refused to believe that he had partaken in the events surrounding it, even if they were harmless fun. He suspected this was a lie he was telling himself because he had felt an inexplicable tug toward Frankie back in the alley, when they were pressed against the wall, and he had to stop himself from tilting forward and kissing her. Out of habit, out of nostalgia, he couldn't say. He'd spent so many years trying to forget Frankie Harriman that now, he couldn't come up with an answer to a question that he didn't even know how to ask. He jiggled his toes to keep them warm and stuffed his hands further into his pockets. Gregory should be here any minute, at least if Ezra had calculated his biathlon time correctly.

He pushed to his feet and checked his watch again. Maybe he'd been too generous with Gregory's physical fitness. Then he saw a figure careening toward him on a mountain bike, waving at him with a mittened hand. He couldn't make out it if it were a man or a woman: all he saw were bright green ear-muffs and loads of layers from the L.L.Bean catalog.

"Hey!" he heard her shout as she got closer. A woman. "Hey!"

She skidded in the snow and hopped off the bike in one fluid motion, then let it give way to gravity, the frame clat-tering against the steps and onto the ground.

At the sound of her voice, Ezra's adrenaline kicked in, or maybe it was his fight-or-flight system. *The girl from Homer with the pepper spray.* He stumbled backward, tripping up the steps, scrambling for the door. If this girl were going to mace him a second time, he had to be better prepared. He honestly didn't think his vision could take another dousing. It was pos-sible, he thought as he swung the doors to Burton Library back open again and the heat from the lobby assaulted him, that he could go permanently blind.

The security guard looked up at the commotion.

"You get your visitor's pass?" he said.

"Please," Ezra panted. "You have to let me in. There's a crazy person tailing me." He felt wild; he felt reckless. He won-dered if this was what Frankie felt like day-to-day. He wanted to recoil from himself, from this baser side of himself, but mostly what he wanted was to avoid being pepper-sprayed. It was incredible, he thought, how you could surprise yourself when the stakes were higher than you ever imagined. He prided himself on being collected, on being the port in a storm; he'd had to be so for his mom, and later, at the card table, and then at all times with Mimi, a couple always in control of themselves. But it turned out that there was only so much pain he could tolerate before his defenses broke down and he became animalistic. Just like Frankie.

The security guard raised his eyebrows toward Ezra like this was at least something intriguing. Then: "So no visitor's pass?" He peered at Ezra over his reading glasses.

"I'm about to be assaulted!" Ezra shrieked, then he heard the clanging of the doors behind him, and he felt himself physically shrivel, as if he could make himself invisible and avoid whatever was about to come next.

The guard looked past him, and his face relaxed. "Oh, Zoe." He gestured as if to indicate that she should just mosey on through. "You have a shift today?"

Ezra turned to face her, this Zoe. His shoulders were hunched, and his chin was tucked into his neck. He held a hand over his eyes and said, "Please, I'm not even bothering you anymore!"

Zoe laughed. *She laughed!* Ezra felt his mouth drop open in surprise—that she could be so casual, so cavalier after actually inflicting physical pain on him, and he lost track of what he'd planned to say next, how he'd planned to beg for mercy.

"Hey, Bruno," she said, then jabbed her thumb toward Ezra. "This dum-dum is with me."

"Been trying to get back into the library twice now." Bruno sniffed. "I've explained the rules." Ezra wanted to scream that all he did was follow the rules! And that anyone who thought he was a rule-breaker was absolutely fucking hilarious.

"I just want my phone," he said, and his voice cracked like he was going through puberty. "I just need to call my girlfriend so I can make sure that she's all right. So"—his voice raised an octave—"I can make sure that I can propose tonight."

He looked from one to the other. "You know, it's New Year's Eve. The turn of the century. I just thought it would be amazing."

Ezra honestly thought he might cry.

"Whoa, whoa," Bruno said, rising to his feet, holding both hands in front of him as if he were guiding a car to a stop. "Just calm down. Calm down now."

Ezra *was* pretty calm, given the set of circumstances.

Zoe's brow wrinkled. "Your girlfriend is literally right outside. She just tried to bribe me with a Night Vixen CD and a Walkman."

"No," Ezra said. "That's not my girlfriend."

At this, Zoe's forehead folded further. "The lady you slept with last night in my bed is *not* your girlfriend?"

Bruno stood up even straighter, as if he were now personally invested.

"It's a long story." Ezra sighed.

"Well, that would certainly explain why she didn't want me to tell you about the condoms," Zoe tutted.

"*Condoms?*" Ezra heard his pitch, knew he was spinning toward hysterical, toward a full-blown panic attack.

"She thought you'd react this way," Zoe said.

"*She knew?*" Ezra's voice bounced off the ceiling of the rotunda, and Bruno turned toward the library's interior to see if anyone had been disturbed. Given that Ezra hadn't seen anyone come or go since he'd arrived and called Gregory (Gregory! Where the hell was Gregory?), he didn't know who on earth Bruno thought he was disturbing.

"Well, she knows now." Zoe shrugged.

Ezra cast around for a bench, for a seat, for something to

steady himself. He thought he was going to be sick. Mimi would never forgive this. He didn't blame her. He wouldn't forgive it either. Fidelity was the bare minimum.

Zoe seemed to take pity on him. "Bruno, how about if he comes back with me for a minute? As my guest." She reached into her messenger bag and pulled out an ID. Then to Ezra: "You're lucky this is my work-study gig. I get special privileges."

Bruno shrugged like the artifice he'd constructed around his tough-guy security image didn't matter one bit.

"Come on," Zoe said, as if she weren't dangerous, as if she hadn't maimed Ezra just a few hours earlier with her pepper spray and her excellent hand-eye coordination that had managed to get him right in both eyes. (And possibly his lungs.) "You look like you could use some luck. I guess, since it is New Year's Eve, I'll try to make that happen."

Ezra nearly fell to his knees in disbelief. Then he remembered that he didn't believe in luck. Luck was what beginners relied on at the card table; luck was leaving something up to chance. What Ezra believed in had nothing to do with luck, but he didn't have a better option, or another hand to play. He shuffled his feet through the turnstile and left the next steps up to chance.

TWENTY-ONE

Frankie

Well, it wasn't glamorous, but Frankie had hidden behind a tree while Zoe approached Ezra, and then watched as he scrambled into the library, with Zoe right behind. Then Frankie pointed herself in the other direction as far away as she could get on foot with a head injury and several inches of snow. She could only imagine how Ezra would hit the marbled rotunda roof if Zoe shared her discovery of a three-pack of condoms, and Frankie wanted to be nowhere near that emotional detonation when the time came. Ezra was, of course, a one-woman man, and Frankie knew he'd never forgive himself for straying, even if she were the party involved. Especially if she were the party involved.

She picked up her pace now, something coming loose in her, and she didn't think she could blame the concussion. She knew herself well enough to know that if she *had* agreed to the scavenger hunt, and if she *had* agreed to partner with Ezra, that she would have gone in whole hog. Even if she begrudged it. Even if she hated him. Frankie had never been one to enact the mercy rule, to wave a fellow competitor over the figurative finish line ahead of her because she'd already won all the other trophies. No, she may have hated that she was a prodigal drone, she may have despised that she felt like a windup toy putting on a performance for the adults who were significantly more invested in her success than she was, but she still wanted to win. She'd always been wired that way.

She reached the outer perimeter of campus and turned toward the athletic complex, a looming concrete eyesore that had once been modern when it was built in the 1970s but now, she could see from a distance, looked as out of place amid the traditional architecture as she probably had when she first arrived on campus. For reasons that were obvious, Frankie hadn't spent much time there over her four years. Occasionally, she would accompany Laila and April to the fitness center and half-heartedly give it a go on the treadmill with the Go-Go's or Duran Duran or Madonna or, when particularly moody, the Cure or the Smiths, blasting out of her cassette Walkman, her spongy headphones soaking up sweat. Once she met Ezra and discovered that he was as disinterested in the fitness center as she was, she abandoned that ruse too.

Still though, she slowed her pace today and lingered. She pulled the Polaroid of the two of them by the pool out of her purse.

"Document each clue," April had announced, clapping her hands as if this were a murder mystery party and she was the lead detective.

Frankie remembered now that she'd groaned, and Ezra, to her left and unable to meet her eyes, finally turned to her and said: "Look, grit your teeth and keep your mouth shut. We're adults. We can do this. We're not going to ruin April and Connor's rehearsal dinner."

Frankie had a slew of witty yet acerbic retorts on her tongue, but he'd already returned his focus to April, who was running down the list of rules. *Rules!* At a rehearsal dinner. This was not what Frankie had signed up for! This was not at all part of the agreement when she'd booked her ticket back east to her old university at risk of seeing her ex-boyfriend with whom she'd had a calamitous breakup. Frankie was just trying to be nice. Showing up. She was just trying to prove that she wasn't the sort of person who walked away from her past after dumping a pool of kerosene on top of it and lighting a match.

Once the rules had been dispatched—there was a clue at each location that would lead them to the next, and photographic evidence was required to move on (*Just so we know there's no cheating!* April had said, ever the professor)—Ezra had been the one to handle the camera. Frankie remembered that now too. She could see that he was a little tipsy, if not significantly wobbly, already in the early evening. Gregory lumbered over, equally foggy, and brought another round of shots.

"This should be interesting," he said, more to Ezra than to Frankie, and when Frankie waved off the alcohol, Gregory drank hers too. Then, he added: "I swear, if you two don't kill each other by the end of the night, maybe you'll find true love."

Frankie exhaled outside the athletic complex. She knew, at the very least, where she'd been at one point last night: she had the Polaroid beside the pool. In college, shortly after their first

Christmas break together junior year, Ezra's mom called and said that her scans were looking uncertain, that the doctors needed to run more tests. Frankie had just nailed a spin at Abel Rink during those skating lessons he'd made her take, and she, high on euphoria, had swung by his room with hoagies and Diet Cokes, when she found him sitting on the floor, the phone in his lap, his face in his hands. That he'd been crying was obvious, and Frankie was surprised to find that she didn't mind. She'd never been a particularly good caretaker, mostly because she'd had no one to tend to, but also because she was so often in self-preservation mode herself. But she found Ezra's vulnerability, at least in that moment, endearing. She found that she loved him more for it, and this revelation startled her. Frankie had always assumed that a hardened exterior was the only way to get through the day-to-day; she'd frankly assumed that it was the only way for anyone to love her. But here was Ezra, his figurative guts on the floor of his dorm room, and she wanted nothing more than to open up his whole heart and to open up hers too.

"Come on," she said finally, as she sung him a bit of "Summer of '69" (it was stuck in her head from the rink, and she was humming it under her breath before she realized what she was doing), and they then sat in silence long enough for the hoagies to warm and the cheese to congeal. She breathed in and out with him; she implored him to exhale. "Let's go do something nuts."

Nuts was a relative term, she realized today, as she swung the door open to the fitness complex. Frankie was still getting her bearings back then, still calibrating how far she could push herself into rebellion. A couple of years ago, she found herself in a Paris hotel with a rooftop pool. Night Vixen was still out doing God knows what with God knows who, but Frankie had called it an early night. She suspected she was getting an ulcer, from either the stress of touring or the stress of managing the world's top female act who also had the maturity of twelve-year-old girls or the stress of eating shit food on the road for nine months. Or maybe all of them. So she slipped out of her jeans and hoody (standard tour uniform) and into the hotel robe, and then out the door of her room, and pressed the elevator up button. It was well past midnight, and she was the only one there, on the roof with a full view of Paris. In the distance, she could see the Eiffel Tower. It was magnificent. She dropped the robe and dived into the pool headfirst, naked. And when she finally surfaced, the first thing—the first person—she thought of was Ezra.

Today, the athletic center was deserted, as expected. In the distance, Frankie could hear the clanking of the weight room—a few athletes who stuck around for break getting in their training. Though the pool was back through the locker room and several long hallways and even a staircase down half a level, the air still smelled of chlorine. Even now, Frankie couldn't disassociate the scent of pool water from Ezra. That night, the night his mother called with the ominous news of her scan, the first time he ever heard her sing for real because belting in his Jeep didn't really count, Frankie had pulled him to his feet from the floor by his twin-sized bed and off the rug he'd probably bought at Bed Bath & Beyond, and they walked out of his dorm room without so much as a word. He had woven his fingers through hers and trusted that wherever she was taking him, whatever she had in mind, it had to feel better than how he felt right now. Frankie didn't remember now—today—why she'd headed toward the pool back then. Maybe she'd been reading some solemn poetry for one of her English seminars about how water was like a baptism, that it could make you feel reborn. Or maybe she was in the middle of her Bruce Springsteen phase and obsessed with "The River" and, in lieu of an actual river on campus, thought the pool water would suffice, even if the song was depressing and had nothing to do with hope, which is exactly what she wanted to offer. Or maybe the idea of skinny-dipping just seemed titillating. The why of it didn't matter then.

They'd discarded their clothes by the diving board, and Frankie jumped in first. When she emerged, Ezra was standing there naked staring down at her, smiling despite the previous few hours, despite the phone call and the scans and the cancer.

"What?" Frankie said. She felt blood rush to her cheeks and felt a little off-kilter that she could be self-conscious in front of an audience.

"Nothing," he said, just before he jumped in. "I just love the shit out of you, Frankie Harriman." Then he cannonballed right next to her, and Frankie had to sink under the water with him so she wasn't blinded by the spray.

Ten years later, Frankie made her way to the back of the athletic center, the scent of chlorine getting stronger and headier as she drew closer. She didn't know what she was looking for. She didn't think that she'd find the answers to the question of their matrimony here, and she doubted their phones were at the bottom of the pool. But she and Ezra had been here last night, just like she and Ezra had been here a decade ago. Maybe that had to mean something.

She knelt down and untied her Doc Martens, which were stained with the salt from the Middleton sidewalks, and she left them outside the pool entrance. The tile flooring felt cool against the pads of her feet. In front of her, the pool was vast and peaceful, the filters churning quietly, near-invisible ripples cresting across the surface.

Frankie rolled up the hems of her jeans, then eased down to the concrete lip of the deep end and plopped her feet in. The water was surprisingly warm, though she didn't know what she expected. That was half of Frankie Harriman's mantra: expect the unexpected! Always be prepared for anything! Which actually, when she thought about it, was basically the Boy Scout's motto, which led her right back to Ezra.

She kicked her feet lazily in the water and considered for the first time how things could have gone differently for them. If she'd been honest with Ezra about who she was, about what she was running from. She'd always blamed him for their split; maybe it had been easier that way, but he was so willfully naive that she couldn't help but use that as an excuse for their messy ending. Well, not the finality of the ending. That was on her. But the messiness of it, yes. Frankie had always assumed that if Ezra had really *known* her, if he'd leaned into the whole of her, they never would have exploded. But, she considered now, maybe she had been focused on the wrong thing for all of these years. That she had blamed Ezra for missing the most funda-mental parts of her—the independence she craved, the freedom she required as much as she needed oxygen—but maybe because she hadn't cracked herself open wide enough, he'd never been able to peer in and get the proper view.

Frankie pulled out the Polaroid picture from her back pocket and stared at it until it made no sense, and then dropped it into the water where it floated to the middle of the pool, out of reach. Then she held up the engagement ring, which was stuffed on her sausaged finger, and found herself moved—*moved*—that it had made its way back into her life. She didn't want it; she never had. But still, she had to admit, a second chance at an old love was the stuff that artists wrote about, the kind of thing that could spark a pretty good song.

TWENTY-TWO

Ezra

Zoe, who Ezra still found quite terrifying, led him back to the private room within the bowels of Burton Library once he explained what he was looking for. She'd half-heartedly apologized for macing him, but she said, as she delayered her various winter accessories—the earmuffs, then a scarf, then the mittens, then her parka to reveal yet another wool sweater below—she didn't think he could blame her. Now she could see that he was harmless, but give her a break, how was she supposed to know?

"That said," she continued, as she wound her way through the reading room and past the hallway with the vending machines stocked with junk food, "I'm a little confused here: your girlfriend is *not* the Night Vixen woman?" She held up a yellow Discman as if this were code for *her.*

"No," he said. "She's my ex."

Zoe stopped and took a long look at him. He knew how that sounded; he deserved it.

"You don't understand," he stammered. "This is the sort of

thing Frankie does. This is the sort of mess she finds herself in. *All the time*."

"So you have no blame for the mess?" Zoe asked, though it wasn't really a question. She doubled back to the vending machines, then kicked one right in the lower left corner, and three seconds later, the machine spit out a bag of Fritos. She grabbed it and said, "Breakfast," offering Ezra none.

Ezra considered this: blame. About his blame with Frankie. He thought, even a decade later, that he'd been a pretty wonderful boyfriend. He'd cheered her when she was sorrowful; he'd given her space when she needed to breathe. He'd brought her Paris, and he hadn't asked too many questions about her life before Middleton because he'd promised her he wouldn't, and he showed up day in, day out, when she was moody, when she was happy, when she was exhausted, when she wasn't. He'd asked so little of her. This, to the best of his understanding, was what a dedicated boyfriend did. He simply stood beside her and wished for her happiness. Still, that hadn't been enough.

He thought of Mimi now too. How even though he'd evolved since twenty-one—he liked to think he'd evolved—the way that he showed up for her as a present partner had not. Something about this bothered him, though he wasn't in any sort of shape—battered and hungover—to articulate exactly what. Relationships were meant to be easy. His dad had left his mom (and him and Henry), and the explanation his mother always gave, with a sigh, was: "It just got too hard for him. He wasn't the type of man to stay when it got hard."

His dad would call on Christmas, and of course on their birthdays, but they would go months without seeing him, sometimes longer. He worked as a longshoreman on boats in

Alaska and who knew where else. He'd literally fled to a north-western territory rather than grit it out through the hard stuff. Ezra—and he knew this was a cliché, ok?—was going to in-oculate himself from the hard stuff, and this way, he'd never have to test if he were the man his father was and then leave. So he'd tried to make Frankie's life seamless in the way that he now tried to make Mimi's life seamless, and thus, that meant that he had zero accountability in their destruction. This was one of the aspects about poker and even blackjack that he found so soothing, at least how he played it: it wasn't that it was pre-dictable, but there were rules and there were strategies, and if you kept your emotions out of it, you rarely got destroyed. Sure, maybe you'd fold, and maybe you'd lose an extra hundred, but if you were careful and held steady, nothing ever happened that you couldn't foresee. If things really went sideways, you got up from the table and walked away unscarred but for whatever you lost in a hand. But with Frankie, so much was unforeseeable. Even ten years out of the explosive breakup in front of this very building, Ezra simply could not dream of the ways that he could have seen any of it coming. He'd kept his head down; he'd loved her. What else was there to know?

By now, they'd reached the private room.

"Here ya go," Zoe said. "And you're welcome."

They both glanced around the room. The cleaning service hadn't yet swept up. There were disposable wineglasses lit-tered on cocktail tables, crumpled-up napkins scattered around too. The flower arrangements had started to wilt, and the ta-blecloths were askew. It was astonishing, Ezra thought, that he was here last night and had absolutely no recollection of it.

"You're leaving?" Ezra asked, moving from table to table, checking for his phone, lifting the linens to search the floor, scooting out the chairs.

"I'm on work-study, dude. I have actual hours to clock in." She gave him another pitying look. "I'm not running a charity." Then: "Also, it's New Year's Eve. I have better things to do than spend it in a library with some old guy."

"Wait," Ezra said, deflating, seeing no sign of a phone. "Just . . . can you look around, see if anything jumps out at you?"

"Like an explanation about why you're cheating on your girlfriend with your ex-girlfriend?" Zoe made a face.

"I'm not . . . I don't . . . I've never been a cheater." Ezra felt a rush of shame. Though what he said was true. But then he remembered how Frankie was right: he *had* been caught in Vegas and yanked out by the elbows and told he was never welcome back at the Bellagio, and then two days later, the MGM. What if he'd been a cheater this whole time? What if the story he told himself was just that? A convenient narrative because it blurred out the messy parts.

Zoe ran her fingers over a shelf of books, tracking them all the way toward the back of the room, where a giant blackboard was adorned with Polaroids. She stopped and stared, and Ezra took ten steps forward—just like he had this morning, pacing back and forth in Homer, he would unconsciously count his steps in his mind—to stand beside her. In front of them were at least a hundred photos, taped up in lines. Seemingly, Ezra thought, by teams or at least by pairs. He squinted and searched the faces, looking for his own.

Zoe spotted him first.

"There." She jabbed her finger. "You're right there. With the *ex*-girlfriend."

Indeed. There he was. In chalk beside the photo, someone had written: TEAM FREZRA.

That's what April used to call them whenever they played all's fair football or foosball in their dorm rec room or just because she thought it was endearingly hilarious. Ezra hadn't thought of that in years. At the top of the board, in the same handwriting, someone had scrawled: APRIL AND CONNOR'S MILLENIUM REUNION WEDDING EPIC SCAVENGER HUNT. He and Frankie were standing rigidly side by side, each of them looking uncomfortable, though Frankie admittedly looking more so. Ezra could tell by the way that his eyes were half-open, the looseness in his jaw, that he must have already been on his way to drunk by then. He couldn't blame Frankie for this, he knew. He could blame Gregory, who he just remembered was probably waiting for him out front. And he could blame himself. He should have known better than to mix a Xanax with booze. He did know better. It had just been so long since he'd had to.

"Shit," he said. "My friend is outside. I totally forgot. I asked him to meet me here."

And Zoe said, "Dude, I think you have a codependence problem."

And Ezra said, "What? No." Then he scanned the photos until he found Gregory with Alec Barstow, hockey star and internet-ordained officiant.

"Look, I have to go to my post," Zoe said.

Ezra took stock of the blackboard. Each team had evidently taken a series of photos around campus. But his and Frankie's petered out after only two. There was the one of them at the start, the uncomfortable one. Then there was one that he must have taken of the two of them. Inexplicably, Frankie kissing him. Or him kissing her. *Kissing her!* His eyes were closed, the angle suggesting that his arm was extended, and the whole thing was a little blurry, but even still, he could see her staring at the camera—at the lens—as if to say, *Just because I'm doing this doesn't mean anything.* Then Ezra remembered the mistletoe, which not even a few minutes ago he was certain he wouldn't have gone along with. He peered more closely at the photo: What if Zoe were right? What if he was a cheater? What if all it took was some Portland booze, a miscalculation with an anti-anxiety pill, and the unfortunate luck to be paired with Frankie for him to forget Mimi altogether?

Ezra felt his breath leave his body for the third time today.

The other teams had seemingly returned to Burton with a stack of photos—evidence, he assumed, that they'd completed the hunt, that they were still in it to win it.

Beside him, he saw Zoe, still not having yet ditched him, inch her nose toward the incriminating photo, then peer toward the doorframe. Then she pointed: "Ah. I was wondering who hung that all over the building. Because it sure as shit wasn't me." She shook her head. "This notion of romance on New Year's Eve, that we can't be alone for the holiday or for, like, the turn of the century, is so outdated. Kissing at midnight. Preposterous." She flopped her shoulders and headed toward the exit. "Anyway, my dude, best of luck with this triangle you have going on, for which you have no responsibility."

Ezra tried to refute her, but only a strangled sort of moan left his mouth.

"Listen," she added, "it's New Year's Eve. Cliché as this may be, it might be time for a reckoning."

He started to protest; he held up a flaccid hand then let it drop. Zoe met his eyes, and something passed between them, a challenge. He dropped his gaze to the floor, and she clucked as if to say, *Exactly what I thought*, and then disappeared around the corner. Gone.

TWENTY-THREE

Frankie

Frankie had sat with the stillness of the pool for as long as she could stand it, and then a little longer because she knew that the quiet was important, was necessary, and too often, she was running from that serenity. She pulled her toes out, wrinkled and pruned by now, and discovered that within the solitude, she had been able to piece together more about the evening than she'd known when she started.

Maybe there was something to simply being still. To working through the discomfort that she so often fled from. For the whole of her life, or at least since she'd first pulled out the piano bench in her parents' apartment when she was five and her parents stumbled into realizing that she had perfect pitch, Frankie had been surrounded by noise. Her dad had inherited a grand piano from his own parents—an antique Steinway that he had tuned twice a year but otherwise went unused in their expansive living room. Her mom had been playing Simon & Garfunkel on the record player, and the story goes, Frankie just sat down at the piano and instinctively began playing "Bridge Over Troubled Water." When she finished, she looked up, and her mom was standing in the precipice between their kitchen and the living room with pink oven mitts on and her mouth agape.

"How did you do that?" her mom said, and Frankie worried that she was mad at her. The truth was that Frankie didn't know how she had done it. It was like she could see the notes the way she saw colors. They were there. Her brain knew that red was red. Her brain knew that "Bridge Over Troubled Water" was set in E-flat minor, even if her brain couldn't tell her that exactly. She started to cry, and her mom rushed over and wrapped her in her arms, the oven mitts still on, and whispered not to cry, that everything was going to be all right. Looking back, Frankie understood that her mom was barely twenty-six. She was playing dress-up as a wife and a mother, numbing herself to the dreary reality of waking up in a life she hadn't planned on. Sometimes, she would stare wistfully at the wall for so long that Frankie, still little, thought maybe she'd mastered the art of falling asleep with her eyes open.

But when Frankie sat down at the piano that day, everything shifted. For the three of them. Now, they were surrounded by noise, and not just noise, they were surrounded by music. *Music!* What a joy that should have been, what a gift. It was only now, by the silence of the pool, with the filter occasionally bubbling and a sporadic hum of a motor, that Frankie felt something untangle in her, just by sitting in peace. Even the lump on her head seemed calmer, like she was beginning to heal from the inside out. She reached up, pressed it, found that it was still sore but less aggressively so.

She dragged her feet, ankle-deep, from the pool, tugged on her socks, and tied her Doc Martens. She unrolled the hems of her jeans and recounted exactly what she knew. These were the facts as Frankie understood them at the moment.

1. She had met Laila in the lobby of the Inn. They had gone to Lemonhead. Just as she had maintained.

2. They proceeded to Burton Library for the rehearsal dinner where—though this part was still a little hazy—she was unceremoniously and unluckily paired with Ezra for a scavenger hunt.

3. At some point, she willingly kissed Ezra Jones under the mistletoe. She thought, perhaps, this was a memory from a long-ago time, but even Frankie wasn't so LA as to believe that déjà vu could be this strong. She'd kissed him. She just needed to accept the facts as they were.

4. She had a photograph of the two of them right here, at the Olympic-sized pool where they once skinny-dipped because his mother's oncologist had discovered lesions on her liver and this felt like the only place to wash Ezra clean.

5. From there, there were gaps. But she knew that at approximately ten o'clock, she and Ezra had linked up with Gregory at Lemonhead, because she had video proof of her leaning into his chest, his arm around her waist (!!!!). How they had gone from sworn enemies (or at the very least, vitriolic exes) to walking arm in arm had yet to be determined.

6. After that, Ezra turned into a card shark and ripped off Joni, the wonderful barista, and as a tour de force to end the evening, they broke into Homer.

7. Oh, Frankie reminded herself, at an undetermined time, Ezra's beloved girlfriend, Mimi, got stranded in . . . she couldn't remember which state, but it was somewhere in the middle of the country, and the two of them—Frankie and Ezra—may have gotten married.

Frankie pushed open the doors to the athletic complex, the cold assaulting her, the wind biting her cheeks. Out of habit, she reached into her bag to grab her Walkman but remembered that Zoe had stolen it. Maybe she could just live in the quiet; maybe she didn't always need to have a melody humming through her brain. What would happen then? If she just kept her head up and her ears open?

Frankie remembered now that Gregory had been partnered with Alec Barstow. Which is precisely how they could have gotten married last night. *Shit. Shit shit shit shit shit.*

She had been whispering to Laila, leaning in close so she didn't cause a scene because she did understand that the rehearsal dinner was not about her (really, she did), and begging Laila to swap partners with her. Laila had heard her out but cocked her head and said something annoyingly maternal like, "Frankie, I kind of think this will be good for you? Just . . . It's been ten years . . . Maybe this can be healing?"

And then Gregory had stepped between them and said to Frankie, "You're a competitive bitch. Let's team up and form an alliance." And Frankie had figured that at least a foursome would provide some breathing room, so she nodded *fine*, and then Gregory clapped and said, "I'm winning this motherfucker," and Alec said, "Excuse me, *we're* winning this motherfucker—you know in college, I set the record for hat tricks," and Frankie recalled then that Alec only ever wanted to talk about hockey back then too. Frankie remembered that Gregory was toting his Portland moonshine, which he held up as if an initiation to their alliance, and that she deflected by making a joke about only drinking top-shelf, which Ezra rolled his eyes at just before he did a shot of his own. Ezra hadn't been much of a drinker in college— that had always fallen to Frankie—and she was surprised to see the alcohol disappear down his throat, how loose he was getting, how messy.

"We're adults here, Frankie," Ezra said. "It's like two hours of your life. I don't want to do this any more than you do." Then he grabbed Gregory's bottle and took a swig directly. Then added, "This is truly disgusting, Greg. It's basically straight kerosene."

Frankie remembered now, as she exited the athletic complex, that their first clue was within the library itself. "*Meet Me Under and you know what to do then*," it read. Well, none of the four of them had any idea what that meant, but Ezra said: "Meet me under the stars?" And Frankie was annoyed because the clue specifically told them to search within the library, and so she said: "Burton does not have a planetarium, you know." So Gregory added, "Maybe in, like, the astrology section?" And Alec said, "I'm a Gemini. We're known to crush it at everything." And Frankie had wanted to scream.

They wandered through the halls, their eyes pointing up, until finally they reached the lobby, and Frankie saw it with dread.

"No," she said, and then the rest of them followed her gaze.

"Jesus," Ezra muttered.

Alec pumped a fist and said, "All right, clue number one accomplished," then he grabbed the Polaroid from Gregory and pulled their faces together and the flash went off. He flopped the picture back and forth in the air until there they were, the two of them, *kissing*, and Gregory squealed a little at the hilarity of it because Alec was as hetero as they came, and said, "I can't lie: I'm a little turned on," and then they sprinted back to the room to deliver the photo for the board and receive their next clue.

Frankie crossed her arms, so Ezra did too. She wanted to win. She really wanted to win because what was the point of this exercise if not?

"Let's just get this over with," she said.

Ezra shook his head *no*. He was definitely drunk by now, his eyes on their way toward half-closed, his posture a little ragged. "I exorcised you, Frankie Harriman. I did."

"Ezra, can we just agree that we are adults and pressing our lips together can just be a ridiculous act of physicality so we can move on from this charade and possibly be crowned champions?" She glanced behind her. Gregory and Alec had at least a minute on them. She didn't know where the other teams were, but so far, it appeared they were in second place. "Like, trust me, I do not want to kiss you any more than you want to kiss me. If there is anything less on this planet I want to do, I

can not think of it. But I want to win more than I do not want
to kiss you, ok?"

Ezra's eyes flitted toward the exit, and he seemed to lose
himself for a beat. They'd never discussed what had happened
outside when they split. She was too heated, even a week later
when they spoke briefly on the phone, and Ezra seemed to just
want to compartmentalize like he always did.

Frankie reached over, grabbed his arm, and swung him
toward her.

"Fine." He sighed. "Fine."

She stood on her tiptoes, and he lowered his chin while
holding the camera aloft, and then suddenly, before she could
give it any more thought, she leaned in and kissed him. And
now, with the wind kicking up but the snow coming to a halt
and the sun beginning to make an appearance on the quiet
Middleton campus, Frankie remembered that she hadn't hated
it. That it had felt familiar, comforting almost. That something
about Ezra Jones sent a charge through her, through her veins,
through her blood, through her guts, and when she kissed him,
that electrical pulse raced inside her just as it always had.

She'd grabbed the photo and run it back to the blackboard
where April had squealed and said, "Oooooh yeah," and she'd
flipped April off because really, come on. April had thrown her
head back and laughed, and said, "The resurrection of Team
Frezra!" and handed her the next clue. Which had led them to
the pool. Which Frankie had already figured out.

At least that answered the question of the mistletoe, she thought
as she shoved her hands into the pockets of her parka. She
wondered where Ezra was, if he'd found his phone, if he'd

tracked down Mimi. The church bells clanged twice in the distance, echoing over the campus, cutting through the quiet. It must have been the turn of the hour, ticking down to the start of the ceremony. She didn't want to drag her problems from last night to the wedding. She could, at the very least, be dignified for April. She had about an hour left before she'd have to abandon hope of solving this mess.

Frankie knew where she was headed next. But she stood there for another minute, the sun on her face, with the church bells as beautiful as any music she'd ever heard. Her eyes blinked back tears. She just didn't know yet what for.

TWENTY-FOUR

Ezra

By the time Ezra had collected himself and woven through the maze of hallways in the depths of Burton and walked past Bruno, the security guard, who wished him a Happy New Year unironically, and under the mistletoe in the front lobby and onto the steps outside, Gregory was nowhere to be found. Ezra blew out his breath, brushed the snow off the steps, and sat down. From across the campus, the church bells clanged twice, a reminder that not only was he losing daylight before the start of the wedding but that time was ticking down on his millennium proposal. In fact—he did the math now, despair taking root in his stomach: there really was no way that Mimi could get here from Kansas City in time: a connecting flight through Chicago, a car ride . . . Ezra could make magic from a bad hand, but there were some deal-ins that one simply needed to fold. The sun

broke through the flat gray sky, illuminating the white landscape in front of him, and Ezra was momentarily blinded. He
held his hand in front of his eyes and saw the gold wedding
band. Maybe it was for the best that she wasn't here. This
notion punctured him, redefined, even if temporarily, the type
of partner he considered himself to be.

What a debacle this was. The wedding band and the condoms and the blackout hangover and the sleepover in Homer.

He pushed himself to his feet. He wished Gregory were
here, but he wasn't. But Ezra didn't want to do this alone. He
never wanted to do most things alone. He knew this was a
squishy area for him; he did know, theoretically, that there was
room for improvement. But still, with the sun brightening the
campus and with Burton at his back, he thought that it
wouldn't be such a bad thing if he found Frankie.

This startled him—admittedly. He'd spent ten years con-
vincing himself that Frankie Harriman was the worst possible
scenario. But now, he allowed for the notion that maybe things
could have been different with them, for them, if he hadn't been
so needy, if he hadn't pushed her outside her comfort zone.

Ezra had always assumed that Frankie would follow him
to New York. They hadn't exactly discussed it, but they hadn't
not discussed it either. She seemed thrilled for him, at the
NYU acceptance, at the scholarship package. It was true that
she kept urging him to wait to hear from Stanford and to take
UCLA or USC more seriously, and Ezra didn't tell her this,
but he'd pulled the rest of his applications once this acceptance
came in. He wanted to be near Henry; he wanted to stay within
driving distance of his mother, who wasn't even close to out of the
woods the winter of his senior year. Though he knew Frankie

had all sorts of issues with her own parents, they didn't seem like anything that would make her flee from Manhattan. For a long time, he blamed her for not opening up about the baggage from her childhood: the pressure and the prodigious gift and how much all of that took from her. How eventually, she just wanted to be normal. But maybe he didn't ask the right questions. Or maybe he didn't ask enough questions, if he were really honest with himself. Maybe he didn't want to make any waves after that initial argument in Steinway Auditorium when he'd caught her playing after her parents had called to say they were making their separation a permanent one.

It takes two to tussle, his own mother had used to say, whenever Ezra would complain about his dad and how he'd dropped out of their lives. She got the idiom wrong, but Ezra loved her all the more for it, and it's not as if he didn't get her meaning. Back then, he had always thought that this was simply her being overly kind toward his father, protecting Ezra from the shit-all truth. But maybe what she meant, it truly just dawned on him now, as he abandoned any hope of Gregory's arrival and descended the steps of Burton, was that everyone shared responsibility in both their triumphs and their failures. *Everyone*—his dad, his mom, him, Frankie, the whole lot of them—always has ownership, for better and worse.

Which meant that the unpleasant truth of whatever happened in the past twenty-four hours, a kiss, a wedding, possibly sex in a twin bed at Homer, couldn't be simply pinned on Frankie. *A reckoning,* Zoe had said. Ezra did not like the sound of that at all. And he didn't think Mimi would either.

But Ezra was a fantastic compartmentalizer—it was certainly part of what also made him an excellent card player. He started down Middie Walk and tried to squelch any sort of hysteria that sprung up when he thought of the consequences of last night. Though there were only two Polaroids of the two of them on the board, he'd noticed what he thought was Abel ice rink in the background of several of the pairings' photos. If they'd been there, maybe he had been too.

Of course, the rink wasn't just another stop in the scavenger hunt; it was another memory piled on top of all the rest. It had been shortly after they'd gone to his place for Christmas break of their junior year. She'd come to stay with him and his mom in Lower Merion, and just by adding her to their table—Henry came too, along with his mother's younger brother whose ex-wife had the kids for the holiday—they'd expanded their family. An extra place setting that plugged a hole Ezra hadn't even been aware of. He remembered that he'd tried to take her to the pond to skate but that Frankie didn't know how, so they saw *Moonstruck* instead, and he was just as happy to do that. Because being anywhere with Frankie was better than being anywhere without her: the movie theater at the Willow Grove mall, the frozen-over pond, the front seat of his Jeep listening to "We Are the World," he didn't really care. When they were packing up to leave and return to campus, his mom pulled him aside and hugged him for a long time, longer than Ezra was used to, and he knew it was because she was so happy that he had found someone to move through life with, whether just in the present or perhaps for longer. They both now knew that there were no guarantees for the longer.

Ezra hadn't thought about any of this in a very long time. How falling in love with Frankie his junior year couldn't be separated from the joy that his mother had during her first stint of hope, of renewed health. She'd been in remission that Christmas, and maybe—it occurred to Ezra now—part of the intensity of his feelings for Frankie had simply been about relief. He shook his head and turned off Middie Walk to the footpath that led downhill to Abel. Not relief. About salvation. Maybe he was so desperate for his mother to be saved that he got things a little mixed-up and thought that Frankie needed to be rescued as well. Or maybe he was trying to save himself. It was hard to remember exactly what was running through his mind, his heart, twelve years ago, but he'd had enough space between then and now to somewhat recognize that it may not have been black and white.

He stopped short once Abel loomed in front of him, and he wondered momentarily if in addition to his blackout, he was now hallucinating. He blinked several times, but it was still there: a Zamboni parked half on the sidewalk, half in the street. One of the side doors of the building was hanging off its hinges, diagonally tilted toward the ground as if waiting for gravity to do its worst.

Ah shit, he thought. But at least he knew he'd been here last night. *Destruction. How fitting.*

TWENTY-FIVE

Frankie

Frankie knew that there were some messes she simply couldn't clean up. She stood in the middle of the rink, with a 360-degree view of the ice and the stands, with her hands on her hips, and honestly had absolutely no clue how to resolve this. From her vantage point, she could see that the Zamboni had plowed clear through the side of the rink's wall—where the little door should have been to allow skaters to enter the ice, there was at present just a gaping hole littered with debris and plaster and shards of wood.

Though now, she at least knew what the keys were for. She pulled them from her pocket. Her options were to drive the Zamboni back through the front door and park it in the middle of the rink, as if it had been here all along. Or wipe down the keys (no fingerprints—all those episodes of *Law & Order* in hotel rooms could finally pay off) and run. Or . . . she chewed the inside of her lip . . . accept accountability and call campus security and offer to write a check for the repairs? *No, no.* She rewound and went back to the previous ideas.

She heard footsteps echoing off the emptiness of the rink and started to scramble toward the bleachers, the keys dropping into her purse. But the ice was slick against her Doc Martens and there was nothing to grab on to, and she slipped and slid and slipped and slid until she more or less careened into part of the side wall that was still intact. The lump on her head was unhappy with this, despite its recovery at the pool, and she could feel the pulse in her neck bleating, beating, angry.

"I figured," was all Ezra said, and then he was standing in front of her. "Of course."

Frankie righted herself. "This wasn't my fault. This was everyone else's fault!"

Ezra scoffed as if this were the most preposterous thing he'd heard all day. Which, Frankie knew, could not have been the most preposterous thing from the day, because she was really starting to think that they'd gotten married.

"The three of you—this was your idea!" Frankie yelped. She yanked the keys out from her bag and threw them at him.

Ezra held out his hand and caught them, then narrowed his eyes.

"You remember?"

"You don't?" Frankie said, her voice still too sharp, and it bounced off the ceiling and back to them. They both quieted and peered around, as if someone else might overhear.

This is what Frankie had ascertained since arriving at the rink from the pool: she remembered that Abel was their next clue after the athletic center, though she couldn't place what the clue had said. That felt irrelevant anyway, and Frankie was not in the business of worrying about irrelevancy; this was at least part of the reason she was so good at her job: if an artist was set to fade into obscurity or not hitting the way they'd anticipated, she simply let them drift off into the figurative musical sea. It wasn't kind, she knew, but then you didn't get to the top of the game in a male-dominated, highly charged industry by being kind. Besides, kindness, she was sure, was overrated.

By the time they'd tripped from the swimming complex through the bone-chilling Western Massachusetts cold to Abel, Ezra and Gregory had been very very drunk. Frankie remembered that too. In some ways, this made being teammates easier. Ezra had never been an emotional drunk; that had been Frankie. Instead, he became quieter, more introverted, so mostly, they slunk down to the rink in silence, a mutually understood pact that saying nothing was better than saying anything, because then, they were really going to get into it. Besides, Gregory was keeping up the conversation for both of them. He and Alec, who was still in top college-athlete form and bigger than all three of them and, therefore, seemed to hold his alcohol the best, belted out a medley of Whitney Houston hits, and it was all Frankie could do not to interject when he got the words wrong.

No one knew exactly what they were looking for when they got there. Probably because no one could remember the clue, which explained why Frankie couldn't remember it today. Alec swore he had stuffed it in his jacket, but alas, it was gone. Frankie emptied her purse on the bleachers while Ezra and Gregory went through their pockets, but their only hope of staying competitive and/or winning, which Frankie very much still wanted to do, was scouring the rink for something that looked amiss. It was then that Ezra noticed that either due to the spotty cell service on campus or due to his inebriation, he had missed three calls from Mimi.

Alec, who Frankie now realized may have been more drunk than she'd been aware of at the time, had pumped his fist and said, "Dudes! Have you ever driven a Zamboni? Let's break into the shed!"

And Gregory threw his head back and yelled, "*Oh, I wanna dance with somebody!*" As if this had anything to do with anything.

And Ezra shrugged, mostly just moving around the bleachers trying to get a signal, his eyes fuzzy, his legs limber, and said: "Cool. A Zamboni." Then to Frankie, "I just remembered that you can skate."

Frankie hadn't known if this meant that she should skate while they took a joyride on the Zamboni or if it meant that he remembered that she'd once took lessons because she'd been too embarrassed to go to the pond near his house. She hadn't even thought about that pond by his house in a decade, though every time *Moonstruck* was on cable as a late-night movie and Frankie couldn't sleep, she did think of Ezra.

Alec disappeared somewhere for a moment, and Gregory shuffled out to the middle of the rink, right at the center circle where the puck gets dropped, and lay flat, as if he were making snow angels. She and Ezra sat in silence, each of their arms still folded, on opposite ends of a bleacher bench, while he punched buttons on his phone and muttered *goddammit*.

Finally, he paused and said, "You know, I know you think you hate me, but I did nothing but try to do right by you." He stopped and seemed to swallow a burp.

Frankie sighed, loud, annoyed. She wished she were as drunk as the rest of them, even though she didn't really, because being clearheaded felt like a marvel right now. Why had she spent so many nights drunk like the rest of them? It wasn't that she was having fun. But at least now she was in control of herself; at least she wasn't mumbling about old wounds from ten years back.

After a minute she said, "You can think whatever you want about me, about doing right by me. Like I care."

She waited for a response because, it turned out, maybe she did care, but Ezra just stood and stumbled down the steps and through the little door that swung open to the rink, and then he threw his body forward, as if he were sliding into home plate, his stomach on the ice, his hands pointed in front of him, toward Gregory. They howled at the hilarity of it. Then she heard Ezra yell, "Wait, I have a signal," and then he tried to stand but slipped and so he pressed the phone to his ear while flat on his back on the ice.

Frankie didn't see how this was getting them any closer to solving their clue and winning.

Just then, there was a rumbling from the back of the rink, and a mechanical door lurched open and a Zamboni emerged. Alec had found the keys. Overhead, the speakers blasted a piercing shot of feedback, and then the unmistakable opening riff to the Beastie Boys: *You gotta fight, for your right, to party!* Gregory let out a cheer and tried to stand but fell flat backward and splatted again. Ezra yelled over the din of the engine and the noise: "What? Shit, Mimi's flight!" And then he let out a primal scream.

Well, Frankie was going to have to be the grown-up here,

that much was clear. That Gregory was having so much fun didn't really surprise her. He was always throwing parties in his room, always egging them on to get an early start at Lemonhead. But Ezra. Ezra was supposed to be the levelheaded one! What had happened in the span of ten years that this had changed?

Frankie considered that a lot had happened, including his mother dying, which could fundamentally shift everything about you, especially a soul like Ezra. Something about this moved her, there in the stands, watching her ex splayed on the ice, listening to his voicemail, seemingly crestfallen but also trying not to be distracted by the hilarity of Gregory. Ezra had always loved everyone so deeply, including her. For a long time after their fight outside Burton just before graduation, this had enraged her, that he had loved her so much.

Gregory had made it to his feet now, then Ezra did too, though in trying to regain his balance, his phone fell from his hand and skittered across the rink. Alec, his eyes closed, started to veer off course, waving his hands in the air and belting out the chorus. Frankie saw the wreckage a few seconds before it happened, but by then, even when she'd yelled, it was too late. The Zamboni crushed Ezra's phone in a mere blink, and then plowed clear through the side wall of the rink, and then Alec was screaming and trying to steer the machine back onto the ice, but soon enough there was an enormous thundering wail beyond the ice, and Frankie was certain the ground shook.

"What the fuck?" Gregory shouted. "Alec? *Alec?*"

He tried to scramble toward the exit, toward the noise, but kept slipping. Ezra had abandoned all hope of standing, so he just crawled in the same direction, stopping to moan and mourn

the shards of his phone in front of him. At some point, Gregory
fell right on top of Ezra, and though Frankie didn't see it, Ezra
must have elbowed him square in his previously broken nose.
The blood spurted out instantly, as if a tap had been turned on,
leaving a round, red crime scene on the ice.

Frankie had always been terrible with blood, and just as
Alec stumbled back toward the rink, threw the keys at Ezra,
and said, "Uh, guys, I think we better split," Frankie herself
staggered down to the ice, holding her hand in front of her
eyes as if this could make anything better at all, but then
Gregory was in front of her, his face mangled like a boxer's.
And there was blood everywhere. On his teeth, on his chin,
down his neck. And Frankie, because this could not be said
enough, really, really was not good with blood, and so the
ground tilted on its axis, and Frankie, the toughest gal around,
unceremoniously fainted.

Today, twelve or fourteen or sixteen hours later, Frankie
sized up Ezra. At least now she knew how she'd been concussed. And she had solved the mystery of the keys. How generous she wanted to be with this information with Ezra was
now the question. She didn't think she owed him anything, but
then she didn't want to be in his debt either.

"I found your phone," she said flatly. Then pointed toward
the ice where only plastic shards and a few buttons were iden-
tifiable. "And that right there is Gregory's blood." Frankie had
discovered her own phone—dead, naturally—under the bleacher
seat where she'd dumped out her purse.

Ezra's gaze followed her gesture. "Gregory's blood? Is
he . . . ok?"

"You elbowed him. Then I fainted." She clicked her tongue

as if she'd taken one on the chin for him. "I must have hit my head." Her hand moved to the lump. "I really shouldn't be out here playing Detective Encyclopedia Brown, you know." Then she cocked her head. "Your face looks better."

He raised his hands to his cheeks as if he'd forgotten that he'd been assaulted by pepper spray. It was amazing, Frankie thought, how quickly we can all move past our trauma.

"We probably shouldn't be here," he said finally. "In my legal opinion."

"No shit," Frankie said. "No wonder you didn't take the bar."

"I didn't take the bar because—"

"I'm kidding, Ezra." Frankie sighed.

Ezra stuffed his hands into his pockets and quieted. Then he said: "If you're going to make a joke, you should at least make it funny." But his heart wasn't really in the reprimand, and Frankie suspected that for the third time in a single day, they had forged a peace.

TWENTY-SIX

Ezra

Time was ticking down, and though Ezra was relieved to have solved at least a few of the smaller mysteries of the morning, the larger ones, the important ones, still loomed. By Ezra's calculation, they had about an hour left before they had to throw in the towel and either accept that they needed to find a divorce lawyer or resolve that since neither of them had a memory of a ceremony, it had never happened in the first place.

"Where to?" he said to Frankie once they were a solid twenty or so feet from Abel Rink's entrance and thus could deflect suspicion should anyone find them there. He glanced over his shoulder toward the Zamboni, which he still could not believe had burst through the front door of the rink. He itched to make it right.

"No. No no no no no," Frankie said, reading him. "There is nothing to be done about this right now. We're not going to turn ourselves in; we're not going to call security."

"I didn't—"

"You did. You were thinking about it," she said. "If you want to anonymously call in a tip and, like, narc out Alec, then be my guest. Tomorrow."

Ezra didn't really want to call in an anonymous tip. He just didn't like the loose end, the messiness of it.

"Fine," he said.

"Fine," she said. They started back up the path to Middie Walk. The snow was beginning to melt under the bright sun, and the branches overhead lurched and groaned and settled. "I think we went to Lemonhead next," Frankie said, surprising him.

"For a clue? To the scavenger thing?" Ezra asked. *Please God make it for a clue and not because he kept drinking.*

"For Gregory's nose. I mean, for ice," Frankie said, then giggled. "Of all the luck—I think you broke his nose for the second time."

Ezra hiccupped out a laugh. "No wonder he stood me up back there."

"Might have to recommend a plastic surgeon." Frankie giggled louder. "I think at this point, he'll be lucky if it doesn't fall off his face like a shriveled-up piece of fruit."

"You're the one in LA. If anyone has a Rolodex of plastic surgeons, I think it'd be you."

Frankie stopped, took a beat to seemingly collect herself. Then, as if it had been building up in her and unexpectedly burst free, she said, "I'm really sorry about your mom, Ez." She blinked quickly. "I guess I should have called. I didn't know—" She stopped, shook her head. "Anyway, I wanted to tell you that. She was always kind to me." She flapped her hands against her sides. "I mean, I'm not a monster."

"You're kind of a monster," he said. Then quieter: "Thank you. I still sometimes can't believe it." Ezra fought the inexplicable urge to move toward her, to touch her, to hold her close. He didn't have to fight it for longer than a moment though because then Frankie was leaning into him too, her arms around his neck, her cheek pressed against his chest. He squeezed her like the hug was a lifeline. She lingered in the embrace, then pulled back.

"Shit, sorry," she said. "I don't know where that came from."

Ezra said nothing, not because he had nothing to say but because he had too much to say. Then, before he could think any of it through, and with her still so close, too close, just inches away, she tipped her head up toward his, raised herself up on her toes, and kissed him.

Frankie Harriman kissed him.

And his brain really did go blank then, as he found himself kissing her back, unsure at first, then desperate, hungry. And he didn't want it to stop because it felt just like it used to and that was comforting, delicious, soul affirming, and then it felt nothing like it used to—because Frankie was a stranger now, and that's when he came to his senses. He opened his eyes and pressed her back gently and said, "No, I mean, I can't." He paused. Tried to breathe. "Shit, this is such a mess."

And Frankie looked as confused as he felt, like she didn't know what had come over her. But it passed quickly, and honestly, Ezra wasn't even sure if he were seeing something he wanted to, something that wasn't even there. Because then she comported herself and said, "Sure, sorry. It was just . . . I don't know. An experiment." Which of course it was to Frankie, Ezra thought. Always cavalier with his heart.

He started forward again, and she followed. They walked side by side in silence, the crunch of the snow and a car alarm off in the distance their only company. He should say something, he knew. He should tell her that she couldn't just kiss him, she couldn't just do something reckless like that. An experiment! He should say that he loved Mimi and he was faithful and loyal and maybe she couldn't understand that, but she needed to respect it all the same. But Ezra found that he didn't have it in him right now. He also found that he hadn't minded the kiss, which was just as troubling as all the rest of it.

He pressed on, back toward Burton, his eyes on his Sambas, her eyes on her Docs. Then he glanced up and stopped cold. Frankie kept going, lost in her own thoughts, then realized he wasn't beside her and stopped as well.

"Holy shit," Ezra said, his heart flying, his pulse skyrocketing. Because there was Gregory, and indeed, his nose was swollen and pink. But there beside him was—again, Ezra had to ensure that he wasn't hallucinating—but no, *there was Mimi.*

Ezra forgot about the kiss and Frankie standing beside him wearing his grandmother's ring and rushed forward.

"Look who I ran into in the lobby," Gregory said dryly. "She wanted to come find you too."

Ezra froze for a beat before Mimi made a face and he realized that he hadn't hugged her, he hadn't kissed her hello. He swooped in and lifted her off her feet. When he rested her back on the ground, he noticed that she looked uncharacteristically rough. Her skin was blotchy; she had bags under her eyes. Ezra wasn't judging. Ezra didn't care. His plan was back on, the proposal still a possibility!

"I'm sorry," she said. "They got me on a direct flight this morning." She gestured to the snow. "I guess you can't mess with God." She managed a smile that was perfectly beguiling, and if Ezra didn't know better (he told himself not to know better), he'd believe her.

Because somewhere in the back of Ezra's mind, which was both muddled and jumping like a live wire now, he remembered that this was a lie. That her flight had taken off and landed on time yesterday. But maybe he'd gotten that wrong. Maybe the American Airlines website had been wrong. It's not like technology was always right! Ezra didn't actually believe that: technology was almost always right—which was part of the reason he'd been so stressed about Y2K and why Google was knocking on his door. But he was so awash in relief, so overjoyed that Mimi was here, at Middleton, and that—this was important—she was not Frankie, and that everything was going to be ok, that he told himself another untruth: that he'd been mistaken about her flight because Mimi would never intentionally deceive him. And he had his own deceits, so what was one more lie when so many had already been told? He'd just kissed his ex-girlfriend! Couldn't they all agree to ignore the various misdeeds and wounds from the past day and just move on? Wouldn't that be the easiest solution?

Gregory looked from Ezra to Frankie to Mimi and back to Ezra again. He appeared decidedly less thrilled than Ezra would have hoped from a dear friend who knew he was set to propose to the theoretical love of his life. Then Ezra remembered the gold band on his left ring finger and wondered if that had anything to do with it. Mimi hadn't yet noticed, so he shoved his hand in his pants pocket and wiggled it off with his thumb. He felt his anxiety spike to level ten again, just as he was smiling at the one thing, the one person, who should have calmed him.

Frankie took a quick step backward, intuitively seeming to understand that this situation did not call for her presence, but inadvertently tripped over a loose brick in the walkway.

"Shit!" she yelped, then quieted, as if she hadn't meant to draw attention, as if she were an interloper. It was only then that Mimi seemed to focus on the woman who was standing behind Ezra and certainly then that she registered who exactly it could be. Ezra figured her Doc Martens and wild hair were unavoidable giveaways: Mimi knew he didn't travel with that type of company, not because he minded, but because the Upper East Side set of her friends (who were now his friends) were the ballet slipper and chunky-highlight types. Most of them had hair that looked exactly like Jennifer Aniston's, and Ezra wondered just now, possibly for the first time, why they all wanted to resemble one another. Frankie scrambled to her feet, and the four of them stood there silently, tensely, like any small movement or quiet word would turn the whole situation combustible.

Finally, Gregory shook his head and said, "Déjà vu," then plodded to the phone booth on the corner to call a cab.

All the lines in Mimi's face had shifted downward into a scowl. But Ezra knew she didn't understand Gregory's reference, the "déjà vu" of it all; Ezra knew that whatever she was peeved about, it couldn't have been the full truth. Because he had never told her, he'd barely told anyone beside his mom,

Henry, and Gregory, that he'd gotten on bended knee right here, outside Burton Library, and asked Frankie Harriman to marry him. And that his proposal would be one of the last things he'd say to her, because from there, it all went to shit. At least until last night. Possibly including last night too.

TWENTY-SEVEN

Frankie

Gregory sat up front with the driver, so the three of them—Frankie, Ezra, and Mimi—were squished in the back. Frankie wondered if she were expected to make small talk, but Ezra glared and then blinked furiously at her when she asked if Mimi's flight had gone smoothly, so now she just fidgeted with her hands and listened to the radio, which was playing the top songs of the year, counting down to number one. Frankie knew that Night Vixen's summer banger would be somewhere in the top five, and strikingly, this brought her no joy.

She tried not to think about what had just happened—that she and Ezra Jones had kissed, no, they had made out—*made out!*—smack in the center of Middie Walk. She hadn't been planning on doing it; she certainly didn't think it through, and even if she had, she wasn't expecting Ezra to reciprocate with such heady commitment. But she supposed that she'd been curious if it would feel like it used to, if he would taste like he used to. It did. He did. And then she found that she didn't want to stop, so she didn't. She pulled back only because he pushed her away. Frankie wanted to talk to him about all of this, she *needed* to talk to him about all of this. But now, here was Mimi.

Ezra's leg was bouncing beside her, jittery and taking on a life of its own. A decade ago, she'd have placed her hand on his thigh, a weight to remind him that she was there, that he should breathe. Now, she waited for Mimi to do the same, but she never did. Instead, she regaled them with calamities of her trip: the canceled flight, the night at the airport Holiday Inn, the middle seat by the toilet this morning.

Ezra, Frankie could tell, was trying to be engaged, but he kept turning his head toward her window, his attention else-where. Maybe it was because of the kiss. Maybe it was because of the ring that was still stuck on Frankie's finger. Maybe it was because of his hangover. Maybe he was nervous because now he had to pull off the turn-of-the-century proposal, and after last night's shit show, he was beginning to doubt that he could pull off anything smoothly. Frankie thought it might be any one of those things—but she reminded herself that Ezra's problems weren't her problems anymore. She again tried to quell the instinct to palm his thigh.

Frankie took a long look at Mimi, who was not what she was expecting, though she didn't know what she was ex-pecting, to be honest. She was beautiful. Certainly. Striking with green eyes and red hair and freckles across both cheeks. This reminded Frankie of Ezra's own band of freckles, that crescent moon that spanned from his left eye to his ear. They would have adorable children, she knew. But there was some-thing about Mimi that repelled Frankie. And it wasn't that Frankie was jealous, though it was possible she was jealous too, which surprised her. But it was something else, something familiar: a layer beneath the surface that Frankie knew too well from LA, from nightclubs and fandom and plenty of circles around the globe with superstars; a frenetic, hungry energy that could be passed off as sociability but in reality was too often desperation. Frankie listened to Mimi ramble about the perils of her trip, seeking reassurance from Ezra, who kept starting sentences and letting them drift.

"But I'm here now, Ez, I'm here," Mimi said. Ezra made a face that Frankie thought was meant to be a smile, but honestly it looked like Ezra was trying not to vomit. "Ez," Mimi said again. "I'm here, despite everything." She finally rested her hand on Ezra's leg. "I know how important that is to you."

At this, she cast a side-eye look at Frankie, as if she were Ezra's white knight, protecting him from the evils of his ex-girlfriend. It was a little on the nose, Frankie thought. Ezra murmured his thanks, and Gregory turned his head just enough to catch Frankie's eye, then rolled his far back into his head. She wondered if he sensed it too: the insecurity, the hunger.

The drive to the hotel was only ten minutes. Gregory gave the driver cash and held the door while the three of them tumbled out. Well, mostly Frankie tumbled out.

"Your head?" Gregory said.

"Oh right, you were there," Frankie replied. It was a relief to have another memory backing hers up. "It's better, thanks." She paused and assessed. "Your nose?"

Gregory shook his head and winced. "I think there is a very decent to probable chance that a deviated septum surgery is in my future." He turned to the side. "But then I can get this bump smoothed out and can tell everyone it was for breathing problems."

Mimi and Ezra had dipped inside the Inn by now, so Frankie took Gregory by the wrist and pulled him to the side, hanging back.

"Hey, did we get married last night?"

Gregory's eyes nearly burst from their sockets. "You and me? We got married last night?"

"No, no, Ezra and me."

Gregory's hand thumped over his chest. "Oh, thank sweet Jesus. You know I'm fully out now, right? Not that my mother wouldn't have been thrilled."

Frankie smiled. "Yes, I know. And I'm sorry about your mom."

His shoulders rose then flopped. "You can't choose your family."

And Frankie nodded because that was the truth. Then the weight of what she asked seemed to sink in for him.

"Wait? *You guys got married?*"

Frankie shoved her hand between them, Ezra's grand-mother's ring still stuck behind a swollen knuckle. "Ezra said that Alec Barstow is, like, ordained or something?"

"Jesus Christ!" Both of Gregory's hands flew over his mouth. Then he turned toward the hotel entrance and then back toward Frankie. "And she . . . and you . . . and . . . holy shit! This is incredible!"

"No, *no*. It's not incredible," Frankie said. "Between my head and his intoxication . . ." Her voice wandered. Then: "So to be clear, you do *not* know if we're married?"

"I left you guys at Lemonhead," Gregory said. "You were

hurt. I was hurt. We headed there to get some ice for the both of us. When I last saw you, you were barely speaking. You were definitely not married."

Frankie exhaled and sank into what she expected to be relief but was also unsettling confusion. The image she had of the two of them, her and Ezra, while Gregory spoke into the mic at Lemonhead's entrance was just that: a passing glance of a moment that she had seemingly misread. She was leaning on Ezra, his arm slung around her, because he was literally holding her up. Not because they were heady in love, not because things had been rekindled. Still though, she considered, it was gracious of Ezra to be that foundation, to come to her rescue. Frankie had never ever asked to be rescued, never even wanted it. She thought of their kiss again, of the way that it turned something feral on inside her. Would it really be so terrible if Ezra rescued her every once in a while?

"Shouldn't I have gone to the hospital?" Frankie only just considered this now.

"We tried! You think we didn't try?" he said. "You kept going on about this one time in Bangkok, and how you were totally fine the next day, and in fact, you started singing that—" He shook his hips, shimmied his shoulders. *"One Night in Bangkok makes a hard man humble, not much between—"*

"Gregory." Frankie cut him off.

"Right, sorry. Anyway, we tried, and also neither Ezra nor I were exactly in good shape to make a case for you at the ER." He grimaced. "I think the booze I brought may have actually been, like, legitimate moonshine. Hoo boy. Also, that Xanax he took. In hindsight, an idiotic combination. Oh, and he was ranting and raving about Mimi canceling and how it wasn't even snowing yet, so why would her flight be canceled." He flung open his arms. "So yeah, it was like a level-five shitstorm, and if you didn't want to go to the hospital, we weren't going to drag you."

Frankie chewed all of this over and found that there were no holes in the plot. Gregory, blessedly, appeared to be telling the truth.

"And Alec? What happened to him?"

"Oh, that boy bolted." Gregory laughed, like this was in any way hilarious. "Ran back inside, tossed the keys at us, and fled. He could be in Canada by now."

Frankie rubbed her temples. "So we didn't hook back up with him after Lemonhead?"

"Well, I stayed." Gregory made a face like he knew that had been the wrong decision.

"You stayed?"

"Uh, yeah. The bartender who gave me the ice pack also threw in a shot of tequila, and I thought I was getting a vibe." He flopped his hand. "It turned out that his vibe was just his general vibe and not necessarily a Gregory vibe, but who could have known that at the time?"

"Not your shining moment."

"Your definition of 'shining' is subjective," Gregory said with a grin. "Most people really do like me."

Frankie wasn't going to argue, because he was probably right, and she'd never been granted such a social luxury: to simply be well-liked as soon as she made an entrance. She'd never tried to be well-liked; she'd never tried at all actually.

For a long time, maybe right until this moment, she'd worn that as a badge of honor. But what would be the harm, to have a bartender like you just because, to be amiable because it was the generous thing to be? She looked again toward the hotel. Ezra was almost always amiable because it was the generous thing to be, and Frankie had always thought of this as a weakness. Maybe that was just another lie she told herself because confronting how diametrically opposite she was to that graciousness was too onerous a task.

"And her? Mimi?" Frankie asked.

Gregory sucked in his breath, the air whistling past his teeth. "Well, Ezra really can pick them, that's for sure."

"Hey." Frankie scowled. She thought of the kiss again.

"You decimated his heart." He shrugged. "Just because you don't see yourself as the bad guy doesn't mean that you weren't."

Frankie started to argue but stopped herself. There were so many more important things right now other than relitigating the past. Besides, she didn't know how much Gregory knew, and she also decided—right then—that she wouldn't be judged for whatever he did know. Though surely there was judgment to be made. But first, she knew she had to figure out her own responsibility. Because for the first time in years, she realized that she had some.

"You know, it takes two to tussle." She often said this—to her clients, to roadies, to dickhead executives at record labels— and now, she only just realized that Ezra was the one who used to say this all the time and that he told her it was because his mom used to pester him with it all through his childhood, how he couldn't bring himself to correct her. *Tango, Mom, it's tango.* Something about this pained Frankie: the thought of Ezra as a boy, that his mom was gone, that they had veered so far from each other that she only offered her condolences several years later, that she was wearing his grandmother's ring while he was ensconced in room 303 with Mimi.

"Well, I'll take you over her any day of the week and on Sunday too," Gregory said, which Frankie thought was a compliment but honestly wasn't sure. Then he lowered his voice, as if Mimi or Ezra could hear them all the way on the third floor.

"Two summers ago, I was back from Portland for a week, and Ezra invited me to his summer share." He gave her a look like Frankie should know what and where this was. When she didn't, he said, "South Hampton. He does it every summer."

"Oh, ok," Frankie said, trying to envision Ezra in board shorts and Ray-Bans and eating corn on the cob while drinking a long-necked beer. The Ezra she knew had never been relaxed enough, casual enough to figuratively sink his feet into the sand. She found that she didn't consider the image unappealing; she found, in fact, that she'd like to know that man.

"Anyway, they were pretty new, I think." Gregory scrunched his face up like the math of it mattered. "Maybe a few months in, I don't know. Ezra had sold the company by then—" He stopped. "You know about that, yes? The gajillion-dollar sale?"

Frankie nodded, though the gajillion-dollar sale really meant nothing one way or the other to her.

"Right, well, this wasn't too long after his mom died, and Ezra was putting on a pretty good face, but I wasn't convinced.

But here was this girl who he was super in love with, so I wanted to be super in love with her too." Gregory sighed. "Look, the long and the short of it is—and I say this with no judgment, ok? We all have our shit." He reached up and touched his wonky, still-swollen nose. "I have my shit; you definitely have your shit."

"Yes," Frankie said. "Got it."

"So I'm at the Kmart—Kmart! Because of course, I'd forgotten half my toiletries, and your boy always needs to moisturize. And I see her—Mimi—in the makeup aisle. And I stop because, look, I'm nosy, ok? I'm not going to apologize for getting up in people's business."

"As expected," Frankie said. Then to be clear that she wasn't being snippy, she offered, "I mean, that's great." Which, of course, made no sense, but she was really hoping Gregory would get to the point.

"And I see this girl, the love of Ezra's life, start to pocket things from the shelf! Like, goddamned Maybelline mascara! Revlon nail polish! God knows how many lipsticks she shoved in her bag." Gregory was animated now. "And look, I'm not, like, the world's Kmart police or whatever, but I do know that retail is a bitch. So I must gasp aloud or maybe she catches me staring . . . I can't remember exactly now. But she sees me, and her eyes flick around like she could, maybe, I don't know, *not* see me? But then she shuffles toward me and says, like, in a low, pathetic voice, 'Please don't tell Ezra. He wouldn't understand.' And I'm thinking, *Lady, you're a thief, and not even a very good one! What is there to understand?*" Gregory sighed.

"And did you? Did you tell him?" Frankie asked, though

she already knew the answer. Because Mimi was still here, and Ezra still planned to propose and have a future with this woman. Ezra, *her* Ezra, the lawyer at least, would never have white-knuckled it through a shoplifting charge.

"No," he said, looking a little embarrassed. "I mean, (a) how was I to know that it was going to last? And (b) he'd been through so much with his mom and all of that, I didn't want to make anything worse." He shrugged. "He seemed happy, you know?"

Frankie, who had seen plenty of atrocious behavior over the years, started to defend her. "Look, there are worse things," she said. Because there were. And though Frankie did have plenty of shit of her own—on that Gregory was correct—one of her few redeeming qualities was that she did not judge. She didn't judge her clients' drug indulgences, she didn't judge Ezra's panic attacks, she didn't even judge Mimi's shoplifting habits. If she stood in judgment, she also knew she'd have plenty to answer for, and really, it was easier not to. She reiterated: "I mean, it's not my business, but again, there are really worse things in the world."

"Well, sure. Like turning down his proposal hours before he was set to graduate and then abandoning him for his move to New York."

"Oh, fuck off, Gregory," Frankie snapped. "I never planned to go to New York with him. He just never heard me when I tried to tell him."

Gregory fell silent and turned back toward where campus stood in the distance.

"Come on," he said finally, slipping his arm through hers, as if they were linked now, though Frankie didn't know by what. "Don't you have a bridesmaid's dress to put on? And we have a new century to greet. And I, for one, could use a drink."

Frankie didn't bother saying she was sober. After last night, that felt like a technicality. Or maybe that was worse: that she went ahead and made such a mess of everything here and had nothing and no one to blame but herself.

TWENTY-EIGHT

Ezra

THREE THIRTY P.M.

Mimi kissed him as soon as the door swung closed. And really *kissed* him, which Ezra certainly didn't mind but wasn't really like her if he were being honest with himself. But for a good thirty seconds, as his hand snaked its way up her shirt and then under her bra, he wasn't—wasn't honest with himself, that is.

She tugged her shirt over her head. "I'm going to remind you how much you missed me," she said, her voice low and breathy. "I'm going to blast that girl's name right out of your head forever."

Ezra pulled his lips off her neck. "What? Who? Frankie?" And then he remembered how not even half an hour ago, he was kissing Frankie. His brain buzzed with static, and he wished he'd brought a second Xanax, but then who could have known what a mess he'd make?

Mimi was undoing his belt buckle, then pushed him back

on the bed and plucked his Sambas off, followed by his pants in record time. She straddled him and then placed her hand over his mouth as if she thought he was going to protest, and she wasn't interested in hearing it.

Ezra closed his eyes and tried to refocus. But now his mind was spinning wildly, a whirling buzz of nerves that hit him like a tornado: about Mimi's alleged canceled flight, about the whole shebang with Frankie, about last night's poker game, about the Zamboni and property destruction, about, well, all of it. And he tried to breathe in and out and count to five just as Frankie had done with him in the café earlier this morning, but he couldn't concentrate on kissing Mimi *and* counting, so he must have recoiled or put his hands on her shoulders to push her away and give him a little space. His chest felt like it was going to explode; his stomach had bottomed out.

Mimi rolled off from him and bounced to her feet in one fluid motion.

"Great, so now you're not interested in sex?"

Ezra pushed to his elbows and tried to breathe, tried to stay calm. "What? No. I'm always interested in sex." He extended his hand to draw her back onto the bed, but he didn't cover it well, and she stepped back. He inhaled, felt his pulse slow just enough, and tried again. "Mimi, come on. I'm just really wiped. And I feel like I need to shower, brush my teeth. That stuff." He exhaled, inhaled, exhaled again.

She tapped her foot and crossed her arms.

"Well, were you going to tell me about her? If I hadn't shown up?"

"Why wouldn't you have shown up?" Ezra hadn't meant to ask it. He didn't want to ask it! His pulse spiked all over again.

Shit shit shit shit shit. All he wanted was to kiss his girlfriend, propose at midnight, and *move on.* Why were the past twenty-four hours so packed with emotional land mines, when he had spent a perfectly wonderful, perfectly placid thirty-two years avoiding them? He couldn't even blame Frankie for this last one! He stilled himself and willed Mimi to move on too, not make this any more complicated than he feared it was about to get. They were so compatible, so in sync, that he thought she might float on down the river of denial with him.

"No, I mean, yes, I was always showing up, obviously," Mimi said. "But I thought we agreed? That you would keep your distance?"

Ezra blinked, surprised at the implication, and something roiled in him. That even while she was concealing something, and Ezra was growing increasingly, uneasily sure that she was indeed concealing something, that she could turn it back on him. He squelched his rising agitation. He had to get through this; he would just press through this.

"Hey," he said, extending his hand. "Come here. I'll brush my teeth and all of that later."

She shook her head. "I'm going to take a shower," she said. "I didn't trust the Holiday Inn last night."

Ezra started to ask her what on earth could be wrong with the water at the Holiday Inn, but he supposed they had grown used to finer things, even though he'd never meant to. He didn't mind a roadside motel, like the kind he'd stayed at growing up, or a greasy diner with plastic menus, not the farm-to-table brunches they lingered over every Sunday now. He couldn't fault Mimi for growing used to such things either; what was his was hers, and the world they ran in now, even if she was still paid in those elusive stock options, didn't much resemble the worlds of their youth. Besides, it was easier for him to just acquiesce in the moment and play along and say: "Ok, great. Yeah, we have to walk out of here in an hour anyway." He checked the clock on the nightstand. It was almost four now, and the wedding started at five. Mimi, and this was not a criticism, took forever to get ready.

The bathroom door closed behind her, then he heard the lock spin. He stilled for a moment, waiting to hear the rush of the shower. When he did, he was on his feet, reaching for his laptop, enduring the interminable wait for the hotel internet, and then logging on to the American Airlines site once again. Maybe he'd misunderstood. Maybe he'd been so wonky from the pepper spray and waking up with Frankie and the blackout-drunk situation that he had misread American's page, and in fact, her flight *had* been canceled, and then he could put this all behind him. The site took a good minute to load, then another minute once Ezra had typed in the flight details. He kept turning to check the bathroom, but the water was still running, the door still locked. And he hated—*hated*—that he was doubting Mimi. He hated that he knew he was going to catch her in a lie. He hated even more that this meant that he was going to have to make a fundamental decision: confront her about it or simply live with the knowledge that the untruth existed between them. He did not stop to remind himself that he had plenty of untruths to share with her.

And there it was. Again. Mimi's flight last night had taken off and landed on time. Ezra considered calling the reservations line just to confirm, but then he further considered how pathetic that was: phoning a call center to ask a stranger if his girlfriend was lying to him.

Ezra shuttered the laptop and ran a hand over his face, which had now settled down and mostly looked normal. Mimi hadn't even noticed that his eyelids were still a little puffy, the whites of his eyes still a little pink. Maybe if he just told her what he knew, and not just about the flight, but about his own pile of shit—the gambling, waking up in Homer, the kiss— they could mutually agree that they'd each screwed the pooch and live happily ever after (literally).

He tapped his fingers in a pattern over the desk, unable to slow his brain. The more he thought about it, the more out- raged he was at Frankie. *She had kissed him! As an experiment!* Like he was a frog in biology class who she had the luxury of poking and prodding until she just sliced him straight open. Ezra so rarely found himself angry, but instantly, immediately, he felt a burst of fury run through him. His cheeks ran hot; his guts roiled. He wanted to recoil from the feeling—Ezra was not in the habit of leaning into his rage—and inexplicably, he found that he could not. It was there, like a fever, pulsing stronger and stronger with each heartbeat.

He reached for the phone to call her room, to tell her . . . well, he wasn't exactly sure what he was going to tell her, but he figured he would work it out when the moment came. Some- thing about her selfishness and her audacity and that he was not a frog there for her dissection! But then he heard the shower turn off behind the bathroom door, and he tried to ease the phone back into its cradle as quietly as possible. He didn't want to lie to Mimi any more than he'd already done. What he wanted was to go back in time and refuse Gregory's alcohol and certainly skip the Xanax and have a perfectly normal evening out with his old college friends that didn't involve Frankie Harriman.

He told himself that he could still make this right. That all he had to do was get through a few more hours, and then he'd never have to think about Frankie again. But his anger churned in his belly, and he wondered, if Frankie did dissect him like a frog, if she'd open up his insides and find a red-hot bomb of rage. Then Mimi emerged from the bathroom, and he tried to swallow this all down, as if you could do such a thing with a ticking time bomb, as if he weren't poised to explode.

TWENTY-NINE

Frankie

Frankie lay on her bed with a pillow over her face and replayed the scenes from the past hour again and again, starting with the kiss and ending with the hotel's revolving doors that gulped up Mimi and Ezra without even a glance back. Then she flung the pillow across the room and pressed her hand over her mouth in astonishment. She had willingly kissed, truly *kissed*, Ezra Jones. Forget being married, forget the rest of it. She had been sober and cogent and still possibly concussed (but definitely recovering), and she had leaned into him, raised her face to his, and kissed him. And Ezra! He had kissed her back. Sober and cogent and all the rest of it. She wasn't sure if she were unsettled or comforted by the unexpected turn of events; for Frankie, those two sentiments were so closely aligned that maybe they were interchangeable.

She thought about calling down to his room. She knew they should probably discuss it, come up with some sort of terms for the rest of the night. But Ezra would never want to get into it, and besides, now Mimi was here, and it was probably easiest to just pretend that whatever had happened . . . hadn't. They'd each gotten good at that in their own way, and for a long time, Frankie had blamed Ezra. But she could call him now, she could say difficult things, she could ask herself difficult questions. But to what end? For what purpose? He was going to propose to Mimi and that was that.

Frankie righted herself and headed to the bathroom. She peeled off her clothes, the J.Crew fisherman sweater that had been such a comfort a decade ago, the Levi's from the vintage store that made a decent enough replacement for the Levi's she'd lived in at Middleton. She stood in front of the vanity mirror naked and marveled at all the ways she could dress herself up: as a pianist in a dress from Bloomingdale's as a child, as a moody but autonomous college kid in her oversize wool sweaters, as a slick music manager in baby-doll dresses and blazers that she bought at Urban Outfitters on Beverly. Frankie had always loved this notion: that you could cast aside whoever you were before and reinvent yourself into someone entirely new. She'd done it at Middleton so well that maybe Ezra hadn't even realized what he was getting into. Maybe she hadn't told him or maybe he didn't want to know. For a long time, she'd thought this part was important: the blame of it all. Why her parents had used her as a Band-Aid for their marriage, why no one stopped to ask her if she truly loved performing, whether Ezra's proposal had been an innocent misunderstanding or a grievous fundamental difference between the two of them.

She ran her hands over her hips, up over her breasts, and cradled her cheeks. The steam from the shower was rising, the mirror fogging along with it. Frankie, she couldn't help but nearly laugh, was disappearing. She'd tell her artists that maybe that lyric was a little too much of a trope, but still, she was astute enough to recognize its prescience. Frankie had always assumed she knew exactly who she was, exactly what she wanted. But what if she'd gotten that wrong? What if, just as Ezra had gotten some things wrong and her parents had gotten things wrong, she had just misunderstood herself? And since she didn't want to lay blame at her feet for the destruction of her past, maybe she shouldn't lay blame at their feet either.

This felt heady, too big to embrace right here at the Inn at Middleton, with the shower running and a wedding to get to and a New Year's Eve to celebrate. But it was fodder, food for thought, and Frankie considered that this was something. This was a start. She wondered now if kissing Ezra out there on Middie Walk wasn't meant to be closure. They'd never gotten it, or at least *she'd* never gotten it, even if she'd tricked herself into believing that by running from Middleton to Los Angeles, that by building an expansive, successful existence for herself where she rarely thought of his proposal and the untruths they'd both told themselves about it, she had successfully shed that chapter of her life. So perhaps that's all the kiss was. She nodded to herself in the mirror through the steamy haze. Closure. No one could blame her for that.

She spun the sink faucet on and reached for the bar of hotel soap still in its packaging. She unwrapped it gently, as if it were a Christmas gift, then plunged her left hand under the water and rubbed the soap against her ring finger.

Ezra's grandmother's ring slipped off after just a few seconds. It was easier than she had thought it would be. She placed it by the soap dish and stepped into the shower, the water nearly scalding now. She leaned into it and let it burn.

THIRTY

Ezra

FIVE P.M.

The sun was setting by the time Ezra and Mimi descended from the room to the wedding shuttle that took them to the Middleton Chapel. Ezra had forgotten how early campus grew dark during the winter months: it wasn't yet five o'clock, and the shadows were long all around them, the temperatures dipping too. Mimi, it must be said, looked stunning, as if she knew she were putting on a show. An emerald-green dress with a furry little shoulder thing (Mimi informed Ezra this was called a stole, and she'd laughed because she found it adorable that he didn't know such things, and then she'd kissed him, which alarmed the bejesus out of Ezra because he was now borderline manically both jumpy and furious about the kiss with Frankie), and open-toed heels that seemed ridiculous for the frigid air and the snowy ground. But Mimi, despite her midwestern roots, had never been one for practicality.

The invite had called for New Year's Eve formal, and Ezra didn't know how that was any different than regular formal, so he'd packed his tux and thought he'd cleaned up ok too. Back in college, he hadn't owned a tux—no use for one and too expensive to buy, though he'd rented one for his high school prom, which was all a blur anyway because his mom was sick and like he gave a shit about anything else beyond that. Well, he had given a shit about his high school girlfriend, of course, but she was off to Pomona, and she'd been very clear that they had no future once she hit the state border. Ezra had tried to plead otherwise, but she was firm, and in the end, it had been for the best for him to have a fresh start. He couldn't see that at the time, but Ezra was beginning to understand that he couldn't see a lot of things at the time. Maybe that's what he loved so much about cards: he was fully present, choices made had immediate consequences, and when you walked away from the table, everyone, even if they'd lost, had understood the rules of the game. He lumbered onto the shuttle, his hand on Mimi's back, and wondered why he, a grown adult with a quick brain and an open heart, felt like he so often misunderstood the rules of the game. Why he had so few hobbies other than whatever Mimi was dragging him to for work. Why he so easily acquiesced into abandoning his own life—his harmless poker games with friends, his weekend runs in the park, visits to London to crash with Henry, whom he hadn't seen in months—for things that were of no importance to him like brunches that took up half his Sundays and business class flights to San Francisco to interview for jobs he probably didn't even want.

Frankie was nowhere to be seen when they took their seats in the back of the van, and unlike so many years ago, Ezra was relieved that she was chronically late. Gregory bounced out of the lobby and hopped on too. He was looking dapper in a bow tie and a suit and a bowler hat, though he had slung his red parka on top. He noticed Mimi give him the once-over and said, "This is how we roll in Portland. It's like fusion but for my clothes."

And Mimi smiled and said, "No, you look extremely handsome. Would you consider signing up for Datify?" and Ezra, who was still one catastrophe away from a nervous breakdown, leaned over and kissed her cheek because Mimi could be—*was in fact*—pretty great, even if she were too often in saleswoman mode.

Gregory laughed and said, "Uh, no fucking way, but thanks," and Mimi made a sour face betraying her chipper facade, but only for a second. Then she beamed, though Ezra knew her heart wasn't in it, and said, "I'm always here when you're ready."

The van wound its way through the darkening streets, now illuminated by festive holiday lights, and soon enough, they were back on campus, and Ezra wished he could appreciate its beauty, tried to just appreciate the moment. He knew he absolutely could not afford to come undone with Mimi. He knew that if she had even a whiff of a scent that he'd spent the prior night with Frankie, even if this were all just a massive misunderstanding, a practical joke they'd one day laugh about, that his chance to propose, to propel his life forward, the life he now realized he'd built mostly around the idea of her, would be obliterated.

In the hotel room, he'd been shaky when he dropped the phone back in the cradle, his call to chew out Frankie aborted. Mimi, fresh from the shower, with a towel on top of her head and the hotel bathrobe swaddling her porcelain skin, hadn't seemed to notice that his voice wobbled, that he stepped too quickly into the bathroom for his own shower and closed the door too loudly behind him. If he'd been paying closer attention, maybe he'd have detected she had been distracted too.

It didn't take long—somewhere between the shampoo and conditioner—for his growing rage toward Frankie to plant seeds, take root, and blossom. Ezra was unaccustomed to tapping into his anger, but now that he had, he found it comforting, he found it mature, he wondered what had taken him so long to get here. Of course Frankie would kiss him on Middie Walk, launching an emotional insurrection. Of course she would insert herself into his life just as Ezra was trying to put everything behind him. Of course, of course, of course! By the time he emerged from the shower, he was goddamned steamingly irate, having completely forgotten that Frankie was supposed to hate him too, and if she chose to kiss him honestly and without motive, perhaps it was because she meant it.

The chapel was hushed, reverent. Guests made their way to the pews, heels clacking against the sandstone floor, nothing more than whispers floating around them. Ezra tried to calm himself. Mimi was pressed next to him, their thighs parallel, her shoulder abutting his, and he wanted to just appreciate the moment for what it was: the last few hours before he asked her to marry him, the quiet aura of a chapel on New Year's Eve, with stained glass windows to each side and an arch adorned with white and pink roses in front of them. He wanted to feel at peace. Everything about this moment told him that he should feel at peace. And yet he had to willfully stop his leg from jittering, consciously work to still his hands and slow his pulse.

He peered around. Still, she wasn't here, and now the string quartet was playing, so everyone scurried to the remaining seats and held their breath. Then there she was. He'd forgotten she was a bridesmaid, that she'd done what she came here to do: show up for an old friend, stand beside April while she embarked on a new life chapter.

The bright magenta taffeta dress was outrageous. A bow over one shoulder as large as an anvil; a fabric that swooshed with each step; and honestly, if Ezra weren't so angry with her, he would have been delighted. Then Pachelbel's Canon began, and he watched her, seeing if she'd flinch. She'd hate the musical choice, he knew, and even through his fury, he wanted to see the look of contempt on her face at the predictability of it. If she were sitting next to him, she'd lean over and say something like, *If it were me, I'd do an instrumental of "Love Is a Battlefield,"* and she'd mean it both sincerely and ironically because he'd learned the hard way that Frankie had never wanted to get married, but if she did, she'd do it without all the traditional pomp and circumstance. The quartet played on, and he waited for her disdain, raised eyebrows, clenched jaw, the hint of a sneer, but her face never wavered, never betrayed judgment of the song. She stepped forward, moving down the aisle with grace, with joy, clutching a bouquet of pink flowers, doing it all, he knew, for April. That alone was astonishing.

Mimi reached for his hand, and he turned to face back toward her.

"This is so beautiful," she said. "It's all like a dream."

And the thing of it was, Mimi was right. It was beautiful and it was magic, and for as long as Ezra had ever known, he'd wanted such things for himself too. So why was he staring at

Frankie, the girl who'd never wanted such things for herself, much less with him? She'd made that clear. She'd said *no*. Anger—at her, at himself—bubbled up all over again.

Ezra leaned toward Mimi, her perfume like a balm, and kissed her forehead. *It takes two to tussle.* He thought of his mother now, as they all stood as April entered and walked down the aisle. He wondered what she would say, about Frankie being here, about her kissing him, about his plans for a New Year's Eve proposal. His mom had never met Mimi, though she'd always been fond of Frankie. That his two serious loves were so different might cause his mom to raise her eyebrows, but what he thought she'd really do if she were here was ease toward him, poke his heart, and ask him if he knew what each woman held in *there*.

April and Connor were in front of them now, both of them teary, both seemingly overwhelmed with the enormity of the moment and their love for each other. Ezra blinked back tears too. All he had wanted was for the same such happiness. He watched them vow themselves to each other and considered what was in Mimi's heart and what was in Frankie's. And he surprised himself when he realized that for each of them, perhaps he didn't know.

THIRTY-ONE

Frankie

SEVEN THIRTY P.M.

Frankie hadn't expected that April and Connor's wedding would move her as much as it had. She found herself blinking back tears when they said their vows, choking up when Connor tilted toward April to kiss her. It was much like the few other weddings she'd been to—the poofy white dress and the impersonal vows and the music, oof, the music! But her old friends from another life seemed so genuinely happy, Frankie found herself setting aside her usual marital scorn and simply stood shoulder to shoulder with Laila and embraced it. She'd even cried.

This, needless to say, was new for her.

Alec Barstow hadn't officiated though. No one had heard from him since last night, despite several calls to his hotel room and three pages to his beeper. (Frankie didn't know anyone who still had a beeper, but that was beside the point.)

When they realized he was MIA, Connor's brother, a lawyer in Boston, got ordained thirty minutes prior to the ceremony. Frankie wasn't certain if she should be reassured that Alec was missing or unnerved because she still couldn't remember anything after the ice rink and it was quite possible that they'd run into him later in the evening, and thus it was not out of the realm of possibility that he had indeed married them. But Frankie didn't want to pester April with the rest of her questions; she knew this wasn't the time.

The shuttle buses waited for the guests after the ceremony to whisk them to Steinway Auditorium for the celebration. *Breathe*, Frankie told herself, as she shuffled from one foot to the other, trying to stay warm while she waited to board, also trying desperately to avoid Ezra and his girlfriend, who were a few dozen people behind her in line.

She'd thought, in the heat of the moment when she kissed him, that maybe she'd wanted something different this time, like those Choose Your Own Adventure books she'd read as a kid. Kiss Ezra Jones and turn to page 45! But she'd glanced his way during the ceremony and saw him leaning into Mimi and looking happy. So perhaps Ezra hadn't wanted to jump to page 45 alongside her. Truthfully, if she were being honest, up until that moment, she hadn't known she wanted to either. This was all a startling turn of events, and for the first time in a long time, she didn't know what to do with herself.

The drive to Steinway was less than a few minutes, and soon, just as she had shuffled onto the bus, she shuffled off. A waiter stood by the door in a wool hat and scarf, offering the arrivals champagne. Frankie reached for one, wanting to smooth out the edges of what was to come. But she was still trying; trying for what, she couldn't put her finger on. She knew that getting obliterated probably wouldn't much help with anything, so she kept walking.

She steeled herself and went inside, the chill from the outdoor air dissipating as the heat from the overhead vents assaulted her. It was almost too much at once: the memories and the atmosphere and the cacophony. Frankie took a sharp right to the restrooms, where she did a double take at herself in the mirror. She'd forgotten she had on the ridiculous bridesmaid's dress, forgotten that she had attempted to pull her hair into what she hoped was an elegant bun, forgotten that April had requested a vibrant pink lipstick to complement the magenta dress, which it did not. Nothing about her was recognizable. She gripped the counter and stared into her own eyes and, once again, reminded herself to breathe, as if she were Ezra, as if hers was the mind that needed quieting. For her whole childhood, Frankie Harriman had been trained, like a robot, like a machine, to ward off nerves by leaning into adrenaline, not running from it. But now, alone, vulnerable, and extremely sober, she discovered that the same grit, the same steeliness was no longer accessible. As an adult, she had toiled with the most temperamental musicians, the peskiest of celebrities; she had built careers into superstardom from nothing; she had fought her way through the boys' club and had lived the life she wanted on her terms. And here she was, in the bathroom of Steinway Auditorium, worried that she was about to become totally undone. She angled over the counter and moaned, her face falling into her hands.

She forced herself upward and met her own eyes. *Breathe,*

she told herself again. The door to the bathroom creaked open, and an older woman entered, nodding hello. Frankie didn't want to linger, so she painted on a smile and said, "What an amazing ceremony!" in a voice that didn't sound like hers at all. She saw herself out.

The auditorium had been transformed for the event. The lights were dim over the stadium seating, but the stage itself had been converted into a genuine party space: round tables adorned with gold cloths and white and magenta flower arrangements, a lacquer dance floor in the center, twinkling white lights draped above and around. If Frankie hadn't known the feel of a stage intuitively, she never would have had the sense that this was where performers sat and destroyed themselves for the love of their art. Or maybe that was just Frankie. Plenty of the kids she knew from back then loved it. Or told themselves they did anyway.

She moved down the darkened aisles toward the revelry, a pit blossoming in her stomach. Ezra and Mimi were on the far right at the bar; with her red hair and green dress, she was impossible to miss. Ezra turned to look toward the open stretch of the auditorium, a drink in one hand, and Frankie pulled back, as if he were looking for her. His eyes flitted back to Mimi, then he smiled at whatever she had said. Frankie had never seen Ezra in a tuxedo, and honestly, it kind of took her breath away. Something about seeing him all grown up moved her, set her on fire. She thought of the kiss again. Maybe it shouldn't have come as such a surprise.

Laila was frantically waving to her from downstage. Frankie had been discombobulated after the kiss and Mimi's arrival and had lingered in the shower too long, and only just made the pre-wedding photos. She and Laila hadn't had a proper chance to debrief.

"There you are!" Laila said, pulling her into a hug once Frankie ascended the steps to the stage. "Where were you all day? I tried you four times."

Frankie sighed. She hadn't even bothered to listen to her voicemail once she charged her phone. What she wanted was fewer people talking to her, needing her, not more.

"How much time do you have?" Frankie said. "Because the story keeps going and going." She flopped a hand and grimaced.

"How's your head?"

"You know about my head?" Frankie jolted. This was new information, and new information was exactly what Frankie needed. She'd pored over her own recollection, and after Abel Rink and the Zamboni debacle, most of it remained fuzzy, just out of reach.

"I mean, I saw you at Lemonhead." Laila frowned. "Were you that wasted?"

"I saw you at Lemonhead?"

"Yes? You were at the entrance with Gregory and Ezra, and you were going on and on about the injustice of being paired with him, and couldn't you join my team and who would have to know?" She paused, her eyes casting sidelong glances around them. "Um, is there a reason that Ezra is staring at you?"

Frankie began to turn.

"No, don't look don't look don't look!" Laila said.

Too late. Frankie found Ezra's eyes through the thicket of guests, or he found hers, but it didn't really matter. He held her gaze and then scowled. He glanced to his right, where Mimi was distracted by a conversation with someone Frankie didn't recognize, her hands animated. Then Ezra mouthed: *You!* and jabbed a finger quickly in her direction.

Frankie flung open her own hands as if to say: *What? Me?*

Ezra held up a palm: *Five minutes*. Then he jerked his thumb toward backstage. *There*. He steeled his jaw and popped his eyes as if to say, *Do not make me drag you back there*, and Frankie sighed and mouthed, *Fine*. Then to Laila, she said: "As I was saying."

"Uh," Laila started, then stopped. "What exactly happened last night?'

"What did you see happen last night?" Frankie asked, like she was a guest star on *Law & Order*. It occurred to her that she really needed to start spending less time alone in hotel rooms.

"So you really don't know? This isn't, like, a rhetorical question?" Laila looked delighted at this turn of events, like a romantic mystery meant to be solved was exactly what this wedding needed.

"I mean, I know." She paused. "Some of it, I know."

"I was only in and out of Lemonhead," Laila said. "Oh, we won by the way! Did you know that?" When Frankie looked confused, she said, "The scavenger hunt, we won!"

"Oh. Ok. Congrats."

"Lord," Laila laughed. "I figured the most competitive person I know would at least be impressed."

Frankie nodded, as if to say that she was, though she really was not. A competition that Frankie Harriman was not prepared to slit throats over? She did an internal temperature check to ensure she was still alive.

"Well, anyway," Laila continued, "it was a hi and bye situation there—you were waiting by the front for Gregory to bring you an ice pack, and I guess he didn't, so Ezra popped in and grabbed one, then told me he had it under control." She winced. "Jesus. In hindsight, he was pretty wasted. Should I have stayed?" Her face fell, her voice growing serious. "Shit, Frankie, did something happen?"

Frankie remembered the time their junior year when Laila had been pinned against the back door at Lemonhead by a senior whose name she only recalled as Christopher. How he'd held both of her hands above her head and kissed her neck until Laila, squirming and terrified, raised a knee to his crotch, and then ran all the way back to the dorms. Laila didn't report him because, well, she'd said, nothing *really* happened, and it was the late '80s and this sort of shit just got glossed over, cast aside with, *Maybe you shouldn't have worn such a short dress* or *How many drinks did you have anyway?*

Eleven years later, Frankie couldn't say it was any better, at least not in her industry. But she did what she could. She gave her artists pepper spray. She gifted a few of them with martial arts lessons a few Christmases ago. She thought now about how exhausting that was: the constant sense that you were only one bad move, one laced drink, one stupid evening out away from danger. Certainly, there were men in her life, in the business, who would look out for her or her artists, but not enough. She could quit, she could walk away, but what would that do? Only leave her female artists more vulnerable. So she stood between them and danger like a shield.

She stared at Ezra now—he had refocused his attention back on Mimi—and was grateful that, even while blackout drunk last night, he'd looked out for her. She hadn't known how much she'd needed this—not just last night, but maybe for decades—until this very moment. How much easier everything could be if you had someone acting as that shield, someone who always stood by your side. She'd always assumed that she hated being protected, that his paternalism was repulsive. Maybe what she had hated was that she was in danger—emotionally, mentally—in the first place, and when she was, no one had her best interests at heart.

"Really," Laila was saying. "Did something happen? Do I need to go maim him?" She looked around for a utensil, finding only a discarded skewer on one of the cocktail tables. She picked it up anyway. "I can do a lot of damage with this. You don't even know, like, you don't even understand. You say the word, and I'm basically auditioning for *The Matrix*."

"No," Frankie said. She wanted to reassure Laila because that's how you tucked away your trauma for the time being. "No, nothing happened. I mean, nothing like that."

Laila uncoiled, the tension in her face abating.

"Shit, still though. I shouldn't have left you."

Frankie really didn't want to turn this into a thing when it was so much easier not to. Also, she was ruminating about Ezra's chivalry. She lowered her voice, though the DJ had started up now—the opening riff of "Don't Stop Believin'" cut through the air, and all the guests let out a cheer, so she had to recalibrate.

"I think it's possible . . . we may have gotten married?"

Laila leaned in. *"What?"*

"I THINK IT'S POSSIBLE THAT EZRA AND I GOT MARRIED LAST NIGHT!"

She screamed this loudly, right when Steve Perry was taking a breath after *Just a small town girl, livin' in a lonely world.*

Gregory, who happened to be clustered nearby, spun toward them and said, "Wait, that's true?! You tracked down Alec?"

But Frankie said, "Shit! *Shit!* No, forget you heard that." Then she noticed Ezra disappearing behind the stage, and she didn't want to make him wait, even though she really did want to make him wait, but she was trying to be mature. Besides, now Mimi was heading toward them, and she absolutely did not want to have a girl fight in the middle of April and Connor's wedding because that would be straight out of a terrible '80s movie, and Frankie was repelled by clichés.

Gregory forced a grin and waved to Mimi, then through gritted teeth said, "Make sure your purses are zipped," and Frankie would have laughed but her stomach had dropped, and it was all she could do to say, "I'll be back," and push herself forward to find Ezra backstage.

This wasn't the first time they'd tripped their way back there, and Frankie very much did not like the memories this whole shebang stirred up. This evening, the backstage area had been transformed into the catering hot zone: waiters came and went with trays of hors d'oeuvres, and the chef barked things like, *We're firing the skewers!* as Frankie dodged a young man who looked exasperated with the job and it was only an hour in.

Ten years ago, when she'd last set foot backstage—the only time she'd set foot backstage at Steinway—she'd found only cluttered darkness. Lights resting, ready to be hoisted, scattered parts of sets that had been broken down from whatever musical the theater nerds had put up that spring. She'd scampered back here when she heard the clatter of the doors to the auditorium open; she was hiding, of course. Hiding from Ezra, because ten years ago, that's all she knew how to do.

By then, they were just two weeks away from graduation. It was early May. Ezra had long since made his choice to attend NYU Law, and Frankie made small but empty comments about possibly joining him even though her heart wasn't in it and she knew she never would. In hindsight, she should have told him. She should have just said: *We had something really beautiful for two years, and you're my best friend, but I can't. I can't go back there, I can't relive the life I've already had, even for you.* And maybe they would have figured out a way to do things long-distance or maybe they could have had a clean break, said all sorts of platitudes that they actually meant when you've had your first significant revelatory love, and they could have split from each other with grace. Theoretically, Frankie knew that people could do this. But she didn't know how to; she wasn't one of those people.

So instead she made vague promises about how she could crash at her mom's place until she found a studio in Alphabet City, and she lied and told Ezra that she'd mailed her résumé in to Atlantic Records, where she had some old contacts. She did, indeed, mail her résumé in to Atlantic Records, but to their LA office, along with Universal and Sony. In fact, the very day she later found herself in the bowels of Steinway, hiding from Ezra, she'd just gotten a call in her dorm room from a friend of a friend of her dad's at Sony requesting an interview, which was the only reason she untacked her wall calendar (cute kitties wearing bow ties—she'd hung it ironically) and realized that she couldn't remember the last time she'd gotten her period. Frankie had been on the pill for a solid year now, which meant that she really didn't give her period too much thought: it showed up when she took her week's worth of pink sugar pills and disappeared when she took the green ones that prevented her from growing a human in her uterus.

She flipped the months—April and May—back and forth. Maybe she was just being ridiculous. If she couldn't remember getting her period last month, it was likely because it was so ordinary, so normal that she just hadn't tracked it. But part of her knew this wasn't true. She'd gotten up from her desk and retrieved her current month's pills, then counted backward with her finger alongside the calendar. In fact, she'd gone home the week of the sugar pills. Her mother had called because her grandfather had a heart attack playing golf in Sagaponack, and her mom, who had said only loathsome, terrible things about her grandfather when Frankie was growing up, pleaded for her to come say goodbye. Frankie took the train down to the city and bought some flowers at a deli outside Grand Central Station but discovered, once she was buzzed up to her grandparents' apartment three blocks south of her mother's, that her grandfather was going to live after all. She thought this was good news, though after she handed her grandmother the bouquet and kissed her grandfather's waxy cheek, she found her mother in the library nursing a whiskey, where she said, "I swear to God, that man will outlive us all."

So Frankie thought she'd remember having her period that weekend. She'd have run to Duane Reade for tampons, have rooted around her mother's medicine cabinet for something strong to ward off cramps. (Also just to root around her mother's medicine cabinet because every turn was a surprise.)

She didn't trust student health with her privacy, so she left the calendar abandoned on her desk and ran, shaky with the anticipation of a truth she already knew was coming, to the dinky drugstore by Lemonhead. She paid in cash, and because Burton Library was closer than her dorm, she scuttled into the restroom, locked the door behind her, and waited the three minutes until the stupid stick told her that she was destined to repeat the mistakes of her parents. Pregnant at twenty-two. She was such a fucking cliché that she would have laughed if she hadn't been weeping, there by herself, in the back stall of the school library, where squares of toilet paper littered the floor and floral air freshener made a pitiful attempt to mask the wayward scent of too many students who had too many cups of coffee.

She'd run to Steinway straightaway. She didn't know why, didn't ask herself to consider why. It didn't matter. Looking back, she doubted it was because music brought her peace or comfort or any of those trite little statements that therapists would say. Because it didn't. But she'd been trained to retreat into it, and it was a long time, maybe until tonight at the wedding, that Frankie understood retreating was not at all the same thing as seeking. Frankie retreated to Steinway because she used music, her music, as a crutch. Not as a balm. And those were two different things entirely. For all of her formative years, up until Middleton, music had filled every emotion for her: pain, stress, loneliness, and yes, even joy. Frankie had loved piano for a while; she knew that to be true too. But it was so all-consuming for her, at least until she walked away, that she couldn't differentiate between any of those feelings: she was like a newborn who screamed at everything because she couldn't tell when she was hungry, when she was scared, when she just wanted someone to hold her.

So she'd found herself onstage alone at the piano bench. As she too often found herself as a child. Only now she was pregnant. She hadn't wanted any of it, and she was determined not to be a passenger in her life any longer. Wasn't that the whole point of rejecting Juilliard or a conservatory or the path of a professional musician? Of telling Fred and her mother to go fuck themselves when they begged her to attend Aspen? Of hanging up on her father when he'd called her to ask what it would take—as if she were waiting on a bribe—for her to rejoin the competition circuit just before she left for her freshman year? All she wanted her life through was to be left to her own choices. She'd decided that at seventeen, and she'd never regretted it. She'd defied expectations; she'd pointed herself toward the unknown, even when it terrified her. This was why she'd abandoned her music, and unlike her mom, she wasn't going to put all of that aside for a baby, for a man, not even for a good man.

Tonight, at April and Connor's reception, all of this rushed back in one unwelcome memory. She was upset all over again at Ezra, for forcing her to dredge this up when she'd spent the better part of a decade forgetting it, pretending none of this had happened.

Out front, the DJ dropped "Y.M.C.A.," and Frankie heard the guests let out a cheer.

She didn't see Ezra at first, so she wound further into the hallways, where the bustle from the catering staff had slowed, peering in one dressing room door, then another.

"Frankie." His voice rose up behind her, and she jumped. She'd missed him in the sea of waiters, but there he was, just like he'd been ten years ago. He looked handsome, flawless in his tuxedo, like nothing from his life had stuck to him. His face had fully recovered from the pepper spray, and she couldn't help but think that Ezra looked a little bit like a movie star.

"I'm here," she said.

Ezra took two quick steps toward her, then turned to glance behind him.

"You're not being followed if that's what you're wondering," Frankie said because she just couldn't help herself.

"What were you thinking?" he said, his flawless face going red, his ears turning a bright shade of pink. "You can't just . . . you can't just do that to a person!"

"Kiss you? Marry you? What? I need to know which calamity you're referencing."

"Don't turn this into a joke, Frankie!" He really was furious now, and Frankie had so rarely seen Ezra genuinely rageful that she didn't know what to do or how to respond. "This is exactly like you: you can't leave well enough alone. You just come in, stir up shit, and press the escape button and boom, you're gone." He inhaled, then blew the air out of his nose. "I won't do it. I won't have it. So seriously, I just wanted to tell you to leave me alone. Now. Forever."

Frankie started to protest. She felt like she should at least be able to launch a defense. The kiss had been mutual, even if she'd been the one to start it. *So excuse her if he now wanted to pretend otherwise.*

Ezra saw her sorting through an explanation. She could read it on his face.

"Don't." He held up his hands as if she were approaching him again. "Just don't."

"Fine!" she said. "Let's call this what it was: a mistake. A massive, miscalculated, decade-old mistake."

Ezra shook his head as if he pitied her, which she really didn't think was fair, and then said: "Goodbye forever, Frankie Harriman." And then he turned to go. He had rounded the corner when Frankie remembered the ring.

"Hey!" she called after him. "*Hey!*" She scurried to keep up, turning the corner back to the main artery of the backstage. "Ezra!" She had to raise her voice now, above the blare of "Y.M.C.A." and the waiters and the clinking of plates and glasses. "*Ezra!*"

He stopped but didn't turn, which Frankie found enraging, bordering on insulting. Despite what she had just said—which she hadn't really meant and was just saying to be provocative; my God, surely, Ezra knew that!—they had a whole history between them, a vast, wide-open love for each other that crumbled into wreckage, and yes, she bore half of the responsibility. But he could turn to face her. He could look her in the eye.

"Fine!" She said it too loudly, and a few of the waiters

stopped loading trays with tiny appetizers and stared. "Of course this is how it would end a second time!"

Now he spun toward her. "End? *End?* This was not a *thing*. We were not a thing a second time! The last time I saw you, Frankie, you made it extremely clear that we were barely a thing the first time. You said no. Do I need to remind you? You. Said. No."

Frankie didn't want to get into all of that, even though she realized that she had been the one to raise it. She reached into her purse and wedged her fingers into the tiny satin pocket that sat just below the zipper. She clasped his grandmother's ring and took four long steps toward him. Then she grabbed his right hand and forced it into his palm, then pressed his fingers closed, into a fist.

"And now," she said, even though she knew it was spiteful, "it's about to be a new century, so we're done entirely. A fresh start. As if we never met."

THIRTY-TWO

Ezra

Ezra did not want Frankie to have the last word. Goddammit, he knew he needed to leave it alone. What was even the point of the verbal sparring, of the back-and-forth, when all he wanted—*all he needed*—was to go back out to the party and dance with Mimi and enjoy the buffet and propose at midnight.

Instead, he marched after Frankie and grabbed her arm before she could slide out from backstage.

"What?" she barked. "What else is there possibly to say?"

Ezra didn't know. He hadn't thought it through. Certainly, there was a lot to say, even though most of it should have been said a decade ago, and now, it felt like an emotional excavation. *Leave*, he thought. *Just leave it. Just leave her.* But like so many things with Frankie Harriman, he felt powerless to do so. Surprisingly, he did not feel like panicking; he did not feel the rise of an oncoming anxiety attack. He'd always assumed that Frankie had somehow played a part in his spiral of nerves, but he was here now, with her, facing an incoming shitstorm, and when he surveyed his heart, his mind, he didn't find the usual static that clouded him, that terrified him, that sent him to the floor trying to breathe.

Ten years ago, just a couple of weeks out from graduation, before everything changed, Laila had seen Frankie run from Burton Library crying. Laila had been on the pay phone out front with her mom, she'd told him, so she couldn't chase after her.

"She looked wrecked, like, really, really upset," Laila had said, her face awash in concern. They both knew that Frankie never cried; she rarely, if ever, even lamented. Ezra had never questioned that until now: he'd just assumed she was gifted with a stoic constitution, the very opposite of him. He stood in the lobby with Laila and realized that was one of the reasons he loved her. It would be a long time until he realized that what he thought he'd loved had been make-believe, just a construct.

"I don't know where she went," Laila said, looking helpless. "Do you think it's something with her parents?" Ezra had no idea what to think because she hadn't shared anything about them recently, and well, he hadn't asked. But he did think he knew where to find her.

Steinway was empty when he got there. She wasn't on-stage; she wasn't anywhere. A few students lingered in the lobby with their string instruments, so he circled back out and asked if they'd seen a girl come in. "She'd have been playing the piano? She's incredible?" he added, as if they'd be mesmerized by her talent.

They raised their eyebrows at this, unimpressed, but they didn't know Frankie, didn't know her gift. Ezra barely did, actually, but the lone time he'd seen her a year ago, right in this very spot, it had taken his breath away. He hadn't grown up going to symphonies or paying much mind to music other than whatever was on the radio when they carpooled to school, but he knew enough to know a generational talent when he saw one.

But she had to be there. Intuitively, he knew this. She wouldn't have run to the dorm to be by herself in the silence; she wouldn't have run to his room for comfort because that wasn't the sort of thing she did. Or had ever done, at least. And for once, he wanted to be the one to nurture her, to lean in and say: *How can I help?* And just as important, for her to tell him. Frankie had been clear that she didn't want a white knight, had never wanted a fixer. But just this one time, wouldn't it be nice if he could offer?

He took the stairs up to the stage, his footsteps echoing in the cavernous space of the thousand or so seats behind him. When he got center stage, he turned and stared out. What a marvel it was, he thought, that she could sit here and lose herself in front of such an audience. Or had a long time ago. That took guts. That took discipline. That took a steely spine that he had never been called to rely on. Crushing the LSAT or making dean's list wasn't nearly the same thing as stepping out in front of a rapt audience and willing yourself to make not a single mistake. He looked out into the empty seats and knew there wasn't a thing in the world that he wouldn't do for Frankie. He'd walk to the ends of the earth if he had to.

He heard a clatter from behind the stage and turned with a start. He'd obviously never been back there, so he fumbled a bit through the darkness, over music stands and set pieces, toward the noise that was still reverberating. He found her sitting behind a partially broken down drum set, her hands on either side of a cymbal, trying to quiet it.

"Frankie," he said.

"Shit," she said.

She looked terrible. Her cheeks were spotty, her eyes damp and bloodshot, her nose an angry red. She'd piled her dark hair into a messy bun on top of her head, and though he had seen her just this morning, her hair looked greasier, like this whole thing—whatever it was—also made her in need of a shower. She played with the cuff of her sweatshirt, then grabbed a wayward thread and pulled it until the seam of her sleeve partially unraveled.

"Hey," he said, stepping toward her. "Whatever it is, I'm here."

Frankie took a long look at him. Then hiccupped.

"I'm not moving to New York," she said. "I should have told you that earlier. I mean, I tried to. Really. But I shouldn't have pretended otherwise. I wanted to make you happy." She shrugged. "But I'm moving to LA."

Ezra felt a shock to his system. Even ten years later, with his grandmother's ring in his palm and Mimi out front onstage waiting for him, he could remember that. How he felt like the bottom was falling out.

"What? Wait, LA?" Ezra tried to recalculate, recalibrate. Whether he could go with her, but he knew he couldn't; why would she suddenly have such a change of heart, if it had been changed at all?

She stood quickly. "This isn't how I wanted to tell you."

"This is why you were crying at Burton? Because you are going to LA?" Ezra tried to take comfort in that. "We can fly back and forth; we'll make it work."

Her eyes found his. No, it was more than that. He understood this intuitively. It would take a wrecking ball to break Frankie Harriman, so whatever it was, it was about significantly more than putting three thousand miles between them.

"Do you . . . I mean . . . is it for a job?" Ezra asked.

Frankie nodded. "Yes."

"One you can't do from New York?" He paused. None of this was making any sense.

"I tried to tell you," she said again. "I can't go back there. I can't live the life that my parents did; I don't want the life my parents had." Her voice elevated and cracked.

He stepped toward her, ran his hands over her shoulders, then down her arms.

"Frankie, we're nothing like your parents. Who ever said that we have to be anything like them?"

Her face fell again, and he saw her fight it but she couldn't, and then she started to cry.

"Ezra," she said, right before she dropped the bomb that would change everything. "I'm pregnant."

Tonight, on New Year's Eve, at April and Connor's wedding, Ezra remembered all of this. He remembered how weeks later, and even months and years after, he would wonder if she would have told him. If he hadn't tracked her down at Steinway, if he hadn't tried to help. Even after their ugly split, he'd wanted to give her the benefit of the doubt, but with Frankie, that wasn't easy, and Ezra resented her for never making it so.

He wove his way through the catering stations backstage, knowing she was right behind him but keeping her distance so they could reemerge at the party and not cause a scene. Well, Frankie may have wanted a scene, but he had enough on his plate and firmly did not.

"Ezra?" He heard a different voice from a few feet away.

He turned, and there was Joni, the barista from the coffee shop this morning, in a white shirt and black pants and her hair pulled into a proper low bun, hoisting a tray of what appeared to be mini quiches.

"I thought that was you! Your face! It looks so much better." Her own face opened into a wide grin. "And now here you are, the best poker player in the land, dressed like James Bond." She mock fanned herself. "It's a good thing that guys aren't my deal." Then her eyes opened with alarm. "Oh shit, oh shit. I'm sorry, I know you're married. I'm just a fangirl. Please don't take it the wrong way."

Ezra wanted to be polite. But honestly, he was just trying to keep his focus and get back to Mimi and forget about this whole dumpster of a situation with Frankie and carry on. For reasons inexplicable to him, he thought, right then, of the first time they'd met, of when she plopped down at the bar next to him and he told her his woes about Bethany, and she'd said, *What are you even doing with her, with your life? Don't you know that you're in control of your own destiny?*

Why did it feel like the span of years had risen and ebbed, and still here he was, refusing to take the wheel of his own future? He'd gotten lucky with his gaming program, but now what? Did he really want to be a tech bro amassing more and more money? Spending weekends in Napa or the Hamptons rubbing elbows with the truly terrible combination of pretentious and boring? He knew that was what Mimi wanted, and he didn't even mind that she liked that scene: this was the version of himself he'd always represented to her, the version on the questionnaire the first time they'd met. But what did Ezra Jones want? That question continued to confound him, which at thirty-two felt too late. Maybe he wanted to be a teacher; maybe he wanted to go to medical school. Maybe he wanted to start a charity for children with cancer or for homeless animals. He didn't know; the world was his oyster, and *he still didn't know.*

Joni, having passed her tray to another waiter, kept chattering on. Her hands were animated, her eyes sparkling.

"I'm actually so glad I ran into you!" she said, and then another look of recognition passed over her as she glanced over his shoulder where Frankie had been trailing him. "Frankie! Hi!" She leaned in and hugged her, like they were old friends, and Frankie, oddly, hugged her back. The Frankie he knew would have never. Maybe she'd gotten practice out there in LA, Ezra thought. Air-kisses and fake smiles and cocaine.

"I remembered something from last night," Joni said. "I mean, I know you guys were fuzzy on things, and after you left, it came to me!" She cast her eyes toward his hands, toward his ring finger, which was now bare, the gold band still hidden in the pocket of his jeans back at the hotel.

"Oh well, I guess maybe you realized too," she said. "It wasn't your wedding band, so yeah, I guess that's weird? Did you lose yours?"

At this, Frankie started laughing. It was more of a cackle, and he knew that she was howling not because any of this was funny but because it was all so absurd. It was funny *ha ha*. Meaning not funny at all.

"I'm not really following," Ezra said. Then: "Frankie, can you please just be quiet for once?"

And Frankie made a grimace at Joni, like she was a child who'd been reprimanded but had no intention of abiding the teacher. And Joni, who was only being a Good Samaritan, Ezra knew, looked a little alarmed at his tone.

"Should I tell you? I mean . . . I was just trying to help," she said. "I can get back to work."

"No, I'm sorry," Ezra said because none of this was her fault. "What exactly happened?"

"Well, there was this grad student there. I'd totally spaced," she said. "And obviously, you were hosing him. Like you were the rest of us. But at least that I could root for." She lowered his voice. "I mean, you don't understand. He was being such a dick."

"Oh, been there, done that," Frankie said.

"Anyway, he was out of cash, and well, to be honest, I think maybe he has a gambling problem? So he bet his wedding ring. And you looked skeptical because you didn't really need it, but then Frankie—you were lying on the floor? Which, in hindsight, I guess is pretty weird? But you said something like, 'Oh, take his ring, Ezra. Marriage is all a farce anyway.'" Joni's face folded into confusion. "Wait, maybe I'm not remembering that right."

"I'm sure you are," Ezra said.

"I don't mean to cause problems between you two!" Joni truly looked alarmed.

"Ship has sailed," Frankie said, and Joni gave her a long stare, then another to Ezra, then back to Frankie.

"Anyway, I guess now that I'm saying this aloud, maybe it's not really all that helpful?" Joni sighed. "I just, you know. As I said, you're the best player I've ever seen, so I thought maybe—"

"So, this was essentially your fault." Ezra glared at Frankie.

"My fault? *My fault?* I was half dead from a concussion—"

"You weren't half dead or I would have taken you to the emergency room—"

"I was a quarter dead from a concussion, so how can this be my fault? It seems to me, Ezra Jones"—and at this Frankie raised a finger and jabbed his shoulder—"that you have only yourself to blame for your poker habit and, well, all the rest of it!"

Ezra didn't know what *all the rest of it* meant, but then he remembered how not even a few minutes ago, he had considered agency in his life: how it was easier not to have it but more fulfilling when you did. Before he could reassess and put Frankie in her place, from behind him came another voice, shrill and cutting. He turned and there was Mimi. Another fatal mistake in his planning: Mimi was his plus-one. He shouldn't have left her alone.

"You were playing *poker*?" she said. Ezra had a plummeting sensation that this was all about to go very wrong for him.

"Oh!" Gregory said, inexplicably backstage now too. Why was everyone back here and not out front enjoying the party, enjoying the mini quiches, the DJ, who was now playing "Livin' on a Prayer," Bon Jovi's best anthem, in his opinion. Gregory wedged himself into their circle, then threw both hands over his mouth, his eyes wide and wild. "Oh, oh shit."

"What?" Ezra said. "What," he said again, this time not a question but a demand.

"Shit," Gregory replied. "That *may* have been my fault?"

Frankie made little circles in the air with her hand above her head as if to say: *See I told you and also obviously,* which Ezra thought was pretty rich because, lady, it takes two to tussle.

"Confess," Ezra said to Gregory.

Then Mimi said, higher pitched and louder, "You confess, Ezra!"

He held her gaze and pleaded: "Please, Mimi. Not now." So Mimi scowled and tapped her high-heeled foot but did thankfully quiet.

"I had forgotten until just now," Gregory said. "Someone had told me about the deal-in at Waverly's. And man, you were just so . . . so . . . ." He looked around as if someone could help him, but no one had any idea what adjective he was going to use, so he sighed and took a long sip of whatever it was he was drinking and continued. "Before we went out. Ezra, I mean, it's like you were a vampire, and everyone had sucked the life from you."

"No," Frankie interjected. "That's not right. The vampire is the one who sucks things from other people."

Gregory looked confused then said, "Right, sorry, I'm drunk again. Anyway, I just wanted you to do something fun, to enjoy yourself, you know . . . like you used to. Everything about you now is about—" Gregory stopped himself. But the implication was there, and Ezra did not like it very much. Did not like it at all. *Like you used to before Mimi. Everything about you now is about Mimi.* "I totally forgot, and shit, I stayed at Lemonhead, and you guys moved on." He seemed genuinely contrite. "I didn't realize it was an issue. I mean, I knew, I guess. And I still told you."

Ezra wanted to scream. He wasn't overcome with his usual nerves or a fevered pulse or a heart that was going to beat out of his chest. He was furious. He was so fucking furious. At Frankie. At Mimi. At Gregory and his 1000-proof booze. At himself. At the ridiculous confluence of events that had led to right now. How did he arrive back at Middleton so full of optimism and, just twenty-four hours later, have everything unravel into a mess that he couldn't even imagine he could mend?

"I'm going back to the hotel," Mimi said.

"Mimi, please, don't," Ezra begged. "Or, I mean, I'll come with you."

"No," she said with such certainty that Ezra was genuinely embarrassed in front of his friends, even if he was irate with them, even if some of them—well, ok, Frankie—were not his friends at all. "No! I didn't even want to come here! I left my one vacation week with my family for this. And now I hear that not one day after you're back with old friends . . . you're gambling. And, you're with *her.*"

She gestured to Frankie, who said, "Hey! I'm not part of this."

But Mimi rolled her eyes and said to Ezra, "You and I had an agreement."

Ezra did not interject here because she was right: he had understood her terms from the start—loyalty and honesty, and he had been happy to live with them because those were his terms too. It didn't seem like the right time to raise the outstanding question as to why she was inexplicably lying about missing her flight. He didn't care if she'd been late or distracted or . . . Ezra couldn't think of another reason she wouldn't have landed last night. It didn't matter! He forgave her! He just wanted to slip the ring on her finger at midnight and move on from all of this! Why was it so hard to move on from all of this?

Mimi had turned to go, and Ezra started to protest, but Gregory touched his outstretched arm and said, "Friend, we should probably have a talk." And Ezra was tired, he was so goddamned tired, so he simply watched Mimi leave, and with that, everything that Ezra had planned on, had planned for, disappeared.

THIRTY-THREE

Frankie

Frankie was beginning to think that Steinway Auditorium was actually cursed. Maybe it had been built on sacred burial grounds or maybe it was just infested with significantly awful juju (she lived in LA; she believed these things from time to time whenever the notion struck her), because she had never gotten out of this godforsaken building without a spiral of shit going down.

They were back at the reception now. Gregory and Ezra were huddled in a corner, and Frankie desperately wanted to eavesdrop but instead lingered by the buffet, which had opened while they were all backstage churning up baggage from a decade ago. She gnawed on a rubbery piece of sirloin and watched Laila make a lap around the dance floor, likely looking for Alec Barstow, who really had disappeared entirely. Frankie wondered if they should file a police report, but she didn't want to incriminate herself with the campus police, and besides, she couldn't remember the rest of the story anyway. Then she noticed Joni looking shaky while busing discarded dishes, and she called to her, "Joni, you don't understand, this has nothing to do with you. We were a mess long before this."

Joni tried to look reassured, but Frankie could tell she didn't believe her. It was easy, necessary, to think that grownups got their lives together after college. To learn that life remained as messy at thirty-two as it was at twenty-two was to shatter the illusion that came with post-graduation dreams. Frankie walked over to her, and above the hum of "Bohemian Rhapsody," she placed a hand on her arm and said, "Joni, it's going to be ok. Really. If you're ever in LA or need a job or could use some help, will you call me?" She had a business card in her wallet and placed it in the pocket of Joni's starched white shirt.

"Thank you," Joni whispered, and Frankie thought she might cry.

"This really had nothing to do with you," she said, and she started to explain, but there was so much, too much, and Frankie didn't even have an honest grasp of it herself.

After she'd told Ezra about the pregnancy, which she hadn't even meant to do really, he became even more Ezra than he usually was—already determined to be the most wonderful father to their zygote. Neither of them had good paternal role models, though hers had promised that he would sit nicely with her mother at graduation, even if her mom showed up with Fred. Frankie didn't think she should be the one to tell him that her mom and Fred had split up (and furthermore, Fred had never been the problem in her parents' marriage), and besides, she was done with their grown-up things. But he would show up, she trusted that, because even if her dad were absent and distracted, he wasn't terrible. He loved her, and Frankie, both then and now, knew their problems didn't stem from her parents' lack of love for her. There was loads of other stuff, just like with Ezra.

Frankie couldn't really articulate why Ezra became so frenzied in the weeks that followed after she broke down in Steinway and told him. She herself had only taken the positive test a few hours prior, so she didn't know what she needed, what she wanted. No, that wasn't true. Even a decade later, she knew that wasn't true. She sat at the piano bench before he found her, her fingers lilting over the keys but never catching flight, never making a sound, and understood intrinsically that she could not, would not have this child.

And then she told Ezra, and he started making plans for their future. The pregnancy test wasn't even dry.

"You'll move to New York with me," he said when they had wandered out of their dorm for dinner at the dining hall, though Frankie had lost her appetite. She thought he sounded genuinely happy. "I don't have to live with Henry. It will be the two of us, then the three of us."

"I didn't realize this was something I wanted," he said one night in her room while she started packing up her books into cardboard boxes. "But now, I can see how it makes so much sense."

And Frankie made small protestations. She said she didn't think the job at Sony (which had not yet been offered to her but she'd led with the lie and it'd snowballed) would let her transfer to New York. She half-heartedly shrugged when Ezra suggested they call a real estate agent to find them a rental near NYU. She taped up her boxes and used a Sharpie to label them and never once really considered doing any of that.

She called her mom and told her, and her mom did something right for once: she gasped and said, "Oh, honey." Then she fell silent for a long minute and said: "What can I do to help? You have your whole life in front of you, and I don't regret being a young mom for a second, but I don't get the sense that it's for you." And Frankie cried, truly sobbed, because that's all she had wanted to hear from Ezra, an understanding that she was in over her head here, and instead of telling her what he was going to do, maybe he should have asked what she wanted.

Years later, on the same stage, Frankie watched Ezra and Gregory grow animated in the corner where, presumably, Gregory was informing her ex-boyfriend that his current girlfriend was a thief. *We all hide a whole manner of sins from one another*, Frankie thought. And maybe the key to successfully loving someone wasn't to judge them for their sins, but rather to ask how we could soothe the pains those afflictions cause one another. Mimi didn't steal things because she needed to; she did it as a panacea for something deeper. Frankie didn't push people away because it served her; she did it because loneliness was a safer space than emotional vulnerability. And Ezra—Frankie almost started to cry at this realization. Ezra wasn't overprotective because he thought that she or Mimi or anyone was breakable; he was overprotective because what he really needed was someone looking out for him instead. His mother was gone; his father was gone. And maybe what he'd needed from Frankie back then wasn't a baby but the assurance of companionship. She could have told him that she didn't want to move to New York with him, even before the positive pregnancy test. She could have told him that she was twenty-two and selfish and wanted to sort out her own life. Instead, she hinted and she obfuscated, and she waited for him to give her what she needed instead of just talking honestly with him. She needed space. She needed freedom. She needed to figure out who she was after being told throughout childhood who she was predestined to be and still not having a firm grasp on it after four years of college. Frankie didn't think there was anything wrong with this—who, really, knew who they were going to be for the rest of their lives at twenty-two?

Maybe Ezra did. He was going to be a lawyer and work his way up through the firm so that he never had to worry about money and also build a logical, linear, reassuring existence where bad things didn't happen that he couldn't control like his dad leaving when he was three and his mom getting ovarian cancer.

It dawned on Frankie now, as she saw Gregory throw his hands in the air, and then Ezra turn and march down the steps from the stage and along the left aisle of the auditorium toward the exit, that the only people who knew who they were going to be at twenty-two were people like her mother and father: parents. Her mom had aspirations well beyond giving birth at twenty and then mothering Frankie until she was old enough to have a life of her own. And Frankie knew this wasn't her fault, that her mom had been stunted. But it had happened all the same; once you had a child, you were a parent forever, and at twenty-two, Frankie knew that she wasn't ready to sacrifice for such things.

Gregory saw her staring and pushed through the dance floor toward her.

"Well, I tried," he said. "I mean, I told him."

"About Kmart?" Frankie asked.

Gregory nodded, looking grim.

"It's not the worst thing in the world, the stealing," Frankie said. "I mean, we all have our shit."

"Of course it's not the worst thing in the world!" he snapped. "But wouldn't you think he'd want to know? But he didn't. He did *not*! He was furious with me for telling him."

"Shooting the messenger." Frankie shrugged because that did sound exactly like Ezra: upset at the outcome, not at the cause. Ten years had come and gone, and here they were exactly the same. Frankie reconsidered. She hoped she had evolved, even just in tiny shifts. Brick by brick, Fred used to say when she was learning a new piece, and she was surprised to think of him now. Still though, brick by brick to self-improvement too.

"Well, you can't blame a guy for trying," Gregory said, just as the DJ came on the mic and said, "We are not only celebrating April and Connor, but a new century in ninety minutes! The countdown has begun!" And then cued up "Electric Boogie."

They stood there and watched some middle-aged guests attempt to wiggle their bodies to the choreography, with April and Connor at the center of it, both of them looking overjoyed, truly elated.

The thing was, Frankie *did* blame a guy for trying. She blamed Ezra for a lot a decade ago. Not the pregnancy. That was on her. She had realized on her way back to the dorm from Steinway that she'd skipped two days of her pills when she was deep into her final econ project and lost track of everything else around her. She had only herself to blame for the mess. She'd trudged back to her room, and all around her, students were carrying on with their lives unencumbered. Someone was blasting Depeche Mode too loudly from their window; a group of boys was playing Hacky Sack on the quad. All of them had their whole futures available, wide open. And Frankie, who had tried so hard to chart her own course after high school, realized that with the pregnancy, hers was already written. But Ezra didn't want to hear any of that. He'd wanted to be her savior instead.

By the time she'd made it back to her room and fell onto her bed and smashed her face into the pillow, Frankie was nearly incandescent with rage. The pregnancy she owned. The rest of it was on him. That he didn't stop to ask her what she wanted. That he simply leapt to *their* future and ignored *her* future. That he seemed truly happy at the possibly of her joining him in New York, of their duo becoming a trio. So, yes, she did blame a guy for trying.

Now, with "Electric Boogie" booming behind them, she looked at Gregory and said: "So what's he going to do?"

And he shrugged. "Who knows. Chase after her, apologize, propose." He swallowed the rest of his drink and set his empty glass on a gold-linen-covered table littered with napkins smudged with lipstick and dirty plates with half-eaten buffet bites. *Everything that started out so beautiful eventually fell apart*, Frankie thought.

"And what should I do now?" Frankie asked, though she wasn't sure why.

"Well, you could chase after him," he said after a long beat. "Apologize. Propose."

"Give me a goddamned break," Frankie scoffed. "Also, I think you mean divorce. We may already be married."

"No, I don't mean that at all," he said, then fell silent again. Then: "But chasing after Ezra was never your thing. You always made him do all the work."

THIRTY-FOUR

Ezra

Ezra tried Mimi's phone from a pay phone on the corner, but she wasn't picking up, and there was no shuttle back to the hotel in sight. Ezra paced back and forth on the sidewalk, his breath all around him pillowing in the bitter night air, and tried, *tried*, to pull back from the swirl of combustible emotions that were boiling over inside of him.

So Gregory had seen her stealing. That wasn't great. It wasn't the end of the world, but it admittedly wasn't great. *But we all have our quirks*, he thought. Ezra's quirks were decidedly noncriminal, barring the Bellagio and MGM, but still. This was petty stuff, nothing major. He had his grandmother's engagement ring in his pocket again, and all he wanted to do was propose at midnight and start the next phase of his life.

It was really goddamned freezing out now, he noticed. His ears stung, and his dress shoes were not meant for subarctic temperature, so his toes cried out too. He tried to consider where he would go if he were Mimi. She couldn't make it back to the hotel on foot in her high heels, and from the look of it, the entirety of campus was shuttered for the night. A few stragglers wandered past, on their way to Lemonhead or someone's dorm to celebrate the turn of the new year, and from a distance, a girl shouted to another, "Happy Y2K, bitch!" And someone whooped a reply.

Ezra tucked his hands into his pockets and headed north. He didn't know where he was going, but then what else was new. He was out here, chasing a girl like he'd chased his high school girlfriend before she dumped him, like he'd chased Bethany before she disappeared for one time too many, like he'd chased Frankie, and now Mimi. Why was it so difficult for him to find someone who stayed? He stopped and stared up at the now cloudless sky. The storm had moved through, and the spread of stars above him nearly took his breath away. He'd forgotten how beautiful it was. In New York, there were lights for miles and miles but no stars.

Ezra picked up his pace and saw a light on in the distance and slowed. Burton Library appeared to be open. Which of course it was: Burton was always open, a safe harbor when students needed to pull all-nighters or retreat from a horrible roommate who didn't shower or just lose themselves in the stacks stocked with history. He sped up again, the wind gusting and chapping his cheeks, blowing his hair aloft too.

He swung open the door, and Mimi was there in the lobby, sitting on a low windowsill, staring out at the unfamiliar campus. Bruno, evidently working a double shift, still sat at the security desk and looked up, his reading glasses low on his nose, and said, "Oh, I see you're back. Zoe's gone, so I'm not giving you special access."

And Mimi turned to him, her face ruddy and streaked with mascara, and said, "Zoe? I thought this was about Frankie!" And her voice bounced off the rotunda, and Bruno sighed loudly.

"No, Zoe's just a girl I met—" Ezra stopped. He didn't even know how to explain it. Zoe was just a girl he met when he woke up in her dorm room where he fell asleep spooning Frankie? "Anyway, she's not important. And this isn't about Frankie either, Meems."

"I came all this way for you!" Mimi hiccupped. "You have no idea how difficult it was for me to get here!"

And Ezra didn't; that was true. She still hadn't told him the truth of why she'd missed her flight. What else didn't he know? He felt an uneasy bubble of anxiety rise through him. *No no no.* That was only supposed to be a Frankie Harriman side effect. If he had a full-blown meltdown here, in the marbled lobby of Burton, who would talk him down? Mimi didn't know about the breathing technique. Mimi didn't know how to handle him at his most undone because she'd never had to; he'd never shown her his vulnerabilities.

Maybe we tell each other a multitude of lies, he thought, *just so we can find someone to love us.*

"Why didn't you get on the plane last night, Mimi?" he heard himself ask.

"Because it was canceled! I told you this! You weren't picking up, probably I realize now because you were with her—Zoe or Frankie or whatever—and I had to try to figure it out on my own," she cried. "I mean, which is fine! I'm an independent woman or whatever, but I'm here, and I did the best I could!"

"But I know your flight wasn't canceled," Ezra said quietly because it was the thing he didn't want to say.

"What are you talking about?" Mimi was on her feet now, half crying, half shouting, and Ezra's instinct was to apologize to Bruno for the disturbance. Not because he was sorry but because he didn't want Bruno to see Mimi this way; he didn't want this stranger to see her at her worst. What he wanted to do was protect her, when maybe, it occurred to him suddenly, Ezra Jones should stop trying to look out for everyone else and start looking out for himself. *Maybe he should be in control of his own destiny.*

"Mimi, I checked with the airline. Your flight took off and landed, and I'm not angry, I'm not upset, I'm just trying to understand why there's this gap between us that I wasn't even aware of until now." He paused. "Gregory told me about Kmart."

Mimi's face froze and then crumbled, and she sank back on the windowsill. "Kmart? This is about Kmart?"

And at this Bruno said, "As intriguing as this is, I'm gonna need you to keep your voice down. This is still a library, miss."

And she turned to him and bleated, *"It is New Year's Eve and we are the only ones here, so please forgive me!"*

And now Ezra was truly mortified. "Mimi, please," he whispered. "Please, let's just sit calmly and talk about this."

"Talk about what?" she cried. "Kmart? That, like, your

friend 'Gregory,'"—she said that like it wasn't really his name, which Ezra really did not understand—"saw me taking, like, a lipstick. A lipstick! Who cares? It's Kmart; they have a billion dollars, and I do not!"

"I'm not upset about Kmart," Ezra said.

"Then maybe we should talk about Frankie!" Mimi said, and Ezra saw Bruno cock his head like this was getting interesting. "What ever happened to loyalty? What ever happened to honesty?"

Ezra knew she was deflecting because it was easier to point fingers than be pointed out. He'd never taken the bar, but he'd been to law school, and he recognized the technique. He breathed in, breathed out. Did it one more time. He could do this on his own. He didn't need Frankie there to calm him.

"Mimi, this is about honesty, actually. Just tell me why you didn't get on your flight," he said. "It's a simple question with a simple answer."

Mimi was truly beside herself now. Her cheeks were raging red, her nose dripping, and she was practically levitating with indignation. She reminded Ezra of a cornered animal who was willing to lash out at anything, anyone, even those who meant it no harm.

"Fine! *Fine!* I didn't get on the flight because I missed it, ok?"

Ezra felt his stomach unwind. That was reasonable. That was believable! Then it occurred to him that if the explanation were simply this innocuous, she would have told him. And in the past, he realized, he would have accepted such things: that she'd answered his question, and even if something about it didn't sit quite right, he didn't want to peel back any other layers because he intuitively knew that he wouldn't like what he'd find. He thought again of Frankie, how when she'd told him she was pregnant, he'd started making plans. Maybe he should have peeled back some of her layers. Maybe then he'd have seen the whole of her, and even if it had been ugly, uglier, he could have loved that part of her too. He would have, he knew now, watching Mimi. He would have loved the whole of it, the whole of her.

"If you just missed your flight, why didn't you tell me?" Now, even if it meant confrontation, even if it meant saying difficult things, he wanted to know the truth. He was keenly aware of how profoundly different this was for him, how profoundly new.

Mimi's face fell into something that Ezra had never seen before. Terror or anguish or fury. A combination of all of them. Maybe, actually, it was honesty.

"I did tell you! I left you three messages!" She was sobbing now.

"You didn't tell me, Mimi. Not the truth."

She jumped to her feet and slipped on the slick floor, her heels no match for the marble that was still damp from all the melted snow tracked in. Ezra reached out to grab her, but she caught herself on the windowsill, found her balance, and stood taller.

Then: "Fine," she said, her voice low and flat. "The reason I did not get on the plane is the exact reason that your friend Gregory would love to gossip about. I wanted some earrings, ok? I wanted some earrings, and I was at Neiman's, and I just wanted something nice to impress your *fancy* fucking friends, so I took them." Her mouth contorted as she inhaled. "You don't understand what it's like to never have what you want, to never be able to get what you deserve."

And Ezra pulled back at this because he understood it so completely that he was almost offended that she thought this of him. He knew intellectually that she was speaking about money—that he had it now and she didn't—but so much of his life had been spent in pursuit of seeking something that he didn't have, of filling a void that he couldn't even articulate but that shadowed him all the same. And Mimi hadn't seen that? Mimi hadn't *known* that?

"And the earrings meant you couldn't get on the flight?" Ezra said finally, quietly, resigned.

"No, of course not! Do you have any idea how any of this works?"

Ezra wasn't sure what to say because he didn't think it was necessarily wrong that he wasn't aware of the rules of shoplifting.

"I got caught, ok? Security. And it's not like they sent me to jail, ok? Don't you worry, Ezra Jones, your girlfriend did not spend the night in jail!"

"Mimi, that's not what—"

"I know the drill, ok? Please, do you think this was my first time?"

Ezra, in fact, had no idea how many times she had been apprehended by mall cops. Until an hour ago, he hadn't even known this was in the cards. He wondered now if this was why she was so controlling of his own vices. Maybe it was a kindness on her behalf, not an embarrassment, which he had always assumed.

"Is this why you hate my gambling? The poker? The blackjack?"

"What?" she said. "I mean, no? I told you about my uncle who had to move in with us." She paused. "Also, who loses money for the sport of it? It's just another thing you don't value because you don't realize how much some of us go without."

Ezra nodded and didn't pursue it. He'd gone without plenty. But this wasn't the time, this wasn't the fix.

"So security took me into their little back room and I had to sign some forms saying I wouldn't come back there for a year, and blah blah blah." She made a face like this was an inconvenience to her, not actually a crime. "It took forever, and I missed the flight, ok? And it felt much easier to just show up today, but maybe I shouldn't have done that either because, my God, no good deed goes unpunished!"

"What was the good deed?" Ezra asked. He couldn't even imagine.

"I came here because you didn't want to do this alone." She considered this then laughed. "Which is ironic since you were actually doing it with *her*."

Ezra fell quiet. Then: "I wanted you here because I was going to ask you to marry me. At midnight. For the millennium."

Behind him, he heard Bruno whisper, "Jeeesus," and he turned, and Bruno said, "Sorry, man."

When he turned back, Mimi was frozen, her mouth agape, her eyes wide.

"What?"

"I was going to ask you to marry me," he said again, and

he honestly thought he might cry. He knew the ring in his pocket was never going to be on her finger; he knew that this was all about to end.

"Wait," Mimi whispered, her voice hoarse from yelling. "Wait! Please, you can still ask! I didn't mean to screw it all—"

Ezra waved a hand, cutting her off. "I can't, Mimi. I can't."

"Because I sometimes take things?" She was crying again, the rage sucked out of her. "Because, I mean, sometimes, I want things that aren't mine?"

Ezra felt something splinter in him. It wasn't so bad that she wanted things that weren't hers. But no one was owed anything in this world, and he, more than most, had learned this lesson through simply living. He ran his hands over his face, blew out his breath. This would be the moment to confess his own omissions, the mess of last night, waking up with Frankie in Homer. But maybe they'd done enough damage to each other in the past few hours. He didn't want to hurt her any more than he had to, didn't want to make this any messier than it already was.

"Please, Ezra, come on. I like the life we've built," she pleaded. "I'll stop. You stopped playing poker for me, and I'll stop this for you."

It occurred to Ezra that for all of his years, he'd assumed that loving someone meant sacrifice. Whether it was because his mom sacrificed so much of herself by marrying a shitty man who left them or whether it was simply because that's just how he'd moved through the world, doling out small pieces of himself whenever someone asked him to. Never stopping to consider whether or not this was a part of himself he wanted to relinquish. But what if it didn't have to? What if loving someone meant enhancing your life, not subtracting from it?

He shook his head and said, simply: "Mimi, I think . . . maybe we were a perfect match on paper but—"

She interrupted him. "Ezra, you knew that wasn't real, right?"

"What?"

"The questionnaire, you knew that wasn't real?"

Ezra narrowed his eyes into a squint. *What?*

"None of that is real!" she said, as if she were explaining that the world wasn't flat, as if this should have been the most fundamentally obvious thing to him for the past two years they'd been together. "The questions are bullshit, the match-making is bullshit. It's all just for an algorithm. We just want people to sign up and maybe some of them will have a few decent dates and get laid. Who am I to say who will be a perfect match, who will live happily ever after? It's all fiction. We just wanted their credit cards, their monthly payments. If anything else worked out, that's the fucking cherry on top!"

"But you trotted me out; you told everyone that we were the perfect example." Ezra felt his cheeks flush with heat, embarrassed at his naivete, as soon as the words were out of his mouth. "I hated all of that. And you did it anyway."

"You never told me you hated it!" Mimi scowled. "And you never even looked closely at my form. You never actually saw my answers! You just believed what you wanted to, and I guess I figured that you were smart enough to know that." She crossed her arms, pursed her lips, then quieted. "But that doesn't mean that we can't make this work. That doesn't mean that we aren't actually *wonderful*. We are!" Her eyes swam with tears. Then quieter still, a plea: "*Please.* Even if it started on a lie, I love you, I really do."

"I can't," he said without artifice, his thoughts swarming and swirling then settling. "I just . . . I can't."

And she let out a string of ugly, monstrous wails, and Ezra didn't judge her for it. He only wished he'd seen that part of her sooner, back when he would have found the ugly parts beautiful. Now, he knew, he couldn't pretend he hadn't changed. So there was nothing else to see.

THIRTY-FIVE

Frankie

Frankie watched April and Connor slice into their red velvet cake and delicately feed each other a bite, which was a promising sign. She'd read somewhere that couples who shove the cake into each other's faces have a higher chance of divorce. Honestly, Frankie thought that everyone had a pretty decent chance at divorce, but she was relieved, almost overjoyed, that her friends from so long ago had a shot at making it work.

The DJ invited everyone back onto the dance floor, and April let out a whoop, and Connor, bless his heart, tried to do a little pump with his arms timed to a gyration of his hips, and April laughed until she cried good tears. But the DJ changed it up at the last second—a trap to get reticent couples up from their chairs, a bait and switch for potential twosomes who were left flat-footed, expecting a jam, and being thrown a love song.

The opening intro to the song was unmistakable, and Frankie felt her stomach fall out. She could see the notes in her mind as clearly as she could see April and Connor in front of her. Bono's unmistakable voice cut through the auditorium, and in no time at all, she was back in the bathroom of Lemonhead, and Ezra was bursting through the door because he had been looking for her everywhere.

See the stone set in your eyes

Frankie stared out into the darkened auditorium where Ezra had fled maybe an hour or so ago. She'd lost track of time since. She closed her eyes and listened to the music and the low electric buzz of her friends on the stage where she'd avoided so much for so long.

I can't live, with or without you.

And then Frankie Harriman remembered everything.

THIRTY-SIX

Ezra

Bruno called the campus shuttle, which was still operating on New Year's Eve, and Ezra gave Mimi the room keys. He'd find somewhere else to sleep for the night, he told her. He said to book whatever flight she wanted back home or whichever train she needed if she wanted to go to their apartment in New York instead. He'd pay for it. He didn't want to make this any more difficult than it had to be on her. It had already gotten so difficult.

"I think you're going to regret this," she sniffed, before she walked through the revolving door into the frigid Berkshire air and to the waiting driver. "I think you're going to call me tomorrow and want me back."

Ezra didn't know what was kinder: to tell her that she was wrong or to give her hope that she wasn't. But he knew that he would not.

Instead, he said, "Mimi, I am truly sorry for all of this. I never wanted things to go this way."

And she gave him a long look like she didn't believe him, which she probably didn't, because this had been his choice, and he just as well could have chosen differently. He could have chosen to still get down on one knee and slip his grandmother's ring on her finger and call her boisterous family in Kansas City with the news and try to reach Henry in London to tell him too. And they probably would have had a perfectly fine life together, even if they hadn't actually been the perfect match he'd always assumed them to be. Ezra realized this, but he also realized that he was capable of asking for more than perfectly fine—that he desperately wanted more. He'd been chasing a big, expansive, intoxicating love since he was old enough to seek it. And how he'd convinced himself that anyone simply loving him in return was the same thing as openhearted, mountain-moving adoration, he didn't know. He didn't have it in him, there in Burton Library with Bruno looking on and Mimi falling apart, to dive into that sort of emotional autopsy. It was enough, for now, to know that he needed to let Mimi go. That he could stop chasing her, stop holding on so tightly to all his plans, because what he was really chasing was something else.

Mimi disappeared out the revolving door and onto the shuttle and into the night.

And Ezra sat there, the mistletoe still hanging above the doorway, and stared out the window at the very place where his big, expansive love had turned him down, and felt, actually, for the first time in a long time, at peace.

THIRTY-SEVEN

Frankie

What had happened was Frankie's doing, Frankie's fault.

She ran down the aisle of Steinway, with Bono belting at her back, and knew this with complete certainty.

Gregory had been wrong. Ezra hadn't been playing poker because of him; Ezra had been playing poker because of her.

By the time they got to Lemonhead, the two of them—Gregory and Ezra—had been quite obviously drunk. She was still sober, but the spill at Abel and the lump on her skull had the world spinning. And Ezra, alternately hysterical and self-soothing from Mimi's voicemail, decided that, in lieu of being able to channel his energy into the *world's most perfect proposal*—she remembered he'd said that as they scurried from Abel Rink: *it was going to be the world's most perfect proposal and now she can't get here?*—he was going to channel his energy into ensuring that she, Frankie, did not die of a head injury.

She wouldn't. She kept telling him. *I won't die of a head injury. This has happened before.* Frankie didn't quite know how that was meant to be reassuring: that she'd previously been concussed. Why did she live a lifestyle that led to such things?

They'd made it to Lemonhead for their ice packs, and eventually, it became obvious that Gregory was not emerging from inside the bar. Ezra could have left her too, after also heading inside to grab her the ice. He could have disappeared into the thicket of students who descended from their dorms through the snow to drink pitchers of beer because that's what you did on frigid winter nights in Western Massachusetts. He could have sat her down in the little folding chair by the entrance and plopped the ice pack in her hand and said: *Best of luck, Frankie Harriman.* But that was not Ezra Jones.

With the clock ticking down to a new century, Frankie made it to Steinway's lobby and stopped to catch her breath, a cramp building in her side. No, that would never be Ezra Jones. A swell of emotion rose up in her. Was it gratitude? Was it nostalgia? She shook her head. She didn't know. This was new territory for her: seeking something, someone, out instead of waiting for it to find her.

"I still hate you," Frankie had mumbled last night at the entrance to Lemonhead as she leaned into him, her chin heavy on his chest. Though visibly intoxicated, he was solid on his feet, and he held her weight on him assuredly.

"And I still hate you," Ezra replied, but Frankie hadn't thought it really sounded like he meant it. Perhaps these were just lies they told themselves so that their wounds healed faster. Perhaps when you told yourself a story long enough, often enough, you tricked your mind into believing that it was true. Frankie slid down to the sodden floor of the bar and plopped her head into her hands.

"I would really like to go to sleep," she said.

Ezra lowered himself into a crouch in front of her, then wobbled, then steadied himself.

"No, no, that's the one thing I know: you can't go to sleep. If you have to go to sleep, we have to go to the ER."

"But I did this in Bangkok!" Frankie bleated. Ezra grabbed both of her elbows and pulled her up like she was weightless. She marveled at the feeling: of simply letting someone else literally carry your load. She reminded herself that she had vowed that Ezra Jones was an enemy for life and there had to be something utterly Machiavellian about his behavior.

"Shit, I can't believe this about Mimi," he said.

And Frankie said, "Forget Mimi! All you have done is whine about Mimi! Why don't you take—"

"Don't start with me about 'destiny' and 'taking charge of my life,' Frankie," Ezra snapped. "I'm a grown adult man!"

And Frankie retorted: "Those are all synonyms," and she thought this was a truly great burn, but Ezra looked at her like she was crazy, so she said, "I have a concussion. What do you want from me?!"

The bouncer shuffled his feet and cleared his throat, then said, "If you're not coming in, then you can't clog the door. Fire hazard."

So Ezra said, "Fine, man, just fine! We were leaving anyway."

And Frankie yelled, "No, we weren't. It's, like, negative thirty degrees out!"

And Ezra said, "It's not my fault that you didn't pack for the weather."

Frankie didn't have an answer for this, because she wanted

to blame him for everything, but alas, on this (and probably on many other things), he was correct.

"Let's go to Waverly's," she said. "I want to see my Boy Scout ex-boyfriend play a hand."

Ezra squeezed his eyes closed and swung his head back and forth. "No, no, no."

"So, you're *not* the card legend you are rumored to be?"

They were outside now, the snow just starting to fall, the wind swirling, a harbinger of what came next. The ground tilted beneath Frankie, and she reached for a lamppost to steady her.

"I don't have anything to prove to you," Ezra said, and even though she knew this was true, she couldn't keep herself from pushing the point. If her judgment hadn't been so clouded, maybe she would have considered that part of the reason she kept drawing Ezra into a fight was because something inside of her still sparked around him. But she didn't see any of this then because that would have been a progression toward clarity, and no one finds clarity from a concussion. "And I told Mimi I wouldn't gamble again," Ezra added. "And even if she's not here, I still keep my promises." The intimation was there: *unlike you.* But he was still tap-dancing around confrontation, so he added, just as a buffer, "I mean, it's not her fault her flight got canceled because of a storm."

And Frankie, not thinking clearly and not at all appreciative of his intimation, said: "Or maybe she just didn't want to be blindsided by a proposal she wasn't ready for."

There. She had said it. And as soon as she had, she knew it was cruel; she knew that if she had the chance, she would retract it and bottle it up and send it out to sea.

Ezra went statue-still. No drunken wobbling, no ine-briated fidgeting. Just the cutting edge of her words, slicing the air between them.

"Fuck you, Frankie," he said. And because Ezra never fought back, Ezra never retaliated, she believed the vitriol behind his words. She felt the punch deep in her guts, and she thought that she'd feel victorious—that she'd finally broken him—but what she really felt was hollow. She thought that his anger would make it easier to justify her own anger, but she'd gotten that all wrong.

He turned to go and got as far as twenty or so feet. She stood there with a frozen hand against the lamppost, her head thumping, her heart pounding. But then, because Ezra Jones was always a good guy, the best guy, he turned around and came back for her.

"I can't leave you out here to die," he said.

"I won't die," Frankie said. "I'm basically invisible."

"I think you mean invincible," he said, correcting her even while his words were getting slurry, the Portland brew really taking effect. "But you're not that either."

And then Frankie stared at him and he at her, and she, unbelievably, started laughing. Gut-bursting, side-cramping laughter. So Ezra did too. Soon, they each had tears streaking down their faces, each of them hiccupping for air, faces contorted into utter ridiculousness. Each time Frankie thought she had a grip on herself, she started again.

Finally, Ezra righted himself and gave her a long, piercing stare. And Frankie felt the connection all the way into her heart.

"Let's go," he said.

"Where?" she asked.

"Waverly's. I'm going to show you the new me."

"Wait," she said.

"Why?" he asked.

And Frankie looked at him for a beat, and then another one, and then she said: "Run."

THIRTY-EIGHT

Ezra

Ezra checked the time on the clock over Bruno's shoulder. Thirty minutes until midnight. He could stay here with Bruno, but he didn't think he wanted to usher in the new millennium with a grumpy security guard when he had anticipated proposing to his girlfriend. Ex-girlfriend. He corrected himself and said the word over and over again in his mind and found that unlike every other breakup, he was entirely ok. It was odd, he realized, how he could have been so wrong about someone, and also, having cut it off before it spiraled into an honest-to-God disaster, that he wasn't panicked, wasn't lying flat on the marble floor wondering when the world would stop spinning. He could almost hear Frankie telling him: *this* was progress.

And it was.

He didn't know why Frankie was still clanging around his brain, however. He didn't mind that she was, but it was both too familiar and unfamiliar, and rather than allow it to evolve into something that terrified him, Ezra decided to just let it be. Maybe Frankie Harriman would always rattle around his brain sometimes. Maybe that's just how it would go. Maybe he would be ok with that too.

THIRTY-NINE

Frankie

They had made it about halfway to Waverly's when it became obvious that Frankie really could not, in fact, run. Ezra was ahead of her, sprinting in a janky, drunken stride but still half a block in front, and finally, she threw herself onto a bench bordering the path and cried out, "Ezra, stop, I can't."

He slowed and turned, suspicious because it wouldn't be above her to cheat. "Sure, right."

He plopped his hands on his hips, and Frankie stared at him in the lamplight with snow falling all around. *He is a vision*, she thought. *I should have married him*, she also thought and genuinely startled, gasped at the notion. Never in her life, never ever, had Frankie considered that she had made a mistake with Ezra. Not because she didn't make mistakes, but for her, life was a forward, fluid motion. Looking back meant unearthing her pain, and she had never been in the business of trading on pain.

"Really, Ezra, my head is in bad shape."

He walked back toward her and stood in front of her. She didn't want to meet his eyes, and yet he refused to budge until she did.

"Proposal," he said. "If I run the table—"

"I don't really think you're *that* good," Frankie interrupted. The Ezra she knew would never have been *that* good at poker, at something as risky as gambling.

"If I win, you have to play something for me. On the piano."

Frankie started to protest, which came out more like a moan.

"If I lose," he paused. "I mean, I don't know, is there anything you want from me? I'm not going to lose, so it doesn't matter; it's irrelevant."

Frankie couldn't think of anything she wanted from him either, though she was starting to suspect that there was plenty if she had time to wrap her head around it. She chewed her lip and pressed her hand against the back of her head to stop the throbbing. It didn't help all that much.

"If you lose," she said, "I want an apology."

Ezra's jaw twitched, and she thought (and maybe hoped) that this would ignite a fight because a fight would mean that she didn't have to delve into the very truth of her feelings that were bubbling up louder with each passing minute.

"Fine, whatever," Ezra said. "I won't lose."

"But I can't walk there," she said.

He spun away from her, and she thought, for a fleeting second, that he was going to leave her there, in the falling snow, on a bench in the lower campus. Then he crouched down and said, "Hop on." And she realized that, even while drunk, Ezra Jones was going to carry her on his back.

FORTY

Ezra

Well, good night," Ezra said to Bruno at long last. He knew he couldn't hide out here forever, even if the quiet, the stillness, had been cathartic. A reckoning, just like Zoe had said. "Happy New Year."

Bruno was half-asleep by now at his security post. "Be careful out there," Bruno mumbled, then sipped from a thermos and perked up.

"It's just a little snow," Ezra replied. "Nothing I can't handle."

"That's not what I meant," Bruno said.

And Ezra nodded and pushed through the revolving doors and out into the night. He'd spent so many of his years on this earth tentative and full of worry. Now, he was ready for something else.

FORTY-ONE

Frankie

Ezra, of course, did not lose. Frankie hadn't realized how truly brilliant he was at the whole card counting or laser focus or whatever, but he just kept winning and winning. Initially, she had sat next to him at the table, occasionally resting her head on his shoulder or leaning forward and collapsing into her folded arms, but then an asshole grad student complained that she was a distraction, so she slid to the floor despite a very kind young woman (Frankie would later remember her to be Joni) suggesting she occupy a booth out front. As payback, Ezra won the grad student's gold wedding band, and Frankie, despite lobbing a quick diatribe against matrimony from underneath Ezra's chair, took no small amount of joy from the fact that Ezra played for keeps and without remorse and extracted revenge in her honor. (This was melodramatic, sure, but she was concussed, and it made sense to her at the time.)

Ezra slid the ring on his finger and held it up to the light, then lowered his hand beneath the chair and wiggled his fingers to show Frankie, and she laughed and laughed, and said, "Please stop, this is making my head hurt worse."

And the grad student said, "You don't have to be a dick," and Ezra said, "I don't, but sometimes it feels really great to be one anyway."

Then, because he was drunk and emotions came and went, he remembered Mimi and his aborted plans for the proposal, and he patted down his pockets for his phone, but couldn't find it, and his brain—loose and nonsensical—forgot about that too, and he launched into an emotional plea for his girl-friend that morphed into a long rant about being stood up by the time he was done.

Frankie listened to it with her eyes pressed closed and thought that Ezra Jones was a bit of a mess, and she found that she wanted to be the one to help him clean up. And never in her life had Frankie had the instinct to be a caretaker for anyone who wasn't on her payroll. She didn't mind cleaning up after her artists because there was no emotional cost in doing so: business was business, and being good in business meant being great for business. But personally? No. This was a whole new wheelhouse.

Ezra leaned over, his face hovering above hers, and said, "Well, I won."

And Frankie groaned and said, "Motherfucking fine."

And Ezra put his hands beneath her armpits and hoisted her up to her feet, and they lingered there, close enough that she could feel his breath, could hear his heartbeat when she laid her head against his chest. Just as she had earlier today in the alley where he brought her Paris. No wonder. Muscle memory, even if the brain had forgotten how it had been between them.

Finally, Ezra said: "Steinway?"

That was too much for Frankie, returning to the scene of their heartbreak. Even with a foggy head and a clearer heart, she couldn't bear that. But she had made a promise to Ezra, and this time, she was going to honor it. So she sighed and leaned into him again and said simply, "Yes."

FORTY-TWO

Ezra

Middleton was beautiful at night, Ezra thought. It was close to midnight now, and students, those who had stayed behind for the holiday, were emerging from their rooms, from their parties, from Lemonhead or wherever they had found to stay warm, to toast to the millennium.

A pack of five girls pushed past him, then a couple who were in the throes of making out and walking at the same time. Behind him, someone tooted a noisemaker, and someone else cheered, and for some reason, Ezra thought of his mother. It hit him occasionally that she wouldn't be here for the milestones: welcoming a new century, walking him down the aisle, meeting her first grandchild. He knew she wouldn't want him to live a life shadowed by her memory, and most of the time, Ezra didn't. But every once in a while, it felt safe, it felt *good* to sink into his grief, because only when he emerged from it did he feel a little more healed.

He was headed back to Steinway now, to the cacophony

and merriment of the wedding. He didn't have anywhere else to go, and besides, he owed Gregory an apology. He shook his head and nearly laughed: *earrings at Neiman's.* He never would have thought that would have been the cause of his reckoning.

Someone was running up the path toward him. Her elbows were askew, and her stride was terrible, but then Frankie had never been an athlete. It took him a long beat to figure out that she was calling his name, that she was coming for him. He slowed and then stopped. He'd wait for her here. Now it was her turn.

FORTY-THREE

Frankie

A few minutes before the turn of the century, Frankie saw Ezra in the shadowed lamplight on Middie Walk, and her heart nearly stopped. She knew what she had to do, and yet, old habits were so deeply ingrained that she had to forcibly not turn around and flee. But Gregory had been right: Ezra was always the one chasing her; Frankie was always the one retreating.

So she pushed herself forward. She owed him that. And she owed him the truth.

Steinway had been locked last night. But the light was on behind the door to the auditorium, and Ezra was determined. He pounded on the front door—something new, Frankie took note of, as the old Ezra would have just let it be—until finally, a custodian unlatched the bolt and said, "Yeah?"

Ezra said: "It's urgent. We have an emergency."

"What kind of emergency?" The custodian looked more annoyed than alarmed.

"A ten-year-old grudge emergency?" Ezra tried, looking

serious. He was drunk. Anything could have seemed serious to him.

"It's fine," Frankie said. "We don't have to."

Ezra narrowed and locked his eyes with hers. "Yes, we do. You promised."

So Frankie nodded, and because she was used to cajoling people into doing things in the name of music, she said, "Can we just have five minutes? He'll give you fifty bucks." And Ezra shrugged and said, "Absolutely," then smiled at Frankie like she was brilliant. She wasn't. She just knew how to manipulate the weak spots. Still though, his smile, that smile: it was like it was made just for her, like she was the only person who saw him, like he was the only person who saw her too.

Ezra pulled the cash from his wallet, then stumbled for no reason at all, and the custodian said, "Just don't make a mess. We're setting up for an event." And they each assured him that they would not. Music wasn't messy after all, though the heart of it, the guts of it—Frankie's, at least—were something else entirely. Nothing but mess, really.

The grand piano wasn't center stage, which meant that if they were really going to do this, if Ezra was going to force her to keep her end of the bet, they were going to have to find an upright in one of the rooms backstage.

Frankie stopped at the bottom of the steps, while Ezra patted his pockets in search of his phone, which he hadn't yet realized had been crushed by the Zamboni. "Shit, I really need to call Mimi," he said. Then, as if the thought were there then gone, he turned to Frankie. "Come on. Let's do this."

"I really don't want to," she whispered.

"I know," Ezra said. "And that is why we're doing it." He

was amazingly coherent for someone who was also well over the legal limit of intoxicated.

Frankie thought she might cry, but she had promised, and she wasn't going to give Ezra any reason to accuse her of being the same person she'd been a decade ago. She'd grown! She was an adult! She managed the number one girl band in the world! She told herself all these things while she ascended the steps with heavy legs and then wound her way backstage. Of course, neither of them had been back here since the day in early May a decade ago when she'd watched the pregnancy test turn blue. They walked side by side in silence.

The two weeks between the test and graduation were agony. Frankie knew now that they were agony for the both of them, but she, at the time, could think only of herself. She doubled down on the lie about the job offer in LA: it didn't matter if it were true or not; what mattered was that Ezra believed it, and actually, Frankie came to believe it too. She called up her father's travel agent and booked a one-way ticket the night of graduation, and if she could have left sooner, she would have. Ezra refused to acknowledge that they couldn't find a way to make it work. She knew that he couldn't give up NYU and his scholarship money, which she found reassuring: she hadn't wanted him to recalibrate his whole life for her, and she'd never have expected it. And perhaps that was part of the reason she was so irritated that he wanted as much from her. With each passing day, it became clearer and clearer to Frankie that their two mostly happy years had been pure luck, and they were so diametrically different—all Frankie wanted for her future was freedom, and all Ezra wanted was security.

But they had never argued; they didn't even know how to

really. And eventually, luck ran dry: you couldn't exist together with such opposing desires and forge peace, find common ground. The pregnancy wasn't the wedge that would drive them apart, though on that they were also divided; rather, it was the light bulb that illuminated brighter and brighter for Frankie that what she needed was out. Ezra's notions of the future terrified her, but more than that, they enraged her. He knew she had spent her years at Middleton attempting to break the shackles of her childhood, even if he didn't know the full-dimensional why of it, and here he was, pretending that a baby, that cohabitation, that New York were all on a new road map for the course she had charted, a course she should just rewrite.

It had been a balmy, bright day in May. Ezra's mom was in town for graduation, as were Frankie's parents, though her mom and dad were barely speaking. Frankie's mother had booked a table for the five of them for dinner at the nicest restaurant in town to celebrate. Frankie pulled on her cap and gown, and spun around in front of the mirror a few times, then turned to the side and cupped her belly, which was still flat—she was only seven weeks pregnant—and gave herself one moment to consider shelving LA and her flight out that night and giving in to everything Ezra wanted because she did love him. But she met her eyes in the reflection and knew she had done that for the first seventeen years of her life—played dress-up for someone else's aspirations—and she also knew, even as much as she did love him, even as wide as her love was, that this was simply too much to ask.

Her phone rang on her desk, and she answered it. Ezra was at Burton, calling from a pay phone. *Come meet me*, he said, *then we'll go to the holding area together*. It was too early to line up for the graduation ceremony, but Frankie didn't have anything else to do: her room was packed, she was dressed, and besides, as fraught as these few weeks had been, she wanted to leave for Los Angeles on a good note, with only fond memories. She'd call him from there and say that she couldn't have the baby, that she'd had it taken care of. He'd be angry, she knew, but ultimately, he had his whole life in front of him too. One day, he'd be grateful.

She descended the steps to the dorm and pushed open the metal door into the bright blinding sunshine and wandered through the campus, trying to pinpoint what she was feeling, how she could explain. And then there he was, exactly where he said he'd be in the archway to Burton Library. Her Ezra. He didn't break his promises.

"Hey," he said, smiling at her cap and gown. "You look beautiful."

And before she could even reply, he was down on one knee, his grandmother's ring in a black velvet box.

Frankie didn't remember what he said. White-hot anger was buzzing in her brain, and she was too clouded to focus. Eventually, he stopped talking, and she realized he was waiting for a reply. So she said no.

Then Ezra rose to his feet, clearly stunned, which Frankie didn't understand because she'd never indicated that she had any interest in marriage, much less at twenty-two, which meant she would be exactly like her own mother and father, who were the world's worst example of how to be married.

"No?" Ezra had parroted back.

"No!" Frankie said. "Absolutely, unequivocally *no*."

"But—"

"But what?" she said too loudly. "What about me ever gave you the impression that I wanted to be someone's wife?"

And it was unkind. She knew as soon as it was out of her mouth, but she was so furious at him. After two years, he had totally and wildly misunderstood her. What was the point of loving someone if they refused to see the entirety of you? What was the point of any of it?

"I mean, I love you, Frankie! I want to be with you forever!"

"You can't love me," she shouted, "when it is devastatingly clear that you don't know me!"

"What does that mean?" Ezra yelled back. "I know every single thing about you."

"Then you'd know that I would never in a million years say yes."

They said some ugly things after that: how if he didn't know her, it was because she refused to let him; how if she'd refused to let him, then maybe it was because she'd been the smart one; how she was too childish for motherhood; how he would fuck it all up because he was always in pursuit of his absent dad.

It was an undignified, messy ending, and they both deserved better. But they'd let so much go unsaid for so long that it all spilled out, too much, more than either of them really wanted. A decade later, running up the frozen brick pathway of Middie Walk, Frankie understood that. But back then, she was so angry at him, so offended by what she saw as a betrayal of who she was working so feverishly to become, that she didn't know how else to react.

She made her mom cancel the dinner reservation. April and Laila happened to stop by her room while she was sitting on the floor crying, and they pulled her up, and she told them everything, and they listened with no judgment, then called her a cab and walked her to the curb and hugged her one more time.

"Do you want me to tell Ezra you left?" April had asked. "What can I do to make this easier?"

And it was such a simple question, such a perfect question, that Frankie started crying again. She didn't want anyone telling her what to do, like Ezra had, like Ezra would. She just wanted someone to make it easier. This was what she owed April a decade later: an act of grace. And this was why she showed up for her wedding: because sometimes, you stood beside people to make things easier, to make them complete.

She boarded the late-evening flight to Los Angeles and stared out the window for a solid six hours, her Walkman keeping her company, a mixtape that she had made months back that reminded her of Ezra echoing in her ears. They landed at midnight, and Frankie stopped to pee in the airport bathroom. Her underwear was dotted with bright red blood. She dropped a dime in the tampon machine for a maxi pad, and when she woke up the next morning in the hotel room that she'd put on her dad's credit card, the last vestiges of Ezra Jones had emptied from her.

She called him a week later and said tersely: "I don't want to make this any more drawn out than it needs to be. I'm not pregnant. It was all a mistake."

And Ezra went silent for a long time, like he sometimes used to when they would linger on the phone on those hot summer nights when they were just falling in love and sharing all their secrets. Then finally he said, "Ok, well, it's done."

And that was the last they spoke of it until ten years later when a wedding reunited them back at the place where it all began.

Frankie hadn't thought about any of this in so long, but last night, as Ezra steadied her up the steps to the stage of Steinway, then back to the music rooms behind it, the unresolved pain of their decimating ending came back in a rush. She would have done so much of it differently. If only she had known how. She wouldn't have married him. But maybe she would have been less angry, maybe she could have been less selfish. And as she flipped on a light to a practice room and found an upright there, she gazed into his open face and understood that he would have done the same. They'd both been greedy back then, and now, she knew, they were both sorry.

She sat heavily on the bench in front of her, and Ezra, surprisingly, plopped down beside her. She'd never, in the span of her life, shared a piano bench with anyone other than the times when Fred got close enough that she could smell his spearmint gum and his aftershave, which she came to associate with her mom. And her instinct was to shove Ezra off, to tell him to give her some goddamned space, but she squelched that voice because there was something fragile between them now, and she didn't want to break it.

"Any requests?" she asked.

"I just want to listen," he replied. His eyes were already closed, and he swayed a little, and Frankie found it endearing. *Shit*, she thought. *Shit, shit, shit*.

There was a beanbag in the corner, and as soon as Frankie's fingers found the keys—stiff at first because she was so out of practice—Ezra rose and curled up on top of it. She played a made-up melody; she didn't want to be cheesy and play something from her old mix-tapes: U2 or Pat Benatar or Tina Turner or Prince. She could have played any of them because she saw the notes in front of her like she always did. But she thought she heard Ezra lightly snoring, so she played something of her own, something original because he was half-asleep, and also, she trusted herself to show him. To be honest. Not to hide behind anyone else's version of a masterpiece. Frankie played longer than she'd planned to—she'd talked herself into just one composition, but then time stood still and, just like she used to, she got swallowed up in the notes and the melody and the beauty of making something from nothing, just with your fingers and your heart and the ivory keys. She'd forgotten that once, maybe only at the beginning but indeed once, she'd loved it. And it wasn't that it felt good to abandon herself to it again—it was painful and bittersweet, but it was wonderful too, like waking something inside of her that had been dormant and now was ready to emerge from hibernation.

When she stopped, Ezra mumbled something like: "You're incredible," and she rose from the bench and curled up on the beanbag next to him, mostly because her head really was throbbing, and she wanted to be horizontal, but also because she found that she just wanted to be near him, to get closer to him, in any way that she could.

She said: "I would have done it all differently, you know. And I'm sorry I didn't."

And his eyes fluttered open, and he said: "Me too."

She reached into his jacket pocket and found his grandmother's ring and slid it on her finger. She was curious how the weight of it would feel, because she'd spurned the chance ten years ago. She held it up to the light, and Ezra shook his head and said, "Wow, this is really a mind-fuck," and it wasn't eloquent, but Frankie laughed, and then so did he, because he was right.

And one of them, even now with a few minutes to midnight on New Year's Eve, as Frankie slowed her pace because Ezra was in front of her, she couldn't remember which one, said: "We should start over, go all the way back to Homer and just start over."

And so they did. Ezra slipped the gold band over his finger, and he called her Mrs. Harriman because she said she'd still keep her maiden name, so he said, "Great, I'll be Mr. Harriman because why not," and she said, "No, no, no, Ez, you gotta learn to keep parts of you for yourself," and he nodded because it was true. And then they waited for someone to emerge from the Homer gate, and they tiptoed inside, which was pointless because no one was really around. And then Ezra found his freshman-year room, and it was unlocked because everything at Middleton was safe. And they curled up into bed together and fell asleep, just slept because it was what they needed most and maybe that was the most intimate thing they could do with each other now. His heartbeat like a metronome in her ear, her breath a welcome calm in his busy, ever-anxious brain.

And then they woke up this morning, and everything was forgotten.

FORTY-FOUR

Ezra

Ezra checked his watch, and it was nearly time. On the lawn across the way, some students were setting off shitty makeshift fireworks, and he turned for a minute and fought the urge to run over and tell them to be careful. That they could blow off a finger or an ear. But he didn't need to take care of everyone; he knew this now.

Besides, Frankie was in front of him, out of breath, and it was almost midnight, and he was tired of always being the grown-up. Where had that gotten him? The most success he'd had was when he gave in and followed his passion, quitting law school, building his gaming platform, losing himself to the numbers or the cards or, yes, how much he had loved Frankie Harriman. He'd do it differently now. He'd take the time to listen to her fears; he'd take the time to understand why and how he could love someone whose perspective on their future was so out of sync with his own. She had been awful about the pregnancy, New York, the rest of it, but he'd been awful in his own way too. Maybe that's just who you were at twenty-two, but he'd repeated plenty of those mistakes between then and now all the same.

"We didn't get married last night," Frankie said. She was just a few feet away now, and she looked pained from her run. "I mean, if you need to propose to what's-her-name, we didn't get married last night."

"You know her name," he said.

"Fine," she answered. "To Mimi. If you need to propose to Mimi."

"You remembered?"

She nodded. "We didn't get married officially, I guess I should say. Like there wasn't a paper; we didn't have a priest."

"I'd never have a priest," Ezra said. "And Alec Barstow is definitely no saint."

And Frankie smiled. "Finally, something we agree on." She paused, uncertain. "And Mimi? Where is she?"

"Gone," Ezra said simply. A beat passed. Then: "How'd you know where to find me?"

Frankie took a long look around. At the kids setting off fireworks, at the starry sky above, at Burton in front of her.

"I just knew," she said. Ezra started to speak but she held up a hand. "Let me this time. Let me be the one to finally chase you."

FORTY-FIVE

Frankie

Frankie wasn't sure if she truly had it in her, but she knew she owed it to herself, and to Ezra, to at least try. Maybe it would be ugly and maybe it would be ineloquent, but she'd shown plenty of men her ugly parts; she'd just never asked them to love her in spite of them. Frankie had made a life for herself, a career for herself, with those ugly parts: the brashness, the brazenness, the over-confidence.

But now, she was standing in front of Ezra and saying: love me anyway, choose me anyway.

"We didn't get married," she started. "But I put on the ring, and you put on yours, and well, I guess for a few minutes, it was lovely to think about." She paused because she wanted to get this right. "I don't . . . I don't think that will ever be for me, Ezra. The white picket fence, the two point five kids with a golden retriever and dinner every night at six. And I guess I always knew that but wanted to have you for myself anyway." She was surprised to find herself blinking back tears. "And even though it's been over between us forever, and even though I spent that forever hating you, I just . . ." She sighed. "I owe you an apology. Because I should have tried harder. I should have been better. You didn't deserve to find out that I had a miscarriage three thousand miles away from you, and you didn't deserve to hear the relief in my voice when I told you, even when I could hear the pain in yours."

"Frankie—" Ezra said.

"Please, let me just—" She stopped, blew out her breath. "It's New Year's Eve, you know? And if I don't say this now, I never will." He nodded, so she steadied herself and continued. "I don't expect for you to forgive me; I don't expect for you to come to LA and take me to dinner. But, I mean, I was thinking—last night, we pretended for a minute that we were together, and I had a head injury and you were pretty drunk—"

"Very drunk," Ezra interrupted.

"Right, so even more drunk than what I said. But well, I was wondering, maybe if I came to New York, maybe I could take *you* to dinner? I can't . . . I don't want to lose this before we've even started. So, I mean, maybe I could ask for you to possibly like me again, someday?"

"Frankie," he said, and took a step closer. "I already like you again."

"But I can't be any of those things you want. I need to tell you that now. I don't want to make you unhappy. For a long time, I wanted that—I wanted you to be the most miserable bastard on earth."

Ezra tilted his head back and howled with laughter, so Frankie allowed herself to grin as well.

"I mean, Ezra, I really did hate you."

"It was mutual," he said.

And she took another step closer until they were right there, in front of each other, with nowhere else to look, nowhere else to turn. No pretense, no baggage, no lies, no history but the good kind.

"I won't run again," she said. Ezra nodded because he already knew.

"But is it a hard no on the golden retriever?" he asked with a smile. "I mean, I really would like a dog."

She placed her hands on his cheeks. "I would allow for a dog. And it's possible I'd consider a baby someday, though I don't do diapers, and I can't promise more than that. I just do not want a ring."

Ezra stared down at her, considering it all.

And then, above them, an explosion of real fireworks. They each craned their necks upward, and all around them, reds and purples and golds soared across the night sky. Frankie and Ezra stood there under the cascade of lights as students shouted their countdown. They were at ten, and then nine, and then eight, then seven, then six, then five, then four, then three, then two, and finally, they were on the precipice of a new millennium, a new century, a new start.

And Frankie gazed at Ezra, and Ezra gazed at Frankie, and it was so odd, she thought, how much she already knew she loved him, even the ways he had changed, even when she remembered all the terrible parts. She pressed up onto her tiptoes because she was the one who had to do it now, and she raised her chin and clasped her hands behind his neck, and then, sober, non-concussed, not under the influence of mistletoe, and not riding the adrenaline of the mishaps of earlier in the day, rather simply with the hope of starting over, Frankie Harriman kissed Ezra Jones in the very spot they'd splintered.

Finally, Ezra pulled back and said: "Wow, that was really something."

And Frankie giggled, so Ezra giggled too, and then he leaned down and kissed her again, wholly, taking his time, because it felt exactly like it used to and entirely different as well.

"We should probably go back to the wedding," she said eventually, though neither of them moved.

"So you remembered everything from last night?" Ezra asked.

"I did."

"And you'll tell me?"

Frankie linked her hand in his, and they started toward their old friends at their old school with a new start.

"You told me to call you Mr. Harriman," Frankie said, and Ezra doubled over in laughter. "Because I told you I had to keep my name."

"I like it," Ezra said. "I like it very much."

"But no ring," Frankie repeated.

Ezra pulled her close to him and kissed the top of her head. "No ring," he repeated. "Just a dog."

Frankie looked up at him. "And me."

"No ring, a dog, and Frankie Harriman," he said, and Frankie thought he looked happier than she ever could have imagined.

"No ring, a dog, and Ezra Jones," she said.

It was the twenty-first century now.

The past was behind them and the whole breadth of the world was in front of them. Frankie started to believe that anything was possible. Ezra, she thought, was starting to believe that too. She could be brave enough to leave herself vulnerable; he could be loose enough to trust that they could stumble wherever their road took them. And there was music to be found in that; there was music to be made. A melody, a harmony, a vast grand symphony.

EPILOGUE

Ezra

Ezra was bone-weary when he climbed up the stairs to Frankie's apartment. The flight out of London had been delayed three hours, and the jet lag was making his legs rubbery, his brain a muddled buzz. Still though, the past three weeks with Henry had been nourishing, the type of time that his therapist would call good for his soul. *We only have one family,* Ezra kept saying to his brother. *We need to be better about this.* So Ezra met Henry's fiancée; Henry met Frankie. He'd greeted her at the airport with a bear hug that Ezra was sure Frankie would flinch from, but Frankie leaned into him too, like she wasn't afraid of openhearted affection, like she needed it as much as the rest of them.

Henry pulled back and said, "Finally, the infamous Frankie Harriman!" Ezra thought he saw her blush, but then she said, "My reputation precedes me, and I stand by it all." And then they all laughed because both Henry and Frankie were right:

theirs wasn't the type of history you could shed even when you put it all behind you. And for three weeks, they ate a shit ton of fish and chips; they raised frothy ales in pubs in memory of Ezra and Henry's mom; they played darts and lingered too long in museums and did all the touristy things that he'd missed out on since he really hadn't visited in years and Frankie had missed out on because she worked too much. Most important, they remembered that being family, *having family*, was foundational, not just a footnote to any of their stories.

Ezra unlatched the lock to Frankie's apartment with his set of keys just as his phone buzzed in his back pocket.

"Hello?" He swung the door shut with his foot, dropped the keys on top of the upright piano.

"Happy birthday!" He could hear Frankie smiling on the other end of the line. She hadn't wanted to spend his birthday apart, their first together in so long, but they'd had to diverge at Heathrow—she was on to Stockholm with Night Vixen; he was back in Los Angeles to start grad school at UCLA. He'd turned down Google after April and Connor's wedding; he'd decided that with his whole life ahead of him, he didn't need to keep chasing something he wasn't even sure he wanted. He decided, instead, to teach, which reminded him of his mom for no reason other than he thought she'd like that for him. And actually, he liked that for himself too.

"High schoolers are the worst though," Frankie had said one night last spring. Ezra had just gotten his acceptance letter in the mail—he was using Frankie's mailing address by then—and they were braided into each other in her bed, her apartment smelling of new paint because she'd had a purple wall that she thought no longer suited her. Ezra ran his hands through her hair, back to brunette, just like it had been at Middleton, and grinned. He felt her own grin against his chest too.

"Hormones and zits and attitude," Ezra agreed.

"And you have the misguided notion that you can make a difference," Frankie said. She tilted her chin up and kissed him. "Still a Boy Scout. Some things never change."

Ezra laughed because so many things, in fact, had. He'd returned to New York after the wedding and packed up his stuff, mostly just clothes and mementos—the rest meant nothing to him at all—while Mimi was at work. His lease ran through June, so he called her and told her to stay as long as she needed. He didn't want to be cruel; he never wanted it to end bitterly. That, he supposed, was going to be true forever. He didn't have to reinvent *himself* to reinvent his life.

Frankie had said she'd consider New York; she didn't want him to think that she was repeating old patterns, asking him to move for her. But Ezra surprised them both: he was ready for something new, for the unknown, which had always terrified him. But because he now knew she was willing to meet him halfway, he was willing to meet her halfway too, all the way even. So he took a taxi to JFK, and he boarded a flight, and he started over in Los Angeles. But not really starting over, because he was with Frankie, and that alone gave him the peace of mind not to panic. Though he still hadn't adjusted to the relentless sunshine, the green juice, the traffic that was backed up by 2 p.m.

"Happy birthday!" Frankie said again on the other end of the line. Ezra tried to calculate the time in Sweden. It must have been the middle of the night; she must have stayed up to reach him when he finally got off the plane. He thought something about this likely contented them both—she was tired when he was tired, her happiness was his happiness, they really were in this together. Everything about it felt new; everything about it felt right.

"I left you a present," Frankie said.

"A present? I told you, I don't need anything." Ezra flopped on the bed.

"I know," she said. "But that's the fun of it. Giving you something that you want, not that you need."

Ezra grunted because his face was smashed against a pillow, and his exhaustion was rising like a tide.

"No, no," Frankie cried. "Sit up! Wake up! I made something for you."

At this, Ezra cracked his eyes open. "You made something for me?"

"Stand up. Go to the kitchen."

Ezra lumbered forward and did as he was told.

"Ok," she said, and Ezra thought she sounded nervous, which was actually adorable. "Move the Froot Loops. There's something behind them, just for you."

"You planned all of this in advance?" Ezra asked. "Before we even left for London?"

"Oh, shut up," Frankie deflected.

"Is this, dare I say, a grand gesture?"

Frankie huffed, but her heart wasn't in it, her sincerity overcoming any sense of indignation. "Look, do you see it or not?" she asked.

Ezra moved the Froot Loops and tucked his hand into the back of the pantry shelf, his fingers landing on something smooth and thin. He slid it out and opened the square plastic case. It was a CD. On it, Frankie had written: **Happy Birthday Ezra**. He was so shocked, so moved, that he found himself blinking back tears.

"Is this yours?" he said. "I mean, did you write something, record something?"

"I did," she said quietly. "But only for you, not for anything big."

Lately, mostly on weekends, Frankie had started easing back onto the piano bench, playing again for the joy of it.

"You wrote me a song," Ezra said.

"Oh God, please don't make me regret it," Frankie replied, but they both knew that she wouldn't.

Ezra padded over to the stereo system, just as Frankie said, "Oh no, no, I can't be on the phone when you listen to it. I'd rather die."

"Don't die," Ezra said. "Not when we're just getting started."

"I won't die, but let me hang up first, ok?"

"But to be clear, this *is* a grand gesture," Ezra said.

"It's a medium gesture," Frankie said. And Ezra laughed because he could live with that. Then she told him that the band needed her back in the studio, which was absurd because it was the middle of the night, but he knew she was too embarrassed to linger on the line while he played the music she wrote for him. So he said good night, and she said good night, and then they clicked goodbye, and even though they were five thousand miles apart, it wasn't a goodbye at all.

Then Ezra slipped the CD into the stereo, and he allowed himself to take in the moment, to absorb his righteous, hard-earned happiness. And then, in what felt like a small miracle given how far they'd come, he pressed PLAY.

Acknowledgments

I will forever be indebted to Elisabeth Weed and Laura Dave for insisting that I write this book; for, essentially, forcing me to. We were nine months into the pandemic. Like everyone, I was listless and depleted. I hadn't written a word since early lockdown. I was out taking one of my endless quarantine walks, with Laura in my ear, pitching her ideas that I didn't really have my heart in, but knowing that something was better than nothing. When I stumbled onto the seed of the idea that would eventually be *The Rewind*, she said, "Stop right there, that's the one. But don't pitch it unless you mean it because it's going to be hard to write, and someone's going to make you to write it." Alas, friends, I pitched it. And Elisabeth, my agent and dear friend of nearly fifteen years, made me write it. When I didn't want to. When indeed, it was very, very hard. When I didn't think I could break the story or make it make sense, and when I endlessly complained that I couldn't do it. (Which was often. Elisabeth, I'm sorry.) She and Laura kept me going, page after page, chapter after chapter, and without them, this book would be nothing more than a spark of an idea that I made up on a long walk up my neighborhood hill because I was desperate to get out of the house during lockdown. How lucky am I to have such women in my corner? Too lucky to quantify.

My editor, Kerry Donovan, has been a dream partner from our very first phone call (also on a lockdown walk!). In fact, the entire team at Berkley has been exceptional beyond measure: supportive, enthusiastic, professional, just a total delight. I am so beyond fortunate to have found a new home in publishing this far along in my career and to have had them cheerlead and champion me from the minute the manuscript crossed their desks. Craig Burke, Christine Ball, Claire Zion, Danielle Keir, Dache' Rogers, Jessica Mangicaro, Catherine Barra, Christine Legon, Megan Elmore, Lila Selle, Mary Baker, and plenty more. I am indebted to you all.

Berni Barta and Michelle Weiner at CAA have been behind Frankie and Ezra from the first pitch. I could not be more grateful to Bryan Unkeless and Alyssa Rodrigues at Clubhouse Pictures, as well as the entire Netflix team, including Nirokhi Raychaudhuri, for being so passionate about their vision of the film adaptation from the early days. Jenny Meyer stormed the foreign markets. Dana Murphy, Brettne Bloom, DJ Kim, Andrea Peskind Katz, Rochelle Weinstein, Ashley Spivey, Hitha Palepu, Elyssa Friedland, Michelle Gable, Julie Clark—thank you for your counsel and advice and friendship.

I'd be remiss not to give special and heartfelt thank-yous to everyone who got us through these past few pandemic years—the doctors, nurses, teachers, emergency personnel, essential workers, scientists, and everyday people who looked out for one another, who tried to do their best, who held the line and rolled up their sleeves and loved their neighbors. None of this was easy. It was hard to be a parent and a daughter and a grown-up and a writer and a human. If it was hard for you too, come sit at my table; I'm holding a seat for you.

A quick note (and this may get weird) about my beloved dog, Pele, who passed away shortly after I finished this book. For those of you who have dogs, you understand that they are more than animals in your home: they are parts of your heart, and in the best cases, pieces of your soul. Pele sat with me every day as I wrote, curled up at my feet (all 110 pounds of him), and gave me more than I ever could have imagined. He was the best boy, the sweetest angel, and I honestly could not have written so many books (or survived lockdown) without him or his brother, Mr. Peanut.

Finally, to my family: Adam, Campbell, Amelia. We spent way more time together than we ever anticipated but we got through it as a unit. Thanks for listening to me when I yelled, "Stop talking to me, I have to finish my word count!" and thanks for giving me the space to write when space was hard to come by. My love for you is wide enough to inspire at least three '80s rock ballads, maybe even more.

The Rewind

Allison Winn Scotch

Questions for Discussion

1. Frankie and Ezra broke up a decade ago and haven't spoken since. In your experience, is it possible to forgive and forget? Do you think second chances at love ever work out?

2. Frankie felt confined by her childhood and her musical gift. At what point do adults have to take responsibility for their current behaviors and not just point fingers at their past? Does Frankie do a good job of this? Was there a particular scene where you really rooted for her?

3. Ezra thinks he is a perfect boyfriend because he tries not to challenge Mimi and simply makes her life easier in all respects. Do you see this as the behavior of a perfect partner? If not, how is he dooming himself to repeat the mistakes of his past? What do you think were his best qualities as a boyfriend?

4. Music plays a pivotal role in the book, especially for Frankie. Has music defined any important moments in your own life? If so, which songs? Which bands?

When you hear that music, does it transport you back to that time in your own life?

5. What role and influence do Frankie's and Ezra's friends have in their relationship and their lives? Did you wish Gregory had told Ezra what happened with Mimi at Kmart sooner? Would that have changed anything?

6. Both Ezra and Frankie hurt each other in different ways back in college before their breakup. If you could offer them each one specific word of advice to prevent their implosion, what would it be? Do you hold one of them more accountable than the other?

7. The book is set in the '80s and '90s. What is it about these eras that feels so nostalgic?

8. Even though Ezra and Frankie hurt each other in their own ways in college, they also loved each other. What were your favorite scenes or moments when they showed the other person how much they cared?

9. Ezra and Frankie are quite different from each other. What works best in a relationship—when you are so different that you balance each other out, or when you are quite alike and often see eye to eye?

10. The scavenger hunt is obviously pivotal for both Ezra and Frankie, when something that started out in good fun leads to more serious revelations. Has this ever happened to you in your own life?

11. Frankie openly admits that she is quite competitive. Does this serve her well or is it a detriment? Do you consider yourself competitive? Did you relate more to Frankie or to Ezra?

Don't miss the next romantic comedy from Allison Winn Scotch, in which a world-famous romance writer—who recently blew up both her professional and personal lives—unearths an anonymous love letter on her childhood desk, and despite her better instincts, stakes her future on reconnecting with her exes—to discover if there's such a thing as the one who got away, and what exactly she's going to do about it when she comes face-to-face with him.

Author photo by Kat Tuohy Rosenberg

Allison Winn Scotch is the *New York Times* bestselling author of nine novels, including *Cleo McDougal Regrets Nothing*, *In Twenty Years*, and *Time of My Life*. She lives in Los Angeles with her family and their two rescue dogs, Hugo and Mr. Peanut.

Ready to find
your next great read?

Let us help.

Visit prh.com/nextread

Penguin
Random
House